WAITING FOR KATIE

Further Titles by Elizabeth Webster from Severn House

THE ACORN WINTER
CLOUD SHADOWS
HOME STREET HOME

WAITING
FOR KATIE

Elizabeth Webster

This first world edition published in Great Britain 1996 by
SEVERN HOUSE PUBLISHERS LTD of
9–15 High Street, Sutton, Surrey SM1 1DF.
First published in the USA 1996 by
SEVERN HOUSE PUBLISHERS INC. of
595 Madison Avenue, New York, NY 10022.

British Library Cataloguing in Publication Data

Webster, Elizabeth
  Waiting for Katie
  1. English fiction – 20th century
  I. Title
  823.9'14 [F]

  ISBN 0-7278-4915-8

Typeset by Palimpsest Book Production Limited,
Polmont, Stirlingshire, Scotland.
Printed and bound in Great Britain by
Hartnolls Ltd, Bodmin, Cornwall.

Chapter One

There were wings in the sky. A flight of white doves circled and flashed in the early morning sunlight. They made Isobel want to fly, too. She felt her heart lift to them – so pure and swift in their passing.

It was one of those crisp, diamond-bright mornings of early spring – a hint of frost in the air, and everything looking entirely new, polished and vivid, and somehow brimming with life. The winter-dark trunks of the trees, the painted railings of the front gardens, even the faded elegance of Clifton's tall Victorian houses, sparkled and gleamed with sharp points of light.

I would like to skip, thought Isobel, walking briskly and sedately as was her custom. I should like to jump over the cracks in the pavement, and run after my own shadow, and climb a tree.

A grim smile touched her straight no-nonsense mouth for a moment. Me – Isobel Frazier, retired teacher (well, I did take early retirement, but not by much), tough as old boots, and just as used up. Fifty-seven next birthday, and no getting away from it – but I don't feel a day over thirty! No, not even thirty. More like ten years old, this bright morning.

The doves flashed by again in a dazzle of silver, and Isobel actually gave a small, unobtrusive skip of delight. Alive, alive-O! they said to her. Alive! And, yes! she answered. Thank God, I'm alive!

She wasn't usually out so early – the normal routines of her life didn't include early morning walks. She had never

1

had a dog. Teaching all day had rather precluded it. But she had a cat, and she had forgotten to buy his food and her own breakfast cereal, and the corner shop wasn't far. And anyway, she told herself, why shouldn't she walk in the clear, cool morning and look up at a sky alive with wings? There was even an early lark singing somewhere high over the Downs. She couldn't see it, but she could hear it trilling and soaring up there in the blue air. The sky was filled with singing flight.

So she swung her shopping bag like a child, and gave another small, surreptitious skip of impish delight as the wings swooped over her.

She had just turned the corner into her own quiet road, when she saw the paperboy going up the steps of her house. It wasn't her usual boy, she thought, though she didn't often catch a glimpse of him, he came too early – but this one seemed slightly younger and smaller, and quicker on his feet.

It was neatly done. Three ragged-jeans strides up the white steps, one hand thrusting the morning paper through the letter box, the other reaching down to grab a pint of milk from the wire rack on the top step, three strides back down, one leg over the bar of the bicycle propped by the hedge, and away. Neat and quick.

But not quick enough. Without hesitation, Isobel leant forward and hooked the crook of her umbrella handle round the spokes of the bicycle's back wheel. The effect was catastrophic. Tatty jeans jumped a mile, the milk bottle fell from his hand, and a shrill cry of dismay escaped from beneath the pulled-down peak of the baseball cap on his head.

Shrill? Isobel paused for thought before launching into the attack. For the thin figure had lurched forward in an attempt to catch the falling milk bottle, and as he leant down, the baseball cap fell off, revealing a vivid mass of startlingly feminine red curls.

Not a paperboy at all. A papergirl – and a distressed one at that. The sharp, pointed little face beneath that profusion of glowing russet was like a hunting vixen's: predatory and fierce, but now filled with an expression that Isobel rightly interpreted as horror. Not horror at being caught in the act,

Isobel realized, but horror at the shattered mess of milk and glass on the pavement. What a waste, that shocked glance seemed to say – and Isobel suddenly understood that this child knew all too well the real value of food.

"I'm sorry, Miss." The voice was softer now, and faintly uneven.

Isobel began to snap in her usual crisp, faintly Scottish voice, *"What did you think you were doing?"* But to her surprise, she found herself saying instead, "It was my fault. I startled you."

The slanting, greenish-gold eyes lifted to Isobel's face. They seemed to probe deeply with the wary, cautious glance of someone who has learnt not to trust human beings very much, and never to be off her guard for a moment. She looked more like a little fox cub than ever. But then an expression of relief – almost of recognition – seemed to come into those extraordinary eyes, and the soft voice dared to offer some kind of explanation.

"It was the kids, you see. Trev says they must have breakfast before school, otherwise they can't concentrate. But my Dad was took bad in the night, see, and Trev used up all the milk. . . ." The words came rushing out in a spate of nervous excuses. "I never – never took nothing before," said the child. "Honest. But I thought – I thought p'raps you wouldn't miss one bottle, as you've got three left."

It was on the tip of Isobel's tongue to say, "I mostly only use it for my cat, anyway," but she knew she couldn't say that to those wary, anxious eyes. She stood looking at that pinched, elfin face for a moment in silence. "Who is Trev?" she asked.

"He's my big brother," said the child, and suddenly a renewed look of horror came into her face as she realized what she had done. "It's his paper-round, see, but he couldn't leave my Dad this morning, so I said I'd do it for him – I've done it before – and we need the money, see, he can't afford to lose the job." She looked at Isobel in helpless terror. "You won't . . .?"

"Call the police?" Isobel almost smiled.

The eyes flashed even more terror at her. "Or – or tell the papershop . . .? Trev would kill me." She took a shaky breath. "I could pay for it tomorrow – or bring you another one?"

"No," said Isobel. "That won't be necessary."

The girl had got off her bicycle completely by now, and stooped down rather desperately to pick up the pieces of glass.

"Leave it," ordered Isobel. "You'll cut yourself. If you come with me, I'll get you a dustpan and brush."

She waited to see whether the child would turn and run, but the eyes were looking at her again, rather puzzled now, and eventually the long, thin legs followed her up the steps, waited docilely while she put her key in the lock, and then followed her inside.

Isobel briskly fetched the dustpan and brush from the cupboard in the kitchen, and handed them to the taut young figure in the hall.

"What's your name, child?"

"Georgie. And I'm not a child. I'm eleven. And Trev says I can be quite useful when I'm not being silly." She looked suddenly abashed, and added, blushing, "Or downright wicked, like now."

A faint smile twitched at Isobel's stern mouth. "Well, Georgie, let's sweep up the mess. And then you can tell me a bit more about Trev and the kids. And your Dad."

Georgie looked at her hard again, and then nodded her small head so that all the red curls bobbed and sparked in the sun. "OK," she said, and went quite confidently down the steps and attacked the broken glass with surprising competence.

"Now," commanded Isobel, "wrap it all in this newspaper, and we'll put it in the dustbin."

Georgie did as she was told.

"And now," said Isobel, back once more in her big, sunny kitchen, "sit down a minute."

But Georgie would not do that. "I can't stay, Miss. The kids have to get to school. I'm late as it is." She looked at Isobel with piteous honesty. "I know it's all my fault – but I've got to go."

Isobel recognized the beginnings of panic in the foxy little face, and knew she could not pursue it now. Instead, she simply followed Georgie out on to the step, and reached down for another milk bottle. "Take this one instead. And don't drop it this time."

Georgie looked incredulous. *"Really?* Straight up?"

"Straight up," said Isobel. "And you'd better have this packet of cornflakes. I don't need it."

The gold-flecked green eyes widened and suddenly filled with tears. "Well, *thanks!*" the soft voice whispered. "You're *smashing,* d'you know that?"

In the circumstances, thought Isobel, *smashing* was not the word she would have chosen to use at present. But before she could say any more, the red-gold curls were flying in the wind as Georgie pedalled away for dear life – towards breakfast and the kids.

Georgie's face haunted Isobel all day, but then, belatedly, she remembered that it was Friday, and her friend Gervase was coming to supper. At the beginning of their acquaintance, when they had been wary of each other and determined to 'keep their end up' as Gervase had put it, the special Friday meal had been dinner, and there had been candles, and they had both dressed up for the occasion and 'put on a good show'. (Another of Gervase's unoriginal remarks.) But that phase had long since passed, and now they were as easy with each other as an old pair of slippers – so it was supper once a week, a game of Scrabble, and positively no candles.

Gervase was about Isobel's age, or perhaps a little older, though he never let on, and he was a great deal more set in his ways. He was an antiquarian bookseller, with a small, discreet shop hidden away in one of the quiet cul-de-sacs of back street Clifton. He looked a bit like his books – dry and leathery, with a stiff, unbending spine, parchment-pale skin, and an air of dusty respectability about him. But his brown, snappish eyes were very shrewd and calculating beneath rather sparse, spiky eyebrows, and his mouth was smallish and had a tendency to look a little prudish and petulant if things didn't go his way.

Isobel had long since recognized his faults as well as his virtues, and took care not to contradict him too much. After all, at his best he was pleasant company, and they could discuss books to their heart's content without coming to blows.

This evening, however, Isobel was still disturbed by that strange, desperate child who had appeared on her doorstep, and it showed.

"What's on your mind, Isobel?" he asked, in his precise, slightly pedantic voice. "You are not with us tonight."

"No," agreed Isobel absently. Then she looked up at Gervase with sudden, piercing directness. "Gervase – do you suppose there are still children in this city who are poor enough to need to steal a bottle of milk?"

Gervase blinked at her mildly. "I shouldn't think so. Pure mischief, more like. Why?"

Isobel chose to ignore the slight reproof in his voice, and recounted the morning's incident. When she had finished, Gervase snorted.

"Just as I said. Pure mischief. Or devilment. Children today have no discipline – no moral sense." He was off on his hobby-horse.

Isobel's clear blue eyes snapped sudden fire, but she did not contradict him. Not directly. "I don't know . . ." she murmured. "The child looked – stricken, somehow."

"Not surprising, since she was caught in the act." His voice was dry.

"No," Isobel said, almost to herself. "It wasn't that. . . ." Then she looked again at Gervase's outraged face and laughed a little. "You don't know much about children, do you, Gervase?"

"Not a lot," he admitted. "Tiresome creatures. Sticky fingers on my books."

"But you were a child yourself once."

"I suppose so." He sounded grudging about it.

Isobel was still looking at him. "Have you ever climbed a tree?" she asked suddenly.

He stared. "A tree? No, I don't think so. Why?"

Her smile was curiously compassionate. I wanted to climb a tree today, she thought. And to skip along the pavement. And to fly like a bird. . . . But to Gervase she only said, with sudden gentleness, "I just wondered . . . what your childhood was like?"

6

Gervase was not a fool. It occurred to him that Isobel had been a teacher all her life, and was probably missing the children, her charges, however tiresome and demanding they had been – and she was probably a little bored with her new life of leisure. But he did not say so.

"It was dull," he said, his tone a shade flat. "My father was an academic – always absorbed in something. No time for me. My mother was – er – 'flightly' was the word in those days, I believe. They quarrelled a lot. So I put my head in a book. I've been doing it ever since."

"Shutting out the world?"

"Exactly. More peaceful that way."

"But – *cold*, Gervase? Isn't it?"

He shrugged. "I hadn't noticed. I like an ordered life. I like books. You know where you are with them."

There was a slight emphasis on the word *them*, which gave Isobel to understand that people and their emotional problems confused Gervase and were best kept at arm's length.

She sighed. It was clearly no good trying to enlist his sympathy for young Georgie and her problems, whatever they were. He would run a mile from that foxy little face with its perilous smile. No, she would have to deal with it herself – if she could think of a way to find out what was wrong.

"You know, Isobel," said Gervase, watching her face with unexpected understanding, "you haven't got enough to do."

She looked startled. "Haven't I?"

"No. You've been so active and energetic all your life. I know you've got a part-time job at the library, and you help out in a couple of charity shops – but it probably isn't enough for you."

"So what do you propose?"

He considered, head on one side like an enquiring bird. "How about helping me in the bookshop?"

She glared at him. "You don't need an assistant."

"Yes, I do. When I go to sales. Or even shopping, or to the bank. I have to shut the shop then. It loses sales."

Isobel looked obstinate. "I don't know anything about antiquarian books."

7

"You'd learn. Anyway, most of the prices are marked inside the covers. Simple."

"No," said Isobel. "No, Gervase. Thank you for the offer. But, no."

"Why not?" He was genuinely puzzled.

She could not say that an extra day spent among dry-as-dust books instead of real people would just about kill her. But it would. And Gervase himself, kind as he was, would not be much better. He was almost as dry as his own books. No. She wanted more than that. She wanted the warmth and life, the anguish and conflict and endless demands of a couple of hundred children learning to cope with this stormy world. This world that had bright wings in the sky, and a child with a tangle of red curls and a vulnerable smile. . . .

"It's too easy . . ." she answered, not expecting him to understand her.

"Oh well," said Gervase, and smiled at her without reproach. "Never mind. How about a game of Scrabble?"

"Yes," agreed Isobel. "Yes, of course."

But in her mind she still saw those bright wings turning in the clear morning air.

The next morning, a little later than usual, her regular paperboy came. He pushed the paper through the letter box in his normal fashion, but then, instead of going away, he rang the bell.

Isobel had heard him come. She had intended to lie in wait and watch through the hall window to see if another milk bottle went missing, but at the last moment she could not bring herself to spy on the boy, or to suspect him even in her mind. It wasn't fair to prejudge him, so she went purposefully into the sitting-room and shut the door. The sudden shrilling of the bell startled her, and she came in some surprise to open her front door on the bright morning.

"Yes?" She looked somewhat severely at the boy standing before her.

He was tallish, she saw – nearly as tall as she was, brother and he stood very straight with his head up, as if strung for a challenge or an ordeal. His hair was not red like his young sister's, but a kind of tawny, burnt blond, and his eyes were

8

grey and wide, and (somehow she was sure) entirely honest. She thought also, with a fleeting sense of recognition, that those eyes would have been visionary and full of dreams if they had not been so worried.

"I brought the money for the milk, Miss," he said. "It was good of you to lend it to Georgie."

Isobel stared. The hand held out to her contained the exact price of two pints of milk. The careful precision of it somehow shook her, and she spoke more abruptly than she meant to, "You are Trev, I presume?"

"Yes, Miss."

"*Trevor?*" She liked to get things straight.

He nodded, still holding out the coins in his hand.

"I didn't *lend* it, Trevor." Her voice had softened suddenly. "I gave it – freely. And I don't want any money for it."

But the boy persisted. "*Please*, Miss. What Georgie did was all wrong, I know. But—"

"The money puts it right?" This time her tone was dry.

He still stood very straight and calm, looking at her out of those wide, anxious eyes, but a faint flush came into his face as she spoke. "No," he admitted. "It doesn't. But it makes it a bit better. Especially for Georgie."

Isobel saw that it mattered very much to this hard-pressed boy. That flake-white scraped-looking face of weary fortitude could not be denied. What on earth was he enduring, Isobel wondered, to make him look like that? So tired, and so determined.

"Very well," she said, and held out her hand for the money. "I'll take it on one condition."

"What's that?" He sounded instantly wary.

"That you come inside for a moment and tell me a bit more about Georgie and the kids. She saw him hesitate, and added with swift comprehension, "Have you time?"

He still seemed to hesitate, and that level glance seemed to probe deep down, through layers and layers of human deception, sudden dangers and broken promises to the heart's core that might or might not prove to be the ultimate threat, or the ultimate sanctuary. But at length he seemed to find reassurance in Isobel's equally straight no-nonsense glance,

9

and to accept her (though cautiously) as someone who could probably be trusted.

"All right," he said. It's Saturday, he reminded himself, totting up responsibilities. The kids are home. They'll be all right for a bit longer. . . . He looked round then at his bicycle propped by the gate, and the empty satchel slung over the end of the handlebars. "You were the last on my round," he muttered, as if still arguing with himself about what to do.

"In that case, you can spare the time for a cup of tea," said Isobel briskly, and waited for him to follow her inside.

Isobel's house, being Victorian and from a more opulent age, had one or two good old-fashioned features, including the staircase with its mahogany banisters and polished treads, and the lofty hall with its black and white tiled floor and tall stained-glass window on the landing.

The boy stood staring round him for a moment, his eyes taking in the airy space with obvious delight, and lingering for a brief appreciative glance on the spilled glow of colours reflected from the high window on to the polished floor. "So much light!" he murmured, and followed Isobel dutifully into the kitchen.

The kettle had already boiled once, Isobel remembered thankfully, and set about making tea as swiftly as possible. The boy was still nervous, she told herself. There must be no delay, or he would just panic like his young sister and go.

"Now," she said, planting a mug of tea down in front of him, "sit down for a minute, Trevor, and tell me about your family. How many of you are there?"

Trevor stirred his tea, frowning down at it in sudden intense concentration. It was as if he was mustering all his forces to face some kind of merciless onslaught. Questions. Rules. Regulations. They terrified him. "Well, there's me and Georgie, and then there's Colin, he's nearly ten, and Marigold – Goldie for short – she's the youngest, she's only six . . . Mum's afterthought, she used to call her." A small, reminiscent smile touched him for a moment.

Isobel looked at him questioningly. But when he didn't say any more, she prompted him gently. "And your father?"

Trevor's worn young face seemed to grow even wearier.

10

"He's sick, you see. He's been sick a long time. . . ." He gave Isobel a bleak, tired smile. "Mostly, he's no trouble now. We all look after him. But – but sometimes in the night he gets bad."

Isobel nodded, as if accepting that calm, neutral assessment. "What about your mother?" After all, she told herself sternly, the question had to be asked.

"Oh, she went off." The boy's voice was absurdly offhand and casual.

"*Went off*? When? How long ago?"

The grey eyes slid away from hers with a sort of unwilling evasion. He did not like being less than truthful – nor did he like admitting the truth, even to himself. "Oh . . . it was about seven – no, eight – months ago. . . . When Goldie was still five."

Isobel was silent for a moment, appalled by the pain behind that too-casual voice. "More than eight months ago? And you've been managing on your own all that time?"

He did look at her then, with a sudden flash of pride. "We manage pretty well. All the kids help. It's only – only *temporary*, you see, till Mum comes back." There was a kind of pleading demand for understanding in his glance now. "I tell the kids she'll be home soon. She'll want to see the place looking tidy – and our Dad well cared for, won't she . . .? And they understand that, you see. They mostly do what I tell them – and I mostly tell them what Mum would have told them, anyway. . . ." He sighed, and looked at Isobel with a lopsided grin of apology. "They're good kids – even Georgie. She's not really . . . not really wild."

Isobel smiled, too. "I'm glad to hear it!" Then she looked again at that too-experienced young face and said gently "And how old are you, Trevor?"

"I'm thirteen," he said. "Nearly fourteen." And, as if answering a question she had not asked, "I'm not too young to cope. I know what to do for my Dad." The fierce, defensive pride was back in his voice.

She nodded. "I'm sure you do."

But there was something he had to explain to her before she said any more. It was all very well, these people who wanted to be helpful, they simply didn't understand a thing.

11

"You see, if the Welfare people come in, they'll try to put us all into care – and put Dad in a home or something. We don't want that. We want to stay together."

"So you keep quiet and ask for no help?"

He looked a little confused. "We do get *some* help. It's not so bad."

"What about school, Trevor?"

"They all go now. Georgie takes them. And they all have school dinners," he added, with an earnest attempt at reassurance. "Mum fixed that before she – as soon as Goldie was five. . . . And she fixed a – all the extras she could get from the Welfare. . . . They do all right." He still sounded anxious and on the defensive.

"I wasn't talking about them," said Isobel. "What about you?"

"Me?" He sounded totally blank for a moment. "Oh, school you mean? I go when I can – if Dad's all right. But he doesn't like being left alone much. . . ." He looked worried again for a moment. "They got a bit bothered about me playing truant, but Mr Selwyn told them how it was, and they've laid off since."

"Who's Mr Selwyn?"

"My music master. And my maths master. Well, he *was*. He taught me the cello, but I had to give it up. No time to practise, and anyway, orchestra was on Saturdays and the kids are home. . . ."

Isobel nodded again, accepting his explanations without comment, but making a swift mental note to look up Mr Selwyn, the music and maths master, sometime. "What school is that, Trevor?"

"St Swithin's."

"And the kids?"

"St Swithin's Junior. Mum's a Catholic, see. She's Irish."

An Irish Catholic, and she leaves her four children and her sick husband without a backward glance . . .? "I see," said Isobel, trying not to let her voice sound too censorious. She wondered if she dared ask the most difficult question of all: What is wrong with your father? But somehow she could not ask it yet. The boy was obviously fiercely protective about his father – determined to put a brave face on it and assure

12

everyone that he could cope. . . . She could not destroy that confidence or that touching pride with awkward questions. Not yet. Though there were plenty of questions to be asked. But they would have to wait till she knew him better – and then maybe he would tell her himself without being asked.

"I must go now," he said, starting up. "I've been away long enough." The anxious eyes raked hers again with sudden terror. "You won't . . .?"

"Shop you to the Welfare?" She grinned at him cheerfully. "No, of course I won't. I can see you've got everything under control, and you're managing very well!"

The painful smile came out again, lighting the tired young face. "Thanks. And thanks for the tea." He seemed to hesitate then, as if wanting to say more, but he didn't. Only, strange messages of reassurance seemed to pass between the two of them, totally unsaid.

Isobel smiled. "There's usually a cup of tea going, if you have time to stop."

He grinned – an almost ordinary, boyish grin with a hint of mischief in it. "Thanks," he said again. "I'll remember that."

Flying through the early morning streets on his bike was the best time for Trevor. He was free then. Free of the worry about his Dad and the kids, the washing and tidying and shopping and cooking and all the endless chores of trying to run a family. Was he doing enough? Was he doing it right? Was he being tough enough with the kids when they went wrong? (His Dad used to be too tough, and his Mum, when she was there, was too soft. . . .) It was hard to be the policeman of the family – but Georgie's latest escapade had shaken him. They had never resorted to stealing before. It was only because his Dad had needed soothing down in the night with that extra hot drink, and the fact that it was Friday and he didn't get paid for the paper-round till Saturday. . . . But even so, it oughtn't to have happened. His Mum would have been horrified. All the time she had been there when things got short, she had managed somehow. And so had he – somehow. Till now. But Georgie's disaster had made him realize how perilously close to the edge they were. . . .

Still, here he was, pedalling away through sunlight and blue air, and this was his own time, and he would not waste it worrying. And besides, he thought to himself, with a strange little smile of recollection lighting his face, he thought he had an ally now. Nothing had been said, but he had felt her strength and kindness round him like a cloak – that tall, grey woman with the piercing eyes. And he had not realized till now how much he had missed having someone to talk to, someone to rely on, someone to share his problems with, because he could never let on to the kids or his Dad how worried he sometimes was. But now it was different suddenly. He felt the weight of responsibility lift a little. She would help, he told himself. If I asked her. I have a friend, and she would help.

He pedalled even faster, and looked up for a moment at the clear morning sky. He felt like letting out a whoop of pure joy. It was suddenly so good to be alive and out of doors in the sparkling day. But he didn't. People might think he was off his head. Perhaps he was, for the moment. Freedom was heady stuff.

Sometimes when he was on his bike he dreamed of real freedom. He thought of going on and on, down the grey tarmac ribbon to the end of the line – to the sea. . . . And then . . .? When his Dad was working on the docks, sometimes he would take Trevor with him on a Saturday to look at the ships. They were mostly container ships nowadays – great long, heavy things that his Dad said were pretty powerful but not at all graceful, not like a ship should be on the water. And then he would point out some of the smaller craft – the tramps and small traders, coalers from Colombia, banana boats and deep sea trawlers and the big fish-processing factory ships that the trawler men hated.

Names sang in his head then. Valparaiso . . . Montevideo . . . Cape Town . . . Lorenco Marques . . . Magical names of distant places . . . places he had never seen, but longed to go to. One day, he would. When his dad was better, and his Mum had come back, and the kids were all grown up, or at any rate old enough for him to leave. *Leave* . . .? Would he ever be free to leave? He wondered about that sometimes – especially in the dark nights when he sat up with his Dad.

14

Things always looked black then. . . . But now it was bright day, and he was free to dream – just for a little while.

There were always seagulls flying overhead near the river – near the wide stretch of the old muddy Severn that led to the sea. He could usually hear them calling, even from the windows of the flat if he left them open, and the sound of their voices always made him ache. The sea, they called, wide empty spaces, waves and gales and distant places, far away, far away. . . . There was a poem they did once at school that began: 'News of a foreign country came. . . .' He couldn't remember the rest, but it haunted him, that mysterious line. . . . The seagulls sang it to him.

He nearly fell off his bike, day-dreaming like that and looking up at a pair of tilting wings when he should have been looking at the road. Pull yourself together, he told himself sharply. Time you were home anyway. They'll all be waiting for you. No more time for dreams.

He pedalled on, turned a corner, and reached his own shabby street. It wasn't any good leaving the bike downstairs chained to a railing. People just cut the chain with a pair of pliers. He'd lost one bike like that already, before his Mum went away, and he knew it had been an awful struggle for her to find the money even for a second-hand clapped-out replacement. Couldn't afford to lose another. So he carried it up two flights of stairs to the flat.

Inside, to his relief, everything seemed to be in order, and Georgie was in charge. She was rather chastened after the row about the milk, and had made a special effort to be useful. The breakfast was laid out on the table, the kids were dressed and washed (even Colin, who hated washing) and his Dad had a cup of tea in his hand.

Trevor went over to him first. "OK, Dad?"

The big blond head nodded slowly, the bright, intelligent eyes looked into his, wanting to say all kinds of things that could not be said.

"I've given him his tea," said Georgie, tossing bright curls out of the way. "And emptied his bottle. But I think he wants to get up."

"Yes," Trevor agreed, interpreting one of the messages in

15

those frustrated eyes. "I'll get you into your chair now, Dad. Do you want the bathroom first?"

"Ba – roo," said his father, painfully trying to get his tongue round the difficult word.

Quite cheerfully, Trevor put his arms round the heavy body of his father and heaved him up, skilfully placing his wheelchair behind him so that he could more-or-less fall into it backwards. His arms were perfectly active and useful – and still quite powerful, too – but his legs dragged helplessly below his damaged spine and were already beginning to shrivel a little through lack of use.

Trevor's father was a big man who had been strong and active and proud of his physique in the days when he was working on the docks – and even now, hampered as he was by these heavy, recalcitrant limbs, he struggled to sit upright, to maintain his fierce independence of movement. It was an impossible task, of course, and he suffered many falls and frustrating set-backs because he was so obstinate, but Trevor and the kids understood his need, and tried to let him do things his own way if they could.

In any case, his rages were still unpredictable and frightening, and they had learnt to be wary of a flying fist or a hurled plate if things got too bad to bear. They understood his rages, too, and did not blame him for them. It was hard for a man like their Dad to be stuck in a wheelchair all day. They forgave him everything, with the easy kindness of children, and simply waited till he felt better before they came near him again. And besides, Trevor had told them all, very seriously, that they must not go near him when he was in a fury, and must be sure to keep out of reach of his hands, which were very strong. He did not explain this to them, but they knew that when Trevor commanded something, it usually made sense, so they obeyed him.

Today, though, Trevor judged, his Dad was feeling a bit better, and he helped him in and out of his wheelchair in the bathroom, aware that his movements were steadier and surer than usual. Maybe he was getting better after all.

"What did she say?" asked Georgie, when they were actually sitting down to breakfast and their father was safely

16

back in his wheelchair and at the table beside them. "Was she very cross?"

"No." Trevor frowned at his sister's cheerful face. Nothing daunted Georgie for long. "But she ought to have been."

Georgie hung her head. "I know. . . . Did she take the money?"

"Yes." A faint smile touched his face for a moment. "And she gave me a cup of tea."

"There," grinned Georgie, "I told you she was a nice old stick."

"She's not an old stick," protested Trevor, unsure why he felt obliged to defend her. "She's a – a real lady." He could not explain quite why this was true, but it was. It wasn't only the straight glance of those searching eyes, the dignified manner, and the upright, elegant carriage, it was something else – to do with her refusal to apportion blame, and her calm desire to know more before passing judgement. And her extraordinarily courteous manner to him – a very errant errand boy. He could not explain all this to himself, but Isobel had impressed him.

"I think she's rather special," he murmured, helping himself to cornflakes.

"I told her she was smashing," agreed Georgie, sparking with cheerfulness now that the danger was past. Trevor could be quite fierce when he disapproved of something.

"Smashing," agreed Goldie, with her mouth full.

Colin was running a toy car from the cornflakes packet round and round the table, with appropriate zooming noises. "Smashing," he echoed vaguely.

"I'll give you smashing," growled Trevor, but the kids could tell by his voice that he wasn't angry. In fact, he sounded quite pleased about something.

"Corn – flakes," said his father, quite distinctly.

They all stared at him in amazement. Then Trevor got to his feet, smiling, with the cornflakes packet in his hand. "Cornflakes coming up," he said, rejoicing. His Dad was getting better.

17

Chapter Two

'Get up, old woman, and shake yourself.'

Old Jig

Isobel did not tell Gervase very much about the boy's visit, though she did report (somewhat smugly) that he had paid her the money for the milk. Gervase, if anything, seemed a little put out by this. She fancied he was slightly annoyed to find his fears about 'devilment' and undisciplined children proved to be groundless.

Undisciplined? Trevor's white, bone-weary face and stony determination to do the right thing came into her mind all too clearly. There was nothing undisciplined about that boy – whatever might be said about his volatile young sister. And the load of responsibility he was carrying might well have daunted an adult, let alone a boy of thirteen. *Had* daunted an adult, hadn't it? What other reason could their mother have had for leaving those children?

The problem puzzled her, but she felt very strongly that she could not ask too many questions at present. She had to wait. Sooner or later the boy would tell her about it. In the meantime, though, was there anything she could do to help?

At first she had been inclined to ask in the papershop about the boy and his father. But then she thought that might make the newsagent suspect there had been some kind of trouble, and that might jeopardize the boy's job. No, she mustn't do that.

Then she thought of the music master, Mr Selwyn, at St Swithin's, but she wasn't ready to talk to him yet. That time would come, she told herself, when she had discovered a bit more about them all, and had found out

18

what she ought to do.

I am a bossy, managing old woman, she told herself. (Well, not *old*, exactly. Just into my prime, I think!) And I've been used to organizing children's lives for them, regardless, whether they liked it or not, all my working life. But now I must go carefully. I'm not in charge of anything, or anyone now. And that boy, Trevor, has got his pride. I could see that. If I interfere, the whole perilous structure of his family life may come tumbling down round his ears. I mustn't do that. I must wait.

So she waited. Even though it was hard for someone as strong and competent and well-meaning, and simply itching to do something practical and useful, as she was. Even so, she waited.

And this time it was Archimedes, the cat, who engineered the next meeting. (There was something rather strange about the way Archimedes engineered things.) Usually, she let him out into the garden at first light through the kitchen door, and let him in again when he condescended to return. Archimedes was an opportunist, from the tip of his elegant black tail to the white tufts in his alert black ears, and if something of interest came to his notice outside the garden, he went to investigate before returning to the simple pleasures of breakfast and his customary saucer of milk. So it was that instead of asking to be let into the kitchen as usual, he turned up on the front doorstep after a detour or two, just as that quick-footed paperboy came running up the steps. Archimedes, not caring much for those rushing feet, flattened himself against the door and asked loudly to be admitted.

Isobel, mystified by this imperious voice from the wrong side of the house, came to have a look, and opened the door just as Trevor reached out to put her paper in the letter box.

"Ah, Trevor," said Isobel, quick off the mark, but not so quick as Archimedes who shot past her into the hall, "what about that cup of tea?"

The boy looked at her for a moment in silence, hesitating, but she almost fancied that she saw relief in his grey eyes. Maybe he wanted to be asked in again, but was too shy to ask?

19

"It *is* Saturday," she reminded him. "You've got time. . . ."

Trevor suddenly smiled, like someone throwing off care. "So I have," he admitted, and followed Archimedes inside. "Is he yours?" he asked, stooping to stroke the immaculate black fur coat – a liberty which Archimedes permitted with gracious condescension.

"Yes," Isobel acknowledged, "as much as he is anyone's. But he is his own master."

"What do you call him?"

"His name is Archimedes – which means 'mastermind'. He is very clever. But I'm afraid he mostly gets called Archie."

The boy's eyes were laced with laughter. "Does he mind?"

"Not if I am calling him in for his food." She grinned, and went ahead of Trevor into the kitchen, where she put down a small dish of cat food and a saucer of milk on the floor. "Though at other times," she added, straightening up and turning back to the white worktop where the kettle was boiling, "he has been known to ignore me altogether unless I use his proper name."

Trevor actually laughed, and somehow, before any more doubts and anxieties could overcome him, he was sitting at the kitchen table drinking tea.

"Well, how have you been getting on?" asked Isobel, sounding brisk and cheerful. "Is your father any better?"

Trevor's face grew a little cautious. "Yes – a bit."

Isobel tried to ignore the reluctance in his voice. It was time to find out a few facts. How else could she be any use to him? "Can't the doctors help?"

"Not a lot." Trevor's tone was bleak. Then he seemed to realize that he was not being very approachable, and his eyes met hers in mute entreaty, but he did not say any more.

"Trevor," began Isobel slowly, not sure if she was going too fast, but pursuing it with intent, "could I come and see you all one day? I'd like to meet Colin and Goldie – and your father."

Trevor looked doubtful. "I don't know . . . I'd have to – to know when you were coming." His apologetic grin flashed out again. "So I could tidy up a bit."

20

"You wouldn't have to tidy up for me."

"Yes, I would." His voice was firm. "And – and spruce up my Dad a bit."

"Oh yes, of course." She was looking at him in half-smiling assent, aware of her advantage. "A Saturday or Sunday would be best, wouldn't it?" She was determined to push it further. "You could tell me which would be convenient when you come next Saturday, couldn't you?"

He was still doubtful. "It – it's a bit rough, you know. . . . Not like here." He looked round him at the big white kitchen and the view of green lawns and flowerbeds beyond the garden door.

"*Trevor!*" she protested. And didn't try to say any more.

"Oh, all right," he agreed suddenly, a pale grin returning. "So long as you know what you're in for."

That gave her the opening she wanted. "But I *don't*, Trevor," she said bluntly. "And I think I ought to before I come, don't you?" She waited a moment, and watched the grey eyes cloud with a kind of helpless uncertainty. "What happened to him?" she insisted, her voice grown curiously gentle. "Can't you tell me?"

The boy's cloudy gaze searched hers for a moment, and then seemed to clear into honesty – as if he had made up his mind at last. "He – he had an accident."

"At work?"

"No. Not at work." He seemed to draw a breath of curiously adult resolve before he went on. "He was laid off, you see – made redundant – at the docks. That began it."

"Began what?" Isobel's voice was still gentle.

He looked at her again, rather despairingly. It was so difficult to explain. "He was very good at his job, my Dad. He couldn't bear being idle. It made him angry – terribly angry. . . ." He paused again, unwilling to go on.

But Isobel was persistent. "And so . . .?"

He gave a small, helpless shrug. "And so . . . there were too many late nights at the Red Lion." His tone was absurdly adult and worldly-wise. "Mum used to yell at him – or go and fetch him sometimes." His eyes were pleading now, belying the tough young voice. He was making excuses for both his parents, as he did all the time in his own mind.

21

"He hated not earning, you see – Mum told me. She said even when he – he hit out, it was because he couldn't bear being useless. She always made excuses for him. But this time. . . ."

"This time?"

"She was angry, too, you see. So she didn't go to fetch him home. . . . But when he didn't come back at all, she began to get worried." Once again he stalled, as if the memory of that long night of waiting was too much to bear.

Isobel could see the pattern – the awful disintegration of an active man with no purpose left in life, his masculine pride in ruins. "And then . . .?" she prompted, for it had to be finished now.

Trevor's face had seemed to grow pale as he thought back to that terrible time. "When he didn't come back all night, she decided to ring the police. He. . . ." the boy's too-knowledgeable glance just flicked hers for a moment, "He wasn't – I mean, she knew he wouldn't have just gone off with some girl or other. He wasn't like that. . . . She was sure something had happened to him."

"And it had?"

The boy nodded bleakly. "Yes. It had. Though no one knows what, exactly. He'd fallen down a whole flight of steps into someone's basement. He was lying there unconscious all night."

"Who found him?"

"I did."

"*You* did?" Isobel was shocked.

"Yes. I'd just started on my paper-round job at Mr Harding's, you see. I was too young, but we were getting short of money by then, and Mum persuaded him."

Isobel nodded.

"So I thought I'd just ride round by the Red Lion and have a look. . . . He might've fallen asleep on a bench or something . . . I don't know what made me look down into that basement area place, but I did – and there he was, all sprawled out in a heap." He shut his mouth tight then, so that it couldn't tremble.

"What did you do?"

"I went to Mr Harding's. It was the only place open that

22

early. And he phoned for an ambulance and told the police . . . and I went back to tell Mum." He took another swift, uneven breath. "The police didn't do much. They said they couldn't tell if he'd just fallen or been mugged or something . . . but he'd fractured his skull on the concrete, and his back. . . ." He corrected himself painfully, "His spine was injured. . . . The doctors couldn't tell how badly."

There was a long silence while the boy tried to get back his normal voice, and Isobel tried vainly to think of something positive to say.

But Trevor was determined to get it all out in the open now. Perhaps if he actually said it all, the whole thing would not seem so bad. "He was in hospital quite a long time. At first he was in a c—?"

"Coma?"

He nodded. "Yes. A coma. But when he came round, he knew us all right, but he couldn't speak." The clear, bleak glance settled on her once more. "You could see him wanting to say things to us – especially to Mum – but he couldn't. The doctors said it was a kind of brain damage, and they didn't know if he'd learn to speak again, but it would take time." He sighed, and went on steadily, "And as for his legs – they didn't think he'd ever walk again, but they'd have to wait and see." His voice hardened a little. "So they sent him home."

"Just like that?"

"There wasn't much more they could do for him, I suppose." Once again the pleading glance begged her to make allowances. "And they knew Mum was there to look after him . . ." There was a grim twist to his mouth now. "But the trouble was, he wouldn't let Mum come near him. He used to – to sort of *roar* at her when he couldn't get the words out, and – and knock things out of her hand. He still, does sometimes. . . . Mum *tried*, really she did . . . but in the end she couldn't take any more, I s'pose. So she just – took off."

There was something a bit odd about the way he said this, as if more could have been added. But he did not go on. Isobel was puzzled, but she did not know quite how to press him further. "Leaving you to cope?"

"She left a note," he said, offering pitiful excuses, and

clearly leaving something out that was probably vital. "She said: 'Tell the Welfare. They'll help when I'm not there.'" The grey eyes were more beseeching than ever. "They wouldn't help before, you see, however much she asked, because they said she was there to look after us. But she thought they would if we were left on our own. . . . She never knew we didn't tell them, see?"

Isobel did see. And her heart ached for that little family of gallant children, patiently waiting for their mother to come home.

"What is she like, your mother?" Isobel had almost said, what *was* she like – but she changed it swiftly. If they believed she was coming back, Isobel herself must not shake that belief. It was all they had to cling to at present. "Tell me about her?" she suggested gently.

A faint, reminiscent smile touched Trevor's face for a moment. "She's very pretty. She's got red hair, like Georgie's, and she used to laugh a lot – and sing the old Irish songs . . . and she used to dance."

"Dance?"

"Yes. She taught us all the tunes. Dad used to play the mouth organ. It was something he could take to work in his pocket to amuse his mates. He was quite good at it. And Georgie played the fiddle, and me on the cello. Colin's learning the clarinet at school, but he's even better on the old penny whistle. Even Goldie used to bang a drum, and sing along with the Tunes . . . and Mum danced. You know, that kind of quick heel-and-toe stuff the Irish do. . . . She was very good. Dad loved to see her dance."

He was silent for a moment, remembering those days when his father was well and working, and everyone was happy. There were very nearly tears in his eyes, but of course he couldn't let them come to anything. He glanced at Isobel again, almost apologetically. "I try to make them practise," he said. "The old Tunes, I mean . . . so that they can play them for her when she comes back. . . . It gives them something to – to plan for. Colin would rather play in a group. He wants an electric guitar, only it costs too much, but he keeps up the old stuff if I make him."

He grinned a little lopsidedly. (He was never sure how

24

much he ought to bully the kids to make them practise.) "I think it cheers Dad up to hear Mum's Tunes, but sometimes it makes him sad, so we have to be careful. . . ." He looked at her seriously, issuing a cautious warning. "We – we try not to let things get too gloomy." He had successfully steered himself past the dangerous moment and his eyes were clear again. There was a curious, pain-washed silence between them, and then he said, "So now you know the worst – do you still want to come?"

"Yes," said Isobel. "I do. I shall look forward to it."

He shot her one incredulous, faintly sardonic look, but he made no further protest. If she wanted to come, she would come. He had done his best.

Archimedes, as if the matter had reached a satisfactory conclusion, leapt up on to the table and butted Trevor with his handsome black head.

"I think he wants me to go," said Trevor, laughing.

When Gervase came to supper the next Friday, Isobel found herself telling him about Trevor's problems and her proposed visit to his family.

But Gervase was very disapproving. "You and your lame ducks," he said. "I don't think you ought to get mixed up with a lot of feckless Irish Catholics who would rather play silly tunes and dance than earn a decent living. They sound like real scroungers to me."

"Gervase," said Isobel sternly, finding herself very angry, "four children under fourteen can't earn a living, decent or otherwise. Nor can a sick man in a wheelchair."

"But a wife and mother could – instead of swanning off," retorted Gervase. "Dancing, indeed! No sense of responsibility."

"By all accounts," said Isobel sadly, "she had put up with a good deal. . . . We don't know, Gervase, what finally drove her to do something so desperate."

He merely snorted at this. "Anyway, they seem to be surviving." He gave them a dismissive shrug. "I should leave well alone if I were you."

"But you're not me," snapped Isobel. "And you don't know anything about them – or whether they are surviving adequately or not. And that's what I am going to find out."

Gervase looked at that set, stern mouth and sighed. He knew better than to argue with Isobel when she had made up her mind about something. "Well, don't blame me if they take you for a ride," he warned, only mildly concerned about her unwise course of action.

"I wouldn't mind taking *them* for a ride," said Isobel, the light of battle in her eye. "That's a brilliant idea. Can I borrow your car?"

He was about to explode into outraged refusal when he realized that she was only teasing him, and, catching the faint twitch of laughter at the corner of that grim mouth, he had the grace to laugh as well.

"You are incorrigible," he said.

"I know," agreed Isobel. "I always was."

All the same, with Gervase's doubts in mind, she decided to go and see the newsagent after all. At least she could check up that the bare bones of Trevor's story were true.

"Oh, you must mean Cliff Broadbent's boy, Trevor."

"Yes, Trevor."

"Why? Has he done anything wrong?"

"No, not at all," said Isobel firmly. "On the contrary, he seems to be a very reliable boy."

"Yes, he is. No trouble." The shrewd brown eyes were looking at her with enquiry.

"I just wondered . . ." began Isobel, feeling somehow uncomfortable even to be asking, "if you could tell me a little about his family circumstances. . . . He seems to have certain – er – difficulties at home?"

The newsagent's face seemed to change from suspicion to a kind of tired compassion. "Yes, poor kid. Plenty on his plate, I'm afraid. He does his level best to keep things going."

"What happened exactly, do you know?"

"To Cliff Broadbent?" He shrugged a little, but his reply was not unsympathetic. "I don't suppose we'll ever know exactly. He was on his way home – rather the worse for wear. . . . It was a dark night. My guess is he just missed the way and fell down. . . . His own fault, of course,

26

but that doesn't make it any better." He looked at Isobel apologetically. "It destroys a man, being laid off. There you are, useless. No one wants you. Can't find a job. So you drink yourself silly." His smile was rueful. "We see a lot of it round here."

Isobel nodded. "I can imagine."

The shopkeeper's good-natured face was saddened. "I'm afraid it's a bad lookout for Cliff Broadbent."

"And his wife?"

"Poor young thing – four kids and a crippled husband. . . . She did her best for them all for a long time. But Cliff was – difficult to manage." The kindly expression grew a little wary again. "I never heard her complain . . . but once or twice she came in here looking really rough."

Isobel sighed. "Knocked about?"

"Oh yes. He could be violent, Cliff Broadbent – short fuse, even before the trouble began." He echoed Isobel's sigh. "You can't really blame her for running off. Only," he sounded puzzled, "she was a good mother, you know. Cared a lot about her kids . . . I couldn't really fathom how she could have just left them like that. Out of character, somehow."

Isobel agreed with him. "I thought so, too – from what Trevor has told me about her."

He flashed her a small, reminiscent smile. "Yes. Pretty young thing. Lively, and always laughing . . . at least, she *was*." He sighed again. "But towards the end, she began to look sort of *quenched*, somehow. All that sparkiness gone, if you know what I mean?"

"I do, indeed," said Isobel.

He was looking at her now with the question back in his eyes, but he did not voice it.

"I'm going to see them next week," she said, answering that look of mute enquiry. "There may be something I can do. . . ."

The small smile flashed out again. "That's good of you. They could certainly do with some help round there." He hesitated a moment and then added a little awkwardly, "I pay the boy as much as I can afford, you know. . . . But if there's anything else I could do . . .?"

27

"I'll find out," promised Isobel, liking his reticent kindness. "You've been very helpful already, Mr Harding."

He held out his hand with sudden unexpected friendliness. "Most people call me Mike."

"Thank you, Mike," answered Isobel, formally shaking his hand. "I'll let you know how things go."

She turned away briskly then, and Mike Harding watched with a mixture of amusement and respect in his face as the straight-backed upright figure marched purposefully away up the street.

It was a jewel-bright spring afternoon when Isobel arrived in the street, but that didn't make it look much better. It was undeniably shabby, peeling paint on the doors and windowframes, crumbling front steps and broken railings, a few battered small cars and vans and one burnt-out wreck at the far end where the houses ended in a cul-de-sac, with another even shabbier row backing on to it. No gardens – front or back, just yards with dustbins and a scraggy tree or two.

She stood looking up at Number Twelve with some misgiving, but she was committed to this visit now and she couldn't back out of it. Nor did she want to, for her sympathy for those children was already strong, and her curiosity even stronger. She had to see for herself what the set-up was, and find out as soon as maybe how to be of some practical help to them all.

Second floor, she said, gazing up at the windows. Well, at least they haven't got grubby grey net curtains like the ground floor, and it looks as if they believe in keeping their windows open. . . . Sighing, she shifted the carrier bag with the cake and the sausages into her other hand, and started to climb the steps.

There had been quite an argument with Trevor about the sausages. "We *asked* you to tea," he said, looking pale and obstinate. "You don't have to bring anything."

"Yes, I do, Trevor. I always bring a cake when I go out to tea."

"Well . . ." he still sounded a little affronted, "maybe a cake. . . ."

28

"Home-made?"

A faint grin. "That's different!"

"But," she pointed out, "it's the kids' evening meal, isn't it? Cake won't be enough. What do they usually have?"

He shrugged, the faint grin still flickering. "Mostly baked beans."

Isobel sighed. "What do they like best?"

"Bangers and mash. Or fish and chips."

"Then sausages it is," she decreed. And glared at Trevor's mutinous face. "No arguments. Can't they have a treat?"

There was no way he could refuse after that. Sausages it was. So he gave in gracefully, with a slightly wider and more mischievous grin of assent.

She pushed open the front door and went into the dark hallway. Two shut doors with Yale locks – the downstairs flats, a tangle of prams and pushchairs under the well of the stairs. One thin table and a letter rack on the wall, and a communal pay phone. Uncarpeted stairs, graffiti on the walls, and a smell of damp.

She climbed to the first floor. Two more Yale-locked doors, blank and silent. No, not quite silent. Faint pop music from behind one, a baby crying from the other. The stairs went on up, bare and steep, not much paint left on the banisters or the walls, but no graffiti up here. One small window letting in a shaft of dusty sunlight, and the second landing ahead. No lift. So how did a man in a wheelchair manage?

Number Three. That was it. She straightened her shoulders, took a deep breath, and rang the bell. There was a scatter of footsteps from within, and a voice said shrilly, "No, let *me!*" before the brown door opened and Georgie's vivid little face in its bright tangle of red curls looked out at her. "Come in, Miss," she said, smiling. "Trev's got the kettle on."

"And I've got the sausages," said Isobel, also smiling, and advancing purposefully into the kitchen, which came first into view from the narrow passage behind the front door. Georgie laughed, and the ice was broken.

Trevor looked up from the kitchen table where he was busy spreading margarine on slices of bread, and gave Isobel an anxious smile.

"I'll cook," announced Georgie, rightly interpreting her

29

brother's anxiety. "You go and talk to Dad, Trev. He's waiting."

"Dad's waiting, Dad's waiting," chanted Goldie from the doorway. (She always turned things into songs.)

Colin, close behind her, instantly hushed her, growling, "Quiet, Goldie. You've got to be good, Trev says." She was instantly quiet, and Isobel reflected that these four valiant children were too disciplined, and too anxious to make a good impression. Their lives were too precarious and threatened for them to take any risks.

She looked at them attentively, already disarmed by their well-drilled good manners and their total reliance on each other – and already more than a little enchanted by Goldie's glowing flower face. For she was absurdly like her name – Marigold, the brilliant red-gold fronds of her hair clinging round her head and framing her pointed face like the petals of a sturdy, sun-gilded plant. Wide open eyes, of the same unusual green-gold as her sister's, regarded Isobel with fearless appraisal and seemed to be summing her up with something like approval, for the soft, gentle mouth suddenly curved into a smile that lit up her whole face and clearly offered a welcome. Isobel could not resist smiling back.

Colin, on the other hand, was more wary, and more cautious in his approval. (They were all a bit too cautious, Isobel reflected, except for the flower girl, Goldie.) The boy did not have the same burnt-blond hair as his brother. His unruly thatch was a mixture of blond and red – a kind of sandy gold, and his nose had a dusting of freckles to match. But he had the same clear grey eyes as Trevor's, only they had more mischief in them. And more sharpness, too – as if he was all too aware of the wicked world around him and determined to get out of it everything he could while the going was good. Isobel thought sadly, he has seen too much for a small boy, and he is less of a visionary than his older brother. Less of an idealist, too – and probably less enduring and steady, but then Trevor is the one who has had to take most of the responsibility.

"Hallo," she said, trying to dispel the faint wariness in those watchful eyes. "You must be Colin. And you're Goldie."

"Goldie," agreed the laughing flower face. "I'm Goldie." And

30

she began to dance a small, ceremonial jig of exuberance in the doorway between the small kitchen and the livingroom beyond.

"Come on," said Trevor. "You must meet my Dad."

Obediently, Isobel followed him into the room and stood looking round her. It was a biggish, open room, and sparsely but not badly furnished. There was a sofa-bed against one wall, neatly made up, and two comfortable-looking armchairs covered in a brownish, serviceable material stood on either side of the fireplace which was blocked by a rather old-fashioned-looking gas fire. A square table, already set with cups and plates for tea, stood in the other corner with six plain kitchen chairs placed round it, and there was not much room for anything else. There was a bit of brown and orange patterned carpet on the floor and a couple of sunny prints of bright landscapes hung on the walls, and beyond these small concessions to civilized living, nothing of any value in the room at all.

Isobel's eyes swept round fairly swiftly, assessing as they went, and then came to rest on the face of the man in the wheelchair beside the open window. Blond, like his eldest son, and big and heavy, with powerful arms and shoulders, (useful for the wheelchair, she commented silently to herself) and eyes of the same candid grey as Trevor's, but these – unlike his son's – were dark with pain and with a kind of restless, tormented anger and frustration that could not be disguised.

"Hallo," said Isobel again, and went quickly to his side, with her hand outstretched. "It was kind of you to let me come, Mr Broadbent. I am so glad to meet you."

The burning, desperate eyes looked into hers, but his hand came out automatically to grasp her offered one. "Cliff," he said distinctly, and managed a twisted smile.

"Cliff," she repeated, smiling back. "And I'm Isobel."

"Miss Izzybell, Miss Izzybell, Mizzibell, Mizzibell!" chanted Goldie, dancing about like a small orange flame, and for some reason they all laughed – even Cliff – and Isobel's nickname was chosen there and then.

After tea, when the sausages and most of Isobel's cake

31

had been demolished and even Colin – who was always voraciously hungry – had pronounced himself full, Goldie looked innocently at Trevor and said, "Shall we play Mizzibell the Tunes?"

A quick look of doubt passed between Georgie and Trevor, and then they both turned to look at their father. Cliff Broadbent was sitting at the table in his wheelchair, and doing his best to be part of the cheerful group, though he could not join in the chatter, but now he accepted the children's instant referral to him for permission with calm good humour, nodding his handsome head and even managing a smile. "Yes . . . Tunes," he said.

"Can I use my penny whistle?" asked Colin, turning to Trevor. "It's dancier than the clarinet, and I'm better at it."

Trevor nodded, like his father, and Georgie went to fetch her fiddle from its case in the corner. Cliff was signalling something unintelligible to Trevor, and Isobel saw the frustration growing in his eyes as he tried to make himself understood, but when his two hands came up together, folded round an invisible something close to his mouth, Trevor understood.

"Your mouth organ? You want it?" For a moment he looked worried, and Isobel guessed that he was instantly anxious that Cliff would try to play it and find he could not manage it. The boy was loth to lay his father open to yet another failure.

But Cliff was shaking his head now, quite decisively. "No," he said. "You!" and pointed at Trevor's own hands.

The boy looked astounded at first, and then smiled at his father with extraordinary tenderness. Only he knew what an abdication it was, and what a great gift his father had just given him. It almost made up for having to give up the cello which he loved, and which he had hated handing back to the school. Did that mean that his father understood how much he missed it? Probably, it did. Cliff Broadbent understood a lot more than he could ever get round to saying.

"I'll try," Trevor said, still with a strangely gentle adult smile. "But I won't be as good as you!"

Goldie, meanwhile, had produced a little finger drum, and was already softly thrumming out a beat, and before long they

32

were all playing together. The catchy, infectious rhythms and beguiling tunes of the old Irish dances lilted out on to the air, from twiddling penny whistle, sprightly fiddle and Trevor's background mouth organ chording. They played *'The Three Little Drummers'* and *'Katie's Fancy'* and *'The Priest in his Boots'*, and even had a go at *'The Frost is all over'* which was hardest of all. They were surprisingly good, Isobel found, and even Cliff seized a spoon from the table and began to beat out his own tattoo to complement Goldie's insistent beat.

But Goldie was not content with mere drumming, she had to dance as well. Her small, neat feet simply couldn't keep still, and she twirled and drummed and laughed, like – Isobel suspected – her mother before her. When they came to the end of *'The Frost is all over'* Goldie said, still with the same innocent enthusiasm: "Can we do the *'Kerry Dancing?'*"

Once more the two eldest ones looked at one another in doubt and indecision, and once again they turned to Cliff with instinctive deference. But Isobel fancied they were more uncertain about this one.

"But someone has to sing it," pointed out Colin, who was either not noticing or ignoring the difficult undercurrents.

"I can sing it," piped up Goldie. "I know the words."

There was an awkward little silence, while Georgie and Trevor still looked at their father, and then Cliff said, clearly and distinctly, "Sing it then," and Goldie gave a small skip of joy and set herself primly in front of them all with her hands folded in front of her, like a slightly dishevelled choirboy.

It seemed to Isobel that the others began the famous old tune almost reluctantly, as if it brought back too many memories of their mother singing it with carefree happiness in the golden days before she went away. But after a few hesitant bars, they warmed to it and grew more confident, and Goldie lifted up her small, childish treble and began to sing.

"O the days of the Kerry Dancing,
O the ring of the Piper's Tune,
O for one of those hours of gladness,
Gone, alas, like our youth, too soon.
When the boys began to gather

33

In the glen of a summer night,
And the Kerry Piper's tuning
Made us long with wild delight,
O to think of it, O to dream of it,
Fills my heart with tears."

Goldie, with her small flower face uplifted to the light, was
not really aware of the meaning of those sorrowful nostalgic
words, or of the effect she was having, either on her father
or Isobel, but the others were, and when the song came to an
end, they looked at Cliff anxiously, afraid they might have
upset him. Indeed, there were tears in his eyes, and even
Isobel's were somewhat misted, but he resolutely clapped
his hands together in swift applause and smiled, signalling
urgently and lucidly to Isobel to do the same.

"Bravo!" said Isobel. "That was lovely."

"Smashing," agreed Colin, inaccurately, though certainly
some barriers had come crashing down.

"She'll come back, Trev says," Goldie told her father,
leaning confidingly against his useless knees under their
disguising rug, "if we keep playing the Tunes. . . ." Her
green-gold eyes offered instant solace, and for a curious
moment the small girl seemed to be the adult and her father
the child in need of comfort.

Cliff looked back at his small daughter with a painful
mixture of hope and despair, and struggled to answer her.
"Come – back . . ." he agreed, nodding his heavy blond
head, " . . . better. . . ."

The silence among the children was almost palpable, and
Isobel could not bear it. "Then you must *get* better," she chal-
lenged, and her eyes met the grey, frustrated ones and seemed
to be promising something – or exacting a promise.

They were still looking at each other, not quite certain
what to do next, when there came a quiet knock at the door.
Trevor roused himself from his anxious thoughts and went
to answer it.

"Sorry to disturb you, Trevor," said a pleasant male voice
outside, "can I have a word?"

"Mr Selwyn!" Trevor exclaimed, sounding both glad and
alarmed at once. "Come in."

"I heard the music outside," said Alan Selwyn, coming into the room. "It sounded pretty good to me – particularly the song."

"That was Goldie," said Georgie, sounding pleased and rather proud.

"Lovely voice," the music master said, smiling. "I could do with her in my choir!" And indeed I could, he told himself – a clear, pure treble like that! Like gold. "Gold from Goldie!" he said, aloud. And Goldie laughed.

"Georgie is pretty good on the fiddle," said Colin, loyally offering praise where it was due.

"So I heard," agreed Alan Selwyn, "and you weren't too bad on that penny whistle thing, either!" He laughed a little, and added, "Do you play the recorder, too?"

"Not now. I'm learning the clarinet at school." Colin sounded a bit reluctant about it. "But this is better for the Tunes."

Alan nodded, as from one musician to another. "Yes. More authentic!"

"But I want to learn the electric guitar," added Colin, not leaving out any chance. "Only it costs too much!"

Alan shot him a sharp, humorous glance. "I daresay you will – when you're a bit older."

Colin laughed them, too, good-humouredly accepting the fact that he wasn't going to win that one. Not at the moment. But there would be other chances to get at Mr Selwyn, he felt sure.

Then Alan turned easily to Cliff Broadbent, and held out his hand. "I hope I'm not intruding, Mr Broadbent. There was something I wanted to talk to Trevor about – it won't take long."

Cliff looked at him anxiously, words struggling to reach the surface. It was clear to Isobel, watching, that Cliff knew all too well what a perilous tightrope his children were walking. "G-good kids . . ." he said at last. "No-no . . . trouble?"

"No trouble at all, Mr Broadbent," Alan Selwyn assured him, and winked cheerfully at the children.

But Trevor was not so sure. "What is it, then?" he asked suspiciously.

Alan was about to answer when he seemed suddenly to

35

notice Isobel standing there, also looking a bit anxious. He took in, with one searching glance, her cool, observant gaze which yet did not seek to hide her concern for the children, and which somehow spoke to him of quiet reserves of strength and support as yet untapped. Looking at that upright, uncompromising figure, and that well-shaped fighting head, he decided he liked what he saw.

Isobel, for her part, looked at this man who was Trevor's music master and champion, with equal attention. He was younger than she was, but not by many years, she thought, and he had that aura of mildly exasperated patience and permanent tiredness which is apt to be the hallmark of a good teacher. (She knew it well.) His hair was darkish with flecks of grey and one startlingly white blaze reaching up from the centre of his forehead, and his eyes, even at their most probing, were of a wide and gentle hazel that seemed to her to see much and to forgive everything. It was a compassionate and uncensorious gaze he turned on both Cliff and the children, that did not seek to apportion blame or reproach. Yes, thought Isobel, echoing Alan Selwyn's own thoughts: I like the look of him.

He moved then, suddenly, from his swift assessment and held out his hand. "Alan Selwyn. Trevor's music master – and his maths teacher, too, but it's the music that counts with him."

Isobel laughed, and reached out a firm hand to clasp his. "I'm Isobel Frazier," she said.

"We call her Mizzibell," volunteered Goldie, with an irrepressible little pirouette. "She's Trev's friend."

Isobel looked at her gravely, and then turned to Cliff with careful deference. "Yours too, I hope – all of you?"

Cliff seemed a bit bemused by everything that was going on round him – there were too many undercurrents and they confused him, but he managed a painfully cautious smile at Isobel.

"What is it, then, Mr Selwyn?" repeated Trevor, who was also afraid of those undercurrents and not to be deflected.

"It's the headmaster, Trevor."

"Again?"

Alan sighed. "Yes, well, it's not his fault, you know. The

truancy officer has been having a look at all the registers, you see. . . ."

Trevor's already pale face had gone even paler. "And . . .?"

"We came to an agreement," said Alan, smiling cheerfully. "I promised to come round and see how things were. . . ." He hesitated then for a moment, and carefully did not look directly at Cliff's uneasy face. "But I think – if you could be at school on Monday when the register is taken – he's coming into school then, you see – we can truthfully tell the officer you were back and things were better at home . . .?"

There was a question in his voice, and Trevor knew he had to answer it. But he also knew he could not make rash promises. "I'll come if Dad's OK," he said, sounding obstinate and driven.

Beside him, his father broke into incoherent speech. "M-manage . . ." he said. "No – no p-prob—"

Trevor reached out, quite unselfconsciously and laid one hand on his father's arm. "It's all right, Dad. Mr Selwyn understands."

He did, too, that was clear to Isobel. And she understood too, but she wondered if Alan Selwyn had caught the sudden flick of terror in Cliff Broadbent's eyes as he faced the thought of doing without Trevor's company – even for a day.

"I'd have to come back at lunchtime," muttered Trevor, trying to work out which priorities came first. "He's not too safe with kettles and such. . . ."

"*Can* . . ." contradicted Cliff, explosively. "*Can* c-cope!"

But Trevor just grinned at him and gave his arm another quiet pat.

"I could come over from twelve till three, if that would be any help," said Isobel briskly, offering the most useful clear-cut timing she could think of, "that is, if Cliff would like it?"

The whole family looked at her in astonishment, but Cliff's eyes fastened themselves on her face and seemed to dilate a little and mist with the easy tears of the chronic invalid.

"Would you?" said Trevor, awestruck.

Isobel smiled. "Why not? I'm free, fresh and willing." She thought sadly, watching the light change in Trevor's anxious

37

eyes – and he's neither free nor fresh, but, poor, gallant boy, forever willing.

"Good," said Alan, clinching it before anyone could change their mind. "That's settled then. Trevor pacifies the truancy officer and the headmaster. . . ."

"And I pacify Cliff – if he'll let me!" said Isobel, and everyone gratefully began to laugh.

"Must go now." Alan became all brisk and practical. "Only looked in for a moment. Keep on practising, you lot. It sounded good. And keep singing, Goldie!"

"I will." Goldie sounded entirely confident. "Till Mum comes back."

There was a sudden, tingling small silence, and then Trevor covered it by remembering his good manners. "Thanks for coming, Mr Selwyn, and for – for—"

"Covering up for you," finished Alan, laughing. "Don't worry, Trevor. I do it all the time."

"I must go, too," announced Isobel, and looked at Alan rather hard.

"Perhaps I could walk along with you, Mizzibell?" asked Alan promptly, not missing his cue.

But Cliff was again struggling to say something – something urgent and desperately important. He looked from Alan Selwyn to Isobel Frazier and did not know which of them to approach. "Kids . . ." he got out at last. "Not – not n-neg—" but he couldn't manage that word 'neglected'. Maybe he didn't dare to try. He looked piteously at Isobel and said, "Don't . . . don't take—"

But Trevor understood him and intervened swiftly. "She's not a social worker, Dad. She's just a friend." *Just* a friend? he thought. When she's just offered to come and sit with my Dad? And I know she's already planning other ways of helping, I can see it in her face. "No one's going to take us away," he added softly, answering his father's worst nightmare – and his own. "Are they, Mr Selwyn?"

"Not if I can help it!" said Alan stoutly. "Don't worry. I think you're all managing very well!" and he winked again at the children and turned to go.

Isobel formally shook Cliff's hand again, smiled her farewell at the little family who answered with a chorus of

38

cheerful goodbyes and followed Alan to the door. "Trevor," she said as she left, "don't forget your Saturday cup of tea. I shall be expecting you."

There wasn't any more she could say to him then, but there would be a lot to talk about later, and it was just as well to let him know it.

"I won't forget," said Trevor, and failed to say any more – not even thank you – before the door closed.

But it didn't matter. He had a friend now. Two friends – for Alan Selwyn had always been interested and helpful. But *two* friends! Now he could face anything.

"Mizzibell's gone," said Goldie, sounding sad.

"Yes, but she's coming back," answered Trevor, and secretly rejoiced.

Chapter Three

'Is the Big Man within?'

Long Dance

Out in the street, Isobel and Alan looked at one another rather grimly, and Alan said, "I think we need to talk, don't you?"

"Yes," agreed Isobel. "We do."

He stood looking round him for a moment. "There's a café near here somewhere. It's probably open on Sundays."

"My house isn't far," said Isobel practically. "I could give you a perfectly good cup of coffee – free!"

"Better still," said Alan, grinning, and they walked on companionably together.

When they were sitting opposite one another in Isobel's comfortable sitting-room, Alan said, half smiling "Well, you can see how I got drawn into it, but how did you get involved?"

So Isobel told him, and at the end of her brief recital of facts, she added in a perplexed tone, "What I don't understand is, why the mother went off like that. Can you understand it?"

Alan answered slowly, his compassionate face even more saddened than usual, "I think something else happened – something we don't know about. And I think young Trevor knows more about it than he lets on."

"But you don't like to question him, in case it's something really bad?"

"I don't like to question him, full stop. He'd tell us if he could."

"You don't think she – could have come to any harm?"

"From Cliff Broadbent, you mean? No. I doubt if he's physically capable of it now."

"But he was?"

"Oh yes." He sighed, and made a slight grimace of distaste. "I think she had quite a time of it, even before the accident."

Isobel nodded. "That's what Mike Harding said."

"Who?"

"The newsagent who employs Trevor." She was still thinking about the young mother and her inexplicable disappearance. "Well, if not Cliff's violence – could she have . . .?"

"Jumped off the Suspension Bridge or something?" The corners of Alan's eyes were crinkling a little with faint laughter. "I doubt it. She'd have been found, and we'd have heard. . . . Anyway, I don't think she was that kind of person."

"What *was* she like? Did you know her?"

"Only in so far as she came to a few parents' meetings, and one or two concerts when Trevor was playing." He paused, remembering a bright-haired, laughing girl who praised his young orchestra and his choir and talked of music as if she understood it. "She was – a lit-up sort of girl," he said absently. "That little thing, Goldie, is like her – and musical, too. . . . They all are, by the sound of it."

"And Trevor?"

"Oh yes. A natural. Instinctive phrasing. Pity he had to give up the cello."

Isobel sighed and poured him out more coffee. "He's had to give up a lot of things, by all accounts." Then she voiced her next anxiety. "I don't like this idea that playing the Irish music will bring their mother back."

"Why not?" He did not sound troubled.

"Isn't it rather . . . dangerous?"

Alan considered. "Yes, I suppose it is – if she never returns. But it gives them all some sort of hope – something to look forward to. . . ."

"That's what Trevor said."

"Mmm." He sipped his coffee. "And, you know, there is something a bit fey about the Irish – and their music. You never know – it might work!"

He smiled at Isobel, and she – warmed by that gentle smile – thought to herself: He really is a very nice man. But aloud she only said, "The real question is, what are we going to do about them? I don't know how to help." She looked at Alan for enlightenment. "What are they living on? Does Cliff get a proper disability allowance? They seem desperately short of money."

Alan agreed. "I did talk to their social worker. She's a nice enough woman, but bound by rules and regulations, of course. The latest cutbacks in community care have made things even more difficult. . . . And the kids are terrified she'll put them into care."

"So they won't ask for any more help, in case she investigates too thoroughly?" Isobel's voice was grim.

"I daresay," ventured Alan, with an innocent glance in her direction, "you could ask on their behalf – without subjecting them to too much scrutiny?"

Isobel laughed. "I could try."

Privately, Alan thought if Isobel tried anything, she would almost certainly succeed. "I'll give you her name," he said, grinning.

"But that's only one side of it," persisted Isobel, not to be deflected. "Can't the local authority get them a ground floor flat? That man is a virtual prisoner up there . . . and he needs a better wheelchair, too – something he can propel about the place himself. He doesn't *need* to be so helpless!" She glared at Alan. "And why isn't he having physiotherapy for those legs, anyway? And speech therapy, too? It could help him a lot." Her voice was crisp with indignation. "It strikes me, they've forgotten all about him. He's getting no help at all!"

Alan put up a hand in self-defence. "Don't take it out on me!" But he was smiling, and somehow Isobel could tell he was well pleased with her fury.

"We'll put our heads together," he promised. "Most of these things can be laid on, if we know where to ask."

"Alan, could we get that wheelchair down the stairs?"

"Down, possibly. Up would be more difficult." He paused, considering. "We might do it with a couple of planks. . . ."

Isobel began to laugh again, but guardedly. "It sounds perilous . . . but I would so like to get all that bunch out into the fresh air!" She looked out of her window and waved an expressive hand. "Clifton Down is out there – all that space

42

for the children to run on. It's criminal to have them all cooped up like that!"

"Give me time," begged Alan, smiling, "I'll come up with something. As for the rest – this is what we must do. . . ."

And they put their heads together.

On the whole, Trevor thought Miss Frazier's visit had been a success, but her proposed arrival on Monday to sit with his father filled him with terror. Would she know what to do? And would his father allow her to do *anything* without hitting out or shouting at her . . .? After all, he often did even at Trevor and Georgie when he was in a bad mood – so how would he be with a stranger . . .? And then, there would be so much more to get done in the morning before he left if he was going to get to school in time for that critical register.

But even while he worried, there was still a warm core of reassurance inside him which was somehow connected with Isobel's smile and her calm assumption that all would be well. So it would be, then, he told himself. Yes, it *would*. He would just have to get up earlier, that's all.

So he did his paper-round, got his father up and washed and installed him in his wheelchair, cut some sandwiches for his lunch (and for Miss Isobel's), and put a thermos of tea near to hand. Meanwhile, Georgie got the kids up and saw to the breakfast, and even had time to wash up and lay a tray of tea for Mizzibell when she came. She also remembered to take her violin with her, and her gym shoes, and reminded Colin about his. And Colin, for once doing his best to be useful, collected all their school bags and coats, while Goldie mostly just danced about and got in the way which exasperated everyone, but somehow cheered them up just the same.

Then the children all looked at each other and made for the door. But Trevor lingered a moment, looking anxiously back at his father.

"Dad?" he said, asking all kinds of things that he had no time to say.

"All right—" mumbled Cliff, nodding his blond head vigorously. For once he was determined to seem confident and positive.

43

"You don't mind Mizzibell coming," said Georgie firmly, not allowing it to be a question.

Cliff managed a crooked smile. "No," he told them, with as much conviction as he could master. "Nice . . ." he added, passing slow judgement on a woman who had impressed him with her forthright lack of fuss.

Satisfied, the children clattered out, and Trevor gave his father's arm a gentle, painfully adult squeeze. "Back as soon as I can," he promised, and shut the outside door behind him, still with an anxious feeling that he ought not to be going at all.

Isobel, on the other hand, had no particular qualms. Having made up her mind to come, she wasted no more time worrying about it, and arrived at the door of the flat in a determinedly cheerful and confident mood. (Not too cheerful and confident, though, she told herself – in case Cliff Broadbent resented it. There was nothing worse than an over-bright and breezy helper.)

Cliff himself came to the door, pushing the wheels of his chair with his strong arms and managing to avoid getting caught on the corners or stuck in the living-room doorway, which he did sometimes. Isobel knew there was a key dangling on a string inside the letter box, because Trevor had told her so, but she hesitated to use it this first time. Let Cliff at least appear to be master in his own house.

So she waited patiently for him to open the door and move himself back again to let her in, though she did have a moment of doubt about whether he could reach the Yale lock from his chair.

They looked at each other for a moment in silence, but their eyes met in cautious greeting nonetheless, and at last Cliff said quite clearly, "Glad . . . you came . . ." and carefully propelled himself back into the living-room. "Tea . . .?" he added, over his shoulder, and waved an expressive hand towards the kitchen.

Isobel went to have a look, and was touched to find the little tray laid ready for her – two mugs and a small jug of milk, and two teabags lying usefully on top of the draining board by the kettle. Basic but sensible, she thought. Was that Trevor or Georgie? She noticed that there was no sugar bowl anywhere,

44

and decided to establish a comfortably domestic atmosphere at once by calling out, "Do you take sugar, Cliff?" (*Does* he *take sugar?* Was it too condescending?)

There was a pause, and then the deep, hesitant voice rumbled out, "No."

"That's good," she said, busy with the kettle, "because I can't see any!" and she waited for the kettle to boil before attempting any more chatty conversation.

What can I talk to him about? she wondered. What does he like – besides the docks and the shipping, which he can no longer have in his life? Does he read? Or do crosswords? Or jigsaws? What does he do all day?

She saw that there was a small, unobtrusive television set in the room, though he had not bothered to put it on. There was also a radio close beside him, but that was switched off, too. Why? she wondered. . . . There were such a lot of questions she could not ask – and she had no intention of upsetting him by trying to find out too much at once. So she simply brought in the tea, handed him his mug, and sat down beside him on the nearest chair, with her own mug of tea in her hand.

She had brought her daily paper with her (the same one that Trevor had stuffed through her letter box very early that morning) and now it occurred to her to find the television page and ask Cliff which channel he wanted to watch.

He looked at the list attentively and gave a slightly sardonic grin. "Mornings . . ." he got out slowly, "mostly – c-crap . . ." Then his finger came down on the school programmes. "Those . . ." he murmured, "sometimes. . . ."

Isobel nodded, but he did not seem to want to watch any of them at the moment. She glanced round the room, and saw that he had an old-fashioned record player and some equally old-fashioned LPs stacked under it.

"Music?" she wondered aloud. After all, the children were musical. Was it only their mother they took after?

Cliff was nodding, and he eased his wheelchair over a little so that he could reach his records. After a little scrabbling, he drew out one and handed it to her. "Katie . . . l-liked music . . ." he said, in a dreaming voice.

Isobel looked at the record sleeve. "The New World Symphony?" she said in surprise. "Shall I put it on?"

He nodded again, and added, looking straight at Isobel with his haunted eyes. *"Far. . . ."*

Isobel understood him, and set the famous Dvorak tunes going on the record player. He did not try to speak while the whole nostalgic work played itself through, but when it was over, he sighed and murmured: *"Cabot. . . ."*

Isobel was surprised again. (He was always surprising her, she reflected.) But she knew what he meant. "John Cabot? . . . Who sailed to Newfoundland?"

He smiled assent, pleased at her quick comprehension.

"Cabot's Tower is here in Bristol, isn't it?"

Once again the blond head nodded.

"Have you ever been up to the top?"

The smile flickered out again. "Once . . . t-took Trevor. . . ."

Isobel saw the hidden longing in his eyes. "Would you like to go to America?"

A spasm, almost of pain, crossed his face. *"Anywhere,"* he said.

Anywhere, to get out of this room, this street, this prison of my body. *"Anywhere!"* he repeated, in a savage undertone.

"There is another Cabot Tower in America, you know – in St John's, Newfoundland where he landed," she said, deciding that to talk about far places might be better than ignoring them. "I've been there, once. . . ."

His eyes lit up with distance. "Have you . . .? Tell . . .?" He could not get out any more just then, but Isobel understood him, and began to talk.

She told him about the far, craggy shores of Newfoundland where the small coves still kept their own little fishing fleets. She told him about her journey across Canada – the Rockies and the lakes, the great waterfalls and rivers, and the huge pine forests – and how she came to the sea again on the other side, among clusters of islands, another 3,000 miles to the farthest western point of that vast continent and a different ocean. And she told him about her first job as a teacher – untrained and inexperienced – far away on another continent altogether, where she was teaching African children in a small mud hut on the edge of a village with the wild interior all around them. . . . And Cliff listened, wide-eyed and attentive, like one of her own pupils, spellbound at story time.

46

But at the end of her description of this first primitive job, he said suddenly, "Why?"

Isobel did not misunderstand him. She was beginning to know how his mind worked. "My father was a preacher," she said. "A Scottish Presbyterian preacher. He had a job out there, and I went where he went. *Then*."

A glimmer of a grin touched Cliff's tired mouth. "L-later. . . .?"

"I went my own way," she said, and something about the way she shut her mouth determinedly on that subject made him look at her with unspoken sympathy. He knew when subjects ought to be left alone – who better? There were many things in his life that he could not talk about. So he sought a way to turn the conversation in another direction. Reaching down to the shelf below the record player, he managed to pull out one of the few books lying there. It was an atlas, and he opened it at one of the early pages, and held it out to Isobel. It was a map of Ireland.

"Have you – been – there . . .?" His eyes seemed to reflect a kind of painful urgency this time.

But for some reason, this new direction did not seem to dispel Isobel's shuttered look. She stared down at the map in silence for a few moments, and then at last she sighed and said gently (for she knew why Cliff was so desperate to know more about this green country): "Yes, Cliff, I've been there . . . but it was long ago."

He was still looking at her, still waiting, and when she did not immediately respond, he put his fingers on the map and traced out the word 'Kerry' and left it there, still pointing, while his anxious glance begged for something she could not give him. "*There* . . .?" he asked.

She bent her head again over the map and laid her own finger on the word 'Kerry', and then found Killarney and the Ring of Kerry, and traced the winding coast roads down to the southernmost tip where they became lost in a tangle of islands, the farthest of which said Cape Clear.

"Yes," she said softly, "I've been to Kerry . . . and right down to Cape Clear where only the boats can go and it is beautiful and cool and quiet."

There was something in her voice then that made Cliff

glance up at her in surprise – a note of longing and loss that seemed to echo his own. "Katie . . ." he said dreamily, "Katie – came – from – Kerry . . ."

Isobel was just taking a deep breath, determined to talk cheerfully about Ireland, when there was a sudden rattle of a key in the lock of the front door, and Trevor burst in, out of breath and anxious. When he saw their two heads together bent over the atlas, he seemed to relax visibly, and came over to them in less of a rush.

"How – how are you getting on?" he asked, though he could see already that he had no need to ask.

"I thought you were supposed to be at school?" said Isobel, pretending to be stern.

"I can just about make it home in the lunch break," Trevor said, still slightly out of breath. "If I run."

Isobel and his father were both looking at him, but somehow their faces were not accusing – they were smiling.

"But then you miss your lunch," Isobel protested.

"Oh, I don't have school dinners." His tone was excessively casual, and he avoided his father's eye. "The other kids do," he added hastily, in case anyone should be under any misapprehension about that. He did not add that theirs were free, but he would have to pay for his, since his mother had not had time to arrange about it when he first went to the senior school, and he had never had the heart to remind her.

"So what *do* you eat?" asked Isobel, mildly inquisitive.

"Oh – a bag of crisps or something." He still sounded far too casual.

"In that case," Isobel told him, "you can share ours. I'll put the kettle on," and she marched into the kitchen.

It occurred to her then, while she was getting out Cliff's sandwiches, and her own from her handbag, that Cliff might be glad of a moment's respite from her company, especially if he wanted to use his bottle. Trev would see to that this time, in case the poor man was embarrassed. But she would have to overcome that kind of barrier sooner or later, she reflected. No doubt he would come to accept her in due course, if she approached things practically and without any fuss.

In the meantime, she gave them both a moment, and then

carried in the tray of tea and sandwiches. "Here we are," she grinned. "We can have a picnic."

All at once, it became a kind of party, and they found themselves laughing about nothing in particular, while veils of anxiety and pain seemed to dissolve round them and leave the day clear and bright with promise.

When Trevor had gone back to school (at a run again, but looking much less anxious that when he came), Cliff picked up the atlas again at the open page, and insisted on making Isobel talk about Ireland. He was, Isobel reflected, half smiling at his persistence, like a small boy determined not to be done out of a promised treat.

She wondered whether the so-called 'brain damage' caused by his accident was responsible for this childlike attitude or whether it had always been part of Cliff's character – and whether the increasing signs of improvement in his speech and understanding meant that the damage done was not irreparable. After all, his old, adult personality might soon return and take over the curiously innocent, vulnerable child looking out of his eyes. In a way, she rather wished it wouldn't – for with the return of adult awareness would come all the guilts and frustrations which had beleaguered him before.

However, now he was looking at her expectantly, one finger still pointing to that magic word 'Kerry' on the map, and waiting patiently for her to begin. She didn't want to talk about Ireland, really. Didn't want to remember that time at all. For many years now – more than she cared to admit – she had avoided thinking about those far-off days, but Cliff's beseeching blue eyes were looking into hers and she had to say something.

"I was very young then," she began slowly. "The world was a different place." She smiled at him resolutely. "The colours all seem brighter when you're young," she murmured, half to herself.

Cliff was looking at her intently. Since his illness, his mind played strange tricks on him sometimes, so that he scarcely knew what was real and what was not. Mirages assailed him – faces changed and grew faint and far away, or suddenly too near and frightening. Colours flashed and merged and grew

49

into nimbuses and rainbows, and people he knew became strangers. . . . But this time, as Isobel spoke, he had a sudden clear picture in his mind of the young Isobel in that far off green sanctuary of Ireland. *Sanctuary?* The word floated into his head, and was all mixed up with his memory of Katie, his young wife, who was always laughing and loved to dance . . . *Always laughing, before . . . before . . .?*

But it was Isobel he could see now – young and shy, and surprisingly pretty. He could still see the bones of that early beauty in her face as she looked at him, even though the lines of her face were set now and her mouth was apt to be rather grim. But there was a tenderness about it, too, and this he recognized. It was a quality he had known and loved in Katie . . . and it meant that Isobel was like Katie – someone who could love and be loved. . . . He understood this with extraordinary clarity (as if he were looking into the past with the knowledge of the present) and it somehow made Isobel seem vulnerable and shy, like him. . . . Someone, maybe, he could meet half-way as a friend and not an enemy.

The vision was fading now, though, and Isobel was still speaking of Ireland in that funny, clipped, half-nostalgic, half-reluctant voice. He thought he understood her sadness, though he couldn't grasp it exactly, but it was like his, full of regrets, and therefore he had to listen.

"Things have probably changed a lot by now," she was saying. "But then it was very unspoilt, very green and quiet, and the sea all round, very deep and wild, with tall, steep cliffs and thousands of birds . . . no, more like millions of birds. . . . They stop off there, down by Cape Clear, on their way from the arctic to the southern hemisphere . . ." I sound like a geography teacher, she thought, appalled, why can't I make myself less stiff? "I saw some of the Kerry Dancing once," she said suddenly, a faint, reminiscent smile touching her stern mouth for a moment. "The same tunes the children played for me yesterday. . . . Though I think what I saw when I was there was a bit of a stunt laid on for the summer visitors, rather than the old traditional stuff . . . But it was catchy enough. I know it set my feet dancing. . . ."

Only I couldn't dance, she thought. Not then. Nor even laugh very much. It was not the time for dancing. . . . "There

50

was a convent there," she said, in a softened, dreaming voice that made Cliff look at her again in wonder. "The nuns were lovely people. . . ." But she withdrew from that, even though Cliff was nodding his head vigorously, and trying to search for something among the tangle of books and papers and record sleeves on his shelf.

She was just launching into a description of the perilous boat trip from the mainland to Cape Clear, when Cliff found what he was looking for and held it out to her triumphantly. It was an old school photograph of a well-ordered group of tidy schoolgirls. They sat there, neatly correct in their white school blouses and stripy ties, with one angelically-smiling nun between them in the centre, all of them gazing out at the world with serious, hopeful eyes.

Isobel bent to look where Cliff's finger was pointing now, and saw it had come to rest on the head of one radiant, exceptionally beautiful girl. A wild tangle of curls tumbled round her head – very like Georgie's – and the mouth was just breaking into Georgie's luminous smile, but the eyes looking out with those others so full of hope and promise were like Trevor's when he was at his most serious and appealing, and their innocence troubled Isobel.

"Katie . . ." he said, repeating the name haltingly, as if it was very difficult to say. "Katie – before. . . ."

Before what? wondered Isobel sadly. Before she met Cliff, before marriage was even thought of, before the advent of four children, before her husband was made redundant and became so angry and frustrated . . . Before his accident . . . And where, in God's name, was Katie now?

She turned the picture over in her hand, hoping to find some clue written on it – the name of the convent school, perhaps, or even a scribbled note of the time and place, but there was nothing there. A neat white oblong, telling her nothing.

"She looks lovely," she said gently, handing it back. "The children are very like her, aren't they?"

Then she wondered whether she should have made that comment, or if it might upset him. But he seemed lost now in some kind of dream, and just sat there with the little photo in his hand, staring into some enchanted distance that was happy and unhaunted.

51

Quietly, Isobel left him there, and went to make him some more tea before the children came home. I can't question him yet, she thought. If ever? It would only confuse him. Just let him get to know me and trust me a little – then perhaps I can begin to be some help – at least to Trevor and the others. I'll have to start asking questions soon, but Cliff isn't ready for them yet. I must wait a little longer.

But when she got back with the tea, Cliff had fallen asleep in his chair.

Isobel did possess a car – a small Mini, not nearly so roomy as Gervase's old station waggon – but on this occasion she had decided to walk down to the Broadbent's flat, partly so that she could get some impression of what the neighbourhood and that particular street was like, and partly out of a diffident desire not to appear too affluent in those surroundings. But in fact there were plenty of cars about, she noticed, and some burnt-out wrecks among them. It was not a good neighbourhood. She could understand why Trevor would not let the children play outside in the street. But they were all safely up in the flat now, having tea with their father, and she was walking home through a scent-laden spring evening which even this shabby environment could not spoil.

A thrush was singing somewhere high up in a city plane tree, unperturbed by the traffic rushing by below, and as Isobel walked away towards the open sunny spaces of the Downs, the little town gardens showed splashes of white snowdrops and pale primroses, and the early cherry blossom cascaded a froth of pink over the walls. Yes, it was spring all right, and she longed to get those children – and Cliff, too – out into it somehow.

She stopped for a moment as she passed through a city square not far from the tall column of Cabot's Tower, and stood looking up at its dark shape, stark and challenging against the evening sky. They used to say you could stand on the top and look right out over the Severn Estuary to the sea, she thought. First stop, America. She sighed, remembering Cliff's driven reply to her question: "Would you like to go to America?" "*Anywhere*," he had growled, and all the agonies of disablement and loss were in his deep voice.

52

I'll get them out, she vowed to herself grimly, I will! Somehow. All of them. And she looked up again at the tall tower against that beguilingly soft blue sky of spring, and felt that a promise had been given that could not be broken.

It had not occurred to Isobel that her life was becoming complicated, until Friday came round again. Then she suddenly realized, with only the faintest flick of alarm, that she had got herself double-booked with two separate dates.

My goodness! she said. I'd forgotten all about Gervase. And I've promised to meet Alan Selwyn at the wine bar to discuss Trevor's school plans. A grin of pure mischief came over that severe mouth, and she couldn't resist a little silly twirl of amusement, right there in her kitchen. And I'm supposed to be bored and lonely, with too little to do, according to Gervase, she thought. And twirled again.

Now let me think. It'll have to be a casserole. No time for *cordon bleu* frills this week — however much he likes them. And I'd better make enough for three, in case Alan can stay. We probably won't have finished discussing the Broadbents in an hour, anyway. (But a small voice inside her head said then: Who do you think you're kidding? — and she couldn't help smiling.) She paused to consider, and decided to make an apple pie as well. It was Gervase's favourite.

"Those two men won't get on," she said aloud to Archimedes, who was sitting on a corner of the table inspecting her activities with a critical eye. "Will they, Archie?"

He did not deign to answer, but managed to convey by the flick of his tail and his supercilious glance that he thought the whole idea rather preposterous.

"Never mind," said Isobel, still grinning. "It'll do Gervase good to be gingered up a little. And I'll put some extra cloves in the pie as well."

Archimedes yawned.

She got her small supper party arrangements together with remarkable speed and efficiency, and went out to meet Alan at the wine bar quite jauntily, wearing her newest blue sweater over her neat black skirt.

*   *   *

53

Alan saw her coming, and began to smile even before she reached him. She seemed to radiate cheerful confidence and a kind of inner glow which he found hard to define. He did not know it yet, of course, but he was looking at Isobel's fighting look. He would come to know it well in time – but even now he interpreted it pretty well.

"You look like Boadicea," he said.

She grinned. "Naked on a horse?"

"That was Godiva."

"So it was. Got my fashions mixed. Boadicea wore woad."

Alan was laughing. "Perhaps Joan of Arc would be more appropriate."

Isobel's grin was even wider. "The only thing likely to be burnt at the stake is my supper. And it isn't steak, either," she said with some asperity. And then, suddenly serious, she added; "Alan, I've made a mess of this evening. I'd quite forgotten about Gervase. So can you possibly come to supper, too, because we won't have time to finish our conversation otherwise."

Alan looked a shade bewildered. "Who is Gervase?"

Isobel's grin returned. (Really, she seemed unable to be serious for long this evening.) "He's a lonely, pedantic old man who keeps an antiquarian bookshop and likes to play Scrabble."

"Sounds fascinating." His eyes were laced with laughter, too.

"He comes to supper every Friday – and he doesn't like his routine upset. In fact, I think he's more of an old maid than I am."

Alan's laughter startled the other quiet drinkers in the wine bar. "Nothing old-maidish about you. More like a battle-maiden. I told you."

She sighed, gratefully aware that Alan was being very kind. "I asked him the other day if he'd ever climbed a tree," she said, her voice a mixture of mischief and sadness.

"Had he?"

"No." She looked at him. "It's dreadful, Alan, when people have never learnt to *play*."

"And that's why you're so concerned about Trevor and his family." It was a statement, not a question.

54

"Of course." She picked up her martini and stared at it absently. "Alan – I can still climb a tree. I can skip down the pavements like a two-year-old. I can go out in the sun, and watch a flight of doves flying. I can go anywhere and do anything I want . . . while they—" She drew a sharp breath, surprised by her own eloquence. "We *must* do something," she said, and turned to him for help.

Alan was nodding. "Hold your horses. I've not been idle." He too picked up his drink, and lifted his glass to Isobel's worried face. "First of all, I've asked the woodwork boys to build us a ramp. We can put it over the stairs, I think. It'll be heavy and cumbersome, but we can manage it, I'm sure, the stairs aren't too steep."

She looked at him delightedly. "That's splendid! We could take him on the Downs." She paused, and then added wistfully, "But what I'd really like to do is take them all on an outing – say, to Weston, or somewhere."

He was smiling at her again. "Why not?"

"Do you – how big is your car? Mine's too small for a wheelchair. I did sort of suggest the idea to Gervase – he has a station wagon – but he nearly had a fit!"

Alan did not look perturbed. "Mine is an estate. Plenty of room. I use it a lot for carrying double basses and things about to concerts!"

"But you . . .? Wasting a whole day . . .? It would have to be at the weekend."

"I wouldn't say it was *wasting* a day," said Alan judiciously. "And, don't forget, the Easter holidays are coming up."

"So they are. I'd forgotten." Her glance was guarded, but undeniably hopeful. "D'you think we could?"

"I'm *sure* we could."

She was silent for a moment. Then she went on more soberly: "You said '*first of all*' – what else?"

He seemed to hesitate a little then, but decided to go ahead with his next suggestion and await her reaction. "We struck a sort of deal – the headmaster and I, with Trevor. . . . A way of getting some schooling into him. . . ." Again there was a fractional pause.

"Yes?"

"It would involve you. . . ."

55

She stared at him, and then smiled as if reassuring a rather dimwitted child. "Alan, I *am* involved."

"I know," he muttered. "But – commitments can be – er – rather binding. I don't know if you'd like the idea."

"Try me."

"Well, the headmaster suggested that if Trevor came to school on Mondays and took work home for three days, and then came on Thursdays and took work home for the weekend, that way he might not fall too far behind. . . . It's the curriculum, you see. . . . If he loses too much, he'll have to stay down another year, and he's far too adult already to mix with a lot of idiotic teenagers."

She nodded. "That makes sense."

"It would mean two 'minders' a week. . . ." He glanced at her, tempering his wary look with a conspiratorial grin. "Of course, if you can persuade the Social Services to do something about it – and they *ought* to – you needn't be involved, except as a temporary measure to tide them over."

Isobel glared back. "I don't propose to be a temporary measure!" Then she began to think of the serious implications of such a scheme. "What does Trevor think?"

Alan sighed, and looked down into his drink with troubled eyes. "He's a curious boy. Absurdly loyal. He said, 'I'll take the work home, but I can't promise to do it. My Dad comes first.'"

She nodded again. "We might have expected him to say that."

"Mmm. I could only say let's try it and see what happens." Once again he glanced, almost tentatively, at Isobel's thoughtful face. "What did you make of Cliff Broadbent?"

She paused before she answered, and then looked straight at Alan with her usual candour. "He seems to be a strange mixture of bewildered child and tormented adult at present . . . I don't know what he was really like when he was well."

"Much the same, I should think," Alan said, "if rather more vocal about it."

She agreed with that. "But he is learning to speak again. We had quite a conversation one way and another – though I did most of the talking." A faint grin touched her again. "But that's not unusual for me!"

56

He shot her an appreciative grin to match hers. But she could see that he was still troubled about something.

"We could probably get him speech therapy to help him there," she went on. "I'm sure he'd improve, with help."

Alan was silent for a moment, and then he said, almost as if arguing with himself about something, "Yes. Trevor told me you got on very well together. Cliff even asked when Mizzibell was coming again."

"Did he?" She was very pleased at that. Then she explained carefully, "I didn't offer to come again – not then. I didn't want him to feel pushed, or – or any of them to feel got at, if you know what I mean?"

His nod was relieved and decisive. "Yes, I do."

"Do-gooders can do so much harm, crashing in where they're not wanted," she said, seeming to speak from painful experience. "I thought I'd better go slowly." She looked at him for approval, but her words seemed to have brought his own hidden doubts to the surface.

"I think you may be up against a less simple problem than that with Cliff Broadbent," he said.

"What do you mean?"

"Hasn't it occurred to you that he is *hiding*? He is too proud and obstinate to admit that he needs help, or to accept it, because he doesn't want the outside world to see him in this state."

She looked at him with swift understanding. "Of course – a man who was big and vigorous, and. . . ."

"Macho?"

"Yes, and head of his family, the breadwinner and all that . . . It must be very hard to accept."

"He hasn't accepted it, Isobel. That's the trouble. It's all right for Trevor and the kids to look after him – they're his family and it is his right. But if he accepts help with his speech, help with his legs, help with having a bath and so on, he has to admit to the nurses and therapists, and all his mates and the uncaring world at large that he is a helpless cripple. And he doesn't want to."

She sighed. "I was afraid it was something like that." Her mind was already searching for solutions. "But he accepted me."

57

Alan's glance was warm with approval. "Yes. Believe me, that was a real breakthrough." His smile rested on her like a benediction. "You are very clever."

But she was still pursuing something. "When he said – after the children played the Tunes that day, do you remember? – When he said something about 'come back . . . when I'm better' . . . Or words to that effect. . . ."

"Yes?"

"I began it then," she told him. "I could see it then. That's the only way to get him to co-operate. I told him: 'Then we must get you better,' and I think he understood." She looked at him hopefully. "Didn't he?"

Alan leant forward impulsively and patted her hand. "Yes, I think he did. But you'll have to keep on telling him."

"Oh, I will," promised Isobel firmly. "In roundabout ways. . . ."

"Anyway will do that stops him resenting interference," said Alan, "and makes him accept proper help."

She agreed, and her serious glance looked away for a moment, and suddenly fastened on the clock above the bar. "Oh, my goodness, Alan, look at the time! We'd better go – Gervase will be gnashing his teeth on the doorstep. You are coming too, aren't you?"

"Of course," said Alan, smoothly grinning. "I'll be delighted."

"You may not be," admitted Isobel. "He's a somewhat prickly customer." And she almost ran for the door.

"I'll take the risk," said Alan, pursuing her cheerfully.

"You're good at that, aren't you?" said Isobel, striding off up the street at a very brisk rate indeed.

"Not as good as you are!" retorted Alan, and matched her stride for stride.

Chapter Four

'The Three Sea Captains'

Long Dance

The supper party with Gervase and Alan went rather better than Isobel expected. She introduced Alan merely as a colleague and a musician, and was relieved to find that the two men seemed to have something in common, especially when Alan began to talk very knowledgeably about early music manuscripts and medieval music notation, skilfully leading Gervase to describe some of the valuable early missals he had seen in the museums and collections he had visited. But there was more than a spark of amusement in her glance as she watched the two of them both angling to capture her wandering attention and dazzle her with their sparkling conversation. It was an unexpected experience for her to have two men vying with one another for her approval. Alan was more subtle about it, and did not try to scintillate too hard, but Gervase got positively flushed and flirtatious over his wine – and a trifle possessive, too, which caused slight danger signals to flash in Isobel's free and unfettered mind.

However, the casserole was good (and not overcooked, after all) and the apple pie even better, and by the time they got to the coffee, they were all feeling fairly mellow. But Isobel knew they were going to have to talk about Trevor and his problems in a bit more detail before Alan left – and then, she feared, the fur might fly.

"So what do you want me to say to young Trevor?" she asked, handing Alan his coffee, and trying to avoid Gervase's affronted gaze. "I shall be seeing him tomorrow morning."

Alan sat back in Isobel's comfortable chair and sipped his

coffee, looking thoughtful and not too emphatic. "I think – that is, if you feel able to accept your own involvement in the plan – should find out if he is willing to try the school scheme, and if not, why not."

She nodded. And then added, "I am a teacher, you know. It occurred to me that I might be able to help him with the work if he needed it?"

He stared at her, half smiling at her humility. "Would you?"

"Of course, if it would help. It might stop him getting too far behind." She paused, waiting for further instructions. "What else?"

"Well, before we start gingering up the Social Services people, ask him if he minds us interfering. I think that is important."

Isobel was about to nod again, when Gervase interrupted, rather waspishly, "I presume you are talking about that bunch of undisciplined kids?"

Isobel's glance raked him like steel. "They are *not* undisciplined, Gervase. In fact they are far *too* disciplined. That's the trouble."

"Well, why should they mind you talking to the Social Services people, then? If they need help, it had much better come from official sources, rather than you getting involved."

There was a moment's silence then, while Isobel bitterly reflected that it was hopeless to try to explain the problem to Gervase, and Alan wondered mildly why the man was so antagonistic. At last, Isobel said, with surprising gentleness, "It's not that simple, Gervase. There's such a thing as pride, you know – however much on your beam ends you may be. . . . You must see that."

Gervase, to his credit, paused to consider the matter then, and conceded that she could be right.

"Well, then," said Alan easily, smiling from one to the other, "granting them the sin of pride, if Trevor agrees, we could try Social Services and the Housing Committee next week."

"We?" Isobel was not really asking for help, she told herself, but it would be nice to have Alan's support.

"Of course. We're both concerned, aren't we?" He glanced a

shade warily at Gervase, and added by way of extenuation, "In any case, I promised the headmaster I'd do what I could."

Isobel's fleeting smile was grateful. And to her surprise, Gervase made an effort to show an interest.

"Are there many of these – er – child-carers about, do you suppose?" he asked. "Or is this an exceptional case?"

Alan looked at him with direct and abrupt seriousness. "About 10,000 of them, I believe – and that's only the ones that actually come to light."

"Ten thousand?"

Alan nodded sadly. "And all of 'em missing school, missing sleep, missing freedom and fresh air and playtime. All of 'em taking on too much responsibility too young, growing up too fast, sacrificing too many years of their young lives. . . ."

"How do you know so much about it?" asked Isobel, amazed at his grasp of the subject.

A brief, sorrowful smile touched him for a moment. "Since I became aware of Trevor's plight, I made it my business to find out." Then he added, with a hint of mischief, "And since you came on the scene, I thought I'd better get my facts right."

Isobel laughed, and Gervase, eying them both with a kind of grudging respect, had the grace to laugh, too.

"I must admit," he said ruefully, "if Isobel gets her teeth into anything, I've also learnt to beware of woolly thinking!"

Here, Archimedes, who was always rather wary of raised voices and troublesome undercurrents, decided that there was no imminent storm approaching, and settled himself comfortably, without undue ceremony, on Alan's knee.

"You are privileged," said Isobel, pouring them all out more coffee. "He must consider you harmless."

"I'm glad to hear it," said Alan, trying not to look smug.

Gervase, on the other hand, did look a little put out. He was friends with Archimedes. After all, he had two cats of his own who lived with him over the shop and made valiant efforts to keep the mice off the bookshelves. Archimedes usually favoured him with his attentions. This was treachery.

"I can see why you are both so committed to helping this young family," he said, trying to be fair. "But – forgive me, Isobel – you are a bit apt to dash off after good causes without stopping to think."

"That's the best way to do it," said Isobel stoutly.

"I only – it's only that I don't want you to – to get trapped into a situation that is more than you bargained f-for. . . ." He was actually stammering in his concern, and Isobel was touched.

She leant forward and patted his arm kindly. "It's all right, Gervase. I do know what I'm doing."

"What you're letting yourself in for?" he persisted.

"Yes, I think so."

"Commitments you can't get out of?"

She smiled. "Gervase, my life isn't too full of commitments at the moment, as you know. I could do with something to – as you so aptly put it – get my teeth into."

"Well, don't bite off more than you can chew!" snapped Gervase, stung by her tolerant smile.

Alan intervened then, judging the warning given, and the fragile truce between them in danger of foundering. "We won't make a meal of it," he said, "since we are being so dental!" and they all began to laugh, and Archimedes unexpectedly began to purr.

"You are both dear men," said Isobel, knowing it was time to make peace all round, "and I am truly touched at your concern. Let's all have a brandy with our coffee, and stop being anxious."

So they did.

When Isobel had Trevor beside her at the kitchen table drinking tea, she realized that he was a bit wary and on the defensive today, and decided to tackle the problem head-on and at once.

"I want to say something to you, Trevor, before we go any further," she said, watching the cautious light of unwilling doubt rise and fall in his expressive gaze.

"Yes?" His voice was suspicious, too.

"We only want to help you and your father, Mr Selwyn and I. That's *all* we want. And if you don't want us to, or feel that we are interfering, you've only got to say so. We don't want to do anything that will upset you or your father, or the kids. Is that understood?"

Relief flooded into his eyes. He looked at her in silence, gratefully believing every word she said.

When he did not answer, Isobel insisted. She knew they had to get things clear. "Understood?" she asked again.

He nodded, and looked down at his hands clutching his cup of tea. Then he looked up again, honest gaze probing equally candid one, and said softly, "Yes."

There was a moment of more comfortable silence then before Isobel went on. "So – that being out of the way – what do you think of the headmaster's deal?"

He looked troubled at that. "It's like I said . . . I can take the work home, but I can't promise to do it." He knew that sounded unhelpful, and tried valiantly to explain. "You see, my Dad likes me to talk to him. He can't seem to manage to listen to the telly or the radio much. They muddle him somehow. He says they are too fast. . . ."

Isobel nodded comprehension. Of course. They would sound too fast to a brain struggling to return to normality. A brain that found even ordinary speech an almost insurmountable obstacle.

" . . . so I just talk while I'm with him – sort of slowly and not too loud. It's all right when I'm cleaning the flat, or cooking something, or doing the washing – I can talk round him. But if I was doing schoolwork . . ." he looked at Isobel again with a kind of bleak, tired honesty, "I couldn't do both, could I? . . . And he'd feel left out."

Isobel understood that. "Mightn't he get interested, and sort of try to help you? I mean, you said he was rather clever and good at his job before. . . ."

Trevor sighed. "Yes, he was. But – but, you see, he's not ready for that yet. . . . Maybe he will be sometime soon . . . but not yet. It would faze him."

It was Isobel's turn to sigh. But she did not press the matter.

"And there are times," Trevor went on, sounding a bit driven now, "when he's bad and can't stand anything. I think his legs hurt a lot sometimes – they even jerk and kick out and frighten him. It's usually in the night, but he needs me to talk to then. . . ." His grey, anxious eyes met hers in open appeal. "The doctors said it was a good sign if his legs hurt, but that isn't much help to him, is it? And he gets very – very down sometimes. You do see why I can't promise?"

63

"Yes," said Isobel. "I do. But I think we should try the headmaster's plan and see what happens. If it doesn't work out, no one will blame you."

"Won't they?" His eyes were still asking unanswerable questions. But at last he capitulated and said painfully, "Well, all right. I'll try." He seemed to realize then that he was being very ungrateful, and began to say, with a slowly-growing smile: "It's good of you to say you'll come. He likes you, you know."

"Does he? I'm glad of that." She paused, wondering how much else could be said today. "Trevor, I think we're going to have to talk to the Social Services people – Mr Selwyn and I. There are things they can do for your father, you know – like physiotherapy, and a better wheelchair, and maybe a bigger care allowance or something." She saw him beginning to look alarmed, and hastened to add, "But I promise you faithfully I won't let them come and bother you, or threaten to take you all into care or anything. In fact, if we go and talk to them, they'll see you've got some useful grown-ups helping you already, and they won't be so inclined to make any fuss."

Trevor nodded slowly. That seemed to him to make sense. "All right," he said again. "But don't let them bully my Dad."

"I won't!" promised Isobel, and meant it.

There was one more thing she had to say, and this was the hardest of all. But with characteristic courage she tackled it head on. "Does your Dad *want* to get well?"

Trevor looked at her wide-eyed. But he did not seem altogether surprised by the question. "Yes, of course he does. Why?"

"Isn't he . . . a bit afraid of other people seeing him like that?"

The eyes were still honest, but clouded now with a kind of angry pity. "Yes, he is. Wouldn't you be? . . . But – but he is getting less fierce about it. He wouldn't let my Mum help at all at first. But he lets me . . . and he lets you."

She smiled. "I know. That's a good start."

They were both silent for a moment, both marshalling thoughts. Isobel had meant to go on and ask whether Trevor thought his father really believed Katie, his wife, would come back when he was better – and whether Trevor himself

64

believed it, too. But somehow she could not call his bluff. Could not make him either admit that he knew it was all a fantasy, or staunchly defend a pipe dream that affected them all . . . Better leave it for now. There would be time enough later to discover what they really thought . . . But she could at least find out a little about Ireland.

"He kept on about Ireland – where your mother came from . . ." she began cautiously.

Trevor sighed. "Yes. Did he get the map out? He often does that."

"Does he believe she's gone back there?"

The boy looked suddenly exhausted and bewildered, as if that question had haunted him for too long. "I don't know," he said slowly. "I think he remembers her talking about it a lot. . . . Maybe he just wants to believe it. It's easier to think of her *somewhere*."

Isobel was shocked at the grief in the young voice. "Do you think that's where she is?"

He shook his head sadly, the bleak look of loss and bewilderment still clear in his eyes. "I don't know," he said again. "She used to tell us she was very happy there. . . . Once or twice when things got bad, she would tell my dad she'd go back for some peace and quiet. But she didn't really mean it."

"Are you sure?"

He looked so besieged by doubt and longing now that she felt ashamed to have pushed him so far. But she needed to know – she had to know, if she was to be any help at all.

"No," he said flatly. "I'm not sure about anything . . . I only know she – she *did* need a rest. It was all – all too much for her, you see. . . ." His voice failed him then, and he fell into a black stillness of memory from which it was hard to rouse him.

"What about her parents – your grandparents?" asked Isobel, trying to find something practical to say. "Would she go to them? Wouldn't they help you at all?"

He shook his head doubtfully. "She didn't talk about them much. I think they disapproved of my Dad, or something . . . She said once her own dad wouldn't speak to her. But she talked about the convent quite a lot."

Isobel sighed again. Not much help there, then. "And

your other grandparents – Cliff's parents? Do you ever see them?"

Once again he shook his head. "They're in Australia . . . Mum did write to them when Dad had his accident, and they wrote back saying they were sorry."

"And that was all?"

He looked a little embarrassed. "I don't think they've got much money. . . . They went out there on some scheme that fell through or something . . . I remember Dad talking about it before. . . ." He sighed and did not go on. *Before.* Everything had been possible *before.* But now it was different. . . . There was nothing much more to be said about it now . . . then he remembered something, and added defensively, "Dad loved the docks and working on the boats, you see . . . they wanted him to give it all up and go with them, but he wouldn't . . . I think there was a bit of a row about it. So they took off without him. Katie – my Mum – did keep writing, trying to make it up, but Dad wouldn't join in, so it didn't work very well."

"I see," said Isobel. No help there either, then, she thought. But she could see that Trevor had had enough by now, and she stretched out a gentle hand and laid it on his arm. "I'm sorry if I asked too many questions," she said softly. "Don't mind me . . . I just wanted to be clear about things."

He nodded silently, not resenting her interference, not rejecting her kindness either.

"We'll deal with things one by one as they come up, shall we?" she suggested, still speaking gently. "And not worry about things we can't do anything about . . . I believe it will all come right in the end, and you've got to believe it, too."

"I know," said Trevor, with the sad, clear understanding of an experienced adult deep in his young voice. "I do try."

Isobel had meant to tackle Cliff Broadbent about Trevor's school work during her next visit, but when it came to the point, she found that she could not. She realized that he was still very dependent on Trevor's company, and that the boy had somehow managed to weave a very skilful web of comfort and reliance between the two of them – a delicate and fragile but resilient bond which somehow supported them both, and which it would be wrong to try to break.   She also realized, looking into those cloudy puzzled eyes, that Cliff was not ready to tackle difficult decisions, or even to understand the sacrifices that his eldest son was being forced to make on his behalf. He could not cope with that knowledge yet, and she understood why Trevor would not commit himself, would not promise anything that might confuse or upset his father, that might disturb the careful pattern of his days. She also began to understand, looking round the flat, how difficult it would be for Trevor to find any spare time or any privacy in which to concentrate on anything so irrelevant (in his eyes) and so unimportant as school work.

The flat itself was spotless today. She thought, sadly, that even her coming had made more work for the boy. He was so determined she should not find him wanting as a good manager, a good family provider, a good son and a good eldest brother. . . . It was a lot for one thirteen-year-old boy to take on. As it was, she saw that the carpet had been hoovered, the toys (mostly Colin's cars) put away, the washing stacked in neat clean piles, the T-shirts ironed ready for school, and Cliff's own sofa-bed made up with clean sheets and a freshly washed duvet cover. Where on earth was the boy going to find the time to do anything else, with all this to cope with? It would be too much to ask of him, and when she came to consider the matter, she could well understand why he felt that the whole problem of school was now an irrelevance that had little meaning for him. It was a world he no longer belonged in. He was too busy keeping his father and his family alive and fed to bother about anything else.

At this point in her thoughts, she found Cliff's blue, bewildered gaze fixed on her with curious intensity – and with a look of sad knowledge in them that she found a little startling.

"G-good boy, our Trevor," he said, very slowly and clearly. "C-couldn't do without him."

She nodded quietly, meeting his glance with as much reassurance as she could muster.

"Lot to – lot to c-cope with . . ." he added, an enormous, tired understanding in both his halting voice and his mist-laden blue eyes.

He knows, thought Isobel, relinquishing all desire to put

Trevor's case before him. He knows just how much the boy is giving up, the sum total of his endless chores and responsibilities. And he knows, poor man, that he can do nothing about it.

But he *can*, she thought, rallying from her own despondency. He *can*. We can make him a lot better – a lot more self-reliant – a lot more confident and in charge of his own life. It will take time – but that's what we have to do.

"We must get you well," she said aloud. "Or better, anyway. That will help him most."

The misty eyes filled with too-easy tears then. But he nodded his heavy blond head. "Try . . ." he said.

Isobel thought they had said enough – been sad and resolute enough – for one day. It did no good to weigh the man down with guilt and desperate resolutions. "Music?" she suggested, smiling at him with gentle encouragement. "What shall we have?"

For a moment Cliff looked at her with no change in his expression, and then he leant forward and scrabbled once again among his old records till he found what he was looking for. Then he held it out to her, almost shyly.

She looked curiously at the record sleeve. It was the Vaughan Williams Sea Symphony. *'Behold, the sea itself!'* she remembered . . . and *'Flaunt out your separate flags and ship signals!'* . . . and *'Token of all brave captains and all intrepid sailors and mates. . . .'*

"Where did you hear this?" she asked, amazed, as always, by his musical taste.

"C-Cathedral . . ." he got out. "Katie . . . took me."

Isobel looked at him, understanding the different longings and heart-tuggings that this great celebration of the sea must conjure up in him. And she remembered how it ended, with the last, sad, valedictory song: *'O my brave soul, O farther sail . . . O farther, farther sail. . . .'*

"One day . . ." Cliff said carefully, as if he knew her thoughts. "One day, Trev will go . . . even if. . . ."

Even if I can't, he meant. But he did not need to say it to Isobel.

"You both will," she said softly, and set the great music of Vaughan Williams singing of the sea.

* * *

68

She did not know quite how it happened that she and Alan were sitting in the Housing Office together, confronting a rather defensive man called Brian Evans who had nothing to offer them, and knew it. But Isobel was glad Alan was there, because she was on the verge of losing her temper, and Alan's patient good humour would probably save them all from the kind of fruitless anger that helped no one.

"But you can't leave a man in a wheelchair in a flat on the second floor!" she protested. "Can't you re-house them?"

"We did re-house them," explained Brian Evans wearily, meeting Isobel's furious stare with a kind of bleak resignation. "That's the trouble. We can't do it again. Others must come first."

Isobel was surprised at this. "You *did*? When was that?"

The man, whose thin, long face was set in lines of tired disillusion about the unending problems he was expected to solve and the countless rules and tangles of red tape which prevented him from doing so, answered her in the colourless voice of grey ash that had become his trade mark and his defence against the onslaught of human emotion and human tragedy that might otherwise engulf him in the course of his daily confrontations with desperate supplicants. "They had a house," he said patiently, glancing from Isobel's fiercely snapping eyes to Alan's milder gaze with little hope of being understood. "Quite a nice one – when Cliff Broadbent was working. But then – after he was laid off . . ." he hesitated, and went on more delicately, "I can't say what exactly happened to his money, but he couldn't keep up the mortgage payments, and the building society finally repossessed."

Isobel sighed. Trevor hadn't told her this part of the story. "But if he was out of work, shouldn't you have been paying his mortgage for him?"

Brian Evans did not look confused, only more tired. "Yes. If he had asked. But apparently he didn't—"

"Or maybe didn't know he could?" barked Isobel.

The housing officer shrugged mildly. "It's possible. . . . We can only help if we are informed of the problem, you know." He paused, and then added slowly, "So they were made homeless." A flick of wry humour came into his voice.

69

"They have to be homeless, you see, before we can help them."

Alan and Isobel looked at each other sadly. There wasn't a lot they could say.

"But the second floor!" persisted Isobel, seeing Cliff's trapped body in that confining wheelchair, and the longing in his eyes as he listened to Vaughan Williams conjuring up the restless spirit of the sea.

"He was not disabled then," pointed out Brian Evans reasonably. "Just – homeless. They were glad to be given anything."

"But weren't you told of his accident?" asked Isobel.

Evans glanced again, rather warily, at Isobel's mutinous face. "I must admit, his wife did come here several times to ask for groundfloor accommodation. She was very persistent, I believe. One of my colleagues saw her. She got very upset when we could do nothing for her."

"*Could* you do nothing?" demanded Isobel, in a disbelieving tone.

Evans sighed again. "The only alternative was bed and breakfast accommodation. That is hopeless for a family with a lot of young children. They have to be out of the house all day, and are all crammed into one room. It was out of the question."

Alan said, keeping his voice mild and sympathetic, "It must be difficult for you – we understand that. But surely there are *some* empty properties you could make use of?"

Brian Evans waved an expressive hand at the papers on his desk. "We have a list as long as my arm of deserving cases. And, of course, young pregnant women come first."

"Well," glared Isobel, "I admit Cliff Broadbent isn't *pregnant.*"

But the sarcastic little joke fell flat. There was no spark of amusement in the housing officer's eye. He went on doggedly setting out his case. "There are only a finite number of properties available. Some already have squatters in them, and it is hard to get them out. Some are in such a state of disrepair that they are unsafe, and we don't have the funds to repair them. We are trying to refurbish quite a few old houses now. There has been a reversal of policy there. But

70

it will take time and money – and meantime, our lists go on growing."

There was a defeated silence between the three of them. Isobel and Alan knew they had gone as far as they could. Brian Evans knew he could offer them no more.

"I can understand," he said at last, "how unsatisfactory and frustrating it must be for a man in a wheelchair. I can only say, we will bear his particular problem in mind, and if anything comes up, we will do our best to help him."

They looked at each other helplessly. Then Isobel got to her feet, knowing herself defeated – for the moment. (But I'm not done yet, she told herself. Not by a long chalk! I'll think of something.)

Beside her, Alan said quietly, "Thank you, anyway, for explaining the situation. I do hope you will be able to come up with something soon. It really is rather urgent."

Brian Evans nodded, relieved that these two far too articulate and intelligent people were not going to make a scene. He did seriously wish he could do something about it – but once again he had to shut down his own compassion and let them go away with no promises made.

"Come on," said Alan, "what we need is a drink," and he led Isobel away from the depressing environs of the Housing Office to yet another discreet but cheerful wine bar in a quiet side street.

"You seem to know all the dives," said Isobel, making it sound like an accolade, not a reproach.

Alan grinned. "Comes in useful. I spend quite a lot of time boosting egos – including my own – before and after concerts."

Isobel laughed. "I could certainly do with a boost now," she admitted.

Alan looked at her half seriously. "You mustn't despair yet. We'll find a way round it somehow. And the ramps will be ready soon. Then at least we can take him out."

Isobel sipped her drink and considered the matter. "I hope he'll agree to come."

Alan's glance grew a little sharper. "How did you get on with him this time?"

71

"Very well. He's a curious mixture, Alan. His taste in music is most surprising."

"Is it? Why?"

"Well, I expected it to be pop – or at least country and western or folk, or something. But so far we've had The New World Symphony and Vaughan Williams' Sea Symphony."

"Classical romantic," said Alan, looking thoughtful. "Escape . . ." he added, not missing the implications.

Isobel nodded. "Yes. He longs to travel, I think. And the sea clearly fascinates him."

"Not surprising, I suppose, if you've worked in the docks – and never had a chance to go out with the ships!"

"He needs space," said Isobel fiercely. "Space round him – air to breathe. . . . He's so confined, so claustrophobic, shut in there . . . and Trevor and the kids, too. . . . They all need room to breathe. We've got to do something."

"We will," Alan told her tranquilly. "We *will*. And there's the social worker to see tomorrow."

"Yes," agreed Isobel, somewhat fiercely. "There is. I want to know exactly what they are doing for that little family. How much money do they get? And do Social Security pay their rent? . . . I shall need to know all that before I start looking for somewhere else for them to live, won't I?" She almost glared at Alan. But he was unperturbed.

"We'll get things moving," he promised. He was watching the light of battle rise and fall in Isobel's eyes as she tried to contain her inner rage at being so hamstrung by the housing authority. Finally he said in an unexpectedly softened, searching tone, "Why, Isobel?"

"Why what?"

"Why do you care so much?"

She looked back at him with her clear, straight gaze. "Why do you?"

He made a curious gesture between a shrug and a denial. "I am a teacher."

"So am I. Or I was." She smiled a little. "Doesn't that include getting involved?"

"Unfortunately, yes," admitted Alan, but he was smiling a little, too. And yet, even so, he wasn't satisfied. . . . He leant forward, looking into her face with sudden intensity. "But that isn't all, Isobel, is it?"

She seemed to go a little pale under the subdued pinkish lighting of the bar, but her glance was as firm and steady as ever. "No," she agreed. "Probably not. But it's old history, Alan. Nothing to do with today. . . . Except that—" she paused, and then went on courageously enough, "I looked after my father – and made certain sacrifices. I know what it's like to be trapped." Her eyes, meeting his, were suddenly full of fierce entreaty. "I know what Trevor's life will be like – if we don't do something soon. That's why I—"

"Why you have to wave your sword and shout," said Alan, very softly, his voice almost a caress. And seeing her distress, the weight of memory still haunting her, he picked up her drink for her and put it into her hands. "Forgive me, Isobel. I didn't mean to probe."

She came out of her black thoughts of the distant past then, and smiled at him gratefully. "It's all right," she said, and took a gulp of wine. "But of course the past is never really dead, is it?"

They looked at each other with a kind of mutual trust and acceptance then, as if reassurances and pledges had been given, though nothing was said.

And presently, Alan began to talk of music and his next concert, and Isobel sat back happily and listened with only half a mind. But she was strangely content.

It was while Isobel was sitting quietly at home considering how to proceed in the flat-hunting enterprise, that the next crisis came upon her. The doorbell rang, and she found a wild-eyed Georgie on her doorstep.

"Can you come?" she begged, without preamble. "Trevor sent me. It's Goldie."

"What's the matter with her?"

"We don't know. She keeps on screaming, and shaking her head to and fro, but she won't tell us what's wrong."

"I'll get the car out," decided Isobel promptly. "We may need it. You go on ahead."

Georgie, after one grateful glance, set off again on Trevor's bike, riding in furious haste as if devils were after her. Isobel,

73

on the other hand, drove down to the flat at a fast but not breakneck speed, and was there almost as soon as Georgie. They went up the stairs together, and they could hear Goldie screaming before they got to the door.

Trevor let them in, and at the sight of Isobel heaved a sigh of relief, flashing her all sorts of grateful messages as he led her into the living-room where Goldie was rolling on the floor, clutching a pillow and yelling blue murder.

Cliff was looking down at her in shocked disbelief, not knowing what to do, and Colin was hovering between the two of them, equally uncertain of how to help.

Isobel went straight over to Goldie and picked her up bodily in her arms. "Quiet, now," she said firmly. "Be *quiet* – and tell us what is hurting?"

Goldie paused in the middle of another scream, and gulped instead, "Ears! . . . my ears! . . ." and began to turn her head again from side to side, with the scream reduced to a whimper.

"Get her coat," commanded Isobel. "We'll take her down to casualty at the hospital. It will be quicker than waiting for the doctor."

Georgie fetched her coat and wrapped it round her threshing little body. Then she and Trevor looked at one another, clearly wondering which of them should go with Goldie and which should stay with Cliff.

Isobel saw that agonized look pass between them, and rightly judged that Trevor should be the one to take decisions – if choices had to be made.

"You stay, Georgie, and keep an eye on things. Better make everyone some tea to keep them happy," said Isobel, smiling encouragement. "Trevor and I will take Goldie. It's probably only earache, anyway."

But she was not sure, of course, and the thought of mastoid-itis, or even meningitis hovered at the back of her mind. So she moved pretty swiftly, and together she and Trevor bundled the writhing child into the back seat of the car, with Trevor now holding her close in his own arms for comfort, while Isobel drove with all speed down to casualty.

By dint of a bit of bullying by Isobel, and the clear indication anyway that the child was in acute pain of one sort or another,

74

they got Goldie on to a trolley and being looked at by a doctor in the shortest possible time. Then they had to wait, while the screams subsided a little, and the experts got busy.

Isobel looked at Trevor's white face and said practically, "There's a coffee machine in the corner. Let's get some," and kept him busy pressing knobs and holding plastic beakers until the initial shock of the sudden crisis had worn down a little to the usual ache of anxiety that always clung to Trevor's mind, whatever he did.

"I never thought—" he began, looking guilty and scared.

"Never thought one of the kids might be ill as well?" Isobel's voice was gentle. "It's apt to happen, Trevor – even in the best regulated families."

He sighed. "I suppose so. . . ."

"Haven't any of them ever been ill before?"

"Well, they've had colds . . . and Georgie had a sore throat once and lost her voice. But never anything like this."

"It may not be so bad, Trevor," she said, hoping she was right. "It may be something quite trivial."

He looked at her rather desperately, seeking reassurance. "Do you think so?"

"Children can sound quite terrifyingly ill when they're just frightened," she said, from years of experience of fraught scenes in staff rooms and school sickbays.

The anxiety in Trevor's eyes did not dissolve, but behind it she glimpsed a sort of thankful reliance on her judgement. If Isobel said it would be all right, it probably would. . . . She felt the weight of that reliance, but she said nothing to shake it.

At that point, a young nurse came looking for them, and she was smiling. "It's all right," she said. "There was something lodged in her ear. The doctor is syringing it out now. She'll be fine."

The relief that came over the two of them was almost visible. "Can we see her?" asked Trevor, desperate to confirm the truth.

"In a minute. I expect you can take her home soon, too."

They looked from each other to the smiling young nurse, and began to smile themselves.

"Well, thank God for that!" murmured Isobel.

"Thank Dr Martin," said the nurse, grinning. "He found it – and he got it out!"

They arrived in the small cubicle to find Goldie sitting up on the trolley, still looking a bit flushed and tearful, but – to their enormous surprise – sucking an iced lolly.

"Where did you get that?" growled Trevor, having visions of small girls raiding hospital storerooms.

"I gave it to her," said Dr Martin, who turned out to be a small, smiling man with a shock of prematurely white hair and a calm and cheerful manner. "I keep a stock of 'em in the fridge for my patients when they've been extra good and co-operative, and Goldie has."

He held out a small sterile dish with a tiny dark object lying in it. "I think it's a small stone," he said." God knows how it got in there. Some scuffling in the playground, I should imagine! Anyway, she's all right now."

"All right now," confirmed Goldie, and promptly leapt off the trolley and began to execute a small dance round the cubicle to demonstrate the fact, chanting, "All right now" as she twirled.

The sighs of relief were audible, and Isobel thanked Dr Martin with real warmth. She was surprised at how much it mattered.

"All in a day's work," he said, smiling. "Wish all my cases were as simple!" and he patted Goldie's red-gold aureole of curls, and went hurrying off to his next crisis.

Trevor was almost inclined to shake Goldie for frightening them all to death over a mere bit of gravel in her ear, but he found himself laughing instead, and saying, "Come on, let's get you home before you get into any more trouble."

"Home," agreed Goldie, waving her nearly-demolished iced lolly. "Get me home, get me home!"

And, thankfully, Isobel did. But when they had got her safely back to the flat, and Cliff and the others had been reassured that all was well, and everyone had drunk another cup of tea to relieve the tension, Trevor accompanied Isobel to the door, and said, "You – you didn't mind us coming for you?"

"*Trevor*," protested Isobel, "I thought we understood one another."

"Yes, but—"

"I can't see the point," she told him severely, "of friends, if they can't be relied on in an emergency!"

Trevor grinned, albeit a little painfully. "There may be more of those than you bargained for – before you've done!"

Isobel grinned back. "When that time comes, I'll let you know," she said.

Chapter Five

'The Hag with the Money'
Old Jig

The social worker, Clare Simpson, was young and well meaning, looking at Isobel with eyes that reflected an earnest honesty beneath her straight, dark fringe. She was, Isobel thought from her long years of experience, too young for the job. How could she know what went on in the minds of people like Cliff Broadbent, or his hard-pressed young son, Trevor?

"Katie Broadbent came to see me a number of times," said Clare, trying to justify whatever arrangements she had or had not made. "To discuss her husband's disability allowance, and whether he was entitled to a care allowance, and so on. The trouble was—" she hesitated, not knowing how much she ought to say to this forceful woman in front of her, but not liking to be less than truthful.

"Yes?" Isobel prompted.

"She said Cliff – Mr Broadbent – did not want to be *visited*. He could not bear to be seen like that, she said. He even got violent when people tried to come near him. She said it upset him too much – she could not take the risk."

"I see," Isobel nodded.

"So we – I couldn't go there to see the situation, or send anyone round to assess his needs. She wouldn't let me."

"That must have been some time ago?" said Alan, sounding carefully neutral.

Clare Simpson looked confused and rather anxious. "I – yes, it was. Katie Broadbent hasn't been down to see me lately, and – er – of course I have a very full load of case work."

78

"You are not aware, then," said Isobel, with a swift glance at Alan for reassurance before she took the final risk, "that Katie Broadbent has left home, and the children and their father are looking after each other?"

The social worker looked appalled. "Is that true? How awful. How long has she been gone?"

"More than six months, I believe," said Isobel, her voice dry with hidden anger.

There was a pause, while the harassed social worker tried to take in what this news implied, and how it reflected upon her handling of the case. But she also, as Isobel observed, looked genuinely upset at the thought of that family of children being left to fend for themselves.

Then Isobel decided to mend some fences before the girl started to make the wrong decisions. "Don't misunderstand me," she said firmly, "they are managing pretty well – as far as it goes. They are fed and clothed, their flat is kept remarkably clean, considering. The younger children all go to school and have solid school dinners. But it means that the eldest boy – Trevor – has no life of his own at all." She looked accusingly at Clare's startled face. "He can't leave his father for long. He can't get to school very often. He can't go out, except to do a paper-round to bring in extra cash. He is cook, cleaner, nursemaid and, as far as I can see, mentor to those children, and to their father, too."

She paused, and added the most important part of her recital. "But – let me make this clear – the children don't want to be taken into care. They are terrified of being split up as a family – and if they were, of course, the father would have to go into some kind of institution, too. He couldn't be left on his own at present." She glared at Clare, daring her to interrupt. "That is why they have failed to contact you to ask for help," she said flatly. "In case your only way of offering help was to take them away."

There was a moment of heavy silence while Clare tried to absorb the whole tragic picture of that beleaguered little family. "What do you want me to do?" she asked at last.

Alan, so far, had said very little – leaving it all to Isobel who was more vocal and more forceful. But now he said judicially and kindly, diffusing some of the sense of blame in case it made the girl less co-operative, "Well, we know you are working under rules and guidelines, and that there are limited resources at your disposal – especially now with the cuts in community care. . . ."

She shot him a grateful glance at this.

'But I think what we have to do is find out what are the ways in which you *can* help."

Clare nodded, relieved to find this friendly-looking man so reasonable.

But Isobel was not to be deflected. "Let me just tell you what is needed," she said. "To begin with, the man is in a wheelchair, in a second-floor flat, which means he can't get out, even if he wanted to. Secondly, the wheelchair itself is old-fashioned and unwieldy, gets stuck in the doorways, and is difficult for him to manoeuvre. Then his physical condition – he needs physiotherapy for his legs. The children tell me the ambulance did come for him a couple of times, but then they stopped coming, and no one knew where to ask for them to come back. He also needs occasional check-ups by the doctor, I should think. But that I can lay on myself, if I make enough fuss."

Clare looked at her with respect. Clearly, this dynamic lady was prepared to make quite a lot of fuss.

"And then," Isobel went on remorselessly, "there is the question of income support. You will know, better than I do, how much they are getting now, and how much they are entitled to if they know how to apply. But they are very short of cash, I know. They were even reduced to stealing a pint of milk off my doorstep once."

Clare stared at her in horror. "*A pint of milk?*"

Isobel grunted. "Exactly. So does Cliff Broadbent get a full disability allowance? Do they get their rent paid for them? Who gets the children's allowance, now that the mother is absent? Shouldn't the father get meals on wheels? Shouldn't he get some care attendance – or at least a care allowance?" Her glare was as fierce as ever. "We need to know the answers to all these questions," she pointed out, "if we are to be any help to them. For instance, if we are to get them moved into a downstairs flat or something, we need to know how much rent they can afford to pay – or how much you are able to pay

80

for them?" She paused for breath, and then added, as fairly as she could, "I mean, here are two willing friends anxious to help and be as much use as we can, but we don't know where to start!"

Clare opened her mouth, daring to stem the flow. "I can see you are genuinely concerned about their welfare," she said, "and, believe it or not, so am I. So let us take all your points one by one."

Isobel heaved a sigh of relief. Now they were getting somewhere. . . . The upshot of it was, when Clare Simpson had taken careful note of all their requirements and promised to put every request to the right department – assuring them with genuine warmth that a lot of their requests could be granted if officialdom agreed – the troubled social worker then pushed her fringe out of her eyes and said tentatively, "I shall have to come and see them, of course."

"Of course," agreed Isobel. "But, if you don't mind, I'd like to be there, too – just to make sure they don't panic. And please – unless, of course, you find the children in really desperate plight – make no mention of the possibility of taking them into care."

"No, I understand that," she said, trying a faint, anxious smile. "And, in any case, you know, it is much cheaper for us to leave them where they are, and give what help we can."

Isobel nodded, matching her smile with a brief one of her own. "Cliff Broadbent can't talk very much yet," pointed out Isobel, "though his speech is improving, and he clearly understands very well what is going on." She paused again, and added, "I did wonder if giving him a computer and a screen for him to tap out messages might help, but then I thought it might actually *prevent* him trying to master speech again. Maybe a speech therapist would be more use?"

"Yes, that is possible," agreed Clare guardedly.

But Alan said slowly: "I'm not sure about that. He's shy enough about his disabilities as it is – I think it might set him back, having to be *taught* to speak, like a child."

The three of them pondered the matter.

"Well, we'll leave that for a bit," said Clare, "and if, as you say, he is improving, maybe the problem will resolve itself in time. . . ." She straightened a few papers on her desk, marshalling her thoughts at the same time. "What about the eldest boy's schooling? Isn't the truancy officer after him?"

"Yes," said Alan grimly, "he is. And his only resource is to *prosecute* the boy, or his father."

Clare made an explosive sound of protest. "Stupid!" she muttered.

"Yes, but I'm afraid the answer lies with you," said Isobel. "If he is to get to school, there has to be some other carer available."

Clare looked more troubled than ever. "It would have to be part-time," she said. "We simply haven't the resources."

"And it would have to be someone Cliff would tolerate," added Alan. "He's not an easy customer to please."

Again they all looked at each other in perplexity. Finally, Isobel said, "I think it will have to be a compromise – some school – some extra care. I am quite willing to be of help there." She looked at Alan, signalling curious messages of reassurance. "If you can meet us half-way," she added to Clare, quite sunnily. "I'm sure we can manage something – at least for the time being."

Clare accepted that gratefully, and then voiced the question that was in all their minds but hadn't yet been asked. "How long do you think Katie – the mother – is likely to be away?"

Alan and Isobel exchanged doubtful glances, and shook their heads sadly. "We have no idea," said Isobel at last. "But the children believe she will come back. Trevor – the eldest – said *she just needed a rest* . . . and I am sure that was true."

"Yes, that was certainly true," agreed Clare. "She was often very stressed when she came to see me. . . ." She hesitated, and then decided to be a little less discreet than perhaps she ought to be. "I gathered from her that Cliff Broadbent could be quite violent at times – due to frustration, no doubt."

"No doubt," answered Isobel, in her dry clipped voice. But she did not volunteer any more.

"So – we are faced with a fairly long-term problem?" said Clare, painfully aware in ner own mind that the resources she had to offer would again have to be stretched very thin.

"We are," confirmed Isobel. Then she looked squarely at Clare, challenge sparking from every pore. "So when can you come to see them?"

82

"It would be better at the weekend, I suppose," said Clare, once more sacrificing her free time, "when the children are home. . . . Say, next Saturday? What time would be best, do you think?"

"Teatime," said Isobel promptly. "Make it a friendly social visit. It won't frighten them so much then."

"Right. Teatime it is," accepted Clare. She turned to Alan, and then back to Isobel for confirmation. "Will you be there?"

"We'll be there," they said.

When they got outside into the early spring evening, Alan took one look at Isobel's face and said, "This is all a bit too grey for you, isn't it? Let's go for a walk."

Isobel stood still, confronting him squarely. "Alan, how can you spare so much time for all this? Haven't you anything better to do?"

"No," he said, sounding as blunt as she did. But there was a quirk of mischief lurking at the corner of his mouth which Isobel did not miss. "I doubt if there *is* anything better to do," he added, as if stating an indisputable fact.

It was Isobel's turn to allow a certain flick of humour to escape. "You sound very certain."

"I am."

They were already strolling along together, heading for the green spaces of Clifton Down at the top of the hill. The air was mild and sweet, already laden with the subtle fragrances of the burgeoning year, white clouds chased themselves across a soft spring sky, and a small wind shook the branches of the budding trees.

"This is more fun than marking books or setting equations," said Alan, smiling. "And my next rehearsal isn't until Friday – so what are we worrying about?"

Isobel had to admit that she wasn't worrying about anything at the moment. In fact she seemed to be unable to stop smiling, and she had a great desire to skip again, like a child let out of school.

They walked for a long time, not saying very much, and Isobel felt the frustrating restrictions of the Social Services network recede from her mind and fall away, dispersed by that persistent small spring wind, so that she felt absurdly light and happy.

I don't know what is happening to me, she thought, but it is a new experience to be with a man like Alan, who accepts everything that comes up with such tranquil good sense. . . . No, she admitted, it is more than that. We understand each other in a curious unspoken way – and maybe it is best not to enquire too deeply into how and why, but I feel ridiculously light-hearted!

At that point, Gervase's long, disapproving face intruded into her thoughts, and she felt a momentary pang of guilt. He didn't really like Alan, she knew, in spite of his attempts to be cordial, and he certainly didn't approve of her involvement with the Broadbent family. . . . Well, so what? she asked herself severely. I don't have to please Gervase, do I? I don't owe him anything. And he really has no right to criticize me . . . or to disapprove of my friends.

"I don't know about you," said Alan, aware of the sudden shadow of doubt in her mind, "but I'm starving. Let's find somewhere to eat."

"Alan, I—"

"No excuses," he said, sounding very brisk. "You have to eat. I have to eat. Let's eat together. Even Gervase couldn't object to that."

She looked at him in astonishment. "How did you . . .?"

"Oh, I guessed some snake had crept into Eden," grinned Alan. "Not that Gervase is a snake – he's a very nice fellow." His grin was wide and friendly. There was no judgement in it.

"I'm not – there isn't anything between us, you know. He's just a very good friend. . . . Only, he does rather try to organize my life!"

Alan laughed. "And protect you from other predatory males?"

"Alan!" But she was laughing, too – and there didn't seem to be any need to say any more.

"I don't know why it is," Alan remarked thoughtfully as they sat over their wine and waited for their meal to arrive, "that we always have a twinge of guilt when we are happy." He looked up into her face, quite simply and honestly declaring a multitude of unsaid things.

84

"Perhaps we think we don't deserve to be happy?" Isobel answered, with equal honesty. And the shade of her strict Presbyterian father hovered over her as she spoke.

"But we do," said Alan, and lifted his glass to her with smiling certainty.

Isobel could find no answer to that, but she lifted her glass to him in response, and recklessly matched his smile.

After anxious thought, Isobel decided not to tell Trevor or Cliff about Clare Simpson's proposed visit until the Saturday morning when Trevor stopped by for his usual cup of tea. That way, she reasoned, none of them would have time to be frightened, or suffer sleepless nights of worry about what the social worker would or would not do.

She did, however, decide to wait in the flat for Trevor's return from school on her Thursday visit, and try to assess in her own mind whether the day away from his father was a good idea or not, and whether the extra burden of school work brought home was going to be too much for him, on top of everything else.

She also, cautiously, tried to prepare Cliff for the idea that he could get help in his recovery without somehow losing his own integrity, and go out to face the outside world again without suffering too much humiliation. It was going to be difficult for him, she knew, but she had to try to get through to him somehow.

The music he chose this time was equally surprising to her – Beethoven's Pastoral Symphony – but it also suited her purpose well enough. So when it was over, the thunderstorm had died away and the little bit of blue sky had come back with the uprising flute to usher in the cheerful country dance tune of the last movement, and that in its turn had stomped its way to a sturdy close, she looked at Cliff's unguarded face and said gently, "It's still there, you know."

His eyes focused on her in startled recognition, the question in them clear for her to see.

"The countryside, Cliff. The trees – the flowers – the thunderstorms – the air itself . . . all waiting for you."

He did not try to speak yet. He waited for her to go on.

"Alan is getting some ramps made, so that we can get your

chair down the stairs . . . I would so love to take you out – and it would be such fun for the kids."

She saw the alarm, the sudden flick of terror and refusal in his expression, and she saw him swallow painfully and struggle to overcome it. "*Outside* . . .?" he said, as if trying out the idea in his reluctant mind.

"They could kick a ball about . . . or fly a kite," she suggested, smiling. "Colin and Goldie would like that. They ought to run about in the sun. . . ."

He nodded then, solemnly acknowledging to himself as well as to her that this was true. But a shadow of anxiety came back into his eyes as he followed her reasoning. "Kids. . . ." he got out, struggling to make himself clear, "not . . . not re—?"

"Restricted?" She understood him very well. "No, of course they're not. They go to school. Trevor has his paper-round. But they'd love an outing – and they won't leave you behind!" She let her smile grow a little more hopeful, and waited for a moment before pursuing the argument – if it was an argument. "Cliff," she said carefully, "it isn't weakness to accept help."

He looked at her, a bleak admission growing in his puzzled eyes. "Isn't . . . it . . .?"

"No. It's common sense. You need help. The children need help. It's a tough job they've set themselves, and it's tough for you, too. . . . But you might as well have all the help you can get – and all the money owing to you, too, if it's on offer. Why not?"

He stared into her face, meeting that strong, uncompromising gaze in fascinated respect. At last, he managed a strange, crooked smile, and echoed her words in his deep, uncoordinated rumble: "*Why not?*"

It was a victory, and Isobel knew it. She gripped his arm with sudden warmth and said, "Well, now we're getting somewhere!"

And Cliff actually began to laugh.

It was to this unexpected sound that Trevor and the other kids came home from school. Trevor, Isobel noted, looked tired and white, and his loaded school bag seemed to weigh heavy on his arm. His eyes went at once to his father's face, and he seemed to shed layers of anxiety and tension as he saw Cliff's smile.

"Everything's all right here," said Isobel, watching the boy's weary relief with some misgiving. . . . We are putting too much strain on him, she thought. This school idea is all very well – he'd be much better off with a day out in the sun.

"Are you staying to tea?" asked Georgie, trying to remember what there was for tea, if anything.

"No, not today," smiled Isobel. "But I'm coming on Saturday – and I'll bring some more sausages."

"Smashing!" said Colin. "Bangers and mash again!" He gave Isobel an impish smile, and went over to his father.

She was touched to notice that each child made a special effort to go over and greet Cliff, making it clear to him that he was still the head of their family, and still deserved their first attention.

"I scored a goal," Colin said, leaning against Cliff's wheelchair confidingly.

"An' I gotta star," said Goldie, not to be outdone.

Cliff nodded his head with conscious approval. "Good," he pronounced, and both children seemed entirely satisfied.

"Trevor," said Isobel as she prepared to leave, "stop by as usual on Saturday morning, will you, and we can arrange about tea."

Trevor glanced at her swiftly, still looking a little worried. He guessed at once from her carefully neutral voice that it wasn't only tea they were going to arrange.

"All right," he agreed, equally neutral and quiet. But Isobel was troubled by the wary knowledge in the boy's eyes, and his tired acceptance of even more difficult decisions to come.

She laid a hand on his arm for a moment and said softly, "Nothing to worry about." Her smile was luminous and full of encouragement. "Life can only get better!"

"Better!" chanted Goldie, pirouetting round the room like a small spinning top. "Better and better!"

"Oh, shut it, Goldie," grumbled Colin, though he didn't sound too bothered. "How do you know?"

"Mizzibell says so," stated Goldie, with perfect certainty.

And, at the complete assurance in the young voice, Isobel turned and fled.

*   *   *

That Friday, Isobel had her first real row with Gervase. He had been a bit glum when he arrived and the gloom continued through supper – even though Isobel had made a special effort over the cooking (perhaps because of a lingering faint sense of guilt about Alan, though she couldn't quite explain why).

Conversation was slow and a bit laboured, unlike their usual easy sparring, and Isobel found herself actually trying to think of something to say. This won't do, she thought sadly. Where has all our old easy companionship gone? What is bugging Gervase this evening?

At last, when they had reached the coffee stage, Gervase suddenly decided to launch the attack. "Isobel – I don't think you ought to get drawn into this rescue mission or whatever it is with those tiresome children."

Isobel looked at him levelly. "They are not tiresome, Gervase. On the whole they are coping very well with a difficult situation."

"Maybe," snapped Gervase. "But that doesn't give them the right to take up your time and energy in this way." He glared at her, aware that he was somehow making things worse, not better.

"It is my choice, Gervase," she said mildly, not wanting to make an issue out of it.

"Is it?" His voice was dry and waspish. "Are you sure you are not being influenced by your eager-beaver schoolmaster friend?"

Isobel's eyebrows rose in astonishment. For it occurred to her then that Gervase was in some absurd way jealous of her entirely innocent association with Alan Selwyn. "Gervase!" she protested. "You know very well that I was concerned about those children well before Alan Selwyn came on the scene." She paused, resolving not to let her old friend Gervase succeed in riling her. "Alan is a useful ally," she went on. "He knows more about the social welfare scene than I do. We are pooling our resources, that is all."

And in any case, she thought, why should I explain myself or make excuses? It isn't necessary.

"Really?" The brittle tone grated on Isobel's strung nerves, and she began to feel cross. *Strung nerves?* she thought. What am I strung up about? It's all perfectly simple. Those kids need help, and I am going to find a way to give it, one way or another, if it kills me. Though I hope it won't.

"And I suppose candle-lit dinners in local wine bars are all part of the campaign, are they?"

This time, she was really angry. "Am I to understand, Gervase, that you have been *spying* on me?"

"I – no," he had the grace to look abashed, "I was just – er – passing, and I happened to see you in there. . . ." He hesitated, seeing her shocked disapproval, but somehow he felt compelled to go on. "It's only that – I'm sure he can be very charming and persuasive, Isobel, but do you really *know* him? Are you sure you are not being – er – *manipulated*?"

I wish he wouldn't talk in italics, she thought crossly, and was just about to explode with righteous indignation, when she realized that the little pulse beating in Gervase's flushed temple meant that he was intensely nervous and intensely upset.

The poor man, she thought, suddenly wanting to laugh. He really thinks I am in danger of being seduced or something. At my age! I ask you! . . . But then she thought more soberly and more honestly: Well, perhaps I am. There is more than one kind of seduction, after all, and Alan is certainly persuasive.

"Gervase," she said aloud, sounding firm and rather chilling, "what I choose to do with my own time is my own affair. And my choice of companion is my own affair, too – whether you disapprove or not."

He blinked a little at her uncompromising tone, but he was still brave enough to oppose her. "That's true enough," he agreed, "but it doesn't stop your friends – your *long-standing* friends, I mean – from trying to prevent you making a fool of yourself."

By the flash of fire in Isobel's eyes, he knew he had gone too far this time, but he did not retreat. The two of them stared at each other in silence, while shock waves of anger and embarrassment seemed to vibrate round them.

And then Isobel began to laugh. "Oh, Gervase," she said, shaking with a mixture of helpless amusement and relief, "if you could see your face! You look like – like Nostradamus predicting the end of the world!"

Gervase tried to keep up his stern, accusing expression, but in truth Isobel's sudden laughter had come as a great relief to him, too, and he began to grin in response. It was no good, he couldn't be angry with her for long, and really, playing the part of a kind of heavy father did not suit him.

"Oh – all right," he said at last, beginning to join her in infectious giggles. "I won't lecture you any more. But don't say I didn't warn you!"

"I could never say that," giggled Isobel, wiping her eyes. "Could I? For heaven's sake let's forget the whole thing, and have some more coffee."

So they did. But the difference of view between them was not really resolved, and they knew it. And Archimedes, though he came out from under the sofa when the argument ended, did not immediately re-establish friendly relations with either of them, but went and sat by himself on the windowsill and brooded about the complicated vibrations in the air caused by human relationships. His dark, inscrutable eyes were very sardonic.

"Her name is Clare Simpson," said Isobel, to an anxious-looking Trevor on Saturday morning. "And she's nice, Trevor. Really quite sympathetic. She won't do anything you don't like."

Trevor looked at her. "Are you sure?" he asked, layers of distrust and earlier betrayal vying with a certain hope of understanding in his young voice.

"Yes, I am. And so is Mr Selwyn. That's why he's coming to tea as well – to make sure nothing is done to upset your father." She paused, and seeing the fear still there, deep down in his eyes, added firmly, "We made her promise not to try to take you into care, or do anything to separate the family." Once again she paused, waiting for that bit of reassurance to sink in. "And, as a matter of fact, Trevor, it wouldn't be in her interests to recommend any such thing. From her point of view, you all have a father who is officially in charge, even if he can't do much – and if you were all taken away, it would cost the local authority much more money, and your father would have to go back into hospital or to an institution of some kind, which would also be much more expensive. Do you see? She knows very well that everyone is better off if she leaves you alone."

Trevor looked almost convinced.

"But that doesn't mean she can't arrange to give you all more help," went on Isobel, pointing out the advantages. "There are better allowances to be had: a better wheelchair, better treatment for your father's legs. All sorts of ways that life can be made easier. And you've got to allow her to do everything she can. You owe it to your father – and the kids."

After a pause, Trevor nodded slowly and said, "Yes. That makes sense." He thought for a moment, and then asked with painful anxiety, "What do you want me to do?"

"Nothing," said Isobel. "Just carry on as usual. Don't polish and clean too much – or scrub the kids too much. Let everything look as normal as possible. And as regards the tea – you must let me provide most of it, and we must make it clear to her that you couldn't have managed to provide all of it out of your ordinary budget."

He looked very doubtful about that, and seemed about to protest, but she glared at him, pretending to be very fierce. "Do you understand? We *want* her to know how tight things are. You mustn't be too proud to let her see."

Trevor sighed. He understood the calculated strategy of trying to convince the Social Services of their needs – hadn't he seen his mother trying desperately to do just that? – but even so, he didn't like it.

"All right," he said sadly." But isn't it a bit – dishonest?"

"No," said Isobel firmly. "You are not pretending anything – covering up anything. Your needs are perfectly clear, perfectly obvious to anyone with any sense. And you are *entitled* to everything she can offer. Remember that. It can only help your dad to get better – and all the kids to have a better time. That's what you want, isn't it?"

"Yes," admitted Trevor, still vaguely unconvinced about the rightness of everything. His mother, Katie, had taught him never to be dishonest and never to beg. Was he doing right . . .? But she had said, "Tell the Welfare," so it must be right.

"Don't worry so," reassured Isobel, aware of the complicated processes of Trevor's mind. "You are not asking for anything that is not your right. That is what the Social Services are there for."

He capitulated at last, and gave her a tired smile. "OK," he said, knowing it sounded inadequate and a bit grudging. Then he remembered his manners. "Thanks for taking all this trouble. . . ." His smile got suddenly warm and alive with feeling.

"It's a pleasure," said Isobel, and meant it. And her answering smile was full of comfort and approval.

"I do cookery at school," explained Georgie, as she set the dish of sausages and baked beans down on the table. "And Trev's quite good at it, too. He did the mash." She gave the lady who Trev said was a social worker her most dazzling smile.

"I see," Clare answered, smiling back. "It all looks very good."

"I can do boiled eggs," announced Goldie, executing a little extra twirl and skip before she sat down. "And Colin's good at toast."

"You all sound most efficient!" Clare told them, touched by their determined efforts to be self-sufficient.

"G-good – kids . . ." Cliff got out, as he had once before to Isobel, in the same state of anxiety.

Trevor propelled his father's chair closer to the table, keeping one hand on his shoulder after he got him settled. "It's all right, Dad," he said, and glanced fiercely and meaningfully at Clare Simpson, the social worker, the enemy, daring her to contradict him.

"We're all friends here, Trevor," said Alan Selwyn mildly, and reached out for a piece of bread with deliberate calm. "Those bangers look good. Can we start?"

"Why not?" said Cliff, suddenly becoming the host and remembering how to smile.

The meal progressed pleasantly enough, though the children were still wary and on their best behaviour. . . . But then, they are *always* on their best behaviour, reflected Isobel sadly. Or nearly always. Life is somehow too precarious for them to risk being naughty or silly . . . but I wish they would be sometimes. . . .

"Guess what," said Alan, grinning round cheerfully at the

kids, "The woodwork boys have made you a ramp to go over the stairs. You'll be able to take your father out for a little jaunt. That is, if he likes the idea?" His mild gaze was suddenly full of challenge as it settled on Cliff Broadbent's face.

Cliff glanced wildly at Isobel, and seemed to draw some kind of strength and reassurance from her, though she said nothing to encourage him. That had all been said before, and he knew it. Now he had to take the decision, and face reality. The world outside was waiting for him, and he could not hide from it any longer . . . *The kids would love it . . .*" Isoble's voice said in his mind, and he couldn't ignore it.

"G-good idea . . ." he said at last, and looked at Isobel for confirmation that he had done right.

"Splendid," said Alan, beaming approval. "We could try tomorrow if it's fine."

Trevor was looking cautious. "It would take two of us . . ." he began doubtfully.

"Well, I'll be there," Alan told him. "And they've put struts across the wood to stop the chair from running away. It's bumpier like that, but much safer."

He seemed to have all the answers, and the children looked at each other hopefully. Take their father out? A little jaunt? Could they?

"Do any of you have a kite?" asked Isobel, smiling at their hopeful faces.

There was a moment's silence while they considered the matter. "I did once," admitted Colin. "But it got tangled up in a tree and it broke." He glanced at Trevor, as if making excuses for his elder brother. "Trev said a new one would cost too much."

So it would, thought Isobel, and Clare Simpson, and Alan Selwyn, all in their own way sympathetically assessing the family's resources. What with food to buy, and bills to pay, and clothes. . . .

"It was the shoes," muttered Trevor, sounding unexpectedly driven. "Colin's feet grew . . ." and suddenly everyone was laughing, albeit a little shakily. They were all aware that another perilous moment had successfully passed.

But Trevor still looked a bit pale and anxious, and when tea was over, he turned resolutely to Clare Simpson and said,

93

"Would you like to see the rest of the flat – while Georgie clears away?" and he glared fierce instructions at Georgie, who picked up her cue at once and dragooned the other two into helping her in the kitchen. Isobel and Alan were left to entertain Cliff, and – they both surmised – to keep him from worrying while Trevor tackled his enemy himself.

There were two other rooms in the flat: a very small bedroom with a single bed in it, and a larger room with two pairs of bunk beds ranged along the walls.

"When Dad had his accident," explained Trevor carefully, "my Mum moved him on to the day-bed in the living-room. It's easier to get into from his chair."

Clare nodded.

"So we put the bunk beds in here," he went on, "and she had the little room. It was closer to reach Dad in the night."

Again Clare nodded. "And where do you sleep now, Trevor?"

"Oh, in the little room. Dad often needs me. He doesn't sleep a lot."

And nor do you, I suppose, thought Clare, very much aware of how much this beleaguered boy had to endure.

"Miss Simpson—" began Trevor, mustering strength and courage from whatever source he could find.

"Clare," she interupted gently. "Everyone calls me Clare. It's easier."

"Clare," he repeated obediently, "you won't – you won't say anything to upset Dad, will you? He gets . . . fazed, you see . . . If things seem too difficult. He can't – he can't cope with too much hassle."

Clare looked at the boy with all the reassurance and honesty of purpose she could offer. "Of course not, Trevor. I'm only here to help, you know. I'm not an enemy!"

Not an enemy. Trevor's mind did a quick double take of adjustment. He had lived too long with the bogey of a do-gooding social worker who would come crashing in and destroy everything he had been struggling to build up – the fragile structure of family solidarity he had been at such pains to preserve. . . . Now, seeing this kind, anxious young woman with the untidy fringe, who was clearly falling over herself backwards trying not to be too critical or too interfering, he

94

knew he had been wrong. She wasn't a threat. Isobel Frazier and Alan Selwyn would never allow her to be. He needn't be afraid of her. She might even be some help.

He smiled at her suddenly, and said in a voice of quiet relief, "That's all right, then." And, realizing that it might still sound a bit unfriendly, he added by way of apology, "It's just that I – I worry about him, you see."

"Of course you do," agreed Clare, allowing real warmth to creep into her voice. "And I think you are doing a wonderful job keeping the family together." She met his smile with an encouraging one of her own. "But there are probably things we can do to make life a bit easier all round – you won't object to that, will you?"

He grinned at that. "I'd be a fool if I did, wouldn't I?" he said.

But at that point, Goldie's small fiery head came round the door. "Come on, Trev. We're going to play the Tunes."

Trevor was instantly on the alert. "Does Dad agree?"

"Yes," Goldie told him, dancing about in excitement. "I asked him and he said: 'Play!' Come on."

So Clare and Trevor went back into the livingroom – an enmity over, an allegiance formed – and the music began.

This time, to Isobel's surprise, Alan decided to join in. He did not explain why, but he knew that making music together was a sure way of building up a sense of camaraderie and mutual trust.

"Do any of you have a recorder?" he asked, noting with approval how easily Colin's fingers managed the stops on the penny whistle.

"We've still got Georgie's treble," said Colin, sounding reluctant and a little at bay. "But it doesn't fit the Tunes—"

"Can I borrow it?" Alan interrupted, smiling at him in a conspiratorial manner.

"Yes, if you like," Colin shrugged. "But it's too soft," he added, mutinously.

Alan nodded. "On its own, yes. But not with the other two."

"OK." Colin handed over the golden-brown treble recorder without further question, and Alan began to join in the Tunes with a warm-sounding obbligato of his own. He wove cheerful

95

patterns below Georgie's lively fiddle and Colin's 'twiddly' penny whistle, while Trevor once again took up his father's mouth organ and filled in some background chording with the tune, though secretly longing for the deep voice of his cello that could provide a real singing bass line. His ears told him that the sound they were making was all a bit too light and shrill, in spite of Alan's treble recorder, and that somehow the Irish Tunes needed a core of darkness under the lilt of their beguiling rhythms. But he did not stop to explain this to anyone – only his eyes met Alan's once or twice in a kind of mute apology. Alan understood him, but he too paid no attention to the missing richness, and just supported the others as cheerfully as he could.

They tried 'The Hare in the Corn', and 'Fire on the Mountain', and even 'The Long Strand', which was a bit too hard for them, really. And then Goldie sang 'The Kerry Dancing' again, her small, clear voice uplifted without shyness or any sign of nerves – she was a born performer. Like her mother? Isobel wondered. And once again, as the magical sound enfolded them, several pairs of eyes got rather misted and dim.

But Alan was master of ceremonies now, and he wasn't going to let anyone get too sad or broody today. "Bravo!" he said, smiling at Goldie's enraptured face. "Goldie, our little blackbird! But now, who can play a really fast Irish jig?"

"I can," said Georgie, breaking into 'Saddle the Pony' at once, and sawing away like mad, her fingers trying to catch all the notes.

"I can!" cried Colin, and twirled away on his penny whistle, also determined not to miss a single twiddle.

"I can!" said Cliff suddenly, and began to bang on the table with a spoon, as he had done once before.

And Goldie, feeling the beat get into her toes, began to dance.

They watched her, fascinated. She didn't know all the heel and toe steps, but she made a good guess at them, her small, neat feet moving like lightning, her red-gold head cocked to one side, curls bouncing, skirts flouncing, as she whirled and leapt and pranced round the room. Faster and faster played Alan, and faster and faster the others tried to follow – and faster and faster danced Goldie until she fell at last in a panting heap on the rug at her father's feet, while the music came to a boisterous end in a gale of breathless laughter.

"She'll come back," said Goldie, looking up at Cliff from the floor and offering him instant consolation for the tears in his eyes, as she had done before. No one knew how to keep the blues at bay from her father quite as well as Goldie, who had no inhibitions about offering comfort. "She will, won't she?" she demanded of Alan, who still seemed to be in charge.

"Well, if you all make music like that, anything could happen!" he said, smiling.

"And *dance*," pointed out Goldie.

"And dance like a dervish, of course," he added, laughing.

"What's a dervish?" asked Colin, who was always interested in anything new.

"Someone who whirls round in circles," said Alan, "and goes on till he drops."

"Like me," said Goldie, satisfied that a dervish was a good sort of thing to be.

She climbed to her feet then and leaned against her father, reaching up to pat his face in a totally unselfconscious gesture of affection. "OK, Dad?"

And Cliff merely nodded, and reached out to tug at one red-gold curl.

"What I would like now," said Alan, still keeping up the sense of occasion, "is another cup of tea – just to round things off."

"So would I," admitted Clare, who was so shaken by the music and the general warmth of this astonishing little family that she could scarcely speak.

Georgie sprang into action, and so did Trevor. "Tea coming up," they said.

And Trevor was suddenly aware that it was a party, and everyone was happy. Even the welfare lady was smiling. Goldie has done it again, he thought. She always gets round people somehow. But it was at Isobel he looked, in thankful recognition that all was well.

Chapter Six

'Rolling on the Ryegrass'

Reel

The combined operation to get Cliff's wheelchair down the stairs looked like being more difficult than they had expected – not because of the practical problems of weight and safety, which Alan thought he could overcome easily enough, but because Cliff himself was being difficult.

When Isobel arrived, a white-faced Trevor came up to her and said urgently, "Can we – can we wait a minute?"

"Yes, of course." Isobel smiled reassuringly at his anxious face. "What's the trouble?"

"It's Dad. He doesn't want to go."

Isobel had been half expecting this, and was not unduly surprised. But neither was she going to let Cliff get away with an attack of panic. This battle had got to be fought and won now.

"When did this start?" she asked, aware of the boy's tension, and longing to dissolve it.

Trevor looked at her in desperate apology. "I'm sorry – the kids were so excited – but he got ill in the night and began to shout. . . ." His eyes, looking into hers, were full of a kind of rueful pity. "He – he often does that . . . when things worry him."

Isobel nodded. "And . . .?" She wanted to find out how much of this constant emotional blackmail Trevor had to endure – and how much he understood it.

"Oh well, I got him a hot drink, and sat with him a bit . . . He went off to sleep in the end, but he – he kept saying: 'I *can't.*'"

She saw the weariness and compassion on the boy's expressive face – somehow a much-too-adult awareness of his father's
plight – and she wished with all her heart that she could lift
this weight of uneasy knowledge from him. Was she asking
too much of Cliff too soon? she wondered Or was she right
in thinking one fierce moment of confrontation might resolve
the matter once and for all.

"Where are the kids?" she asked, putting essentials first.

"In the kitchen, making sandwiches."

"Go and help them, Trevor. I want to talk to your father."

The boy hesitated, looking at her with the same driven look
of divided allegiance. "You won't . . .?"

"I won't upset him, no. Trust me."

He did trust her really, he told himself. She knew how to
handle his father somehow, without being told. But she had
never seen him in one of his shouting tantrums or when he had
one of his crying fits afterwards . . . Trevor had, and he knew,
better than anyone else, how hard it was to get Cliff Broadbent
to calm down when he was worked up.

Only now, Trevor thought suddenly, I'm too tired to do any
more. Maybe she can deal with him . . . I'd better let her try.
"All right," he said, his voice heavy with exhaustion, and he
turned away and went into the kitchen and shut the door.

Isobel advanced on Cliff, who was sitting in his chair,
looking frightened and at bay. His shoulders were hunched
against the encroaching world, and his eyes were bleak with
refusal. In fact, Isobel thought, from the many years of her
teaching life, she recognized that look. She had seen it many
times on the faces of many small boys facing their first
day at their new big school, with the fierce, rough world
pressing in all round them, threatening the sheltered safeties
and certainties of their vanishing childhood.

It brought her up short – that look – and she spoke with
sudden gentleness to the small boy inside Cliff Broadbent's
tormented body. "It's like the first day at school, isn't it? And
once it's over, nothing will ever be quite so bad again."

Cliff stared at her, bewildered by her softened tone. He had
expected brusque words and fierce orders.

"You're a bit of a hero to Trevor, you know," she said,
smiling. "And to the other kids, too. But specially to Trevor. He

knows what you're going through." She watched the changing thoughts chase themselves across his puzzled face. "You can't disappoint them, can you?" She saw that new thought take over from the others in his mind. And she waited.

There was a small, tingling silence in the room, while they looked at one another, challenge bright in the air. Each of them seemed to be waiting for a sign.

Everything depends on this moment, thought Isobel. All that we can do for him – and for the kids – his future and theirs. If he can come to terms with accepting help, with admitting that he needs it, and allow other people to see his needs . . . and if he can begin to think of the children first, and not himself. . . . But how can I begin to explain any of this to him?

Cliff, for his part, was trying to adjust his mind to a new thought. When he had thought about the kids being disappointed – and he had – he understood about them not wanting to miss the outing, but it was something they could do without. They were good kids, and they wouldn't really mind much. They were used to doing what their sick father wanted, and it wouldn't hurt them. . . . But the idea that they might be disappointed *in him*, if he refused to go out, that was something different. If, as this nice, bossy woman, Mizzibell, suggested, they thought of him as 'a bit of a hero,' hadn't he better keep it up and go on being 'a bit heroic'? . . . He considered the matter slowly. It took a long time for new ideas to settle into his mind these days. . . . Heroic? Him? A helpless cripple in a wheelchair? And all his mates being sorry for him, if he ever did venture out and risk meeting them in the street?

He was sorry enough for himself, he admitted, with a rare flash of insight, without anyone else adding to it. But maybe it was time he stopped moping indoors and tried to get his act together. Maybe, if he forced himself to get going again somehow, he wouldn't see pity in their eyes – only respect?

"Sorry?" he said suddenly, and it was a question, not an apology.

Isobel did not misunderstand him. "*Sorry*? For you?" She laughed, a little fiercely. "*Proud*, more like! Once we get you out there!"

To her surprise, he began to smile at her vehemence, and she saw that the battle was somehow over before anything more had been said. *"Out there!"* he repeated, and nodded his head in acceptance.

And at that point, as if on cue, Goldie came in, carefully carrying a bright yellow daffodil in her hand. "Buttonhole," she said, and reached up to fix it in the lapel of his best jacket, which Trevor had carefully helped him into earlier. "When you go out, you've got to look smart!"

"Smart!" agreed Cliff, admiring the daffodil, and his smile grew steadily wider.

The doorbell rang then, and Alan arrived with two large and cheerful boys from the woodwork class. "We've brought the ramp," he said, smiling round at everyone, "and two likely lads to help us with the chair."

The boys came forward, open and friendly, each of them holding out a firm, warm hand to Cliff. (If they had been briefed by Alan, Isobel reflected, he had done it very well.)

"Hallo, Mr Broadbent. Bit of an adventure this, isn't it?" said Dave, the tallest and fairest.

"We thought we'd better make sure the chair didn't run away with you!" added Mitch, the shorter, darker one. And everyone began to laugh.

But Cliff looked at Isobel, and then at Trevor who was already standing protectively by his chair, and said very clearly and distinctly, *"Adventure!"*

So they wheeled him out of the door and began the perilous journey downstairs.

The first thing that happened was the unexpected opening of neighbours' doors. Hearing the commotion, they came out of their first-floor flats and their ground-floor flats to see what was going on.

The couple on the first floor were elderly and shy – not aggressive at all, but just anxious about the fuss. The woman, who was slight and rather fragile, looked at Isobel from behind a wispy grey fringe and said in a gentle, apologetic voice, "If I'd known what to do to help, I would've . . . but Mrs Broadbent said he didn't want visitors. . . ."

Isobel watched Alan and the two boys, with Trevor still manfully holding on to the handles of the wheelchair, bump Cliff Broadbent slowly down the first flight of stairs. "Yes,

I know," she said, smiling at the woman's worried face. "He doesn't find it easy to let people help!"

"It's a disgrace," her husband said, sounding quite angry, "leaving a man in his condition on the second floor. What is he supposed to do?"

"Not this, anyway," Isobel admitted ruefully. "I hope the council landlord won't complain."

"How can he?" retorted the man, his ruff of white hair standing up with indignation. "It's the council's fault there's no lift." He squared his shoulders, and looked absurdly ready for a fight.

The chair went on bumping down, and on the ground floor another, younger couple came out with several children round them. The father was in his shirtsleeves, wiry and practical-looking, with a thin, lined face lit by bright, observant eyes. "Good for you!" he said, in cheerful approval. "About time someone did something about this place. It's like a morgue."

"Frank!" remonstrated his wife, sounding a shade scared. "It's not all that bad. Suppose Mr Grant heard you?"

"Serve 'im right!" growled Frank. "The council never spends a penny on this place. Putting in a lift wouldn't hurt them!"

By this time, the chair had crossed the hall, and was making for the front door and the steps outside. Trevor was still doggedly holding on to the handles, and Cliff was watching everything that went on with a curiously detached interest – almost as if it was happening to someone else.

"If they ever want a hand . . ." said Frank, looking at Isobel, assuming – like everyone else – that she was in charge, "tell the boy to let me know."

"I will," smiled Isobel, thankfully aware that the bumpy ride had broken down more barriers than that steep, awkward staircase had presented.

Getting down the front steps was the most hazardous part of the whole exercise, but they managed it successfully without spilling Cliff out of his chair. He bore it all without saying a word, grimly determined not to make a fuss, but Isobel saw a flash of relief in his eyes as the whole little party assembled round him on the pavement.

"I'll take the ramp down," volunteered Frank. "And help you put it up again when you come back."

"*Thanks*," said Alan, aware that real signals of goodwill had been made.

The two boys, Dave and Mitch, had clearly decided to be part of the whole expedition "in case you need a hand," as they put it to Alan Selwyn. And it was clear to him, and to Isobel and Trevor, that they certainly would need a hand to get Cliff back upstairs when the time came. So they all started off in a cheerful party, with Goldie and Colin darting about in front, Georgie hovering between them and her father, and Trevor, now in charge again on his own, pushing the chair. Cliff did not seem unduly shaken by the first part of the journey, and now, Isobel observed, he was beginning to look about him with real interest, and there was a small flush of excitement – or was it just pleasure? – on his pale cheeks as he felt the sun and the spring wind on his face.

And then a neighbour came up to speak to him, and Isobel froze with terror in case he showed any sign of the pity that Cliff so dreaded, or used those fatal words: "*I'm sorry.*" But he didn't. He clapped Cliff on the shoulder, none too gently, and said heartily, "Good to see you out and about again, Cliff," and went on his way, tactfully not waiting for a reply.

Isobel breathed a sigh of relief, and met Cliff's eyes in thankful reassurance.

"*Out . . . and . . . about!*" said Cliff, and actually laughed.

They went on up the hill till they reached the grassy open spaces of the Downs, and here Trevor actually let Dave and Mitch take it in turns to push the chair while he walked free in the sun. *Walked free*, he thought, and Dad can only sit and look at it . . . though I suppose this is better than nothing. But when he turned to look at his father, Cliff was smiling, and watching Goldie and Colin chase each other through sunshine and shadow on the new spring grass. They even rolled about on the springy turf like frolicking puppies, and got up again in a splutter of laughter and a tangle of wildly flailing limbs. . . . Georgie still hovered between Cliff's chair and the laughing kids – not quite sure where her allegiance lay. But her little foxy face was sharp with longing – the wide open spaces of the Downs were very inviting.

"I brought a kite," said Alan, winking at Isobel. "Someone else in the woodwork class made it." He unfolded the package he had been carrying under his arm and spread it out on the grass. It was blue and gold, shaped like a bird with wings outspread, with two long streamers for its tail.

"Ooh, smashing!" said Colin, who had a one-track mind.

"Now then," Alan protested severely, "that is *not* the idea at all. Dave, you show him how to get it flying . . ." and before he could say any more, they were all running about the grass and the blue and gold wings were high in the air.

"Come on," said Alan, master of ceremonies again, "there's a bench over here in the sun. We can all sit and watch the fun."

"*Fun* . . ." agreed Cliff, a sparkle in his eye, and Isobel realized he was trying very hard to make this first expedition a success.

So far, Trevor had shown little desire to leave his father's side, but once Isobel and Alan had settled Cliff's chair beside them and sat down together to admire the antics of the kite-flyers, he hesitated and stood wondering what to do.

Isobel understood his reluctance and uncertainty – and her heart seemed to clench with a kind of angry pity inside her. It was all wrong that a boy of thirteen should be so anxious and so dutiful that he had almost forgotten how to play. "Go on," she urged. "Go and join them. Cliff will be all right with us – won't you?" she added, turning to him with deliberate challenge.

"All – right . . ." agreed Cliff, nodding and smiling. And then he managed a whole sentence specially for Trevor, who never let him down and who so needed to be let off the leash a little. "Go – and – fly . . ." he said.

Trevor gave him one incredulous look, and went. Because he was at school so little, he did not have many friends there, and Dave and Mitch were older anyway, and in a much more senior class. But they seemed to accept him quite cheerfully – as they did Colin and little Goldie, not to mention Georgie whom they clearly found rather attractive with her wild red hair and elfin face. So they took a lot of trouble to make the kite fly, and keep everyone happy. It was a new experience for Trevor, and he was rather amazed at the whole situation.

On the street where he lived, he had no time to mix with the other boys who hung about after school and at weekends, mostly getting up to mischief of one kind or another. He did not let the kids play out in the street either, afraid they would get drawn into the usual petty crime, joy-riding and ram-raiding, and uneasy experiments with drugs. He didn't want his kids to get into trouble – his Mum would never have allowed it, and nor would his father when he was well. It meant that Trevor had to be a bit of a heavy father himself, and he wondered sometimes if they resented it, but they didn't complain about it, and usually obeyed him without question, though Colin sometimes liked to argue the toss a bit.

As for the street kids – he half expected them to be suspicious and unfriendly, or even downright antagonistic – he wasn't one of the gang and never could be – but for some reason he did not understand, they did not pick on him, and let him alone. Two things affected his 'street cred', as they called it – and gave him enough status to make them accept him without question. One was the paper-round which he did every morning, wet or fine (unless Georgie did it for him in an emergency) and the other was his care for his father, Cliff. They knew about Cliff in the street. They knew about his redundancy – his all-too-frequent visits to the Red Lion – his accident – and his young wife going off like that without a word. . . . They knew about it all – and though they didn't say anything, or do anything, they did afford Trevor a grudging respect for the way he kept things together.

That did not mean, though, that they were all that friendly and approachable – or all that playful, either – so it was a rather strange, heady experience to be dashing about in the sun with two laughing boys who didn't seem to have a care in the world.

But he didn't forget his father for long. Presently, he arrived holding the string of the kite, and carefully transferred it to Cliff's inexperienced hand. "It's quite high now," he said. "You can feel it tug in the wind. Doesn't it look beautiful up there?"

They all looked up into the spring sky where the blue and

105

gold bird swooped and darted in the fickle wind, and something about its straining upward flight seemed to stir them all into half-forgotten dreams and longings.

"Time to eat," said Alan, not allowing anyone to get too full of visions. "Call the others, Trevor, while I go and get some hot dogs from the stall."

It became a picnic then – with the children's sandwiches, and hot dogs and coke, and finally ice-cream cones all round. Even Cliff accepted everything he was given without demur, and seemed to be enjoying himself.

My goodness, I believe it's a success! thought Isobel, admitting to herself how frightened she had been about the whole enterprise. But Alan did not make the mistake of allowing the outing to go on too long. Even unexpected pleasure could be tiring, he knew – and Cliff had a lot of adjusting to do, one way and another. The bright sunlight and capricious spring wind were enough in themselves to tire a man who was not used to them – and though Cliff tried gallantly to look pleased with everything, it was clear to both Alan and Isobel that he was beginning to flag.

It was clear to Trevor, too. After all, he knew his father best, and was always watching for signs of weariness or failing strength. "I think we ought to go home now," he said, and looked urgently at Isobel.

"So we should," she agreed cheerfully, and turned to Alan for confirmation.

"Home, troops," said Alan. "Furl your wings," and he and Trevor took hold of Cliff's chair and turned it onto the homeward path. Georgie came up to them then, still out of breath from running and laughing in the sun, and quietly took up her protective station by her father's side.

"There are lots of daisies," panted Goldie, arriving with a fistful of them, which she solemnly presented to her father.

"If you can put your foot on seven, it's spring," Isobel told her.

Goldie tried, but her feet were too small.

"Mine's big enough," said Dave, who had rather fallen for Goldie. "Look! Seven!"

"It's spring!" cried Goldie, capering about round her

106

father's chair. "It's spring, it's spring . . ." and she went on, dancing and chanting, all the way home.

They got him up the stairs – with help from the cheerful boys, and sympathetic glances from the spectators in the hall and on the landings – but it was certainly harder than going down. And finally they stacked the new ramp against the wall inside the narrow hall of the flat, ready for future use, and Alan and the Likely Lads turned to go.

Isobel had gone straight to the kitchen to put the kettle on, but now she felt as sure as Alan that they should all go away and leave Cliff and his children in peace. It had been an eventful – even a stressful afternoon, and they needed time to recover. She only hoped they hadn't tired Cliff out too much. But then she reflected, understanding him a lot more than she ever let on, he would probably be quite glad to be tired. To be really, physically stretched enough to be tired. . . . Well, there would be more chances for that to come, now that the barriers were down and the first step was taken. Let them all get used to the idea, and not feel too pushed around. There was plenty of time for future outings – future improvements . . . better not push it now.

So she went quietly up to Cliff, and looked at him with all the warmth and approval her face could reflect. "Well done," she said softly. "Was it worth it?"

"Yes," said Cliff, and looked back at her with honest admission. But he did not say any more.

Then Isobel turned to Trevor, smiling, and added, still speaking gently, "It's been a good day. We've achieved a lot. Now everyone deserves a rest."

Trevor tried to thank her and Alan and the Likely Lads, but a sudden enormous tiredness and relief seemed to wash over him, and all he could get out was a sort of croak of appreciation. But they understood him well enough.

"Goodbye, Mr Broadbent," said the Likely Lads. "We'll come again when Mr Selwyn says," and they went off, smiling, with Alan and Isobel behind them.

Outside in the street, they all looked at each other and laughed. "Phew!" said Alan. "Well, I think it was a success!" Then he looked at Isobel, and added with sudden firmness,

107

"Get in the car, Isobel. We'll run you home before you fall down in a heap."

"I'm not that tired," protested Isobel.

"Oh yes you are." Alan winked at her. "Playing God is the most exhausting thing in the world."

Isobel sighed and meekly got into the car. "It's the responsibility," she murmured.

"Yes, well it worked. Didn't it, boys? And now we can all go home and put our feet up, and plan the next move!"

The Likely Lads gave a general growl of approval at this, clearly opting in to the next operation, and Isobel failed to say anything. She was, she suddenly realized, just about as enormously tired as she guessed young Trevor was when they finally got his father safely home. Oh well, she thought, it was worth it. I'm sure it was.

Alan dropped her off at her house, and did not wait to come in. But he did smile at her weary face and say softly; "That social worker will want to see us again. I'll be in touch soon."

Isobel smiled back, and was astonished when he added even more softly before he turned away, "New flight paths on the way."

And before Isobel could answer, he had got back into the car and driven away.

On Monday morning when Trevor delivered the paper, he rang Isobel's bell. She came to the door, looking a little surprised, and he said at once, "Don't come today – I'm going to stay with Dad. I think he needs to feel things are back to normal – otherwise he might panic."

Isobel nodded, well understanding Trevor's anxiety.

"In any case," added Trevor, with a sudden grin in lieu of unspoken thanks, "you've given up two days of your time already this weekend."

She grinned back. "Shall I come on Thursday, then?"

"Yes, please – if you can." He sighed a little, and added, "Though I don't know how much school work I'll get done."

"Never mind," said Isobel, wanting only to ease the pressure a little for this anxious boy. "It's more important for you not to be tired."

He looked at her, still faintly smiling. "That'll be the day!" he said, and ran down the steps to his bicycle and rode away.

When Isobel considered the matter, she knew perfectly well that the perilous arrangement with the ramp, and several able-bodied people to make use of it, could never be a permanent solution for Cliff Broadbent. It meant that he was always dependent on other people's goodwill, and permanently isolated without their help. Or, even worse, constantly at risk if he tried to take matters into his own hands and used his children for the dangerous descent of the stairs. They were not strong enough. Even Trevor, who was both sturdy and determined, could not hope to hold Cliff's weight if the chair started to go too fast. It simply would not do.

With this in mind, therefore, she went back to the housing officer, and protested about Cliff's plight all over again.

Brian Evans was a bit alarmed to see Isobel returning to do battle so soon. But he did his best to be cordial, even if he couldn't be very helpful. "I know," he said regretfully. "I have also had a visit from the social worker in charge of the case."

"Clare Simpson? What did she think of the situation?"

"Somewhat the same as you," Brian admitted, with a rueful grin. "She told me that Cliff Broadbent's situation in that flat was untenable."

"So it is," glared Isobel. "It took four people all of half an hour to get him down the stairs on a ramp, and even longer to get him back up again."

Brian Evans sighed. "I realize it is difficult—"

"Don't you have a statutory obligation to provide adequate housing accommodation for the disabled?" she demanded.

"Yes," he said. "We do. But we also, nowadays, have a standing obligation to meet our budget."

"What does that mean?" Her eyes flashed challenge.

He looked at her with painful honesty. Really, he was doing his best. "It means that we don't have the funds to renovate all the properties on our hands – whether flats or houses. And if we can't afford to put them into a proper state of repair, we are not allowed to let them to any of our council tenants – however desperate their case."

109

"So what *can* you do?"

He shrugged uneasily, but his eyes were sympathetic. "Just put Cliff Broadbent as high on the list as we can – and hope something comes up soon."

"Is that all you can offer?"

"I'm afraid so." He shook his head in mute apology. "I know it's unsatisfactory—"

"*Unsatisfactory*? It's downright disgraceful!" raged Isobel. "That poor man needs urgent help. There must be something you can do."

Brian sighed again, and reached for his lists on his littered desk. "Look," he said wearily, "the red asterisks indicate priority assessments: disabled, single parents with young children—"

"Well, he qualifies for both of those," Isobel snapped.

"Certainly," agreed Brian. "But so do about fifty others. And properties come in – if at all – at about the rate of one in three months. . . ."

It was Isobel's turn to sigh. She could see that the problem was insoluble – at least for the time being. But she wasn't done yet. "What would happen if I found suitable private accommodation? Would Social Services pay the rent?"

He hesitated. "It would have to come up to Housing Authority standards – but yes, we would pay the rent, if it was not too exorbitant."

Isobel nodded and rose to her feet. "Then I'll start looking," she said.

But it was not easy. After three fruitless days of tramping up and down streets and following house agents' directions, she had to admit that she had not found anywhere suitable. They either had too many steps, or too narrow doorways, or were too dark and cramped, with no proper facilities for anyone disabled – or they were altogether too smart and expensive for the Social Services ever to consider paying the rent. She began to understand what the housing officer meant when he said there was a dearth of suitable accommodation available – especially when funds for renovation were also being cut.

She was just walking wearily away from her last fruitless call, when a car drew up beside her, and Alan's voice said

110

cheerfully, "You look as if you could do with a cup of tea. Get in."

Thankfully, Isobel climbed in beside him, and then turned to glare in only moderate indignation. "Are you by any chance following me?"

"Yes," said Alan. "I saw you come out of the house agents." He grinned at her sideways. "It seemed to me that you needed support."

She laughed. "I must admit that pavements are hard on the feet!"

They went to a quiet, rather chintzy café where the lights were low and pink, but the china tea was heavenly. Isobel sat back and relaxed, allowing warmth and comfort to enfold her. Really, Alan was extraordinarily kind and thoughtful . . . but what was he doing out of school at this hour?

"Finished early," he said, interpreting her questioning look. "Rehearsal this evening." He took a grateful gulp of tea and added, "Ah! That's better." Then he looked at Isobel with a question of his own. "This concert – the Broadbent kids are playing – the junior and senior schools have combined forces. Do you think we could get Cliff to come?"

Isobel looked doubtful. "A wheelchair?"

"Oh, we can manage that. There are ramps at school, and the hall has wide aisles." He considered. "And the Likely Lads could come and get him and take him back." He was still looking hopefully at Isobel. "And I think I could persuade Trevor to play in the orchestra just that once – we need an extra cello."

Isobel thought about it. "We'd have to consult Trevor – on both counts."

"Yes, of course." He paused, and then put forward the serious intention behind his appeal. "It would be very good for Cliff to feel part of the show. Proud father and all that."

Isobel nodded. "Yes. It would." She smiled at Alan, touched by his concern. "Well, I'm going there tomorrow. I'll ask him – and you can ask Trevor at school."

He agreed cheerfully. "And then we can pool our resources."

Isobel was on the brink of protesting then that Alan was giving up altogether too much of his time to her and the Broadbent problems, but something about the sudden firmness of his straight look deterred her.

"How did you get on with the housing people?" he asked.

"Not very well," she admitted, and found herself telling him all about it. She also found herself agreeing to meet him again on Saturday to discuss the concert proposal and Cliff's and Trevor's reaction to it. But here at last she managed to get in a slight protest. "Alan, you must be awfully busy with all this going on. I really don't see how you can spare the time."

"Time," said Alan sententiously, "is relative. Especially *musical* time." He laughed. "And life would be pretty boring if we couldn't fit in what we *want* to do among the things that we *have* to do!"

There didn't seem to be any answer to that, and they glared at each other for a moment in mutual resistance, and then burst out laughing.

"That's better," said Alan. "You don't look half so formidable when you laugh."

She grinned. "Do I look formidable?"

"Sometimes – yes. I bet Brian Evans is scared stiff when you start bullying him!"

Laughter still bubbled between them, but Isobel could not quite shake off her concern about the housing situation. "I seem to be getting nowhere," she said.

"Don't worry so," Alan answered gently. "Something will turn up."

"You're such an optimist," she protested.

"Of course." He crinkled up the corners of his eyes at her in a kind of teasing affection. "One of us has to be." He was still smiling. "But two of us might work wonders."

Isobel shook her head at him. But she could not help smiling either.

Cliff, when approached about the concert, looked frightened again for a moment, and then began to think about it seriously. It took him a long time to get his thoughts in order, sometimes they seemed to slide away from him like slippery eels that couldn't be grasped . . . And sometimes a sort of fog of panic came down, and his brain refused to think at all. But this time things became clear to him quite soon, and he was able to put his fears into words that Isobel could understand.

"How – long?" he asked, his eyes looking anxious again.

"There'll be an interval, Cliff. You could go at half time if you got tired."

He shook his head. "Not – *tired* . . ." He seemed to hesitate, and Isobel suddenly understood his dilemma.

"There'll be a gents. You can bring your bottle – like you did the other day on the Downs."

He gave her a crooked smile of relief. This woman, Mizzibell, didn't seem to mind anything. His expression changed then, for he was now seriously considering the concert. "K-Katie. . ." he said painfully. "Music m-mattered. . . ."

Isobel nodded. "It does to the children, too."

He clearly understood that. "Ought to – ought to . . .?"

She did not press him, but she smiled. "They'd love it if you came."

He sighed. Life seemed to be all battles lately. But he knew he ought to go. Somewhere far at the back of his reluctant mind, he knew that Katie would want him to go . . . But that thought was among the terrors of memory that he could not dare to have. . . . Better to shut it down and try to concentrate on the kids and what was wanted of him now.

"If – I can . . .?" he said, acquiescing as gracefully as he could, though he was still a bit scared at the prospect.

"We'll get you there," promised Isobel. "And I'll stay with you, in case you need anything." Her voice was calm and reassuringly practical. "And everyone can push you home in a triumphal procession," she added, grinning.

Cliff did his best to grin, too. He knew he was being manipulated by someone very clever, but somehow he didn't mind. It would be a bit of an ordeal, but she would see him through. "Rely – on you," he said, suddenly speaking very clearly.

And Isobel did not know whether to be glad or sorry. The responsibility was hers.

Trevor's reaction was predictably anxious. "Won't it be too much for him?"

"I don't think so," said Isobel judiciously. "Alan Selwyn thinks he will like being a proud father."

Trevor grinned, but he was still a bit worried. "We're only a small part of the show – not soloists."

113

"That doesn't matter," said Isobel. "You'll be performing. He can bask in your glory!"

Trevor laughed then. "Some glory. Second fiddle. Fourth cello!"

Isobel was pleased. "You are going to play, then?"

He shrugged. "Seems like it. Mr Selwyn gave me back my cello. I've got a week to learn the pieces." He looked at her, a light of cautious happiness in his eyes. "It'll be good to be playing again . . ."

They were sitting opposite each other over their customary Saturday morning cup of tea (it was becoming a cherished ceremony between them that they both looked forward to) and Trevor was visibly relaxing in Isobel's warm kitchen.

"You miss your music, don't you?" she said, passing the plate of chocolate biscuits.

Trevor sighed. "Yes, but it doesn't matter."

She could have contradicted him, but she didn't. Instead, she asked how Cliff had been after his day out on the Downs.

"Pretty good," he said, sounding rather amazed. "He slept all night."

Isobel privately took note of that remark, which gave her a very clear picture of the sort of interrupted nights that Trevor had to endure.

"He was a bit – a bit clingy the next day," he went on, trying to be fair. "But I think he's only scared of things changing too much . . ." He looked at Isobel with honest eyes. "He needs to feel *safe*," he explained.

Isobel understood him, and she also understood the sad wisdom that clung to the boy's young voice. It made her ache. "The holidays are coming up," she said, deliberately changing the subject. "And Mr Selwyn wants to take you all out for a day at the seaside. Do you think that's a good idea?"

His smile was suddenly vivid and boyish. "I think it's a super idea – if we can manage it."

"He likes the sea, doesn't he?"

"Oh yes!" He sounded quite positive. He knew his father had dreams, too.

"Well, then," said Isobel, "that'll be something to look forward to – for all of us.

It seemed to Trevor that all of a sudden, the grey exhausting

114

routine of his life was full of new horizons and things to look forward to. . . . Nothing would ever be quite the same again. He looked at Isobel through a blur of unexpected tears and said obscurely, "Horizons. . . ."

"Yes," agreed Isobel, smiling. "Wide ones."

It was rather uncanny of Alan, therefore, Isobel reflected, that he arrived soon after Trevor left, and said, "Come on. I think you need some new horizons. We're going to the sea."

She stared at him, amazed. "Today?"

"Today. Now. It's a fine day. Why not?"

"But I thought—"

"Casing the joint," he explained, grinning at her like a naughty schoolboy. "Got to get things haven't we?" He stood in her hallway, laughing at her, with bright flecks of sunlight in his eyes.

Isobel capitulated. "All right. But I think you're mad."

"Mad as a hatter. Crazy as a coot. Get your sunhat and your bucket and spade." He was still laughing, but a sudden gentleness crept into his voice as he added softly, "You know perfectly well you are suffering from a surfeit of grey cobwebs. A sea breeze will do you good, and we can decide which is the best place to take them."

Isobel could not think of any way to answer this. It was extraordinarily reassuring to realize that he understood what was so daunting about the whole social services scene and the plight of the little Broadbent family. So she meekly fetched her coat (no hat – the wind blowing in her hair would be a joy in itself), stuffed the rest of the packet of chocolate biscuits into her pocket, and followed Alan down the steps to his car.

They went first to Weston-super-Mare, where Alan drove patiently up and down looking for the best car-park for a wheelchair – near the beach, no steps but a gentle slope, and a convenient gents nearby.

Then they went down the slope to the sands, watching for difficulties or hazards all the way. It must be easy for Cliff and his helpers, not a nightmare of perilous obstacles. . . . The tide was coming in that morning, so there were no long stretches of wet sand or mud – only a fairly empty, clean expanse of firm sand below the built-up esplanade.

"We'll have to ask about the tides," said Alan. "We don't want the kids floundering knee-deep in Weston mud – or Cliff's chair, either."

Isobel stood looking about her, pleasantly surprised by the view. The sea was actually blue this morning – or nearly blue – beneath a palely azure spring sky. It sparkled prettily like a picture postcard round the struts of the pier, and small waves lapped lazily against the shoreline, creaming themselves into lacy patterns on the wet sand. And it stretched for miles – that gentle, estuary sea. You would never know, looking out, that Wales was just across the bay. It seemed just as enormous and powerful as it ought to – not tame at all – and you could sail all the way to America without sighting land at all. . . .

She gave a sigh of relief and pleasure. "I haven't been to Weston for years. I'd forgotten how *wide* it is."

He grinned. "Weed wide enough to wrap a fairy in." He lobbed a small pebble into the sea. "What would you like to do?"

Isobel looked at him and decided to be reckless. "What I'd like to do is take off my shoes and socks like a child, and run."

"Well, come on then," he agreed, unperturbed. "Let's run."

So Isobel threw down her shoes and socks, rolled up her neat trousers, and ran laughing after Alan across the beach, into the cold, sun-laced shallows and out again in a scatter of sea foam and sparkles, and on across the new, tide-swept reaches of the clean wet sand above the waterline, on and on, till they both stopped, breathless and laughing, once more at the edge of the sea.

"It's absurd," said Isobel, gasping. "I feel like a child of six!"

Alan crinkled up his eyes at her in the old, teasing way. "I reckon there's a child of six inside each one of us, trying to get out," he said. "How about an iced lolly?"

It was, thought Isobel, ridiculous to be so happy – so entirely carefree. But why not enjoy it while it lasted?

So they had their iced lollies, and strolled up and down, still casing the joint, as Alan insisted, and looked at suitable cafés that could accommodate wheelchairs and lots of kids, and all the different amusements that the children might want to sample.

116

"And donkey rides," said Isobel suddenly, remembering what children liked. "Surely there must still be donkey rides?"

There would be by Easter, the deck chair attendant told her. The donkeys all came back from their winter holiday by then.

"Oh good," she said, smiling. "Weston wouldn't be the same without donkey rides."

Alan was looking at her with laughing affection. "Well, that's another important thing settled. Now I think we can go on somewhere else."

She looked surprised. "Where?"

"Brean Down . . . it's a bit wilder and emptier – and the dunes have lovely curves."

So they went on to Brean Down, and looked at more sparkling sea, and walked on the pale, fine sand of the dunes, and watched the seabirds fly up and sail on the wind.

"Farther horizons here," said Alan, "but I reckon Cliff and Trevor would really rather look at the great ships coming in and out of the docks from the wide Atlantic."

"How do you know so much about those two?" asked Isobel, astonished at his insight.

"You told me about Cliff and the Sea Symphony, remember? And Cabot. . . ." His face this time, looking out to sea, was grave and compassionate, all laughter quenched. "I can imagine what it must feel like – to be cooped up there. Cliff's been used to ships and the docks for most of his working life. And Trevor . . ." He glanced at Isobel. "Trevor is a visionary sort of boy, isn't he? Though he hides it well from the uncaring world."

Isobel sighed. "Not ships this time, Alan. It would make them both too restless!"

He smiled. "Yes, I know . . . we must widen their sights bit by bit!" He grasped her arm for a moment in a comforting squeeze of reassurance. "Don't worry – we'll give them a happy day."

If it's as happy as this, thought Isobel, they can't complain. And then, greatly daring, she said it aloud. Why not? It was true. She was happy. Today. It wasn't something you could ignore.

"That's what I wanted to hear," he said, smiling and looking straight into her eyes. "Come on. Let's go and find lunch."

Chapter Seven

'The Chorus Jig'

Kerry Dance

The social worker, Clare Simpson, elected to call the next meeting on a weekday afternoon, and for once Alan could not arrange his school duties to coincide. So Isobel had to outface her with enough fierce arguments of her own. This didn't trouble her, but what did worry her was the lack of Alan's calm, neutral assessment of the situation, and his unshakeable good humour.

Clare faced Isobel in a friendly and helpful manner, but she was a shade on the defensive. What had emerged at that meeting in Cliff Broadbent's flat had made it clear to her that the man's needs had been ignored or neglected, and she ought to have made more effort to go and see for herself before. Now, she did her best to explain what extra help the family could get, and how much pressure could be put on the housing department to get them more workable accommodation.

"He is entitled to Income Support and Disability Living Allowance," she explained. "His wife arranged all that, but of course it has to be re-applied for every time the period runs out. Is he doing that?"

Isobel looked uncertain. "I suppose so – they've got nothing much else to live on, have they? Trevor told me he usually filled in the various forms for his father and then got him to sign them. Cliff hasn't been up to dealing with them himself – though he is improving rapidly now."

Clare nodded. "The rules and regulations have changed, of course, with this new drive to cut back on entitlement to disability allowances." She frowned, well aware that the new

118

directives were wholly wrong and unworkable, as usual, and led to many deserving cases getting no help at all. "He should have another medical assessment," she said at last. "We can arrange that – if he'll accept it?"

"Yes," agreed Isobel firmly. "He is much more co-operative these days."

"A report from his own GP, or the hospital, would help," added Clare. "Could you arrange that?"

"I could," Isobel said, mouth set firm with determination.

"Good. That would help in several ways. He should be getting a Community Care Allowance, to help him become more independent—"

"But that is surely dependent on him having ground-floor accommodation?" pointed out Isobel. "How can he become more independent trapped up there on the second floor?"

"Quite," agreed Clare. "I have already pointed that out to the housing officer." She paused, and added, "It also affects the question of physiotherapy for his legs and arms. That could probably be laid on, especially if his doctor recommends it, but we'd have to be able to get him in and out of the ambulance on a regular basis."

Isobel refrained from saying that she had been demanding this extra help for Cliff all along, and merely said, "Yes, we would, wouldn't we?" in a carefully neutral voice.

"He gets child benefit now," pursued Clare, "and the children get free school dinners at the Junior school, I've checked that. But the eldest boy is entitled to them, too, at the Senior school, only he hasn't applied for them."

"Probably didn't know he could," said Isobel drily.

"Or," Clare admitted, "he didn't want to admit to his peers that he needed them. Though we get round that problem these days by having a 'payment in advance' system for those who *do* pay – which covers the question of payment for those who don't."

Isobel understood this – she had met it before many times in her teaching life. But she fancied that Trevor would not have been bothered by this, if he had thought of it. It was just that he was at school so little, he didn't think of it at all, or if he did, he didn't want to draw attention to the fact that he was hardly ever there.

"They might get some Family Credit for extra things like shoes and clothes," Clare added, remembering Trevor's painful admission about Colin's demand for a new kite, "*It was the shoes . . . Colin's feet grew.*" "They get housing benefit now," Clare went on, "with their income support, so the rent is paid for them."

"And would that continue if they found private accommodation?" demanded Isobel, wanting to confirm what she had already been told by Brian Evans.

"Oh yes. Provided it was adequate and suitable – and not excessively expensive."

"Well, almost anything would be adequate and more suitable than where they are now," growled Isobel.

Clare glanced at her apologetically. "I know." She seemed to hesitate then, and waited a few moments before continuing. "There is one thing that bothers me – about the wife, Katie. . . ."

"Yes?"

"You say you don't know how long she is likely to be away?"

"No. But they all insist that it is only a temporary absence. Why?"

"Because if it is a permanent situation, Cliff Broadbent ought to be registered as a one-parent family," said Clare. "And though it seems unfair, it would mean that he actually got *less* income support."

Isobel stared at her. "I am sure he does not think of himself as a single parent – and nor do the children."

"Yes, but—" began Clare.

"They are all perfectly certain their mother will return soon," stated Isobel, in a flat, no-nonsense tone that she hoped carried conviction. "And we must believe them."

Clare looked into that implacable face and sighed. "Well, I just hope she turns up soon," she said, admitting defeat, and at the same time indicating that she would do nothing about it at present.

"So do I," said Isobel, and a small conspiratorial smile of thanks lit that formidable face.

They were silent for a moment, marshalling facts, and tacitly admitting a working alliance.

"He could get meals on wheels," Clare suggested, "and a care allowance to cover assistance with baths and dressing and so on. But since the Community Care budget has been so drastically cut in this area, it is getting very difficult to promise anything."

Isobel nodded. "So I understand."

"Do you know," said Clare, eyes wide with indignation, "our care helpers have all had a directive which says they can no longer shop for the elderly, or draw their pensions for them, or fetch their prescriptions – and they are not allowed to do any cleaning or washing. It's absolutely ridiclous. Those are all the things that disabled and housebound people need most!"

Isobel joined her in a sigh of exasperation.

"I sometimes wonder whether the bureaucrats who send out these orders have lived in the real world at all!" exploded Clare, pushing her fringe out of her eyes in a gesture of fierce frustration. "I'm speaking out of turn, of course . . ." she muttered. "But in any case, I rather thought Cliff Broadbent would resent that kind of help from anyone else, since Trevor does most of it for him?" There was a faint question in her glance.

"I'm afraid you're right," said Isobel sadly. "I did suggest meals on wheels myself, but Trevor said they all preferred to eat together in the evening, and his father could not manage two hot meals a day. Sandwiches suit him better, he says . . . I suspect the man has a certain amount of digestive trouble and so on, being so inactive."

Clare looked sympathetic, but helpless about that. "Yes, I expect so . . ." She paused, painfully considering the options and restraints of her complicated job. "The trouble is, Trevor can't get a carer's allowance – he is too young – even though I am sure he does the full work of an adult carer."

"And more," said Isobel grimly. "I think he hardly ever gets a full night's sleep."

"Maybe if we could increase his father's care allowance as part of his disability grant, he could use some of it for outside help?"

Isobel shook her head. "I doubt it. He relies heavily on Trevor. Much too heavily, really. But the boy himself will not hear of allowing a stranger to deal with his father. It's as

121

much as he can do to accept me – and I'm not allowed to do much more than keep him company."

Once more they looked at one another, quietly acknowledging the difficulties involved in helping proud and independent people.

"But things may improve," Isobel added. "We are making progress. We persuaded Cliff to go out on Clifton Down last Saturday. And he has agreed to attend the school concert. That's a great step forward."

"That's very good news," said Clare, pleased. "I do hope you will be able to keep it up."

"So do I," said Isobel fervently – as fervently as she had hoped, earlier, that Katie Broadbent would return soon. . . . It was all hope – all full of imponderables, she reflected. They could only press on with their task of lessening the load bit by bit.

At this moment in their discussion, the door of Clare's office burst open suddenly and a furious man rushed in and leant over Clare's desk, literally waving his fist at her. "How dare you!" he yelled. "How dare you come snooping round, frightening my wife to death and asking all those questions!"

Clare regarded him calmly and apparently without surprise or shock. "It's my job, Mr Williams," she said. "I have to ask questions."

"Not in my bloody house, you don't!" he blustered. "I'll have you done for trespassing!"

The social worker merely smiled. "Really? I should think bringing in the police would be the last thing you would want . . . all things considered."

He glared at her, rage making him even stupider than normal. "What's that supposed to mean?"

"I was sent round to investigate reports of child neglect and violence, Mr Williams – as you well know. So far, we have been reluctant to bring the police into it, and so has your wife. But if the children are at risk, we may have to. And that's what I came round to find out. Do you understand?"

"I understand all right," he shouted. "It's a disgrace – coming to my house and making accusations! I'll – I'll have the law on you for slander, just see if I don't!" and he stormed out of the office again, muttering and swearing as he went.

Clare sighed, and looked at Isobel ruefully. "Sorry about that."

Isobel looked at her with sympathy. "Does it often happen?"

The social worker shrugged sadly. "It's an occupational hazard!" Then she seemed to recollect that she was still in the middle of another difficult interview, and ought to do something to reassure this worried and persistent woman. "Well, I'll do everything I can to push things through all the right departments," she said, looking at Isobel almost with appeal. She really did want to help, if she could disentangle herself from all the new rules and regulations she was up against.

"I'm sure you will," agreed Isobel, thereby skilfully binding Clare to a promise. "And I'll do everything I can, too. Between us, we should be able to come up with something useful for the Broadbents!"

Their smiles were tentative and cautious, but it was a bargain that had been struck, and they knew it. Isobel reached out a hand, sealing the bargain. "Thanks for all your help," she said, with a faint grin. "I can see you have quite a lot on your plate without me as well!"

"We'll keep in touch," said Clare, offering as much as she dared. But her grin was also warm and faintly tinged with mischief.

Isobel went away then, slightly less beset by grey cobwebs than usual. But she still looked a little like an avenging angel, striding off up Clifton hill.

Relations with Gervase had not improved much since his argument with Isobel about the Broadbent family. In fact, they had not progressed at all, for Gervase had phoned to cancel his Friday visit, saying he had a cold and did not want to pass it on.

Isobel was not sure whether to believe him or not. Gervase was rather good at avoiding issues when they got too difficult – and he might well have thought it politic to stay away for a while. He might even be really annoyed with her, and not want to continue their long-term friendship at all. This thought troubled her a little. Gervase was a bit old-fashioned and conventional, she knew, but he was not unkind, and she had grown quite fond of him over the years. It would be a pity to see their normally easy relationship founder because of a stupid misunderstanding.

Of course, on the other hand, he could be genuinely suffering from a cold, and in that case she ought to go round and see how he was. The man was a fool about creature comforts, and lived an absurdly spartan life in which he often forgot to eat, or to heat his own flat over the shop.

With this in mind, therefore, Isobel decided to call in at the shop on her way home. Even if he was still annoyed, he would scarcely refuse to speak to her – and if he was really ill, he might need help.

She pushed open the door, and waited for the old-fashioned bell above it to ping as she went in. The crowded little bookshop smelled of old leather, dust and camphor – a mixture induced by Gervase's obsessive dusting and his belief that moths were likely to attack his most precious bindings. It was dim in the shop, and sunlight filtered palely through the windows in shafts of illuminated motes of more flying dust which seemed to cling in iridescent haloes round every shelf. The reason for this was evident. At the back of the shop, Gervase stood perched precariously on a stepladder, ineffectually waving a feather duster at his shelves of brown leather and gilt. And with every wave a new cloud of dust flew up, and Gervase sneezed.

"Gervase, what on earth are you doing?" she said, half laughing at the spectacle.

"Dusting," said Gervase, and sneezed again. "What do you suppose?"

"If I may say so," protested Isobel mildly, "I think you are only making matters worse."

Gervase sneezed even more explosively, and began to climb down the stepladder. "I expect you're right," he sighed in a resigned tone, and added, a shade tartly, "as usual."

Isobel recognized the faint irritation as mere tiredness – he was clearly not well – but she was determined to put things right between them today and not waste any more time, so she went towards him, smiling. "But I'm not always right, Gervase – and I really came in to tell you so. We

124

can't start falling out over differences of opinion at our age, can we?"

Gervase's parchment-coloured face looked even paler than usual when he came into the light, but he smiled back at her with sudden relief. "No," he agreed. "It does seem a bit silly, doesn't it?" And he sneezed again.

"You really do look under the weather," she said severely. "Shouldn't you be in bed?"

"Nonsense," he snapped. "It's only a cold."

"Well, come on upstairs to the flat," she commanded. "At least I can make you a hot drink."

"The shop—"

"Don't be silly, Gervase. I'll put the sign up. It's nearly closing time, anyway." She went across to the door, and put the 'Closed' sign against the glass. "Now," she said, shooing Gervase ahead of her, "what's it to be? Ovaltine, or whisky and hot lemon?"

He gave her a wan grin over his shoulder. "You know I hate milky drinks."

"Hot toddy, then," she said briskly. "And a couple of aspirins, I should think." She looked at him more attentively as he went before her up the stairs, and thought he seemed to be weaving on his feet a little.

"Gervase, do go to bed. You're not fit to be up."

He stopped and looked round in horror. "Bed?"

"Oh, for God's sake," said Isobel, exasperated. "I'm not making improper suggestions! Go and get into bed – keep your clothes on if you think your honour is at stake – but get under the blankets and *lie down!*" And then, hearing the pseudo-rage in her own voice, she began to giggle, and to her surprise, Gervase began to giggle too, and went meekly off to his bedroom and closed the door.

By the time Isobel had made the drink and switched on his central heating, which he had forgotten, and had a quick look in his fridge to see what there was to eat, he was safely in bed and calling out in a slightly apologetic voice; "I'm in bed, you bully. You can come in."

He was sitting up in bed, wearing elegant dark blue pyjamas which looked suspiciously like silk, but clutching the sheet over them with one convulsive hand while he looked over the

125

top of it at Isobel like a bashful small boy who didn't quite know what he had let himself in for.

A smile twitched at Isobel's stern mouth – he really was too absurd – but she only said in a practical voice, "I could do you some soup? Or a boiled egg and toast?"

He began to protest. "I don't need—"

But she interrupted impatiently, "Oh, come on, Gervase. You'd better have *something*."

He sighed in a defeated sort of way, and said peevishly, "All right . . . a boiled egg, then," and lay back against his pillows, looking quenched.

But when she returned in a little while with the tray, he seemed less exhausted, and there was a gleam of humour in his eyes.

"Isobel . . . that bunch of flowers—"

"What bunch of flowers?"

"In the jug – on my kitchen windowsill. . . ."

"What about them?"

He looked almost shy for a moment. "I – er – bought them for you."

"*What*?"

"I meant to bring them round . . . on Friday. . . ."

They looked at each other, and simultaneously began to laugh.

"Oh, Gervase – how touching!"

"Peace offering!" he spluttered, and went on giggling.

But in truth, Isobel really was rather touched. She patted his arm and said, smiling, "Eat up your egg . . . *My* peace offering!"

And they could neither of them resist a couple of extra giggles. It really was rather absurd. But they also both knew that the rift was well and truly mended.

"I'll leave you now," she said at last. "You'd better get some sleep. I'll look in tomorrow and see how you are."

He smiled, no longer looking apprehensive or bashful. "You'd better lock up and take the key."

She agreed cheerfully, though recognizing by this that Gervase must be feeling pretty ill. He had never relinquished the keys to his shop before.

"It's probably only one of those three-day flu's," he

muttered, rightly interpreting her raised eyebrows. "Go away, Isobel, before you get it, too."

"All right, I'm going!" she grinned. "Your honour is still intact!" And she left him then, chuckling to herself at the outraged snort that followed her down the stairs.

True to her word, Isobel did call in the next day, bringing a casserole, and also arranged, after a certain amount of argument with a slightly tetchy Gervase, to come in on Friday evening and cook supper for him in his own flat.

"It makes sense," she said severely. "You're ill and I'm not. Why struggle out in the cold to come to me? We can just as well eat here."

"Oh, all right," said Gervase, none too graciously, being not quite sure whether he liked all this cosseting.

"We can still play Scrabble!" grinned Isobel, enjoying his confusion with only slightly malicious glee.

"Oh, ah, yes, Scrabble . . ." he agreed faintly. "I hope I'm up to it."

"If you're not," Isobel threatened, "I'll have to put you back to bed." And she went away, laughing, before he could reply.

But during the rest of the week while she pursued her fruit-less task of looking for a ground-floor flat for the Broadbent family, she didn't feel much like laughing. She went to a lot of unsuitable places, driving her little red Mini up and down the hills and tortuous streets of Bristol and its outlying districts – but nothing seemed possible. It was either too expensive or too shabby, or too full of steps and hazards, or too big or too small. . . . By the time the weekend came, she had to admit that she was tired and discouraged, and because Alan was busy with the last rehearsals for the school concert, she had not had his cheerful optimism to sustain her, and she missed it badly.

So it was with a sense of curious relief that she opened the door to Trevor on Saturday morning, and found Alan beside him on the step.

"Can I join you for a cuppa?" he asked, smiling. "Things to arrange."

"Come in, both of you," said Isobel, rejoicing secretly. "Tea coming up. Biscuits in the tin."

The three of them settled down happily at the kitchen table.

"About your father," said Alan, turning to Trevor. "Is he still game to come tonight?"

Trevor nodded, though he looked a little doubtful. "He said 'yes' when I asked last night." He looked from one to the other of them with a bleak, far-too-knowledgeable smile. "But I can't guarantee he'll say the same tonight."

Alan was undismayed. "Well, let's just assume he's coming, and then he probably will." He glanced fleetingly at Isobel, and then went on cheerfully; "What I suggest is this: if the lads and I come early, we can get all of you into my car—"

"And the wheelchair?" Trevor was making sure of essentials.

"Of course. We did before. . . . Then we can wheel him into the hall before the crowd arrives . . . get him settled in quietly . . . and you lot can go off to your appointed places without worrying."

"Who will stay with Dad?" Trevor's voice was still anxious.

"I will," said Isobel. "I promised him that, anyway."

Trevor smiled at her a little tremulously. The debt he owed to Isobel was getting almost too great to bear. "Thanks," he murmured, and seemed reasonably reassured.

"And if he stays there when the concert's over and the audience have gone, I'll be free by then to drive you all home," Alan continued, announcing his plans like a general going into battle.

"But, Alan, how can you have time for all this?" asked Isobel. "You'll have more than enough to organize with the whole concert on your hands."

Alan grinned. "Last rehearsal was OK. Run-through this afternoon. Nothing more to do after that till this evening. Got it all taped."

Isobel and Trevor looked at each other and laughed. There was no point in arguing with Mr Selwyn when he had made up his mind about something. A certain course of action had been decreed. Then it would happen according to plan.

"Well, I hope you know what you're doing," said Isobel.

Alan nodded briskly. "I'd have left it to the Likely Lads," he explained. "But I wasn't too happy about those stairs. . . .

Better this way." He seemed to think that the discussion was over then, and smilingly asked for a second cup of tea. "Thirsty work, organizing people," he said, and winked at Trevor.

"You can say that again!" agreed Isobel, and filled his cup to the brim.

So there they were, Cliff Broadbent and Isobel, alone in the empty school hall, the difficult journey behind them, and the cool silence of the half-dark auditorium like balm on their anxious minds.

Isobel knew it had been an ordeal for Cliff – and still was, come to that. There was the whole concert to get through, and the noisy, inquisitive audience to brave as well. She wondered, glancing at Cliff's still, rather bewildered profile, whether she and Alan were right to insist on this expedition. Was it going to be too much for him? . . . She just didn't know.

But Alan had been so sure about it – so certain it would boost Cliff's confidence and make him more part of his own family scene.

"Are you all right, Cliff?" she asked, allowing her own anxiety to show for once.

The blond head nodded slowly. "All right—" he answered, and essayed a lopsided smile. "Quiet . . ." he added, with appreciation.

"It won't be for long," she warned. "But you may actually *like* the music," she admitted, as an afterthought.

"Might," he agreed, the smile twitching a little.

"And it'll make their day, having you here," Isobel told him, just in case he needed reminding.

Cliff actually laughed. "A – about . . . time . . ." he said, with sudden clarity, and there was a rueful understanding in his cloudy gaze.

At that moment, the headmaster, John Sullivan, grey-haired and permanently tired but always pleasant, came purposefully up to Cliff's chair, hand outstretched in careful welcome.

"Mr Broadbent, how nice to see you here. It was good of you to make the effort, we do appreciate it." His shrewd grey eyes rested on Cliff in a brief, friendly glance. "I hope you enjoy the concert," he added, and hurried away again before Cliff could answer.

"Phew!" said Cliff, sounding very much on the spot, and rather like a naughty small boy having been let off an expected punishment. "VIP stuff!"

And he and Isobel both began to giggle. Then the audience started to trickle in, and Trevor reappeared for a brief moment, looking strung up and anxious. "OK, Dad?" he asked, touching him on the arm.

"Fine," said Cliff distinctly. *"Fine*. Go – and – play!"

Trevor gave him one searching look and then disappeared again backstage. The others had not come back to see Cliff, but since they were in the junior half of the programme, they came on first, and could not risk being late on stage. The hall was filling up now, and the excited chatter was rising in a steady crescendo. Isobel stole a quick anxious glance at Cliff, but he did not seem to be troubled by the noise.

"Cliff," said a cheerful man's voice close beside them. "Good to see you, mate! Your kids performing?"

Isobel turned sharply to look at the newcomer, but he was smiling comfortably at Cliff, and his voice remained reassuringly casual and unconcerned. He was a big man, broad and solid, with receding greyish hair above a round, easy-going face, and he was clearly not going to make any awkward comments about Cliff's disability or his sudden reappearance in the outside world.

"All – of – them!" pronounced Cliff, proudly, and beamed at his friend.

"That's great!" The man gave him an appreciative nod, and went off to his own seat across the aisle.

The lights dipped then, and slowly dimmed in the auditorium as the stage lights came on, and the Junior choir filed on to the platform.

They sang three songs, and one Easter hymn, and then they re-arranged themselves for the last song, and Isobel saw that the small figure of Goldie had been carefully placed in front. Her red-gold aureole of curls shone in the lights, and she stood perfectly still, perfectly at ease, with her face lifted to the glow of the spotlights. The song was a setting of 'Tomorrow Shall Be My Dancing Day' – and Isobel reflected that nothing could be more suitable for a small girl who already knew all about dancing her way through life, and for whom 'tomorrow' was a magical time that was always just coming. She only had one short verse as a solo before the choir joined in, but she sang it with such perfect clarity, and such innocent confidence that she won all hearts, and Cliff beamed and clapped his approval with the best of them.

After the applause had died away, the Junior orchestra came on, and there was Georgie with her violin among the strings, and Colin with his clarinet among the woodwind. The choir did not go off, but stayed in position on the raised rostrum at the back, listening entranced while their friends played 'The Sheep May Safely Graze'.

It was a tune that Cliff knew well, like most of the audience, and he smiled when he heard it begin. As for Isobel, that particular piece of familiar Bach always reminded her of her childhood in Scotland, and how the hill farmers brought the patient ewes down to the lower pastures before lambing, so that they could in truth safely graze while they waited their time. It always reminded her of early spring in the highlands, and it always made her ache.

Next came a very competent recorder group who played some lively folk tunes, and Isobel noted (and hoped that Cliff did, too) that Colin had laid down his clarinet and crossed over to join them with his treble recorder.

After this came more songs from the choir, including a couple of recent hit pop songs which Isobel did not know. (Out of date, that's me! she thought ruefully, and turned to see Cliff grinning at her and whispering: *"Trendy. . . ."*) And here again, young Colin crossed over and joined the percussion section on some bongo drums. He seems to be a jack of all trades, she thought. Well, why not? He looks happy enough, banging away up there.

For the last items choir and orchestra combined, first of all in a cheerful version of 'Strawberry Fair', where everyone seemed to be 'singing, singing, buttercups and daisies' – and finally in a swinging, joyous account of the famous round 'Sumer is icumen in', in which even the orchestra divided into three parts, and one small girl had the enviable task of playing the cuckoo's notes on a kind of sawn-off recorder, a special instrument of which she was enormously proud. The whole room seemed to be singing then – even the audience – and

131

even Isobel and Cliff managed 'Sing cuckoo!' and joined in the laughter over the cheeky cuckoo instrument's last word.

And then it was the interval. Cliff had joined in all the applause, and he was still smiling and pleased, but Isobel thought there was a hint of tired bewilderment back in his eyes. She was about to ask him again if he felt all right, when Trevor arrived, brisk and efficient, if a shade anxious, and without stopping to make any explanation, simply wheeled his father away towards the long corridor leading to the men's toilets. And presently he brought him back to his place next to Isobel, and left him there, with the whispered words, "My turn now. Keep your ears pinned back!"

Cliff looked across at Isobel and grinned. *"Pinned back!"* he repeated, a tremor of laughter in his voice.

This time the Senior choir began the proceedings with two Bach chorales and a chorus from the St Matthew Passion, followed by a group of modern songs with fascinating harmonies which intrigued Isobel's ear. And then the Senior orchestra came on, and there was Trevor with the cellos, and their first piece was Mendelssohn's Overture, Fingal's Cave. . . . More seascapes, thought Isobel, and watched Cliff's dreaming face – for this was clearly another of his favourites.

Various solos followed, and then the stage filled up with all the Junior choir and orchestra performers as well, and the whole gathering joined together in Vaughan Williams' great shout of praise: *'Let all the world in every corner sing – my God and King!'* The strings sawed away like mad at the accompaniment, and the voices rose in triumph, and everyone in the hall felt as if they were being lifted off their feet by the sound of pure, white-hot rejoicing.

"Bravo!" said Alan Selwyn under his breath, to his young performers.

"Bravo!" yelled some of the less inhibited audience – and then many more followed suit, throwing discretion to the winds.

"Bravo!" murmured Cliff and Isobel, smiling at each other.

It was a splendid evening, and a glorious finale.

Eventually, Alan managed to escape from the congratulations of the departing audience, and came up to Isobel and Cliff, looking sparkling and elated – the adrenalin still flowing. By this time, the four children had arrived, and Cliff had nodded and smiled at them all and said "Bravo" several times, and so had Isobel, so everyone was happy.

"The Lads are cycling over," said Alan. "They'll meet us there. Come on."

The whole party saw Cliff safely into Alan's car and then climbed in beside him. The old station wagon cruised gently through night-time Bristol so that everyone could look at the lights that transformed even the meanest street into something approaching mystery and elegance.

"It's different in the dark," said Goldie, who didn't often go out at night. "Did you hear me sing?"

"We did indeed," said Isobel, speaking for Cliff as well, since he seemed a bit silent and distant now. "Every note. Didn't we, Cliff?"

"*Every note*," he repeated, not sounding distant at all.

They arrived at the flat and found the Likely Lads waiting for them, and Cliff was heaved and hoisted up the stairs and deposited – safe, if rather tired – in his own front room. Isobel thought they ought to leave the family to their own devices pretty smartly, but Cliff looked at her with sudden appeal and said very clearly and distinctly, "Stay – for – tea?"

Then she understood that he wanted to round off this special evening with some sort of attempt at hospitality – some final heart-warming little ceremony.

"Why not?" said Alan, who was probably much more tired than Cliff. "What about you guys?"

Dave and Mitch made silent signals to each other and said cheerfully, "Why not?" and everyone laughed.

It was only a small party, and it did not last long, but it somehow set a seal upon the whole perilous undertaking.

"That was a wonderful concert, Alan," said Isobel. "I think we should all drink your health," and she lifted her cup to him in smiling recognition.

Everyone followed suit, but Alan promptly turned it all round by saying, "Don't the performers count? And what about the listeners?" So it became a general toast to each other, and in the ensuing laughter the little gathering broke up and went home. Dave and Mitch switched on their cycle lamps and rode off into the night, calling out cheerful goodbyes, and left Alan and Isobel together on the pavement.

"Why are they so nice?" Isobel asked, looking after them in wonder.

Alan laughed. "Don't tell me you've never met any nice boys in all your teaching life?"

Isobel giggled. "Of course – but. . . ."

He answered her seriously then, understanding her question. "It's a Catholic school, remember. There's a tradition of service – especially among the sixth-formers." He saw her doubt, and added for good measure; "But they volunteered, you know. I didn't have to ask."

By this time he had opened the door of the car and skilfully steered Isobel inside before she could protest. And when she did start to say something about walking home, he interrupted with smiling firmness, "Don't be silly. You know you're tired."

"So are you!"

"A few extra yards in the car is no hardship."

Isobel looked at him curiously in the light of the passing street-lamps. "What do you usually do after a concert?"

"Go home and have a large whisky."

She laughed. "It sounds a bit tame."

He grinned at her sideways. "Yes," he said. "It is."

They drove on in companionable silence until they came to Isobel's door, and there she said rather too brusquely, "I've got some whisky, if that's what you want."

"I thought you'd never ask," said Alan, and they went up the steps together, laughing at nothing.

By the time Isobel had found the whisky and made some sandwiches in case Alan was feeling peckish (which he was), Alan himself had put a match to the fire, and Isobel's sitting-room was lit by a rosy glow. It was a long, elegant room, with tall windows and glass doors, all looking out over a neat terrace and green lawns at the back of the house. Isobel had furnished it with typical unfussy spareness – a few good pieces with well-polished mahogany surfaces, a couple of chairs and a sofa covered in creamy unbleached linen, and several jewel-coloured Indian rugs on the floor.

Alan eyed it appreciatively, and sat back in his chair, visibly relaxing in the calm and undemanding atmosphere of Isobel's house. "This is nice," he said, sipping his drink.

They talked for a while about the concert – since Alan was clearly still in the withdrawal symptons of high endeavour, and Isobel found herself curiously reluctant to see him come down out of the clouds.

"It had to be a fairly obvious programme," he said, seeming to apologize about something. "What with Easter coming up. And with our kind of parents, popular classics and well-loved favourites are the order of the day."

Isobel smiled. "I'm not complaining! Did you plan the whole programme?"

"Oh no. Stella – that's the Junior school music girl, Stella Richards – organized her own items, of course. But we did – er – collaborate on the final plan." He grinned at Isobel, admitting without words that he was really the master planner. "The Junior school is quite separate," he explained, "though its building is just across the road. But we usually get together in something once or twice a year. Parents often have kids at both schools, and it makes for good relations all round." A thought struck him then, and he added, "By the way, Georgie will be moving on next September. I hope it won't make it difficult for her to see the other two home?"

"Don't the times correspond?"

"Not always. Seniors are apt to stay on late for this and that . . . I know Trevor had difficulty about music lessons. That's really why he stopped learning the cello."

Isobel sighed. "Is he really good?"

Alan shrugged a little sadly. "Could be – with practice. The way things are at the moment, he can't really progress."

They were both silent for a moment, thinking of that over-burdened boy and his family problems.

"But it was a lovely evening for all of them," said Isobel, refusing to let doubts dispel Alan's glow of achievement. "And Cliff really did enjoy it. He didn't miss a thing."

Alan nodded, smiling. "I think his grasp of things has improved a lot."

"So do I." She glanced at him appreciatively. "Thanks to you."

He disclaimed that. "Oh, I don't know . . . I think it was

coming back anyway." He paused, considering the matter. "We've got the Weston outing to plan next, haven't we? Term ends next week."

Isobel looked at him enquiringly. "Aren't you going away?"

"No." He held his glass up to the light and squinted through the golden whisky, admiring the colour. "Not this time."

Isobel was still looking at him, with some curiosity. "I don't know, Alan. You spend far too much of your time dealing with the problems of just one of your pupils – let alone all the rest. Don't you have any private life of your own?"

He grinned back at her, crinkling up his eyes again in what was becoming a familiar expression of teasing tenderness. "As much as I want," he said.

Isobel shook her head at him. "You haven't told me anything about your home life. I don't even know where you live!"

He laughed. "Not much to tell. I have a flat in a staff house belonging to the school. It's small and neat, and all I really need. I'm out most evenings at rehearsals and choir practice and so on . . . and I give a few private lessons here and there. Plenty to do!"

"And you can still afford to waste all that time on the Broadbents?"

"It isn't *wasted*," stated Alan. "I told you before. And they are rather a special case."

"I should hope so," retorted Isobel. "Otherwise you'd have no time left for your work at all!" She glared at him, and added slyly, "Let alone any personal commitments."

"I don't have any personal commitments," said Alan, grinning.

"Why not?"

Alan knew what she was up to, and his grin got wider. "Don't need 'em. Wedded to my art."

Isobel laughed. "I don't believe it!"

He grew sober for a moment. "I was married – once."

"What happened?"

"Oh . . . I suppose we outgrew each other. I liked my work, and was seldom at home. She liked to play – not always music." He paused, not wanting to discuss that failure very much. "Eventually, she decided to go off with someone else,

136

and I didn't try to stop her." He glanced at Isobel and added honestly, "As much my fault as hers."

"Do you still keep in touch?"

His smile was easier now. "Not a lot. . . . But we parted friends." Then he looked at Isobel very straight and said deliberately, "So I am fancy free – and glad of good company. . . ." He let the silence flow on a moment, and then added softly, "And, believe me, Isobel, good company is hard to find."

"Yes," said Isobel simply. "I know."

They looked at each other, intentions clearly stated, and found themselves smiling in spite of themselves.

"Well," said Alan, at last getting to his feet, "now that the battle-lines have been drawn up, I'd better go home!"

"Not battle-lines, surely?" protested Isobel.

"Oh yes. Battle-lines," Alan insisted, laughing. "Only we're allies, not enemies."

"Yes, I suppose even allies have to take up strategic positions and plan their campaign," conceded Isobel, joining in his laughter.

"Of course," agreed Alan. "United we stand!" and he gave Isobel a brief, surprising hug of affection, before turning his back on the firelit room and making for the door.

Chapter Eight

'The Piper's Picnic'

Double Jig

The interviews with the two doctors took place in the following week. The Social Services doctor agreed to make his assessment visit after Cliff's own GP had reported on his present condition in relation to what he had been like when first sent home from hospital. The GP himself – John Barry – was less co-operative initially. In fact, Isobel had to make an appointment to see him herself before he would agree to a home visit at all. But when confronted by an irate, handsome elderly woman who looked at him with icy incredulity and said, "I thought a general practitioner was supposed to be concerned about his patient's welfare!" he became both defensive and apologetic.

He was a small man, crisp and clever, and permanently tired, but in spite of his slightly exasperated manner, his eyes were kind. "You must understand, Miss – er – Frazier, that we are all rather overworked here, and we rather expect the patients to come to us – or *ask* us for help if they think they need a visit."

"Well, Cliff Broadbent can't come to you, can he?" Isobel snapped.

"That's true. But his wife should tell us if he needs a visit."

"No doubt she did, when she was here," said Isobel drily.

"*When she was here?*" Dr Barry looked at her sharply. "What do you mean?"

"I mean that Katie Broadbent left her husband and young family more than six months ago, and since that time Cliff

138

Broadbent has been looked after by his children – the eldest of which, Trevor, is just thirteen years old."

The doctor looked appalled. "I had no idea."

"No. Well, to do you justice, they did not ask you for help – they probably didn't know how. But you might conceivably have called round to see how your patient was getting on . . . though I suppose those days are gone."

He sighed, honestly admitting a failure of duty. "Yes. You're right. It's just that – my days are pretty full anyway with more-or-less urgent cases, and it slipped my mind. . . . There are so many calls on my time – all of them deserving." He spread his hands out in a helpless gesture. "I need a reminder – especially for a chronic case where no one expects much change."

Isobel nodded. "Well, I think you'll find there is a change now. And that's why I want you to come and see him. I don't know whether anything further can be done about his legs – Trevor says they do occasionally twitch and kick out, so there must be some movement there, even if involuntary . . . but his speech is returning quite fast now, there are more words every day, and his thinking capacity seems to be remarkably on the spot. We've managed to take him out twice – once just for an airing on the Downs, and once to his children's school concert. Both events were big occasions for him, requiring a lot of effort – especially getting him down the stairs in his wheelchair!"

John Barry stared at her. "*Down the stairs?*"

"They are marooned on the second floor, with no lift. Didn't you realize that?"

He shook his head. "I knew they were there when he first came out of hospital, yes. But I thought the Social Services would have moved him."

"So they should," agreed Isobel grimly. "But they haven't. So far. They say there is no ground-floor accommodation available at present."

"That's outrageous."

"Yes, it is rather. Especially as it also means Cliff can't get downstairs to go to physiotherapy sessions or anything else. And I believe he could be a lot more independent now that his wits and his speech are returning. After all, he has the use of his arms. He could manoeuvre a wheelchair quite

139

well on the level." She looked at him severely. "I was hoping, among other things, that you would put in a strong word to the housing department. It might help them make up their minds to do something."

He nodded slowly. "Yes. I'll come and see him, of course. There may indeed be more we can do for him . . ." He looked at Isobel, almost with appeal now. "Will you be there?"

"Yes, if you like. But I think you must talk to the boy, Trevor. He does everything for his father. In fact, he hardly ever leaves him, even to go to school." She sighed. "He knows more about Cliff Broadbent's condition than anyone."

Dr Barry sighed too, realizing for the first time what a responsibility all this must be to a thirteen-year-old boy. "What happened to the mother?" he asked.

"No one seems to know. Or at least, no one is saying anything," Isobel told him. "Though I rather suspect Trevor knows more about it than he lets on."

"But there must be some explanation?"

"Yes, there must," Isobel agreed. "But all he will say is: 'She needed a rest.'" She paused, and then, seeong his doubtful expression, added further explanation. "Apparently, she left a note telling them to 'ask the Welfare' for help. . . . Trevor thinks she expected the Social Services to take care of the children, and presumably put Cliff Broadbent into residential care."

"But they didn't?"

Isobel sighed again. "No. Because, like you, they were not *asked* to help."

"And they've been struggling on their own ever since?"

"Yes. Struggling." Her glance was still grim and accusing.

"I'll come tomorrow," he said.

So when Dr Barry came, Isobel was there as requested, but it was Trevor who hovered anxiously at his father's side, and remained watchful and protective throughout the doctor's careful examination and his equally careful questions.

"Tell him I'll talk to him afterwards – in the kitchen," Trevor had said urgently to Isobel before Barry came. "I don't want to – to talk over Dad's head. . . ."

Isobel understood him. "I'll tell him . . . just be there while he talks to Cliff – that's all you need do."

And this Trevor certainly did.

The doctor seemed well aware of this, and was careful to include Trevor in his questioning assessment. "Do you have any pain now?" he asked Cliff, looking from him to Trevor, not knowing which of them would answer.

"More . . . *now*," said Cliff, quite distinctly.

Barry looked interested. "Really? Where?"

Cliff's hands, which were clenched a little fiercely on the arms of his chair, relaxed a little, and he let his left hand move down to the small of his back near the bottom of his spine. "Here," he said. And added again, without rancour or complaint, "*More.*"

John Barry glanced from Trevor to Isobel, and back to Cliff's face. "That might be a good sign, you know – even if it is more uncomfortable. Do you take any painkillers now?"

Cliff shook his head, this time with a hint of impatience. "No." And he looked at Trevor in mute appeal.

Trevor decided to explain, then. "He used to take them. Mum used to get them for him. . . . He had a repeat prescription. But he got fed up with them. Said they didn't do any good – so he stopped."

Dr Barry nodded quietly, and made no further comment. He just went on patiently with his examination, trying out each of Cliff's wasted legs and looking for reflex action or any sign of returning movement.

Cliff bore it all docilely enough without protest, but his eyes were fixed anxiously on the doctor's face, and he finally said, with slow, painstaking clarity, "Get-ting – better?"

John Barry smiled and patted him encouragingly on the arm. "Yes," he said. "Definitely getting better. A great improvement since I saw you last. But now we must try to get those legs moving – if we can."

"Try," echoed Cliff, still gazing at the doctor in fierce appeal. "*I – will – try.*"

"We'll all try," promised the doctor, and looked from Trevor to Isobel for confirmation.

"I'll make Dad some tea," said Trevor. "Would you like some?"

141

Dr Barry was about to decline – he never had time for cups of tea or socializing with his patients – but something about the boy's insistent look got through to him, and he followed Trevor into the kitchen, saying, "Good idea." After all, he thought, why not? Am I really so pushed I can't spare five minutes for this loyal, overworked boy?

Isobel had meant to stay tactfully out of the way, but Trevor's eyes flashed equally insistent messages to her, so she gave Cliff a reassuring wink, and followed the others. It was clear that Trevor wanted her to hear the doctor's opinion.

"What is he like at night?" asked Barry, watching Trevor put the kettle on and lay out the mugs on a tray. (Efficient and unfussy, he commented to himself. Not making too much song and dance about it. A good carer.)

Trevor hesitated, and then looked squarely at the doctor's neutral, listening face. "He doesn't sleep a lot. He can't get very comfortable . . . and when he does sleep, he has bad dreams."

"Bad dreams?"

"Nightmares . . ." Trevor glanced fleetingly at Isobel. "Shouting ones. . . ."

The doctor nodded. "What does he say?"

Again there was that fractional hesitation. "Nothing much . . . Sometimes it's just a sort of yell . . . or a roar, if he's really upset." He paused, and added carefully, "Or sometimes it's *'No!'* His straight glance wavered a little, and then settled firmly again, but this time on Isobel's face as if seeking support. "At least, I think it's 'No'."

"What else might it be?" Barry was interested now.

"Oh, I don't know . . . I thought it might be *'GO!'*'" He was looking away from both of them now, as if caught in some dark dream of his father's. "But he's not very clear when he's frightened," he added, almost to himself.

"Frightened?"

Trevor looked at him with bleak honesty. "I think so. That's what it sounds like."

John Barry did not comment on this directly, but he was following up a line of enquiry of his own, and trying to be tactful about it.

"Does he . . .? I know he used to have bouts of frustration

142

and – er – so he hit out at things. . . . Your mother told me. Does he still do that?"

"Sometimes," admitted Trevor, and clamped his mouth tight shut. Then he thought he sounded too abrupt, and added with a faint grin of reassurance. "Not so often now." He took a deep breath and made his first admission of help from outside sources. "Especially since Miss Isobel came."

Isobel looked at him in amazement. Trevor had never told her that – although his appreciative glance had often signalled recognition of the trust and understanding that was growing between his father and his friend, Mizzibell. Not that he ever used the children's nickname aloud. He always called her Miss Isobel – most correctly and politely.

"Well," said the doctor, seeing that the tea was now made and it was time to return to a suspicious Cliff Broadbent, "I think your father is definitely improving – in various ways. We now have to discover what else we can do to help him. And maybe make your own job a little easier."

"I don't mind it," said Trevor swiftly. "He's not really any trouble."

Dr Barry and Isobel looked at each other in disbelief.

"He must be heavy to lift?" Barry suggested.

Trevor admitted that. "Yes. But we've worked out how to do it. His arms are very strong." He picked up the tray and purposefully marched out of the kitchen, making it very clear that everyone had said enough.

"It's all right," murmured the doctor to Trevor's retreating back. "I think you're doing splendidly." He went quite deliberately up to Cliff, who was looking a bit mutinous, marooned in his chair, and said, "You must be very proud of Trevor, Mr Broadbent. He's an excellent manager."

Cliff's dark expression changed then, and a curiously vulnerable smile lit his face. "Yes," he nodded. "Good – boy – our Trev."

The other two agreed with him wholeheartedly, but they knew better than to say so. Let Cliff have the last word.

Isobel had just finished having a few final words with John Barry, and watched him drive away in his car, when the children came rushing up the front steps. At least, two of

143

them did. There was Colin, out of breath and dishevelled, with one heavily bruised cheek and a bloody nose – and there was Georgie, equally out of breath and dishevelled, with her red hair on end, and a darkening bruise on her determined little chin.

"Has Goldie come home?" they chorused urgently.

"No." Isobel looked surprised. "Wasn't she with you?"

The two of them looked at each other and groaned. "I told her to run," blurted out Colin. "I thought she'd run home – she knows the way. . . ."

"Then where *is* she?" gasped Georgie, in a voice of horror. "Where's she got to? She shouldn't be out on her own – Trev will kill me!"

By this time, Trevor, hearing their voices in the street below the open window, and somehow guessing that something was wrong, came down the stairs to find out what was happening.

"What's going on?" he demanded, sounding sharp and anxious.

"It was Terry – Terry Blatchford," began Colin.

"And Tony . . ." added Georgie, rubbing her jaw.

"Hadn't you better start at the beginning?" suggested Isobel.

They looked at her gratefully, and tried to snatch a couple of shaky breaths. "They set on us," said Colin, sounding aggrieved and belligerent both at once.

"All of 'em," added Georgie, backing him up.

"Terry and Tony Blatchford?" Trevor's voice was still sharp. "And who else?"

"His gang . . . don't know 'em all – Mick and Jinty – you know. . . ."

Trevor's face was grim. He did know that gang. Most people in the street did.

"We fought 'em off," panted Colin, who had clearly been in quite a fight.

"Gave as good as we got!" corroborated Georgie.

"Sent 'em packing in the end," Colin boasted, but then remembered Goldie, with an awful jolt of terror. "I thought – better get Goldie out of it – so I told her to run, and she did. But I didn't see which way she went . . . they were all over me by then, and I couldn't stop to look—" He sounded desperately at bay.

144

"It's all right, Colin," Isobel intervened. "Take your time."

"It wasn't his fault," said Georgie, looking from Trevor to Isobel with equal desperation. "Honest – we didn't say anything to them. We didn't even see them coming—"

"What did they want?" asked Trevor, a curious dread in his voice now.

Colin looked up at his big brother and tried to shrug. But his shoulder seemed to be hurt as well, and he winced. "Dunno . . . They kept on about Dad talking. . . ."

"*What?*"

"'Talking, is he?' they said. 'Well, he'd better not, see? You tell him that, Colin,' and then they thumped me."

"We thumped them back," added Georgie. "Good and hard." Then she, too, thought of Goldie, out in the streets alone. "Where can she *be?*" she wailed, suddenly near to tears.

"Let's stop and think," said Isobel. "She'd be a bit frightened, wouldn't she? What sort of places does she know where she would feel safe?"

They looked at each other doubtfully. "There's the swings and roundabouts," suggested Colin.

"But we passed them on the way home," pointed out Georgie. "She'd have come out if she'd seen us running by."

"Or the sweetshop?" Colin wondered.

"But she hadn't any money," said Georgie practically.

"She wouldn't go to the arcade, would she?" Trevor demanded.

"No." Colin was quite definite. "Terry's gang hang out there – she'd never go near it."

"Where else, then?" Trevor insisted.

"Has she any special friend at school?" asked Isobel, looking for possibilities.

Georgie sighed. "There's Trudy – but she lives in the same street as Terry. Goldie wouldn't go there."

"She must have gone somewhere," persisted Colin, sounding more upset minute by minute.

"Then we must find her," Trevor said, not knowing in the least how to set about it.

"I've got my car here," volunteered Isobel. "We could cover a lot more ground that way . . .?"

The children all shook their heads vehemently. "She

145

wouldn't just be *walking about* – she'd be hiding some-where," Georgie explained. "We might miss her altogether, driving by."

Isobel saw the sense in that. "Well then, where are the sort of places she might hide in?"

They considered the matter. "We don't usually stop any-where," Georgie said worriedly. "It's safer not to . . ." All at once, hearing her own voice saying that word '*safer*', she was overwhelmed with anxiety about her small sister, and had to gulp back tears.

"You've had about enough," said Trevor, not missing a thing. "You'd better go up and keep Dad happy, while we look—"

"But you won't know where to look!" she protested, very near tears now.

"Nor do you," retorted Trevor. "But Colin will show me the likeliest places. . . . Go on, Georgie, Dad will be getting worried."

"What shall I tell him?" she asked, afraid to put the frightful possibilities into words.

"Tell him Goldie stopped to play with a friend," said Trevor firmly. "And we've gone to fetch her home."

Georgie looked from him to Isobel, as if seeking guidance.

"That sounds sensible," agreed Isobel. "Go and make him some tea, Georgina. And wash your face, or your father will—"

"Smell a rat," put in Colin flatly, and managed a pale grin. "Go on, Georgie – we'll manage."

Trevor looked at Isobel. "You don't have to—" he began.

"Don't be silly," snapped Isobel. "Of course I'm coming." She turned to Colin. "You'd better take us back to where the fight began. We'll start from there." A thought struck her then, and she went over to her car, unlocked it, and seized her umbrella from the back seat. "And if we meet your gang again," she added with grim humour, "I'll have something to say to them!"

"So will I!" growled Trevor.

Then Georgie, unwillingly admitting defeat, went back upstairs to her father, and the other three set out to look for Goldie.

*　　*　　*

They tried the sweetshop on the corner, and the pet shop where Goldie loved to watch the guinea-pigs and rabbits, and the disused bandstand near the swings in the sooty little recreation ground, and the broken verandah round the deserted sports club that was no longer used except as a useful expanse of wall for graffiti – but there was no sign of Goldie anywhere.

Colin was looking at the broken rails of the wooden verandah with a frown of concentration, as if it reminded him of something. It looked sad and forgotten – derelict, really. . . .

"*Derelict*," he said suddenly. "Old Nick."

"What?" Trevor was mystified.

"Old Nick's a sort of tramp," Colin explained.

"You don't really call him that to his face, do you?" asked Isobel, half smiling.

"Oh yes, he likes it. He says it frightens off the kids and keeps them from bothering him . . . but it doesn't frighten Goldie. We often see him on our way to school, he sits on the steps and plays his penny whistle. Goldie always talks to him. . . ."

"Well?" Trevor sounded quite fierce. "What's he got to do with it?"

"'*Derelict*,' he said," Colin repeated slowly. "'Derelict, I am, little Goldie, and derelict is where I lives . . .'." He turned to Trevor urgently. "That empty place behind the shoe factory – you know the one."

"But it's falling down." Trevor was horrified.

"I know – but he lives there – and Goldie might go to him. She likes Old Nick."

"Come on, then," said Trevor, and began to run.

So did Colin. So did Isobel – pleased to note that she could keep up with the boys quite easily without getting too out of breath.

The old building was indeed falling down. Holes gaped in the brickwork, and dark empty spaces loomed where the windows should have been. One lot of glassless gaps on the ground floor had been boarded up, and so had the front door, but even this attempt at security (or shutting out squatters) had failed, and the boards hung drunkenly sideways, leaving

147

a narrow, crooked sliver of space just wide enough for a thin man – or a child – to squeeze through.

The three of them paused and looked at each other.

"I'll go in first," said Colin.

"No, you won't. I will," contradicted Trevor.

"There's room enough for me to get through," countered Isobel.

"It doesn't look very safe—" Trevor began.

"All the more reason to get Goldie out – if she's there," pointed out Isobel.

"Old Nick isn't dangerous," said Colin. "Not like the gang, I mean."

Isobel took note of that admission, and admired the boy's courage even more. "Come on," she said. "We'll all go in," and she went first up to the drunken doorway and sidled her way in past the sagging planks. Behind her came Trevor and Colin, silent now in the gloom.

There was glass underfoot, and broken bricks littered the hallway, with bits of broken banister from the rotten staircase.

I hope we don't have to go up there, thought Isobel. It looks very unsafe to me. I wonder if I can persuade the boys to stay downstairs while I have a look?

I hope we don't have to go up there, thought Trevor. I wonder if I can go up on my own and leave Colin and Mizzibell downstairs while I have a look?

Colin did not think that far. There was a faint smell of woodsmoke and cooking coming from somewhere, and he followed his nose. As he got nearer to the smell, he could hear an old voice talking softly to itself, and just now and then a small voice answering.

"I think they're here," he said, calling the others, and walked rather cautiously into the room at the end of the unlit passage.

It was like a scene out of Dickens, thought Isobel, pausing in the doorway. The shabby, forgotten room was faintly lit by firelight from a small, bright blaze of broken bits of wood in the old-fashioned grate. Bending over this glowing heart, was an old, tattered figure in a long, mud-coloured khaki overcoat with frayed edges, his grey hair and beard almost in danger of

148

catching alight, he stooped so low over his cooking pot. And beside him, half-lit into a kind of haloed stillness, was Goldie, holding a long toasting fork to the fire. Her face, beneath its bright nimbus of red-gold hair which was lit into fiery flames by the reflected glow from the grate, seemed serious about the task in hand, but otherwise untroubled. She was clearly not afraid of Old Nick in his shadowy home.

"So there you are," said Colin, trying not to sound alarmed or excited. And Trevor and Isobel, taking their cue from him, said nothing at all.

The old man, Nick, looked round and gave a rheumy cackle. "Ar, there she is – safe with Old Nick," he said. "And a good bitta tea comin' up, an' all, isn't it, little 'un?"

Goldie had also looked round, rather fearfully for a moment, Isobel thought, but was now staring hard at Colin in something like relief. "Have they gone?" she asked.

"Quite gone," Colin told her. "Scrammed. Vermoosed. Me and Georgie sent 'em packing."

Goldie was still looking at him. "What happened to your nose?"

"It got hit," said Colin, and did not enlarge on the subject. (It was large enough already.)

"Only got one mug," said Nick hospitably, "but you're welcome." He poured some water from his blackened kettle into his tin mug and dropped a teabag in. Then he picked up an open tin of condensed milk and carefully tilted some in on top of the teabag. Having got this far with his tea-making, he looked again, more carefully, at his visitors, and offered the mug to Isobel, belatedly remembering to drop a rather grey lump of sugar into it, and finding a battered spoon to stir it vigorously.

Isobel knew better than to refuse. Instead, she sipped the rapidly darkening liquid, and handed the mug on to Trevor, who did the same with perfect manners and passed it on to Colin.

"Can't I have some?" demanded Goldie.

So Colin passed it on to Goldie, who took a sip, made a slight face at the hot, bitter liquid, and passed it back to Nick who took a hearty swig.

It was a ceremony, thought Isobel, as important as any

149

passing round of peace-pipe or loving-cup. They were all brothers now – and sisters too.

"You can have the toast," said Goldie, offering it back to Nick with one of her most radiant smiles.

Nick also knew better than to refuse. He spread a thick layer of jam on it from another opened tin standing in the hearth, and took a large, satisfying crunch.

"Ar," he said. "Good, that is." Then he winked at Isobel, and added in a perfectly rational, reasoned tone, "Reckoned ordinary things'd be less frightening – like."

Isobel understood him. So did Trevor. It was rather over Colin's head, but he gathered that Old Nick was somehow explaining why he had let Goldie stay with him and help him get his frightful tea.

"I knew she'd be safe with you," Trevor said aloud, and then, honestly admitting the truth, "when I remembered."

Old Nick cackled again. "When you remembered, was it? . . . No one remembers Old Nick, unless they wants to throw him out of somewheres. . . . Except the little 'un, here. She allus remembers Old Nick – especially when the devil is after her!" He gave Goldie a small, friendly nudge and added gently, "Don't you, my lovely?"

Goldie smiled, and went over to Trevor who was still standing near the doorway, not wanting to rush things. "Can we go home now?"

"We'd better," Trevor agreed, smiling. "Dad will be wondering where you've got to."

"*Safe?*" Goldie enquired, looking from him to Isobel with big eyes.

"*Quite safe,*" said Isobel. "No one about at all. And anyway, I've got my umbrella!" and she waved it fiercely in the air like a sword – and everyone laughed. Old Nick loudest of all.

"You go on home now, little 'un," he said. "You got a whole army there to keep you safe." He turned back to his fire, and added over his shoulder, "Give us a wave when you goes by, and I'll know everything's all right – see?"

He did not look round as they prepared to leave, but Isobel and Trevor spoke together from the doorway, as if compelled by a single impulse. "Thank you, Nick," they said, and began

150

to crunch their way back down the littered corridor, with Colin leading the way.

But Goldie looked back at the old man bending over his fire, with his face so determinedly turned away, and she ran back across the room and put her arms round his neck and planted a kiss on his bushy grey beard.

Then she followed the others, with Colin still confidently leading, and presently took Isobel and Trevor each by the hand for reassurance while they walked home through the dove-coloured dusk of a terror-free spring evening.

Chapter Nine

'There is a Beech-Tree Grove'

Ancient Kerry Air

Isobel had to wait till Saturday morning to ask Trevor about the implications of the Blatchford Gang attack, and even then she was not sure that he would tell her what it was all about – if he knew. After Dr Barry's visit and the scare about Goldie, she had returned for her usual 'minder' stint on the Thursday, but she had not liked to ask Trevor any awkward questions in front of his father, so she had contented herself with reminding him to call in for his Saturday cup of tea, and hoped that he would be in a confiding mood.

In the meantime, she and Alan had agreed to wait a few days before planning the next outing for Cliff, in case he was feeling a bit pushed around by the various disruptions to his quiet, enclosed routine. In any case, the second doctor's visit hadn't taken place yet – and that in itself would probably be disturbing enough, however pleasant the Community Care assessor was.

So they decided to put off the trip to Weston till the following week. But that didn't stop Alan arranging to meet Isobel on Sunday 'to discuss ways and means'.

Feeling a shade guilty about all these excuses for what were, after all, perfectly ordinary meetings, Isobel went to rather more trouble than usual over Gervase's Friday supper. And when he arrived, newly recovered from his feverish cold, and bearing yet another bunch of flowers, she felt guiltier than ever. But Gervase was in a sunny mood and did not seem to notice the absurd confusion of loyalties in Isobel's divided mind, and she carefully said as little as possible about Alan

152

or Cliff Broadbent and his problems, or the frightening little episode of the gang attack on the children.

But now, here was Trevor, hands clasped round his mug of tea, looking at her with the same candid trust as usual, while she wondered how much she ought to ask.

"That business about your father *talking*," she said at last, "What did they mean?"

Trevor was still looking at her, but now he bent his head and stared down into his half-empty mug. "I don't know . . ." he said slowly. "At least . . . I *hope* I don't." He did not say any more, and did not look up, but Isobel knew he was holding something back.

She waited for a few moments, but when he did not speak again, she prodded him gently. "Trevor? What are you suggesting?"

He glanced up at her again then, with a bleak, unwilling admission in his eyes. "Well – none of us knows exactly what happened to Dad that night, do we? . . . If it was an accident, or a fight, or whatever . . .? I mean, he couldn't tell us, could he?" He paused, and then went on even more painfully, "But if – if someone is getting worried about what Dad *could* tell us . . .?" He didn't finish the question. There was no need.

Isobel sighed. The situation had a rather ominous ring.

"It makes it even more dicey for them to play outside," he said slowly. "I'll have to – have a bit of a talk with Terry Blatchford."

"Will that do any good?"

He shrugged sadly. "Shouldn't think so. Not with that lot. But I'd better try."

"Won't you get beaten up, too?"

Trevor smiled. "Probably. But I'm bigger than Colin or Georgie – as big as Terry, really." His smile looked a little dangerous to Isobel. "Can't have the kids frightened to walk home," he muttered, sounding both fierce and determined, if a little weary about it.

"I know it's the end of term," began Isobel, working her way cautiously towards the next step, "but I was thinking – if I kept on coming twice a week as usual, at least you could take the kids out for a bit yourself. You could all do with a breather." She smiled at the protest rising in Trevor's expressive face.

153

"And as your father is just getting used to me, it seems a pity to stop now."

Trevor shook his head at her in disbelief. "Why should—" he began.

But Isobel interrupted. "They wouldn't be scared if you were with them, would they? And they can't be cooped up indoors all through the holidays, can they? It wouldn't be fair."

Trevor had no answer to this. He knew it wouldn't be fair. But it wasn't fair that a small gang of thugs should terrorize them either. It wasn't fair that his Dad was stuck in a wheelchair – or that his mother wasn't there. Nothing was fair. When was life ever fair?

"I – it would be great to get out a bit," he agreed, but he sounded almost ashamed to admit it.

"We're going to take Cliff with us all to Weston," Isobel reminded him, knowing the reason for his reluctance. "And there'll be other outings. . . ."

Trevor met her smile with a doubtful one of his own. "It's – a bit of a hassle—"

"For your father?"

"No, for you."

Isobel grinned. "Not really – with all our willing helpers." She saw that he was still looking doubtful, and went on cheerfully, "And it may get easier if the housing people wake up and actually do something. We're working on it!"

Trevor was still looking unconvinced.

"You do need a break sometimes, Trevor. You know you do," she persisted reasonably. "Everyone does."

He sighed, admitting defeat all at once with a kind of tired acceptance. "I suppose so. . . ."

"Re-charging batteries," she told him, half seriously, "is no bad thing."

"So long as you don't blow a fuse!" countered Trevor, and began to laugh.

They looked at each other then, with mutual relief and gladness. They both knew that an agreement had been reached that was somehow valuable to all of them.

"That's all right, then," smiled Isobel. "More tea?"

*   *   *

So when Alan arrived on Sunday, full of plans for a day in the country, Isobel had plenty to tell him, and refused to go out until he had heard the whole story.

"This Terry Blatchford and his gang," said Isobel worriedly, "what do you know about him?"

"Not much." Alan was also looking slightly worried. "They don't go to our school – don't go to school much at all, by all accounts." He sighed." And not for any good reason, either."

"So what do they do?"

"Mostly terrorize the neighbourhood – pinch cars, snatch handbags, stage small break-ins . . . any local petty crime, they're likely to be mixed up in it."

Isobel also sighed. "No wonder Trevor doesn't let the kids play outside."

"Yes. A constant hazard, I'd say. . . ."

"Is there a father?"

"Oh yes." He made a faint grimace. "But if you were thinking of appealing to him, you won't get very far."

"Why not?"

Alan hesitated, and then decided to be frank. "He has a reputation for being a trouble maker. Supposed to be involved in various shady deals, and when people don't co-operate, he – er – leans on them!" He shook his head sadly. "There have been various incidents involving fights or unexplained muggings or beatings-up. . . . But the police can never pin anything on him."

"They know what he's up to?"

"Oh yes. Most of the time. But you have to have proof – or witnesses. And no one seems very willing to come forward, when pressed."

"I can imagine," said Isobel drily. The picture Alan was presenting filled her with a sort of cold dread. "Could – do you think he could have had anything to do with Cliff Broadbent's accident?"

"I don't know," said Alan slowly. "It's possible. . . ." He paused to consider. "Did anyone ever enquire, I wonder, if there had been some sort of fight at the Red Lion that night?"

Isobel shook her head. "I don't know, either." The possibility did nothing to reassure her. "But it seems a bit odd – these threats about *talking* . . . I don't like it."

155

"Nor do I," agreed Alan. "Sounds a bit like instructions from their tiresome father."

"What can we do about it?" asked Isobel, always on the lookout for solutions to problems rather than letting them simmer on unchecked.

Alan grinned and laid a restraining hand on her arm. "Hold your horses. They may not do anything else – especially as, by all accounts, the kids put up a good fight."

Isobel grinned back, though with reservations. "Sent 'em packing, Colin said!"

He laughed. "Well, that may be enough. They are bullies, after all, and that means they mostly run screaming at any real opposition."

"But Trevor is threatening to 'talk' to them."

Alan looked only faintly alarmed. "I'm afraid we can't stop him. He feels he is the kids' guardian – in place of his father. He's bound to want to protect them somehow."

"I only hope it doesn't lead to more trouble," said Isobel, sounding distinctly doubtful.

Alan still had his hand on her arm, and now he gave it a small squeeze of reassurance. "You can't fight all their battles for them, Isobel. They wouldn't like it if you did."

"Yes, but—"

"Just be there to pick up the pieces," he said, smiling at her troubled face. "That's all we can do at present."

She had to admit that he was right, and wasted no more time on vain forbodings. "But it's all the more important that we get them out of that place as soon as possible," she said, her mind already made up to an even more exhaustive search for a new flat for them to move to – somewhere – somehow – and to hell with the housing authority.

"Come on," said Alan. "That's enough worrying for one day. We can't do anything for them now. And you'll be going there tomorrow, anyway"

She looked at him almost reluctantly. "Alan – I feel guilty, going off and enjoying myself, when they—"

He answered her seriously, not dismissing her qualms at all lightly. "You are going there so that they can have their time off. This is yours. And I happen to think you need it."

"Why?"

156

He shook his head at her, half laughing. "I don't know . . . something to do with greyness – and the flame of the spirit . . ." His eyes, looking into hers, were suddenly piercing and full of knowledge. "The *oriflamme* . . ." he said obscurely. "Can't let it be quenched."

Isobel stared at him, astonished. "Alan – you're a poet as well as a musician."

"Only sometimes," he said, "when pushed. And I'm pushed now. So come out into the sun."

And, much to her surprise, Isobel obeyed him.

They went to a place of rolling green hills and tall beechwoods, where spring was a potent force, far removed from the pale promise of the town. The delicate stars of wood anemones laced the winter-dark forest floor of dead leaves, making a frieze of white petals against the new green of woodspurge and wild arum. Small clumps of primroses lit sheltered corners, lifting transparent faces to the sun, and the bright new green of the unfurling hawthorn leaves was just beginning to colour the hedgerows.

They walked for a long time through the dappled shade of the beech woods, and Alan led her unerringly to a wide clearing among the tall, silver-grey trees where one enormous old beech spread its branches in solitary state, bigger and older than all its companions, and somehow more kingly and powerful, too.

"There!" he said in triumph. "You said you wanted to climb a tree."

Isobel looked at him in disbelief, and then her glance travelled up the great girth of the tree and its wide-spread smooth limbs. They were evenly spaced at the bottom, easy to reach and easy to climb, with each gap between possible to bridge with a comfortable stride. But beyond the first main fork of the trunk, the gaps got wider, and the branches more slender and whippy in the soft spring wind.

"*Up there?*" she said, awestruck, and then suddenly began to laugh. Well, why not? she thought. If Alan is determined to call my bluff, I'll show him! And, eyes sparkling with mischief, she kicked off her sensible shoes and reached out to swing herself up onto the first branch she could reach.

Once on that strong, firm base, she found the going quite

157

easy. Step by step, branch by branch, she made her way upwards, feet planted firmly on each new rounded surface, fingers grasping each knobby handhold as it came within reach. She did not waste time looking down, but fixed her eyes ahead, assessing each next step, each reachable bough, and each hazard or gap to be negotiated as she climbed. She decided she wasn't in the least afraid, and in fact the climb was rather exhilarating, reminding her of her youth, and there was something immensely strong and comforting about those smooth, grey, living branches under the clasp of her hands.

Her progress up the tree had been in a kind of circular pattern as the easiest ways up presented themselves, and now Isobel suddenly found herself at the top of the great tree, where the last fork divided into its graceful crown of smaller branches. I must just put my head out of the top, she thought. Am I tall enough if I stand in the fork? I don't think those thin bits would hold me. . . .

Very cautiously, but with an enormous sense of elation, she planted both feet firmly on either side of the final fork of the tree, stretched herself tall and lifted her head high to look over the top of the highest twigs as they swayed in the scented wind. And as she gazed upwards past each fragile, pointing finger of growing tree, she found she was looking at nothing but sky. It stretched above her, limitless and pure, the pale, milky blue of early spring awash with light – and below her were the silver-grey beechwoods rooted in the rich brown earth, solid and strong. And she was poised, breathless and filled with wonder, between the two.

"I'm here!" she said aloud. "I've arrived. I'm at the top!" and she wanted to sing, or to fly – or both.

"Don't take off altogether," warned Alan, just below her, and his voice was laced with affectionate laughter.

She looked down then, straight into his eyes, and laughed back. "I didn't know you'd followed me up."

"Whither thou goest, I will go," he said, grinning. "And besides, I'd be softer to fall on than the ground."

"I am *not* going to fall," said Isobel, with dignity.

"What are you going to do, then?" he enquired. "Fly?"

"No," she said, considering the matter judicially. "I think I should like to sing."

"Well, go on," he urged. "I'll join you. What's it to be?"

Isobel grinned. "Daft or not, and with apologies to the last night of the Proms, it'll have to be 'Jerusalem'. Nothing else is exalted enough up here!" and she launched straight away into the first verse.

> *"And did those feet in ancient time*
> *Walk upon England's mountains green . . ."*

Even up here, she managed to produce a clear, vigorous contralto, and Alan joined in with a surprisingly rich and uninhibited baritone. Neither of them seemed to think it at all odd to be belting out 'Jerusalem' at the top of their voices from the top of a tree.

But when they got to the second verse, Alan almost forgot to sing, he was so entranced at the sight of Isobel standing astride the topmost fork of the swaying tree, singing with such absurd and spirited fervour, and at the way the famous words seemed to fit her fighting mood.

"Bring me my bow of burning gold!" she sang, looking up into the flawless spring sky above the tree's spreading crown.

> *"Bring me my arrows of desire.*
> *Bring me my spear, O clouds unfold,*
> *Bring me my chariot of fire!"*

and Alan almost expected the listening sky to oblige.

> *"I will not cease from mental fight,*
> *Nor shall my sword sleep in my hand!"*

promised Isobel, still looking up and singing with all her might – and Alan followed her, thinking she looked more like a fiery Joan of Arc than ever, with her head uplifted, challenging the sky. And at that point the sun, glancing through a moving cloud, shot a ray of piercing radiance down through the trees, lighting her upturned face, as if with approval.

> *"Till we have built Jerusalem*
> *In England's green and pleasant land!"*

159

they finished together, on a note of curious triumph, and the silence afterwards seemed full of echoes and strange overtones.

But moments of pure elation cannot last, and Isobel sighed and said sadly to Alan, "Though I don't know what Blake's Industrial Revolution has got to do with what I'm fighting for!"

"Oh, I don't know," said Alan slowly. "Why did Cliff Broadbent get made redundant? Mechanization and container shipping are all part of the same thing, aren't they? . . . And industry is still laying waste the land."

Isobel looked down at him half seriously. "You're absolutely right. We're still fighting the same war!" Her eyes went past Alan and saw the whole sweep of the beautiful unspoilt woodlands below her, and the swelling curves of the empty hills beyond . . . "Poor Blake," she said, "it isn't over yet!"

It didn't seem to occur to either of them that it was a bit crazy to be discussing the Industrial Revolution at the top of a tree.

"Come down, Isobel, before you declare war on anything else," Alan begged. "You can't stay on the heights for ever."

"True," agreed Isobel, and gave a last, valedictory look at all that glory spread around her. Then she glanced down again at Alan's face enquiringly, and added, "But don't you want to go to the top as well?"

"No." He smiled at her cheerfully. "You've done it for me. And if we try to pass each other up here, we'll probably both fall off!" and he began to climb down again, slowly and carefully, with Isobel following behind him.

When they got about half-way down, where there was a slightly thicker fork in the trunk, they both paused for a breather, and Alan suddenly began to sing again.

> "The grand old Duke of York
> He had ten thousand men,"

and Isobel responded, grinning:

> "He marched them up to the top of the hill,
> And he marched them down again."

Both voices joined together then, in delighted unison:

"And when they were up, they were up,
And when they were down, they were down,
And when they were only halfway up
They were neither up nor down!"

"You are a fool, Alan," said Isobel, laughing.

"Who's talking?" he retorted. "Singing 'Jerusalem' fit to bust at the top of a tree!"

And they went on climbing down, giggling helplessly at each other as they went. At the bottom of the tree, among the wood anemones and bluebell shoots, they stopped and looked at each other, half afraid to come down to earth.

"Alan – am I quite mad?"

"Yes," he said, smiling. "Utterly bonkers. But it's all right. I know the sky's the limit so far as you are concerned!"

"And for you?"

He crinkled up his eyes again in the old, teasing manner. "Well, it's like I said, if you go to the top, I won't be far behind!"

They were silent for a moment, aware that another threshold had been crossed, and then Alan deliberately broke the spell.

"Come on, I'm starving. After the heights, you need ballast to keep your feet on the ground!" and he led her away between the trees towards Blake's still embattled real world.

The interview with the Community Care assessor was very nearly a disaster. To begin with, the doctor who came was a woman. And Cliff, all his painful masculine pride aroused, refused to let her come near him.

"Dr Barclay," she said, hand outstretched. "Ruth Barclay. Hallo, Mr Broadbent."

But Cliff only backed away, hands stiff on the wheels of his chair, and roared like a lion.

Isobel was there, at Trevor's request, but even she could not pacify Cliff. She had never seen him in a rage before (a tantrum, she called it to herself) though Trevor had told her earlier about how difficult his father could be. But now she saw for herself what it was like when he 'lost his cool,'

161

as Trevor called it – and why the children were so wary of upsetting him.

He roared, *"Go away!"* at everyone in sight – at Isobel – at the startled woman doctor – even at Trevor – and shouted *"NO! NO!"* to the company at large, and backed his wheelchair into a corner of the living-room, and finally put the rug from his knees over his head and hid from the encroaching world like a frightened child.

"He can't bear to be seen like this," explained a white-faced Trevor. "Let alone be examined . . . by a lady." He looked rather desperately from the concerned face of the woman doctor to Isobel's more understanding one. "He wouldn't even let my Mum come near him – on the bad days. . . ."

Isobel turned to the puzzled doctor with some urgency. "You won't do any good while he's like this. Is there anyone else you could send?"

"You mean a *man*?" said Ruth Barclay, beginning to sound rather clipped and angry. "I can't see the necessity."

"It's just – old-fashioned macho pride," murmured Isobel, like Trevor, doing her best to explain.

"Well, he'll have to get over it, won't he?" said the affronted doctor, sounding distinctly impatient. "I'm only doing my job. And I've got plenty of others to attend to."

Isobel sighed, realizing that she was up against two obstinate people. Then she thought fleetingly of Cliff Broadbent's young wife Katie, and the shoutings and roarings of bitter rejection she had had to endure before she went away. . . . If that poor girl is ever to come back, Isobel thought, Cliff has got to get over this stupid hang-up. The young doctor is right.

She turned back to Ruth Barclay, appeal in her glance. "Give me a moment with him. Trevor, take Dr barclay into the kitchen. I'm sure we could all do with a cup of tea."

Trevor hesitated. He knew they meant well – Miss Frazier and the doctor – but they didn't understand his Dad like he did. They didn't seem to realize that they were stripping away his dignity and his privacy with every new approach – with every offer of help. . . . It was all so loaded, and he couldn't explain to them why his father was so at bay, and so frightened. Yes, *frightened*, Trevor told himself, understanding very well how Cliff Broadbent felt. . . . But how

162

could he tell these two uncomprehending people what the trouble was?

"I – I don't think he'll listen," he said to Isobel, speaking very softly, "not while he's *scared*." He did not know if either of the women would understand him, but he had done his best to make things clear.

Isobel nodded quietly. "It's all right," she replied, speaking just as softly. "Leave it to me," and something about the clear compassion in her glance seemed to reassure him, and he turned away with Dr Barclay beside him, and went into the kitchen.

Well, at least I can talk to the boy about how much care he has to provide for his father, thought Ruth Barclay.

Well, at least I can explain to her what my Dad needs, thought Trevor, as he put the kettle on.

Isobel waited a few moments before going over to Cliff, hunched rigid and furious in his chair.

"You're not a coward, Cliff," she said. "You've done some pretty brave things in the last couple of weeks. . . ." She paused, waiting for those brief words of praise to sink in before she dared to put the next, crucial decision before him. "But you've got to get over this before Katie comes back, haven't you?"

There was a long, agonized silence while Isobel waited, in some trepidation, for Cliff's reaction, and he stayed absolutely still under his rug. But all at once she saw that his shoulders were beginning to shake, and she realized that he was crying.

"A – ashamed," he got out at last, "ashamed. . . ."

"No, Cliff." She spoke quite firmly. "You are *not* ashamed. Your body got damaged, that's all. And doctors are trained to put it right. Just like engineers are with machines. It's a skilled job, just like yours. Why should you mind what they see? To them, you are just another machine that needs mending – legs and arms, wheels and cogs. It's all the same."

His head began to emerge from behind the rug. He looked, she thought, very like a naughty child who didn't know how to admit his tantrum was over. "*Wheels . . . and cogs?*" he repeated, wondering.

Isobel smiled. "A very complicated and precious machine, the human body. They spend *years* learning how to mend it. You've got to give them a chance."

163

"Chance?" he said. Isobel wondered if he wanted to say 'Chance would be a fine thing,' but she saw returning sanity growing in his cloudy gaze and decided to press on with one more appeal.

"Let her see you, Cliff – for Katie's sake, if not for the kids. . . ."

It was a risk, she thought. He might start to cry again, or shout and rage at her – but it was time he understood what his bitter pride had done – what damage it might still do, if he let it continue to dominate his frail will to recover.

"*Job?*" he said, trying to get things clear.

"Just her job, Cliff. She only wants to help you." She looked at him very straight then, her mouth a grim line, and added deliberately, "At least she doesn't have to *love* you as well."

"Wh – *what?*" He stared at her, shaken and bewildered.

"Katie loved you, as well as wanting to help you," Isobel said, spelling it out very loud and clear. "It was much harder for her."

Cliff did not try to answer that, he was too shocked. But Isobel could see him straining to understand, while the slow tears gathered again in his eyes. At last he shook his head helplessly and said in a strange, gruff voice of unwilling recognition, "Much . . . harder?"

"Much," repeated Isobel.

"Sorry . . ." he whispered, tears in his voice, too. "So sorry. . . ."

Isobel went close to him them, and – greatly daring – laid an arm round his shoulders and gave him a small, encouraging hug. "*You* can be sorry – but we can't – is that right?" And when he began, painfully, to smile, she said simply, "Shall we let her do her worst?"

"Yes," agreed Cliff, his smile growing less fragile. "*Worst!*"

164

Chapter Ten

'Be easy, you Rogue'
Old Jig or March

It was a couple of days after Ruth Barclay's visit, when Isobel was at home, that her doorbell rang quite early in the morning. Puzzled, she came down the stairs, wondering who it could be. It wasn't Saturday, so it wouldn't be Trevor, and it was too early for the postman unless he had changed his route.

Still slightly surprised, she opened the door and looked out, just as the crumpled figure of a battered Trevor lurched forward and fell in a heap on the threshold.

"Trevor? What on earth . . .?" began Isobel. But then, wasting no more time on words, she gathered him up in her arms and half dragged, half carried him across the hall and into her sitting-room where she laid him down on the sofa.

"Thanks . . ." he muttered, "Sorry . . ." and sank back in weary relief. But then all at once his eyes flew open, and he said urgently, "My bike . . .?"

"Where is it, Trevor?"

"Down the road . . . by the railings. . . ." His voice was fading, but he forced himself back to consciousness. "They ran me down," he said, sounding tired and angry – and only faintly surprised. "If it's smashed. . . ." He turned his head restlessly from side to side. *"Can't* do without it," he murmured. *"Must* have it . . ." and this time his voice did fade altogether, and his face went even paler and more ashen.

Isobel looked at him anxiously, and then tried, very cautiously, to find out the damage. His pulse was all right, she thought – a bit fast, but not fluttering or uneven, and his

165

breathing, though it had a faint catch in it, was not desperate or laboured.

"Where does it hurt?" she asked.

A thin smile twitched his mouth. *"Everywhere."* Then he added swiftly. "But nowhere really bad."

Isobel was not convinced. She took another look at him, and then left him lying there for a moment while she went into the hall to telephone for an ambulance. She thought the boy had better be examined by experts. After this, she filled a hot bottle and fetched two blankets to wrap round the shocked boy, and wondered what to do for him while she waited for help to arrive.

"My bike . . ." he said again, sounding even more distressed about it.

"All right, I'll go and get it," Isobel reassured him. "Lie still, Trevor. Don't try to move," and she hurried out of the door, through the hall, and out into the road where she stood looking up and down, searching for the smashed bike. Yes, there it was, lying sideways up against the railings of the little square of public garden on the corner.

There was a woman standing beside it, looking anxiously up and down the road. Isobel went towards her, and bent down to pick up the mangled remains of the bicycle.

"Did you see what happened?" she asked.

The woman nodded. She was youngish and pleasant-looking, Isobel observed, probably in her thirties, and just now her face was sharp with indignation. "I did, indeed!" she told Isobel. "Young hooligans! Joy-riding, they call it. But not much joy for that poor boy." She turned to Isobel, stiff with outrage. "They came right at him, knocked him flying – drove him off the road straight into the railings. He didn't have a chance." She shook her head in disbelief. "Was the boy hurt?"

"I'm not sure yet," said Isobel grimly. "I've sent for the ambulance."

The woman looked relieved. "I saw him limp off to your door. I was upstairs at the window when it happened, and by the time I got down here, he'd gone." She gave Isobel a cautious smile. "Do you know him?"

"Yes," Isobel said. "And I probably know the joy-riders, too. Did you get the number of the car?"

"Sorry," the woman shook her head. "It all happened so quickly. They shot off down the road like the clappers . . . I think it was a Ford Escort. But that wouldn't be much help to the police. They'll probably have abandoned it by now – or burnt it out."

Isobel nodded agreement. "Would you know them again?"

The woman looked doubtful. "I don't know . . . I might recognize the driver. He was big and dark – and he was laughing."

Isobel sighed. It sounded very like Colin's description of Terry Blatchford. "The police might want a witness?" she suggested.

The woman agreed, and held out her hand. "Gregg. Sheila Gregg. I'd be glad to oblige. Time we caught some of these louts. Let me know if I can help."

"I will," promised Isobel, smiling her thanks, and then remembered she had left Trevor alone for too long, and hurried back, pushing the bent bike before her on the pavement.

She arrived just as the ambulance was pulling up at her door, and led the two paramedics up the steps, explaining the situation as she went.

"I'd have brought him down to the hospital myself," she said, "but I didn't like to move him more than necessary."

"Quite right," said one of the ambulance men, giving her an approving smile. "What's his name? Trevor?"

He went into the sitting-room with his companion beside him, and stood looking down at the pale, bruised face below him. "Well now, Trevor, let's see what the damage is, shall we?"

But Trevor refused to co-operate. He shot one wild, accusing glance at Isobel and said, "I *can't* – the kids will wonder where I am . . . I'm late already. . . ."

Isobel had not thought of this. But now she reacted swiftly and decisively. "Trevor – you *must* be checked over by a doctor. It's important – especially if you want to get over this quickly. I'll drive round to see your father and the kids, and tell them you're delayed – and then follow you down to the hospital in my car. That way, I can be on hand to run you back when they've examined you. All right?"

167

He looked bewildered and uncertain. "What will you tell them?"

"That you've fallen off your bike. Will that do?"

He tried to smile. "Fair enough . . . but Colin will smell a rat."

Isobel grinned, relieved to see even the glimmer of a smile on the boy's face. "He's good at smelling rats, your brother. But I'll try to convince him."

"Come on now," said the kindly paramedic. "Sooner you get there, the sooner you'll get back," and before Trevor could make any further protest, he was lifted on to a stretcher and carried out to the waiting ambulance.

Isobel went with them to the open doors, and gave Trevor's hand an encouraging squeeze as he was lifted inside. "I'll be there almost as soon as you are," she said. "Don't worry – I'll reassure the kids."

She watched them close the doors, and then went to fetch her own small car, and drove smartly away towards the Broadbents' flat.

Cliff and the children were certainly startled by her arrival, but she managed to make her errand sound very matter-of-fact and ordinary. Trevor had fallen off his bike. He was just having a check-up. He wouldn't be long. Would they be all right till he got back?

Georgie, instantly taking charge, assured Isobel that they would. She had already got breakfast ready. They would all manage perfectly well without Trevor. He always went on as if no one else could do *anything* useful! And she shot Isobel a bright, shrewd glance and murmured, "Is he all right, then?" as she followed her to the door.

"Yes," said Isobel firmly, and hoped to God it was true.

When she got to the hospital, they told her that Trevor was being X-rayed, but they thought he was all right, it was just a precaution, and she could see the doctor soon.

She sat down to wait, and then suddenly thought of ringing Alan, for it was clear to her that there were going to be repercussions about this attack on Trevor. It couldn't be allowed to pass without anything being done, or anything said. The question was, what would be the best course of action to take? Bringing the police into it might do more harm that good – and threats and intimidation were hard to prove. . . .

Yes, Alan must be told. For he was the one person experienced enough (and fair-minded enough, and cool enough, she added to herself) to know what to do. So she found a telephone and rang him – and of course he responded with instant support, and said he would come to the hospital right away. By the time he arrived, Trevor had just got back from X-ray and the duty doctor was ready to give his report, so Isobel and Alan went to hear his verdict together.

"A couple of cracked ribs," said the Casualty doctor, "a badly wrenched arm and one fractured finger. He must have put out a hand to save himself. And he twisted an ankle too, probably as his foot got caught in a pedal. . . . Apart from that, he has had quite a bang on his head, but there's no hairline fracture, and no internal injuries, so far as we can see. . . ." He looked from Isobel to Alan, wondering what relationship there was between these two concerned people and the injured boy. "He's been lucky, I would say . . . But we'd like to keep him in overnight, just as a precaution."

Alan nodded consent, and Isobel was just about to do the same when Trevor protested from his temporary bed in the casualty cubicle. "I can't! I must go home. What will happen to my Dad, and the kids?"

Isobel glanced from Alan to the doctor, and took a swift decision to be firm about this. The boy badly needed a rest, whatever else, and he would never get it at home. She was tempted to say she would take him home with her, but she knew he would never agree to stay. Here, at least, he might accept hospital care, if they were all decisive enough.

"No, Trevor. You've got to do as the doctor says. We don't know yet how much damage has been done, and you are going to feel very stiff and sore by tomorrow anyway."

"But—"

"I will look after your father and the kids," she added, recklessly promising whatever would keep him safely in hospital for the night. "You don't have to worry about a thing."

Trevor looked at her and sighed. It was too much for him to cope with – all this care and kindness. He wasn't used to it. For

169

too long now, he had been the one giving these things to others without regard for his own needs. Now, suddenly, he realized he could let go. For a little while, other people would deal with his problems. *For a little while*, he could just lie down and sleep. . . . He closed his eyes to hide the tears of shock and relief that threatened to overcome him. "Just . . . till tomorrow," he murmured, for once admitting defeat. But then his eyes flew open again and he said urgently, "The paper-round . . . Mr Harding . . .?"

"We'll tell him," Isobel reassured. "He'll understand."

Trevor shut his eyes again and gave up. He really did feel rather strange and swimmy.

But Alan was not yet ready to let him sleep. "Trevor," he said, "just tell me one thing. Do you know who it was who ran you down?"

"Yes." Trevor's eyes opened reluctantly this time, and fixed themselves anxiously on Isobel's face, not Alan's. "It was Terry Blatchford." He looked painfully into Isobel's worried eyes, as if apologizing for something. "I tried to tell him – to lay off the kids. . . ."

"When was that?" Alan's voice was sharp.

"Yesterday. I – I thought he might listen, and just – just take it out on me instead." He swallowed uneasily. "But he just laughed."

Isobel remembered the woman, Sheila Gregg, saying: *"He was big and dark, and he was laughing . . ."*

"Well, I suppose he did, in a way . . ." added Trevor as an afterthought, with a faint attempt at a grin. "take it out on me, I mean—"

"Trevor, it's a criminal offence," said Alan. "We ought to tell the police."

The boy looked alarmed. "I don't want – it will only make things worse."

"No. It *won't*." Alan's voice was as firm as Isobel's. "We'll make sure of that. Just trust us."

Trevor sighed again, fretfully shaking his head in mute protest. "I do," he admitted, once again attempting a tired smile. "But the Blatchford gang are . . ." He hesitated, as if not quite sure how to describe them. "Tricky," he said at last.

You can say that again, thought Isobel, and looked at

Alan. "It's all right, Trevor," she told him gently. "We'll sort everything out. Go to sleep."

And, with a vague feeling that he was giving way too easily, Trevor did.

"Are we going to the police?" asked Isobel, as they left the hospital.

"Not yet." Alan's mouth was set in a curiously grim line. "I have an idea how to deal with these characters."

Isobel looked at him doubtfully. "How?"

"Call their bluff," he said shortly, and refused to enlarge on it.

"Alan, be careful. They seem to be pretty dangerous people."

He laughed. "Do you know, Isobel, I am too – when roused." But he saw her look of alarm, and hastened to reassure her. "Don't worry – I'll walk warily." His smile was full of cheerful confidence. "What will you do about Cliff and the kids?"

"Probably stay the night," said Isobel, unable to resist smiling back. "Since I promised Trevor to look after them."

He nodded. "That's what I thought. So shall I fetch Trevor back from hospital tomorrow?"

"Yes, if they let him go . . . I'd better hold the fort till you come."

"All right," he assented. But I'll probably look in to report progress before then."

"Aren't you going to tell me any more than that?"

"Not at the moment. You'll have to trust me."

Isobel snorted. "Alan Selwyn, I don't trust you an inch."

"Sorry," he grinned. "Then you'll have to do the other thing," and he gave her a comforting pat on the arm, and got into his car and drove away.

Isobel, full of misgiving, watched him go, and then resolutely climbed into her own car and made her way back to the Broadbents' flat.

Alan's first task was to stop off at Mike Harding's papershop to tell him about Trevor's mishap. But he found that the newsagent knew all about it already, and was full of righteous indignation. He was also, Alan discovered to his surprise,

171

another useful witness, for he had seen the joy-riders go hurtling by, still laughing, just after they had knocked Trevor off his bike – and had recognized Terry Blatchford at the wheel.

"Are you sure of that?" Alan asked, patiently checking his facts.

"Oh yes. No question. I'd know that face anywhere. I've had dealings with him before."

Alan did not try to hide his satisfaction. "That may help a lot."

Mike Harding grunted. "If we could put that yobbo behind bars, we'd be doing the whole neighbourhood a service."

Alan laughed. "You never know – we may manage it yet!"

Then Mike Harding grew serious. "How is young Trevor, then? Is he hurt much?"

"Nothing too serious," Alan told him. "But it might have been. They're keeping him in overnight, just to make sure."

The newsagent shook his head. "Poor kid. He's got enough on his plate already, without that." He paused, and looked at Alan with kindly concern. "Tell him not to worry about the paper-round. Someone else can cover it till he gets back. . . . He won't lose the job. I know he needs it."

Alan smiled. "Thanks. I'll tell him."

"And if he wants that bike repaired, tell him to take it down to Woody's – by the Chinese take-away on the corner. He'll fix it for him – and he'll probably lend him an old one for a day or two, if he needs it."

Alan nodded gratefully. "Thanks again. You've been a great help. Now all I want is Ron Blatchford's address."

Mike looked alarmed. "Asking for trouble, aren't you?"

"Afraid so," admitted Alan, still smiling, albeit a trifle grimly. "Someone's got to call his bluff sometime."

"Rather you than me," Mike said. But he gave him the address nevertheless, with the added admonition, "Mind how you go!"

"Oh, I will," promised Alan, and went cheerfully on his way.

Ron Blatchford lived in an ordinary, respectable-looking house in an ordinary, respectable street that was more than a little up-market from Cliff Broadbent's present address. Alan

172

rang the bell, and wondered whether anyone would be at home at all, or if both Ron and his tearaway son, Terry, would be out pursuing their various nefarious schemes. But Ron Blatchford came to the door himself, looking formidably suspicious.

"Yes?"

"I'm glad to find you in, Mr Blatchford," said Alan pleasantly. "I want to talk to you for a moment about Cliff Broadbent and his son, Trevor, who is currently lying in hospital, having been knocked off his bike by some joy-riders in a stolen car. Can I come in?"

He thought at first that Ron was either going to slam the door in his face, or hit him, but he watched the doubt beginning to grow in the man's belligerent gaze as he tried to work out how much this stranger really knew, and Alan was quick to follow up his advantage. "Is your son, Terry, at home, too?"

Ron glared, but there was uncertainty behind the furious stare. "What's he got to do with it?"

"Quite a lot, I think," said Alan, still sounding extremely smooth and pleasant. "I really do think we should have a little talk, don't you?"

The two men seemed to measure each other up for a long moment, and then Ron stepped ungraciously back and growled, "You'd better come in, then."

He was a big man, Alan observed, and heavy with it – a lot heavier than Alan himself – but he was also rather soft-looking and somewhat out of condition, and Alan was neither . . . I could probably give him as good as I got, Alan thought. But it won't come to that if I play my cards right. He looked again at the flaccid, rather petulant face, the too-long wispy dark hair (receding badly at the edges) and the small, shifty brown eyes that were already a trifle on the defensive, and decided that the man was a has-been whose bullying methods were just a cover-up for weakness. No real threat at all.

"Now then," said Ron, rounding on Alan as soon as they got inside the living-room. "What's all this about?"

"It's about two things, Mr Blatchford, which I think you will agree are connected." Alan paused, taking his time, aware that this sly, rather stupid man was already getting slightly rattled. "The first is Cliff Broadbent, now permanently in a wheelchair, as you know – and a certain fight that took place at the Red Lion

173

on the same night as his mysterious – er – accident. . . ." Once again he paused, watching the small flick of alarm deep down in Ron Blatchford's wary gaze. "And the second, as I have said, is young Trevor Broadbent's accident – if that is the right word for it. Odd, isn't it, that two members of the family should have such bad luck? And the other three children, I am told, have also been set upon by an unruly gang of thugs. Unfortunate, isn't it?"

"What are you suggesting?" Ron's glare was still baleful, but it was less sure of itself.

"I am not suggesting anything, Mr Blatchford. I am merely stating a few facts. First, two separate witnesses have insisted that they recognized your son, Terry, as the driver of a certain stolen Ford Escort when it inexplicably rode down Trevor Broadbent, smashed his bike to pieces, and caused him considerable injury. I'm told he is lucky to be alive – and your son, Terry – if it *was* your son, Terry – is lucky not to be up on a charge of manslaughter, or murder. Of course it could still be GBH or attempted murder, if the evidence is sufficient. . . ." He waited to let his words sink in for a moment, and then continued steadily, "And, referring to the earlier incident, I think you should know that another witness has come forward who can not only identify the other man involved in the fight at the Red Lion, but who also testifies that the fracas continued *as a running fight all down the road.*"

There was a tingling silence while Ron Blatchford absorbed this.

"So?" he said at last, sounding as menacing as possible.

"So I suggest," Alan answered sunnily, "that it might be in everyone's best interests if the Broadbent family did not suffer any more unexpected accidents, or harassments – or anything that might draw attention to their plight – such as rather forceful questions about the state of Cliff Broadbent's health and his renewed ability to talk."

Ron Blatchford's eyes widened at that, as if in shock. "He didn't . . .?" he began.

Alan stared blandly back. "So it was reported to me." He paused, and then added calmly, "As a matter of fact, he is talking again quite well now, and I am sure we *all* wish him a complete recovery." He was still looking at Ron's blank, slightly stunned expression, and smiled again. "Of course, no one knows whether he will ever remember *exactly* what happened that night – *but others may.*"

Ron was doing his best not to get really rattled, though Alan's excessive sweetness did worry him more than he cared to admit. He decided to bluff it out. "I don't know what you're talking about."

"I am talking about the police," said Alan, spelling it out politely. "Young Trevor's accident will probably be reported by someone – there were several witnesses. And one piece of information often leads to another, doesn't it . . .? And I am told that the file on Cliff's earlier accident has never been closed."

"Really?"

"Really," Alan confirmed, and now allowed his voice to get suddenly cold and hard. "And if anything further should happen to any of the Broadbents, I shall, of course, feel obliged to inform the police of *all* these facts at my disposal – if the witnesses don't do it first. No doubt the police will draw their own conclusions." He paused again then, and added softly, "Maybe I should make myself clear, Mr Blatchford – in case Terry or anyone should think of driving a car in the wrong direction again. I have already left a full statement of all these facts with my solicitor, with instructions to pass it on to the police if I should be – er – incapacitated in any way."

The silence this time was almost palpable. "I see," said Ron heavily.

It occurred to Alan then, with a twitch of amusement, that the plausible small-time crook was really at a loss for words. "I'm sure you do," he said, and looked him straight in the eye.

But the big, uneasy man was still truculent. "I don't know who the hell you are," he grumbled.

"No, you don't, do you?" agreed Alan. "But I know you." Then he relented a little. After all, he reasoned, it was better to have things out in the open – and Ron Blatchford was less likely to try anything on now that he understood the situation. Besides, a teacher at a local school, and rather too much in the public eye what with his concerts and his outside teaching, was not a very safe target. He was

175

too well known locally. There would be too many repercussions.

"My name is Alan Selwyn," he said. "I teach at St Swithin's. Young Trevor is a pupil of mine – and I happen to care about the boys in my charge, that's all."

Ron's sliding, unstable gaze settled on Alan's face for a moment with grudging respect. He rather liked a man who stood up to him. "Can't say I'm pleased to meet you," he growled.

Alan grinned. "No. But at least we know where we stand." He regarded his scowling antagonist in a considering, faintly quizzical manner. "You know, it's a funny thing," he said chattily, "Trevor is only trying to protect his dad and keep his family together – and I suppose you could say your Terry is doing the same. Only his methods are rather extreme."

Ron stared at him, saying nothing, but far down in his eyes a faint gleam of recognition stirred.

Alan moved past him then, and turned to go out of the door. "Oh, by the way," he added casually as he crossed the hall, "about the boy's bike . . .?" He stopped and glanced back at Ron with polite enquiry.

"Yeah?" But Ron clearly knew what was coming.

"A replacement would be in order, wouldn't it? Tell Terry to leave it with Mike Harding at the papershop, will you? The boy needs that job." He did not wait for Ron's reply, grudging or otherwise. He simply went out of the door and down the steps without looking back. He thought the job was done now – and not too badly at that. At least they hadn't come to blows. . . . Better not push his luck any further.

Behind him, Ron Blatchford watched him go and did not say a word. He was very confused.

Isobel found the children, as Georgie said, 'managing perfectly well,' and not particularly worried about Trevor's absence. But she fancied that Cliff was not so untroubled as the rest of them, and when she explained that Trevor wouldn't be back till the next day, there was a brief moment when panic loked out of Cliff's eyes. However, he said nothing about how he felt, only asked, rather cautiously, exactly what was happening to Trevor.

176

"Check – up?"

Isobel explained as casually as she could. "His finger needed attention, and there were various bumps and bruises to be looked at. . . . The doctors just want to make sure he's all right before they send him home."

Cliff nodded, accepting it. "Tomorrow?"

"Yes. Tomorrow morning. Alan Selwyn will bring him. And I shall stay here tonight."

"There's no need," protested Georgie indignantly. "I can deal with Dad just as well as Trev."

"I know," Isobel agreed. "But I promised Trevor, you see. He wouldn't stay in hospital unless I did."

Georgie seemed to understand that. "Oh, all right," she said, none too graciously. "But you needn't do anything. *We* can." Then she suddenly smiled and added, "But it's nice if you can just *be* here."

Isobel smiled back, touched that tough young Georgie could make such a concession.

"*Be here,*" agreed Goldie, doing one of her little twirls. "*Be here!*" Then she looked at Isobel very earnestly and said, "Trev *is* coming back, isn't he?"

"Of course," Isobel told her, suddenly realizing that this child was all too aware of the precarious uncertainties of her existence, of the unreliability of people who should have been as solid and safe a part of your life as the sun that shone, but who went away without a word . . . "Of *course,*" Isobel said again, and put an arm round Goldie in a small hug of reassurance. "Tomorrow morning – without fail!"

Colin, who had been watching this small exchange, now turned to his father and said quickly, "Shall we put on a record?"

Cliff nodded and reached down to sort among his old LPs, and finally handed one over to Colin.

"He used to have a proper music centre," Colin remarked to Isobel as he put the record on the turntable, "you know, one that took CDs and tapes and everything. . . ."

"What happened to it?" asked Isobel, and then realized that it was a rather loaded question, and wished she hadn't.

Colin and Georgie looked at each other and then at their father. "Mum sold it," said Georgie shortly.

177

"We needed the money, see!" added Colin, loyally.

"And Dad didn't really want it," explained Georgie. "Not then."

"*Put it on,*" said Cliff, as if closing the conversation.

Colin obliged, and the cheerful strains of Vivaldi filled the room. "He doesn't like the telly, so we don't have it on much," explained Colin, under cover of the music. "He says the people drive him mad, they talk so much. And football only drives him even madder!" He grinned at Isobel. "But he likes the music programmes on radio."

Isobel nodded. "More peaceful?"

Colin agreed, waving vaguely at the spinning record. "This always calms him down."

"Don't you others miss the telly?" asked Isobel, wondering how a young, modern family managed to get on without it, and whether it affected their conversations with their friends, and their lack of knowledge of the current jokes and crazes.

Colin shrugged. "Not much. Too busy . . . Goldie likes the music to dance to, anyway, and Trev makes us all play the tunes, to keep in practice. . . ." He made a slight, humorous grimace, and added slyly, "And Georgie just falls about laughing at the sexy bits and makes us turn it off!"

Isobel's own mouth began to twitch with laughter then, but before the Four Seasons had wound their vigorous way to the end, Alan arrived, bearing fish and chips for everyone, accompanied by a wide smile of reassurance.

"All's well," he told Isobel, under cover of the general chatter. "I don't think there'll be any more trouble. . . . Talk about it later."

Isobel nodded, and went on doling out chips to everyone in sight. But Georgie's ears were much too sharp, and she went after Alan as he dived into the kitchen to fetch another plate.

"What did you mean – no more trouble?" she demanded.

Alan looked at that clever little face, and knew he couldn't lie to it. "I went to see Ron Blatchford," he said quietly. "It's all right. I think he's got the message."

"What message?" She was still confronting him, hands on her hips like a small fishwife.

Alan smiled. "Don't look like that. I'm on *your* side, remember?" But he saw the anxiety still in her eyes, and went on reassuringly, "We think Terry and his gang were mixed up in Trevor's bike accident – but it won't happen again – any of it."

"Why not?"

"Because Terry went too far this time, and it's a police matter. Ron doesn't want any trouble – not of *that* kind, so he'll make sure Terry toes the line from now on. OK?"

She looked at him hard, wondering whether to believe him, and whether a nice, kind man like Mr Selwyn could have any idea how dangerous and slippery a customer Terry Blatchford was . . . Georgie was used to street life and gang warfare – or she had been until Trevor got tough and made her stay in. And in a way, she was more streetwise than her brother, though she never told him so. There were bullies at school, and sometimes on the way home, too – but she could deal with those. She had learned how to kick back, and one of the older boys who rather liked her had taught her a couple of judo tricks . . . She was well able to take care of herself, and of Colin and Goldie, too, if the need arose. But Terry Blatchford and his gang were different. To begin with, they were older and tougher than she was – much older and much tougher – and they were sly with it. You never knew when they would turn up out of nowhere, or what they would do. Even Trevor, who was clever *and* strong, couldn't really deal with them, not if they all came at him at once. . . .

And now, Mr Selwyn thought he had persuaded them to lay off – got the whole thing sewn up, he said. . . . Well, she hoped he was right, that's all.

"OK," she answered at last, realizing she had taken a very long time to respond. Then her singularly vivid smile flashed out and she added cheerfully, "Thanks!" and went to fill up the kettle for some more tea all round.

But Alan saw and understood her doubts, and hoped to God he had really got through to the Blatchfords, and that the uneasy truce would last.

"Come on," said Colin, hovering in the doorway, and well aware that serious matters had been discussed. "Your chips are getting cold."

Trevor came home the next morning, as promised, with a

rather bruised face and his arm in a sling, but seeming unexpectedly relaxed and cheerful. That this was due more to Alan's handling of the situation than the doctor's, Isobel was certain, but she said nothing to Alan at the time. It was enough to see the boy smiling and apparently over the shock.

He went straight across to his father, and the two pairs of eyes met in mutual enquiry. "You all right?" asked Trevor.

Cliff nodded. "You?"

"I'm fine," Trevor lied cheerfully, and promptly took off his sling and waved his arm about to demonstrate.

"Those docs'll be after you!" scolded Georgie, and promptly put it on for him again.

"Who's boss around here?" growled Trevor.

Colin and Georgie laughed, while Goldie pranced up and down chanting, "*Who's boss? Who's boss?*"

"I am this morning," said Alan, sounding surprisingly firm. "And I decree that we all sit down and discuss the trip to the sea, over coke and sticky buns provided by Trevor and me." And he winked at Georgie and handed her a bulging carrier bag.

"*Sticky buns and coke, sticky buns and coke!*" lilted Goldie, who couldn't resist making a song about everything.

"And after that," went on Alan, "Mizzibell and I will leave you all in peace – provided you all wait on Trevor hand and foot and make him go to bed early."

"That'll be the day!" snorted Georgie.

"How?" queried Colin practically.

"*Hand and foot,*" danced Goldie, demonstrating wildly. "*Hand and foot!*"

"Who's going to make me?" glared Trevor.

And to everyone's surprise, Cliff laughed, and said in a new, deep voice of command, "I am."

Alan and Isobel glanced at one another. It seemed to them that the little family was suddenly happy – and their closeness and reliance on each other seemed to create an atmosphere of touching warmth.

"Monday," said Alan, knowing that he and Isobel ought to go now, while this glow of happiness lasted. "Ten o'clock sharp. All right?"

He looked at Cliff for confirmation, and received a smiling nod of consent. "All – right."

180

"All right, Trevor?"

Trevor also nodded, smiling.

"All right, you guys?" He glanced round at the other three, innocently enquiring.

"All right!" they choroused, and Goldie threatened to do another twirl, but Colin restrained her.

"Good – then we'll be off," Alan said, and signalled several things at once to Isobel as he got to his feet. "And take it easy, Trevor – that's an order!"

"Yes, sir," said Trevor meekly, but he was still smiling. Then he looked at Isobel, who had been taking care of his family for him so calmly and kindly, and had received no word of thanks. "I wish—" he began.

But Isobel forestalled him. "You won't have your bike, Trevor, but if you could call in on Saturday, we've got things to discuss."

She saw an expression of relief come into his eyes. He need not say anything. She understood anyway.

"Yes," he said quietly. "I will."

And Isobel followed Alan out of the door.

"You'd better tell me what you've been up to," said Isobel severely, as they sat over their usual glass of wine in their usual wine bar.

"All right," agreed Alan equably. "I will." And he did.

Isobel listened intently, her face unguardedly expressing her concern at the risks he had been taking. "Do you think it'll do any good?" she asked, getting to the heart of the matter at once.

Alan looked at her seriously. "Yes – for a time. I think Ron Blatchford was genuinely shocked to hear what Terry had been up to – especially the questions about Cliff *talking*. . . . It was clearly news to him – and I got the impression he was really rather scared of any police enquiries – especially about Cliff's accident." His straight glance held Isobel's with quiet determination. "Isobel, I think you've got to get Trevor to tell you what he knows . . . I'm sure he's holding something back."

Isobel sighed. "Yes, I think so, too. I'll see what I can do." Then she returned to the most urgent question. "What about the police?"

181

Alan was still looking at her, but now his glance shifted a little, and he answered quietly, "I think you should report it now – rather late. Tell them you didn't know a car was involved until Trevor was able to tell you."

She sighed. "That's true, at least."

"And you could add that Trevor was afraid of repercussions if he reported it. They're used to that round here."

"Will that help?"

"It'll add another notch to the Blatchford gang tally. They're bound to find out who was driving, one way or another – even if Trevor doesn't tell them, the other witnesses probably will. It'll be too late to pin it on Terry – this time. But all these things add up."

Isobel nodded, but she still looked doubtful. "Will they want to question Trevor? I don't want him harried."

"My guess is, they'll do nothing – unless anyone is going to press charges. They have a mass of such incidents to follow up. But if they do, you can always ask them to see the boy at your house, and tell them about his invalid dad, if they don't know already."

Isobel agreed to that – it made sense, after all. "Will you – could you be there too?"

He shook his head. "Better not. I'd better keep a low profile – considering my so-called pact with Ron Blatchford." He saw her dubious expression and tried to reassure her. Isobel was always too painfully honest. "We have those witnesses, Isobel. We can always call on them later, if need be. I just feel that it's better to keep the Blatchfords guessing at present than to pounce on them too soon."

Isobel shook her head at him. "Alan Selwyn, you're a devious and dangerous man. I don't think I know you at all!"

"Just as well," he grinned. "But I really am on the side of the angels."

"I know that," said Isobel, and suddenly smiled back.

They were still sitting there, smiling rather foolishly at one another, when Isobel remembered it was Friday.

"Gervase night!" she exclaimed. "And I nearly forgot it again. I must go shopping. Do you want to come to supper too?"

"I don't think so," Alan said, though there was regret in his

182

voice. "The fur nearly flew last time, and if he thinks I've got you mixed up in all this Blatchford business, he'll be more disapproving than ever!"

Isobel laughed. "But you didn't have anything to do with it."

"I know," Alan agreed. "But I do now!"

Isobel looked at him with sudden concern. "Alan – I hope you haven't laid yourself open to real danger?" There was an anxious question behind her quiet voice.

"I doubt it," He sounded quite cheerful. "Ron Blatchford doesn't want trouble any more than I do. Don't worry!"

Isobel smiled at his confident certainty, but she was not entirely convinced. "Well, mind how you go," she said as she set off in search of supper for Gervase.

"And you mind how you go with that predatory old book-seller!" retorted Alan, laughing. And when he saw her outraged expression, he added gently, "I'll come round tomorrow afternoon to hear how you got on, shall I?"

"Yes," smiled Isobel. "Do that," and she went off, curiously heartened by the laughter in his gentle voice.

Chapter Eleven

'The Little House Under the Hill'

Old Jig

It was Archimedes who found the solution – though he didn't know it. But then he was in no position to show off his extraordinary sagacity at the time. He got lost.

Isobel did not worry very much when he didn't come in for his supper. He was often a bit late on these beguiling spring evenings. But when the leisurely evening with Gervase was drawing to its usual close, the Scrabble game over, and the last coffee and brandy consumed – and Archimedes still hadn't returned – she began to wonder where he had got to.

"I'll give him another call in the garden," she said, and went out into the warm, starless night and stood on the lawn and called.

Gervase had followed her, and now also stood peering into the shadows among the shrubs at the end of the garden wall. He liked cats. He had two of his own who were supposed to keep the mice down in the shop, and he was, if anything, more concerned than Isobel. They both called again, but nothing stirred in the garden.

"Oh well," said Isobel, turning back to the lighted sitting-room, whose French windows stood open to the soft spring air, "I expect he'll turn up when he wants to," and she went inside again, with Gervase beside her, and closed the windows.

"Wait a minute," Gervase said, stopping suddenly just inside the room. "I thought I heard something."

Isobel stopped too, and listened intently.

"There!" said Gervase, triumphantly. "Can't you hear it?"

And Isobel, still listening hard, thought she could detect a faint meow coming from somewhere.

"It sounds as if it's right under our feet," said Gervase, puzzled. "Could he have got trapped under the floorboards? Or do you have a cellar?"

"The basement!" exclaimed Isobel. "Why didn't I think of it before?" And she hurried out into the hall and went over to a tall, narrow door concealed in the dark alcove beneath the staircase. "But it's never used," she said, wrenching open the wooden door which stuck a little in its frame. "I can't imagine how he could have got down there. . . ." She reached inside the door for the light switch, and a flood of pale amber light disclosed a downward-slanting flight of steps flanked by yellowish painted walls. "Where are you, Archie?" she called. "Are you down there?"

There was a relieved answering chirrup – a cross between a complaint and a purr – and the big black cat streaked up the steps and rubbed himself happily against Isobel's legs.

"Well, that's all right then," said Gervase, sounding pleased and a shade complacent because he had been the one who heard the cat first. "You naughty puss, frightening your mistress like that," and he stooped to fondle the velvet ears.

Isobel did not tell him that she had been much more frightened by Trevor's accident, and by Alan's deliberate courting of danger in the Blatchford affair. In fact, she had told Gervase nothing about it at all. Not even when he said (somewhat pettishly) "I tried to ring you last night, just to confirm this evening's supper – but you were out."

"Yes," Isobel told him calmly. "I was out last night." And did not enlarge on it.

But now, here was soft-hearted Gervase, all pleased and rosy about finding her cat, about to go home in a comfortable glow of achievement, and she had no intention of disturbing his mellow mood by even mentioning her own private anxieties.

"I must go now," said Gervase. "Busy day tomorrow. A very pleasant evening, Isobel – and a happy ending, too! Good-night!"

"Good-night!" echoed Isobel, and watched him go down the front steps and out into the quiet night. But behind her eyes she saw the lurching, battered figure of Trevor

185

struggling up the steps towards her and collapsing in a heap at the door. . . .

"Now," she said, turning away and shutting the door on all the phantoms of the night, "let's see what you've discovered, you clever cat." And she went back to the open wooden door beneath the stairs, switched on the light again and descended the steps to the forgotten basement below.

It had been converted to a self-contained flat once, long before Isobel came to live there, and the original fittings were still in place – plain and out-of-date, but functional. There was a biggish, old-fashioned kitchen, opening into what had once been a scullery, with a modern cooker and sink at one end, a smallish, shabby bathroom and adjoining lavatory, and three other moderate-sized rooms that had probably originally been store rooms and larders and laundry rooms. But they would make perfectly adequate bedrooms, Isobel told herself – and the big kitchen would make a very reasonable living-room, especially if the adjoining scullery was screened off to make the kitchen separate but easily reachable with a wheelchair. . . .

The only trouble was the access. The stairs from the ground floor were impossible. The front of the basement looked out on to an enclosed area with steep sides, a formidable pile of rocks pretending to be a rock garden, and more steep steps up to the garden level. But I could build a ramp, Isobel said to herself. That's it – a ramp. Get rid of all those heavy stones – slope the ground up gently – let in some light, and make a long, gentle ramp up to the lawn . . . and from the lawn I could build another ramp outside my French windows, also reachable from the lawn. And it's level ground from there out into the street. . . .

But it's very dark, she thought, looking round and shivering a little. Could it be made pleasant enough to live in? Would white paint all round be enough? And would the slopes for the ramp let enough light in through the windows? It's very shut in at present.

There were dozens of questions to be answered – but a slow, growing excitement was building up inside her, and she gave a small twirl of enthusiasm (rather like Goldie) as her thoughts began to take shape. It might work, she thought. It might be the answer. There would be a lot to plan, a lot to do, but it might be feasible. . . .

"What do you think, Archie?" she said to the handsome black statue sitting on the bottom step. "Would it do?"

Archimedes looked a bit supercilious about it, and made a curious growling noise and rubbed his eyes with one immaculate paw.

"You are quite right," said Isobel, smiling. "We'd better sleep on it. We can ask Alan tomorrow."

And she followed the cat up the stairs, and put out the light.

Trevor arrived on Saturday morning a little later than usual, still looking rather bruised and white-faced, but with a kind of glow about him that Isobel did not quite expect.

"Guess what," he said as soon as he got inside the door, "I've just been down to see Mike Harding about the job, and he says all his customers have clubbed together to pay for a week's sick leave for me!"

Isobel beamed with pleasure. "That's wonderful!"

"And that's not all," Trevor went on, still glowing. "Some total stranger walked into Woody's shop and told him to let me have whatever new bike I chose, to replace the old one. But Mr Harding says I can't have it till the end of the week because I'm not fit to ride a bike yet, but I can go down and fetch it next Saturday if I promise to behave myself this week, and then I'll be ready for work again!"

He had been talking so fast and with so much excitement that he was out of breath, and Isobel couldn't get a word in edgeways. But now he subsided, breathless and happy, on to his usual chair in the kitchen and looked at Isobel with his clear, intelligent gaze.

"I suppose it's all Mr Selwyn's doing, isn't it? He told me he'd been to see Ron Blatchford . . . and – and sort of hinted at various things!"

Isobel nodded, smiling, and put a cup of tea in front of him. "Yes, he did. And it seems to have had results!"

Trevor grinned. Then he grew more serious, as he thought of the various implications of Alan's confrontation with that tricky rogue Ron Blatchford.

187

"Do you think it will work – what Mr Selwyn said to him, I mean? Will he really get Terry to lay off bothering us?"

"I think so, yes," said Isobel, trying to sound entirely certain. "Alan Selwyn seemed to think Ron Blatchford didn't want any more trouble – especially with the police."

She handed Trevor a chocolate biscuit and waited to see whether she had convinced him.

He glanced up at her a shade anxiously. "Do you think the police will try to follow it up?"

Here, Isobel knew, she had to tread even more cautiously. "They may want to hear your account of the accident – just for the record. But Alan thinks they'll do nothing else until the next time – unless we want to press charges. And he doesn't think we've got enough evidence for that." She smiled at him encouragingly. "But he certainly did put the fear of God into Ron Blatchford!"

"It was pretty brave of him, I think," said Trevor. "Could have been nasty."

She agreed with that soberly, and then looked into Trevor's face with searching attention. It was hard to have to quench that cheerful glow with awkward questions about the past – but there were things she needed to know about Blatchford and Cliff Broadbent – especially if the police might be coming to question him.

"Trevor," she said at last, "I hate to bother you about a whole lot of past history – but it may be important. What was the trouble between Ron Blatchford and your father – do you know?"

Trevor's bright gaze clouded a little, but he seemed to understand why Isobel was asking, and did not refuse to answer. "I don't know a lot," he said slowly. "They didn't tell me – but I – I couldn't help overhearing some of it." He hesitated, not quite knowing where to start.

"Go on," prompted Isobel gently.

He glanced up at her, struggling again with his own painful honesty, and his loyalty to his family. "Well, it began before – before we lost the house. Money had got more and more difficult. Mum simply couldn't manage to pay the mortgage payments as well as everything else. She kept on at Dad about spending too much down at the pub, and he kept saying he'd go mad if he didn't, and anyway she was a bad manager. . . ." He paused again, and then added in a small, shamed voice, "There were terrible rows . . . I used to come home from school and hear them shouting at each other . . . and sometimes Dad – well, he got rough. . . ." He stopped then for a moment, looking back into those times of darkness, and then seemed to shake them from him. Miss Isobel wanted to know. Then he would tell her.

"I knew Mum was desperate. She'd sold almost everything that would fetch any cash – including the big telly and the video and the camcorder, and Dad's music centre – and that caused another row. . . . But she had to . . . and so she borrowed some money from Ron Blatchford."

"I see," breathed Isobel, light beginning to dawn.

Trevor looked away from her now, remembering how things were with a kind of bitter clarity. "It was all right at first – but she still couldn't manage on Dad's dole money, and she got more into debt . . . and Ron Blatchford kept coming round and bothering her. . . . She told me about it once, and said, 'Trev, never get to owe more than you've got. It's *awful*.'" He sighed a little. "So then we lost the house and moved into the flat – and Mum sold a whole lot more things and tried to pay off Mr Blatchford. But he kept on coming round and – and sort of hinting that he'd be easy about the money if she was nice to him. . . ." His glance reflected a sardonic awareness of the uneasy pressures of the adult world. "And Dad began to get – well, *jealous*, I suppose – though there was no need to be. Mum hated Ron Blatchford. But Dad wouldn't believe her. . . ." He looked helplessly at Isobel. "You can see how it was . . .?"

"Yes," Isobel agreed. "I can."

"Dad has a – a rather short fuse," Trevor explained, trying as usual to make excuses for him. "He didn't understand what was happening – and he got an absolute thing about Mum seeing Ron Blatchford. . . . He kept on and on at her . . . and then – that night – the night of his accident, they'd been arguing about it again, and he stormed off, saying he was going to teach Ron a lesson. . . ." He stopped again there, as if he had said enough, and indeed he almost had, for Isobel could see the picture very clearly.

189

"I don't know what happened," Trevor said slowly. "But if they had a fight . . .? Dad could be quite – quite violent, especially when he was drunk. . . ." The young voice was somehow cold with knowledge. "And Ron Blatchford was the same. . . ."

Isobel laid a hand on his arm. "That's enough. I've got the picture."

Trevor looked at her with a kind of sad understanding. "My bet is, it was just a fight that went wrong. Not anything *on purpose.*"

She nodded again. "I expect you're right."

"It won't do Dad any good to bring it all up again now," he added, sounding old and wise and rather weary.

There was something else Isobel wanted to know – about those months in the flat with their mother, Katie, and the final row – if row it was – that drove her away . . . But looking into that stoical, tired young face, she knew she could not ask about it now. He had had enough of all those dark memories for one day.

She was just about to pour out another cup of tea when the doorbell rang, and she left Trevor alone for a moment's respite while she went to answer it.

A young policewoman stood there, looking shy and decidedly unthreatening. She approached Isobel with an apologetic smile. "PC Janice Brown. I believe you have young Trevor Broadbent here with you – is that right?"

"Yes. He's here."

"Could I see him for a few moments?"

"Of course. Come in." She led the young woman into the kitchen, and signalled reassuringly to Trevor not to get up. "Would you like a cup of tea?" she suggested, making everything seem as normal as possible. "You can see that Trevor is a bit the worse for wear – so we're taking it easy this morning." It was a warning, clearly given, and the policewoman did not fail to understand it.

"I'd love a cup of tea," she said, smiling at Trevor. "This won't take long. I just want your version of what happened to you. Is that all right?"

Trevor nodded. "I can tell you up to when I got knocked off the bike. The rest is rather hazy!"

190

"I'm listening," she said, and got out her notebook.

So Trevor went through it again, and once again the vital question was asked, "Did you see who was driving the car?"

"Oh yes," Trevor told her quite calmly. "It was Terry Blatchford. He even called out something – and he was laughing. . . ." But then his innate fairness took over suddenly and he added, "I think it was just a joke – only it went wrong. He probably didn't see there was nowhere left for me to go but into the railings!"

Isobel looked at him in surprise. But she didn't say anything.

"I wonder – could we look at the place where it happened? Is it far from here?" the policewoman asked.

"No. A few yards," said Isobel. "He just about staggered to my door." She grinned encouragingly at Trevor. "And you can see the bits of bike, too, if you like?"

"You really should have left the bicycle on the spot, and called the police straight away," said the policewoman severely, though she was half smiling at Trevor.

"I wasn't in a state to call anyone," he answered. "And Miss Isobel was. . . ." he hesitated then, clearly not wanting to get her into trouble.

"I was too concerned about getting him to hospital to think of anything else," admitted Isobel.

"Well, it's too late now," Janice Brown told them resignedly. "Let's look at that bike, shall we?"

So the three of them went and inspected the wrecked bicycle, and then went on to the bent railings by the little town square, and Janice Brown looked up and down the road and said, "Did you see which way they went afterwards?"

"No," Trevor answered, grinning. "I was all of a heap by then."

Isobel wondered whether the nice young woman, Sheila Gregg, would come out of the house again to corroborate Trevor's story, but she didn't, and, remembering Alan's curious deal with Ron Blatchford, Isobel did not mention it. Better wait to use that weapon when it was needed.

"Well, I think that will do for the moment," said the young policewoman, smiling again at Trevor. "You've been very co-operative. I hope you get well soon." She turned to Isobel and added: "Thank you for your help," and went briskly off to her car and drove away.

"Phew!" said Trevor. "I'm glad that's over. Did I do all right?"

"Fine," said Isobel. "But what possessed you to say it was just a joke?"

"I don't know." He sounded vaguely puzzled himself, and then added drily, "It probably was, to him."

They looked at each other, and both began to laugh.

"Well," said Isobel, still smiling, "it's another nail in his coffin. They'll catch him in the end!"

And they went off, companionably, to have yet another cup of tea.

Isobel had not dared to mention the idea of the basement flat to Trevor yet. There were so many questions to be answered – so many drawbacks to be overcome – and she was still not at all sure that the place could be made habitable or suitable for a wheelchair. Better talk to Alan first and see what he thought of the idea. At least he would be able to point out the snags, and be fair enough to consider the advantages with an open mind. If she tried to ask Gervase about it, there would be fireworks – and she didn't want to quarrel with Gervase again.

So she waited with some impatience until Alan arrived, and then launched into a careful account of all that Trevor had said about the trouble between Cliff Broadbent and Ron Blatchford.

Alan listened attentively, and nodded comprehension. "I thought it must be something like that. As a matter of fact, I'm glad it was nothing more serious than a bit of male jealousy – that makes it less likely that Ron Blatchford was taking conscious revenge. . . . I think Trevor's right – it was probably just a fight that went wrong." He paused, thinking about it, and then added soberly, "But Cliff was left lying down those steps all night without help – and that might well be on Ron's conscience, too."

Isobel agreed, and then told him what Trevor had said to the nice young policewoman, Janice Brown. "She seemed reasonably satisfied," she told him, "and our vital witness didn't come forward, so I didn't push it."

Alan grinned approval. "It may seem wrong to let Terry get away with it this time, but I think it may be safer for the kids."

"Oh, that reminds me," Isobel added, "He's already come up with a new bicycle. Isn't that rather soon?"

Alan laughed. "He was in a bit of a cleft stick, you know. If he ignored my suggestion, he would expect us to go to the police and press charges and sue for compensation – much more costly than one bike. But if he agreed, he was more-or-less admitting that Terry was responsible." He looked at Isobel, eyes bright with amusement. "He must be more scared of the police than I thought!"

Isobel laughed too, then, though she was still not entirely happy about the situation. There was something unresolved and a bit ominous about the whole Blatchford affair, and it bothered her. Then she thought of the basement flat, and decided it was time to talk about it.

"Alan, I want to show you something – and I want you to use all your soundest judgement and your most far-seeing wisdom to help me decide about it. Will you?"

"That's a tall order," said Alan, smiling. "And very flattering!"

"But *will you*?" Isobel persisted.

"Of course," he said, still smiling. "How could I refuse?" He was looking at her rather quizzically. "What is it, Isobel? You're like a small girl with a secret."

"Come with me," said Isobel. "It's really all Archie's fault." And she led the way to the warped wooden door under the stairs.

They went down the steps together, and Isobel began to talk in a kind of breathless explanation long before they got to the empty rooms below.

"I don't know why I didn't think of it before," she said. "I had thought about the attic rooms – they are hardly ever used – but the access is impossible there, and anyway, I didn't think they'd like being on top of me, as it were. . . ." She took another breath. "They do so need to be independent. But down here, they could be. If I could fix the access and make the place habitable. It would need more light – and ramps and things—"

"Hold on," said Alan, beginning to get the drift. "Let's consider this slowly, shall we? Are we talking about the Broadbents?"

"Of course."

He grinned. "Well, go on – where shall we start?"

Isobel sighed with relief. He understood her at once, and didn't seem to want to throw out the whole idea as ridiculous. (Or preposterous. She could imagine Gervase saying it.)

"It's the outside that matters most," she explained. "If we could get all those rocks shifted, and make a long, shallow ramp up into the garden. . . . It would mean moving quite a lot of earth to make the slope gentler – and that would bring in more light. . . . And then we could make another ramp into the house through my french windows, if we wanted them to come in and see us sometimes. But once they could get the wheelchair up and down to the garden, they could reach the road and take Cliff anywhere. There's a side gate they could use. . . ."

He nodded, and stood looking out of the dusty window at the glimpses of green garden above the rampart of offending rocks. "It's possible. . . ." he agreed slowly.

"We needn't bother about the front entrance to the basement at all – the steps down are too steep, and there's no room for a long ramp out into the street," Isobel went on. "But we could paint it all white to let in a bit more light, and stick in a few pots of geraniums or something. What do you think?"

"I think you'd better ask your bank manager first."

She laughed. "Oh, that's no problem. I've got more than enough money for my own needs – and nothing much else to spend it on." She looked at Alan questioningly, sensing his doubt. "What's the matter? Don't you think it would work?"

Alan hesitated. "It's not that, Isobel. It's whether you ought to take on all this. It may make a lot of difference to your own peace and quiet. Are you sure you want to do it?"

"Of course I'm sure," snapped Isobel. "I've been thinking about it all night! It's just the question of whether it would be feasible – and whether they would like it."

Alan sighed. He could see that Isobel was not going to be dissuaded – at least not by arguments about her own interrupted lifestyle. "Would you charge them rent?" he asked.

Isobel had thought of that, too. "Yes. They wouldn't come otherwise. But the housing people have already said they'd pay the rent if I found somewhere suitable."

"Suitable is the operative word," said Alan. "They'd have to come round and approve it."

"Well, it couldn't be much less suitable than the one they've got now, could it?" Isobel retorted. "Let 'em come. They can tell me where to put the ramps, and handles on the bath and so on. . . . Bring them into the scheme right away. They won't say no then – especially if I am offering to do all the conversion."

Alan looked at her with humorous despair. "You've got it all worked out, haven't you?"

"Not all," she told him briskly. "Come and look at the rooms properly. . . . There are three that would make quite good bedrooms – especially if we brought the kids' bunk beds with them. . . . And the big kitchen could be the living-room, if we put in a sort of breakfast bar screening off the scullery and make that into the cooking area . . . and the bathroom isn't bad. Of course it all wants a coat of paint." She led him from room to room, and finally out into the garden, where they stood together looking down at the steps beyond the pile of rocks and the formidable drop where the ramp should be.

"The kids would love the garden . . ." she murmured, looking down the expanse of her tidy green lawns. "And Cliff, too . . . Imagine them all able to get out here into the sun whenever they liked. . . ."

"It would be the end of peace for you," he said, but he could not disguise the smile in his eyes when he saw her wistful look.

"Oh, *peace!*" she snorted. "Life's meant for living – not avoiding!" She turned to him then, her face challenging and bright with resolve. "Well – what's the verdict? Shall I do it or not?"

Alan shook his head at her. "How can I answer that? It's your life – and your decision."

"But you'll help me, if I do it?"

He laughed helplessly. "Isobel, you know I will. But you must ask the housing people for their opinion first – and then you'll have to ask Trevor and his father. And then you'll have to get an estimate on the cost of all this – especially the ramps. It may come to more than you think . . . And after all that, if it's still possible and everyone wants to go ahead, I'll do everything in the world I can to make it work."

"But – do you approve?"

He looked at her then, a warm, smiling look of approval. "I think it's a wonderful idea – and only you would be crazy enough to suggest it!"

"Oh, that's all right, then," said Isobel, as if the whole thing had been solved there and then. "Now let's go and plan this day by the sea . . . Alan, let's make it a *simply splendid* day! They all need a break so much."

"Right," said Alan, tucking his arm through hers and strolling back with her towards the house. "A splendid day it shall be."

And they went indoors, heads together, already deep in cheerful plans.

Chapter Twelve

'Scatter the Mud'

Double Jig

It was one of those blue and gold days with racing clouds and seagulls careening on the wind, sunshine and shadow on the sands, the sea looking nearly blue and the tide nearly in, so that the vast expanse of estuary mud was covered in shallow sparkles of light. It was one of those days that somehow made the heart lift, and even the most sober person feel like doing something silly.

Isobel wasn't a sober person, and nor was Alan, come to that, so they were quite prepared for the most absurd happenings to overtake them, and they did.

First of all, there was a small, fierce hailstorm out of a bright, innocent sky, and when Isobel put up her umbrella, the wind blew it inside out and she nearly took off like Mary Poppins. The kids didn't seem to mind the hail, in fact Goldie danced in it, lifting her face to the sky, and Trevor simply tucked the rug more firmly round Cliff's knees and laughed.

Then Cliff's wheelchair got stuck in a grating at the edge of the promenade, and the Likely Lads (who had insisted on coming too, 'in case') had an awful job to get it moving again. But while they were manoeuvring it back onto firmer ground, a band came marching by, cornets braying like mad, and they seized Cliff's chair and swept him and the Likely Lads along with them, and went marching on, with Cliff riding at their head like a triumphant soldier coming home from war.

Goldie took one delighted look, and danced to the music all the way along the promenade, and the other three, having exchanged helpless glances, followed in the procession, with

197

Trevor keeping an anxious eye on Cliff's chair in case it got tipped over in the excitement. Alan and Isobel simply followed after. What else could they do?

At length the band arrived at its appointed spot for the ensuing concert and smilingly released Cliff from their clutches – but not before someone had given him a balloon and a huge swirl of candyfloss which he promptly gave to Goldie.

"Phew!" said Alan, casting a swift glance at Cliff to see whether he was too shaken up by all the unusual goings-on. "I thought you were being kidnapped!"

"Kidnapped!" twirled Goldie. "Dad's being kidnapped!"

At that point, the band struck up '*O what a beautiful morning,*' with trumpets and trombones at full blast, and everyone – including Isobel – began to sing. They hadn't got much further than '*Everything's going my way,*' when a clown stepped out of the crowd and politely gave Isobel a red nose, so she put it on, and her singing voice came out in a sort of nasal croak, which reduced the rest of the party to helpless laughter.

"Ice-creams," said Alan. "After exercising your vocal cords, eat lots of ice-cream. All the best singers do."

"We'll get them," volunteered the Likely Lads, beaming with goodwill (and primed with a surreptitious donation by Alan). "Will Cliff be all right here in the sun? It's sheltered from the wind."

They looked from Cliff to Trevor enquiringly, and then at Alan and Isobel for confirmation, but it was Cliff who spoke. "Be – fine – here . . . Warm!"

By now, the tide had come in as far as it ever did, and the three younger children had already got down to the beach and were running down to the edge of the water to have a look. Trevor did not find it easy to leave his father, still feeling vaguely uncertain about his safety, and hovered a little awkwardly by his side. Isobel thought the boy looked a little grey and tired today, and guessed that those cracked ribs of his were still hurting him a bit.

Alan, meanwhile, had found some deck chairs from somewhere, and even a windbreak, and was busy setting them up in a comfortable little group round Cliff.

"Can we paddle?" asked Goldie, rushing back to them to ask

permission, but she was already pulling off shoes and socks, eyes alight with adventure. And Colin and Georgie were not far behind. There followed a lot of splashing and laughing, until Goldie put one foot in some true Weston-super-Mare mud and brought it up looking as if it had been dipped in melted chocolate.

"Choc-ice?" called one of the Likely Lads, balancing a variety of ice-cream cones and tubs and packets.

"Better than mud any day!" added the other, grinning, and gave Goldie the first choice.

After that it was cricket on the beach, and then football, and then someone produced a boomerang which Alan had bought at one of the beach shops, and it came back and hit him on the head. Everyone played and ran about laughing, including Isobel and Alan, and even Trevor, though he moved with some caution – and they kept Cliff in the middle of their games so that he got things to throw from time to time and didn't get left out. Goldie, in particular, was most insistent that her father should be part of the fun.

And there *were* donkey rides. Isobel rejoiced secretly, and set about organizing things for the three children. Trevor refused, saying the jolts might jar his ribs, but he stayed to watch the others, and smiled to see Goldie trying to persuade her placid mount to race Georgie's and Colin's.

"Coffee now," announced Alan, as if producing a rabbit out of a hat, and promptly did produce a picnic basket and a large thermos. "If we're going to be trippers," he said, grinning, "we might as well do it properly."

The wind seemed to die down then, though there were still seagulls tilting their wings into the blue air above their heads, and the sun came out brighter than ever and felt warm on their faces.

Cliff had been following the donkey rides with his eyes, but now he was looking straight out to sea – as far as the curve of the estuary would let him – and his expression was rapt and lit with distance.

"Ireland . . . over there?" he said.

Alan nodded, keeping things cheerful. "Wales first, and then Ireland – and then America!"

But it was Ireland Cliff was looking for across the sea, Isobel knew. Ireland, and nowhere else. . . .

I wonder where she is, she thought, that young woman whom everyone misses and needs so badly? Where is she? Why doesn't she come home?

The Likely Lads came back then, from some foray of their own, bringing a whole batch of toffee apples they had found on a stall – and from the other side of the beach there came a brown-skinned gypsy woman in a bright headscarf, carrying sprigs of white heather for luck.

"There you are, luv," she said to Cliff, and laid the white sprig on his knee. "Heather from across the water brings the roamer home." And she went on walking away across the beach, not asking for any payment.

Isobel and Alan looked at each other, but it was the kind of day for strange happenings, and they saw that Cliff was holding the heather in his hand but not looking really surprised, and his eyes were still far and fixed on the sunlit horizon.

In the afternoon, someone suggested the amusement arcade at the end of the pier, but to Isobel's surprise, the children refused to leave the beach, and Trevor explained carefully that they were a bit wary of those sort of places because they were where gangs like the Blatchford boys were apt to hang about. . . . It was only a hint of the tightrope of caution that the Broadbent children had learnt to walk, but it troubled Isobel, and she wished she had not mentioned the pier at all.

But then the Likely Lads came back from yet another foray and announced that there was a small fun fair set up for the Easter holidays, and it looked like being a lot of fun. So then it was the dodgems, and the Tunnel of Terror, and the Fantasy Ride, not to mention the rifle range and the coconut shy and the bowling alley. . . . They tried everything, and Alan won a china pig, while Colin won six free goes on the rifle range, and Georgie won a green plush dinosaur on the pinball game, and Goldie got given a fluffy pink rabbit simply for standing there and looking wistful. (She was good at that.) And Trevor persuaded Cliff to try throwing rings on to hooks, and his prize was (surprisingly) a string of Spanish onions.

"Come in useful for tea," said Georgie, always practical, "especially with hamburgers."

"Talking of which . . ." said Alan, and went in search of the next reinforcements.

While he was gone, the Fortune Telling Lady, Madame Elvira, came out of her tent and fixed Isobel with a beady eye. "Change is coming," she said darkly. "Upheaval. No stone unturned. And a journey across the sea. But it will be worth it. Good will come." She smiled dazzlingly from behind her orange fringe, and added, "That will be fifty pence."

Isobel was so astonished that she paid up without a word.

It went on like that all day. Alan bought Isobel a red rose in a plastic phial of special plant food to keep it fresh. Trevor bought the kids some more candyfloss (hoping Goldie wouldn't be sick). Colin found a crab and tried to put it down Georgie's neck. Amid screams, Goldie dropped her second ice-cream down Colin's neck instead.

The Likely Lads came and went, pursuing their own devices, but returning from time to time to see whether their services were required. The tide began to go out. The wet sand became wet mud. The donkeys went home . . . and Cliff held on to his sprig of white heather, and gazed out to sea.

And last of all, the band came marching back again, playing 'Colonel Bogey', stopped for a brief serenade beside Cliff, wound a bright paper streamer round his chair and gave him a cardboard bowler hat to wear on his head, and went marching on into the distance, playing fit to bust.

"Time to go home, I think," said Alan softly. It seemed like a fitting end to the day.

"Look," said Goldie, who had been busy collecting things as the treacherous tide receded, but had not been silly enough to fall into the mud again, "here's the seaside . . ." and she laid her treasures on her father's knee. There was a white seagull's feather, a creamy, fluted cockle shell, a feathery frond of pink sea fern, a glistening round pebble with black and white speckles like a bird's egg, and Colin's tiny crab (now dead) for good measure.

Has it been a good day for Cliff too, I wonder? thought Isobel. Or has it merely made him sad? Perhaps the sea – and the passage to Ireland – is all too fraught with hopes and dreams for him?

But Cliff was looking down at Goldie's offerings, and saying in a soft, bemused kind of voice: "The sea . . . itself . . ."

Then he looked up at them all and said simply, *"Magic – a magic day!"*

The housing officer was due to come at eleven, and Alan had promised to be there too, in order to be a 'wise and impartial observer' as Isobel told him. In the meantime, she had gone out into the garden to inspect the stone steps and steep sides of the basement area, and was considering how difficult the change to a ramp might be.

Isobel's garden was long and pleasantly informal, with two sides backing on to the road, as her house was on a corner site. There were two long herbaceous borders full of well-cared-for perennials, for Isobel loved flowers and had reasonably 'green' fingers. On the shorter side at the end, there was a small vegetable patch, and a compost heap underneath the shade of a silver birch and two old apple trees.

The garage was next to the vegetable patch, with its doors opening on to a small tarmac strip leading to gates out into the road. There was also a smaller gate leading out to the other road, and this neat white escape route was the one she envisaged getting Cliff Broadbent's chair through, once the ramp was built.

There were other trees in the garden – notably an old mulberry that had probably been there for many generations of fruit-loving householders, and a couple of small maples for autumn colour. And besides these eyecatchers, there were two lilac trees, one laburnum, and several old-fashioned standard roses that had been allowed to grow too tall.

Now, at the beginning of spring, there were early daffodils nodding in the breeze, and several milky clumps of primroses in the hedge mixed up with some pale lilac cuckoo flowers, and a whole lot of cheerful crocuses along the paths.

It was a pleasant place – green and calm, and reasonably spacious for a town garden, and Isobel was wondering how much its graceful outlines and its peaceful atmosphere would be changed by the churning up of mechanical diggers and the insertion of two concrete ramps. Two – because she was determined to be able to invite the young family into her own

202

part of the house from time to time, and they would never come without their father. So her own little terrace outside the french windows would have to go, or part of it anyway and that might mean that the wisteria would have to be cut back. But it wouldn't matter, she told herself. It could be sort of diverted sideways and re-trained, not cut down. . . .

She was contemplating all this with some misgiving, standing alone on the green lawn, when Alan arrived and stood smiling at her over the garden gate from the road.

"Shall I come in? Or are you about to repel all borders?"

She went across to him, gladness clear in her face. "Of course not! Did I look so forbidding?" She smiled at him. "But I do need an ally."

He came in through the gate and stood beside her, admiring the garden. "*Not* an ally, Isobel, remember? You told me I'd got to be impartial."

She grinned. "I've changed my mind. I just want your support in what you *know* is a damn good idea."

Alan shook his head at her. "Are you sure you want to disturb all this?" He looked round him at the tranquil green spaces – the trees and shrubs and dappled shade of the quiet garden. "It's such a peaceful place."

Isobel sighed. "I know, Alan, I know . . . but those children need it more than I do – and so does Cliff. How can I have a monopoly on *fresh air*!"

He was looking back at the house now, and considering, as she had, where the ramps could go, and how much disturbance there would have to be.

"How long have you lived here, Isobel?" he asked.

"Only four years . . . I bought it when I took early retirement." She glanced at Alan, and then, feeling that perhaps she owed him a further explanation, she added, "My father died, and I was tired of Scotland. . . . So I sold his house and came south."

"I see," he said absently. "So perhaps you won't mind churning up the garden so much as you would if you'd always lived here?"

"I hope not," Isobel said, with a faint, absent smile.

But at that moment the doorbell rang, and they went together to let the housing officer in for his inspection.

203

"I had it checked for damp and dry rot and so on when I moved in," said Isobel, putting first things first. "And it seems dry enough."

The housing officer nodded briefly, and put one hand on the wall as he passed. It was certainly dry, and there was no sign of mould.

They went from room to room, assessing and discussing possibilities, and finally ended up looking out of the big kitchen window at the area steps and the rocky bank leading up to the green garden beyond.

"It would have a lot more light without those infernal rocks," said Isobel. "And the sloping ramp would help to let in the sun, too."

Brian Evans, the same hard-pressed housing official they had met before, nodded patiently.

"Maybe we could enlarge the kitchen door for the wheelchair, and put some glass in the top?" suggested Alan.

Isobel glanced at him swiftly, noting that small word 'we'. "That's a good idea." She turned to Brian Evans. "What do you think?"

He smiled at Isobel, surprised by the anxiety in her eyes. This competent, kindly woman really minded about that young family and their future mattered to her. It was a bit incomprehensible to him, but nevertheless, he was impressed by her sincerity.

"You'll have to get planning permission, of course," he told her cautiously. "But I think they'll grant it, especially for a disabled person. Then, if you can get the ramps built as you propose, the accommodation should be perfectly adequate." Her permitted himself a small smile. "In fact, it would be much better than what they have now. . . . We could help in putting up extra supports and handrails and various aids suitable for wheelchair tenants," he went on, offering what small assistance he could. "That at least we can do . . . and I think you might get a small conversion grant for 'disabled access'. That might help with the ramps."

"That's not important," said Isobel recklessly. "What matters is, will the Social Services pay the rent for the Broadbents? Because they won't accept charity from me – and they can't afford it on their own."

Brian Evans understood her. "I think they will agree to that," he said. "I shall have to come and see it again when it is finished, of course."

"Of course," agreed Isobel.

"And you shouldn't dismiss the possibility of a conversion grant as unimportant," said Alan severely. "It would be very useful."

They all looked at one another, and Brian Evans actually laughed. "I can see you have a good adviser here," he said. And they understood that the basement flat had passed the first test – with provisos – and Brian Evans was already an ally prepared to help in any way he could to see the scheme through.

"By the way," said Alan, as they all trooped up the stairs to have a cup of tea in Isobel's own kitchen, "how did that clever cat get down here in the first place? Do you know?"

Isobel laughed. "He's like Houdini, that cat. There is a loose board under the stairs. He could push it forward to get in, but he couldn't push it back to get out!"

"Well," grinned Alan, "it's an ill cat that blows nobody any good!"

And even Brian Evans laughed again.

"Look here, Isobel, you've got to be sensible about this," Alan said, when they were alone. "I mean, I can get you an estimate for the ramps and so on – but you've got to talk to Trevor first. And then his father."

Isobel nodded. "Yes, I know." She looked a little alarmed. "Do you think they might not want to come?"

He looked at Isobel's suddenly anxious face and almost smiled. She was so eager, so full of her new scheme and all that it entailed – like a child planning a birthday party, suddenly terrified that no one would come to it.

"It's possible," he said slowly.

"Why?" She had not really begun to think in those terms yet.

"Well, they might feel that they were losing their independence. Or that they were being manipulated. . . ."

She stared at him, silent and troubled.

"Or Trevor might feel that you were too kind-hearted, and they were taking advantage of you."

Isobel snorted.

"Or Cliff might just dig his toes in and refuse to move. He doesn't much like change . . . and he doesn't much like charity, either."

She sighed. "Do you think any of these objections are likely?"

He hesitated, and then answered firmly, "No. I don't. But you have to consider them as possibilities." He did allow himself to smile then. "But on the whole I think they'll love the idea."

Isobel was still looking doubtful. "They ought to see it all – all of them . . . But how could we get Cliff down the steps?"

"We could bring the home-made ramp over – just for once."

"But aren't the steps too steep?"

He considered. "No worse than the stairs at the flat . . . but we might need the Likely Lads again." He seemed to think all that side of it was possible, but he was clearly being cautious about the Broadbent family's reaction. Then he saw Isobel's worried expression and relented suddenly. "It's only a precaution, Isobel . . . I just don't want you to go ahead with your plans, only to be disappointed."

Isobel suddenly met his smile with a brave one of her own. "I'll talk to Trevor . . . as soon as I can."

He nodded approval, and then steered her cheerfully out of her own front door and into his waiting car. "Come on, then, let's go and visit a builder I know."

She had to wait till Trevor's usual Saturday visit before mentioning the basement flat. She had gone over for her usual Thursday 'minding' session, even though Trevor protested that she had already spent Monday with them at Weston. But she had insisted on coming, and on making Trevor go out with the other children for a while. He was still a bit pale and tired after the bicycle episode, and he clearly needed a rest which he couldn't have. Those cracked ribs were still painful, and she guessed his hand was a nuisance when he was trying to lift his father in and out of his chair. A few hours of respite would at least take some of the pressure off, and now that the Social Security people had woken up, there was a little more leeway in the weekly budget for the occasional treat. He argued that he didn't need it, but he went – egged on by Georgie, who was well aware of the problems that would arise 'if Trev got too tired to cope,' and therefore scolded and fussed round him like a little mother.

So it was Saturday morning, and they were having their usual cup of tea, before Isobel broached the subject of the new flat.

"Trevor," she said at last, "I have something to show you – and I want you to think very hard about it before coming to any decision. All right?"

He looked a bit mystified. But he had learnt to trust Isobel by now, and the curious unspoken bond between them had grown much stronger over the past few weeks – especially since the accident with the Blatchford boys. It was to Isobel's house he had staggered that day, to Isobel he had gone instinctively for help, knowing it would be given. And it was to Isobel he turned now when the problems of his father and his family became insoluble.

So he smiled now and said carefully, "OK. I'll think!" and followed her, uncomprehending, into the hall and down the stone steps to the empty flat below. Isobel took him quietly from room to room, and finally to the kitchen window and the door out to the area steps.

"We can put in a ramp here, d'you see? Leading up to the garden. That would mean your father could get in and out safely, and sit in the garden in the sun . . . and get out to the road without any difficulty. What do you think?"

Trevor was silent for a moment, his eyes fixed on her face, not on the way out to the garden beyond. "You – would do all that?" he said, in a voice of disbelief.

"It's not a lot of work, Trevor. Only a ramp and some decorating. . . . And the Council would put in some handles and things for Cliff, and they'd pay the rent, just like they do now . . ." She paused, and added gently, "But it is really a question of what *you* would like, and whether you think it would do?"

He was still looking at her, and now the anxious grey eyes seemed to dilate and to reflect a sheen of tears. "I – you *know* I would like it," he said unevenly, "but I – I will have to think. . . ."

"Yes, of course you must think. That's what I said." She opened the door out into the narrow 'area' and led him up the steps into the garden. "Plenty of room out here," she said, "for the kids to play . . . They'd be safe out here – and away from the Blatchford's stamping ground."

He nodded and stood looking round the soft green spaces of the garden, an expression of startled awareness on his face now. Yes, how the kids would love it here – so much space – so much green – so much freedom . . . And how his father would love it, too . . . But – was it right? Was it fair? Ought he to let this happen? . . . He did not know.

"It would be farther for the kids to go to school, of course," said Isobel, wondering if that was one of his worries.

He shook his head at that. "The school bus comes this way – almost to the end of the road."

So that was one problem out of the way.

"It's bigger than our own flat," he said slowly, trying to work things out in his mind. "Wouldn't it cost more?"

"No," said Isobel. "The same rent. The Council agreed to that. And the heating would come from the house boiler, anyway. I don't think your expenses would be any higher." And as an afterthought she added, "You could still do your paper-round from here, couldn't you?"

He nodded, almost absently. There were so many things to think about, and he was trying so hard to be practical and sensible, and not get carried away by joy. Yes, joy – for the idea of being under the same roof as Isobel, with her care and kindness to turn to in emergencies, filled him with a dreadful admission of relief and gladness. He wouldn't have to battle on alone – not altogether. He wouldn't have to worry about the kids whenever they went out to play. He wouldn't have to worry about his father feeling cooped up and frustrated. . . . Or about him being ill in the night. . . .

"And it would be easier for Cliff to get the physiotherapy treatment he needs," pointed out Isobel, for this was really an important asset. "The ambulance people could collect him and bring him back without any hassle."

Trevor sighed. He was almost defeated by all the wonders

208

and advantages heaped upon him. It was all much too easy, much too good to be true. And then a thought came to him with awful force, and his eyes clouded. They couldn't leave the flat. *What would their mother do when she came back and found them gone?*

He turned to Isobel, a desperate appeal in those misted eyes now. "How – how would Mum know where to find us – if she came back?"

Isobel had not thought of this. But the answer was simple – and direct. "We would leave an address at the old flat – and with the landlord, and the other tenants, to make sure. And the Council would know, wouldn't they? If your mother came back to look for you, she would go straight to them."

Trevor considered. It seemed to make sense. After all, she *had* told him to go to the Welfare people. She would expect to get news of them there . . . "I – I should have to talk to my Dad," he said cautiously.

"Of course. And the kids . . . and you could bring them all round to have a look." She smiled at him now, seeing signs of wary acceptance in his softened glance. "Alan Selwyn says we could use the home-made ramp on the steps, just for once, so that Cliff could have a look inside. . . ."

She waited then, wondering if the boy was feeling too pressurized – if the whole project sounded too daunting. "You'd be quite separate – quite independent down here," she explained. "Your *own* place. You needn't be afraid that your private family life would be interfered with. . . ."

A gleam of humour came into his face then. "I should think it might be the other way round," he said.

And then the two of them began to laugh – as if a decision had been made and a pact sealed and signed between them.

It was a day of sunshine and sparkle when Cliff and his family came to look at the basement flat and the garden. It had rained earlier, and everything shone with a new brilliance – the colours of the flowers – the grass and the trees – all seemed to glow with a vivid life of their own.

Alan parked his car near the garden gate, and he and the Likely Lads helped Cliff into his wheelchair and brought him into the garden, followed by a gaggle of eager children. Trevor had ridden over on his new bike – being much too proud of it to leave it behind, and he now appeared close beside the rest of the party, and carefully parked his bike just inside the garden gate where it wouldn't get stolen. He went straight over to his father and stood protectively beside him while the whole family looked around them in fascinated disbelief.

"All this . . .?" said Colin.

"The trees!" exclaimed Georgie.

"Lovely grass!" laughed Goldie, and promptly began to dance on it.

Cliff said nothing – but his eyes swept over the gentle green spaces and did not reject them.

Trevor was also silent – but he was waiting for everyone else's reaction. Meanwhile Alan and the Likely Lads had gone back to the car for the ramp, and now they reappeared, carrying it between them.

But when they got to the basement steps, they found that Isobel had forestalled them. The steps had gone, the rocks and the high, steep wall supporting them had gone, and there was a new, shallow slope of freshly raked earth leading up from the old kitchen door.

"It isn't finished yet," explained Isobel, who had been waiting for them by the door, "but it will be much easier to put your ramp on than those awful steps . . ." She grinned at Alan's accusing face, and added softly, "And I thought – I was afraid those steep area steps might remind Cliff of something. . . ."

Alan nodded, and accepted her explanation, though he still looked a bit disapproving.

"It only took him a day," she said, still vaguely justifying herself. "And I thought, what the hell – whether they come or not, I hate those rocks!"

Then Alan laughed and forgave her.

The Likely Lads had laid the wooden ramp down on the new soil by now, and were testing it for firmness before they let Cliff's wheelchair go down it. "Seems OK," they said, smiling. "It'll be dead easy for him when it's concreted."

The two boys looked round appreciatively at the garden and the open door into the basement, now flooded with spring sunlight, and added: "Nice place!" in cheerful tones.

By this time, Trevor had pushed Cliff across the grass and

stood looking at Isobel over the top of the wheelchair with eyes that signalled both reassurance and hope. "He likes it so far," he said, risking a smile. "Don't you, Dad?"

"Cliff nodded, also risking a smile, though his was more laboured. "Yes. L-lovely garden. . . ." he said.

"Where are the rest of you?" asked Isobel.

They all turned to look for the children in surprise. But the three of them were otherwise engaged – already far out in their own new worlds. Goldie had met Archimedes, and had instantly and totally and irrevocably fallen in love. Colin had met a garden for the first time and was almost as in love as Goldie. While she was sitting cross-legged beside Archimedes on the garden bench, stroking his black velvet coat, Colin was stooping to touch each daffodil and primrose, and even the daisies, with reverent fingers. An Georgie? She was already half-way up one of the old apple trees in the corner, gazing up at the sky and singing softly to herself about buttercups and daisies. . . .

"Come on," called Trevor, "we're going inside."

But Isobel smiled when she saw how absorbed and happy they were, and murmured softly, "Don't hurry them. . . ."

Eventually, they all trooped round the rooms, and Isobel explained everything all over again very carefully and courteously to Cliff as they went, with the children following, wide-eyed and inquisitive, exploring every nook and cranny and cupboard. And, to Isobel's surprise though she made no comment, accompanying them on their voyage of discovery came Archimedes, walking sedately beside Goldie and waving his tail in a lordly manner like a victorious banner.

At last they all arrived back in the kitchen, as Isobel and Alan had done with the housing officer, and stood in a group round Cliff's chair while he looked out of the window.

And, yes, Isobel was pleased to see that the view of the garden was very much better now that the rocks had gone, and there was much more light streaming in from the clear spring sky beyond. "It will all need painting, of course . . ." she murmured, more to herself than anyone else.

"We could give you a hand with that," volunteered Dave, the tall fair one of the Likely Lads. "Couldn't we, Mitch?"

"Good idea," agreed Mitch, smiling.

Isobel looked at them in amazement. It was on the tip of her tongue to ask them why on earth they should bother, but she thought that leading question had better wait till later.

Trevor was just about to join in with, "We could help with that, too," when – as so often in his life these days – he had to think twice. He could not leave his father long enough to be much use as a decorator, and the others were really too young to be much help, even if they came without him. And, clearly, the painting had to be done before they moved in, so he couldn't wait till Cliff was safely installed in the new flat. Once again, he had to think of his father first, and keep quiet when he longed to take part in something outside. . . . Well, he told himself philosophically, it will be easier when we are here – much easier.

But Alan was no fool, and he saw the regret in Trevor's eyes. "I daresay you'll be able to put the finishing touches to the rooms yourselves when you've moved in," he suggested, signalling all sorts of things to Isobel above Trevor's head. "Won't they, Isobel?"

She caught the flecks of laughter behind his meaning glance, and answered him with the same cheerful response as Mitch. "Good idea!"

There was a moment's silence then, while everyone waited and wondered what Cliff Broadbent's verdict would be.

But Isobel wasn't going to have him rushed into anything. "Why don't you all go out in the garden again, while I go upstairs and fetch everyone a cup of tea?" she suggested.

The children needed no prompting. They were outside and up the ramp on to the grass like small streaks of summer lightning.

Trevor and Cliff, with the Likely Lads helping to push the chair up the ramp, followed more slowly, and stopped beside the garden bench where Archimedes had been sunning himself before – as if it were the focal point of all that tranquil space.

Then the Likely Lads, with enormous tact, left Trevor alone with his father and went to inspect the rest of the garden.

Alan, meanwhile, had followed Isobel upstairs and was making himself useful loading a tray with mugs and spoons and sugar, and a plate of chocolate biscuits.

"Well?" said Isobel. "What do you think?"

"Hard to tell," he shrugged. "He seems happy enough about all the plans. . . ." He glanced at her hopeful face, and added gently, "Better wait and see . . ."

But while he was speaking, Trevor came into the kitchen and looked at them both with cautious optimism. "He likes the idea," he said. "But he wants to talk to Miss Isobel first."

"Of course," agreed Isobel, and set off at once, leaving Trevor and Alan to bring out the tray of tea.

Cliff was sitting alone where Trevor had left him, his blond head glinting in the sun as he gazed round the garden and looked back at the house that was soon to be his home. He found it difficult to adjust his mind to this new circumstance yet, but he knew quite clearly that it would be a good move. Good for everyone, especially his children, and he knew he must not refuse. But there was still some vague residue of doubt in his mind – some reluctance to give in, to admit that he needed help or that his children needed more space and more light and air, more protection, even, than he could give them. He knew, obscurely, that this was unreasonable and selfish of him, and that he ought to be grateful to Isobel for her offer. But he felt a little as if the last of his independence was going – as if he was sinking under the weight of his own needs and the needs of his family, especially Trevor who carried most of the burdens of the day – sinking helplessly into a sea of dependence and perpetual gratitude that he could not escape . . . into a deep, unfathomable sea where he was drowning, not waving. . . .

"Cliff," said Isobel softly. "It's not a surrender."

"Isn't it?" He looked up at her, amazed that she understood him.

"No," she said. "Something new. More independence. The kids can take you *anywhere* from here. And who knows what the physiotherapy might do? You will be your own man again, here."

His eyes misted over with the far-too-easy tears of weakness, but he tried to make sense of the words. "Not . . .?"

"Taking the easy way out? No. Believe me, it will be hard enough. But you have to go on, Cliff, not *back*!"

He nodded, accepting that. "Will you . . .?"

213

"Come and see you? Only if you want me. The place will be yours. Totally private. No one can interfere."

He smiled at that, and got out a few important words. "We *would* want you." But there were still words he did not know how to say. "I don't know – how to—"

But Isobel forestalled him. "I don't want thanks, Cliff," she said briskly. "I want you to get well – and the kids to be safe and happy. That's all."

He sighed. That was all he wanted, too. All but one thing. And he had to speak of that, too. *"Katie . . .?"*

"Yes. Trevor asked me about that. We'll make sure everyone has the new address: the old flat, the landlord, the Council. She won't have any trouble finding you." She smiled at him then, with all the confidence she could muster. "And you might be well by then."

He understood then, suddenly, that she was right. It wasn't a surrender. It was a new battleground he was going to – and the battle wasn't over yet. And that being so, maybe he didn't mind going after all. There was no disgrace in finding a new place to fight.

"I – tell the kids it's 'yes'," he said, and leant back in his chair as if he had fought the first new skirmish already.

But Trevor was standing beside him now, with the tray of tea in his hands, and he heard what his father said. Carefully, he put the tray down, and laid a hand on Cliff's shoulder. "I'll tell them, Dad," he said.

Chapter Thirteen

'The Garden of Daisies'
Set Dance

Things began to move on the home front. Isobel had a strong feeling that she ought to get those children out of the Blatchford Gang district before anything else happened, so she pushed ahead with her plans for the flat as fast as she could.

The young builder came back and concreted the new ramp from the kitchen door, smoothed out the raw, churned-up slope that had once been a fortresslike rock facade, sowed the newly turned earth with grass seed, and then began on the other ramp leading up to Isobel's sitting-room. Drawing-room it still was in Isobel's vocabulary, but she never called it that nowadays in case people thought she was putting on airs. Gervase thought the opposite, and accused her of inverted snobbery. It was a beautiful room, he said, a room to withdraw into for respite and peace. Of course it was a drawing-room – why pretend otherwise?

Gervase! she thought. I shall have to tell him soon. Next time he comes, he will see the ramps and all the chaos in the garden. And he will be furious! Just like Archimedes. His quiet haven of peace utterly ruined. For Archimedes, who, after all, had started all this in the first place, had been deeply affronted by the ensuing upheaval, and had taken to sitting on the first branch of the silver birch tree, well out of harm's way, and refusing to come down until the evening when everyone went home.

Once the ramps were dealt with, there was the breakfast bar in the old scullery to install, a face-lift and a new shower for the bathroom, several new cupboards to build, and a new kitchen door with glass panels to replace the old one. And after all that, lots and lots of white paint over every dingy surface. . . . And this was where the Likely Lads came in, for they had insisted on making good their offer, and arrived one day, complete with overalls and buckets, to wash down all the walls before they began.

Isobel welcomed their help, and offered them tea and buns at frequent intervals – and during one of these friendly tea-breaks, asked the question that had been troubling her.

"Why?" she said, looking from one to the other with half smiling curiosity. "Why are you doing this? I mean, you've already been towers of strength – almost literally!" she added, grinning. "But why?"

Dave looked at Mitch, and then grinned back at Isobel. "Look, I'm not in a wheelchair. I haven't got a whole family on my back, like Trevor. Nor has Mitch."

Mitch nodded agreement. "We're the lucky ones," he explained.

"Besides," added Dave, almost as an afterthought, "we like Alan Sewyn. As teachers go, he's not half bad."

There didn't seem to be any more to say – at least not by their reckoning – and they both took another swig of hot tea and grinned even wider at Isobel. "We're happy if you are," they said.

Isobel had to admit she *was* happy. They were good workers, and the grey basement rooms were already looking transformed. All she could do was offer them another sticky bun. They had already refused payment – even below the going rate, saying that this was their contribution to the grand plan and anyway they enjoyed it.

And then it was Friday evening, and Gervase came. He stood by the open french windows of the drawing-room, as was his custom, with a glass of dry sherry in his hand, and gazed out at the gently curving sweep of lawn and the shadowy trees at the end of the garden. And then his glance came sharply into focus on the newly-raked earth on the sloping ramp that viciously slashed through the middle of Isobel's ruined terrace.

"What on earth are you doing to the garden?" His voice was almost a squeak of outrage.

Isobel sighed. Now was the time to tell him all about it,

and she didn't really want to. Upsetting her old friend was not something she enjoyed, and the thought of his indignation and dismay filled her with dread.

"I'm doing up the basement flat," she said. "I'm going to have tenants."

Gervase's long face looked instantly suspicious. But then another thought seemed to strike him, and his expression softened. "Are you short of money? I said you ought to come and work for me."

Isobel laughed. "No, I'm not short of money. This is quite a different matter. Sit down a minute, and I'll tell you all about it."

And she did, but in a carefully edited version, not mentioning Trevor's bike accident or Alan's subsequent visit to Ron Blatchford. It would never do to let Gervase know that her new, deserving tenants were all mixed up with one of the toughest street gangs in the city. So she concentrated on Cliff's need for more freedom of movement, and the children's need for fresh air and space, and Trevor's need for respite from his demanding rôle as carer and manager of his struggling family.

Gervase listened in silence, his mouth getting steadily grimmer, but he did not interrupt or explode into furious splutters of disbelief. He just sat there, looking at Isobel with grave attention, and waited for her to come to an end of her explanations.

"It wasn't being used, Gervase – and it seemed such a waste," she pleaded. "Especially when I looked round for other flats and found out how difficult it was. . . . This will be ideal for them, really – and they need it so badly." She stopped there – not being able to think of anything else to say. And Gervase was still silent, which surprised her very much.

At last he said slowly, in a strange, rather diffident voice, "You never married, did you, Isobel?"

She looked at him, startled, and far down in her eyes something seemed to flash and smoulder, and then become instantly suppressed by saving laughter. "No, Gervase dear, I didn't. But that isn't to say I haven't lived!"

His glance met hers in mutual amusement. "I'm sure you have!"

217

She considered. "Are you saying that I am suffering from a frustrated maternal instinct?" There was a definite gleam in her eyes now.

"Could be," he allowed, matching the gleam with one of his own. "You were very maternal over me when I had flu."

She laughed. "Did you mind?"

"No," he admitted honestly. "I loved it."

They grinned at each other.

"Well, then," said Isobel, as if that clinched it. "There's no harm in being a bit maternal sometimes. It's an occupational hazard in teaching, anyway." She paused then, and her face grew serious and curiously bleak and stern. "But that isn't really the point in this case, Gervase. . . ." Once again she seemed to pause, as if marshalling her facts and drawing on long-hidden reserves of steady resolve. "I've never told you much about my early life, Gervase, and I'm not going to now. But I – I was trapped into a carer's situation very much like Trevor's – only I was older . . . I looked after my father till he died. And I . . . there were sacrifices that had to be made. . . ." The sternness was very marked in her straight mouth now. "I just don't want to see it happen to that boy – or any of his family. And I don't want to see that man trapped in his wheelchair for life, either. . . . That's all."

Gervase nodded quietly, impressed by her sudden gravity. "In that case," he said, quite gently and kindly, "I won't argue."

She stared at him in amazement. "You won't?"

"No. I can see why it matters to you." He sighed. "But it will be the end of peace."

"No, it won't, Gervase. They aren't hooligans. In fact, they're rather too good and quiet on the whole. . . ." She smiled at him with swift appeal. "D'you remember me asking you if you'd ever climbed a tree?"

"Yes?"

"And you thought I was slightly mad to ask," she added, grinning. (I wonder what he would think if I told him about Alan and me up that beech tree, she thought.) "Well, these children have never climbed a tree," she went on. "It was the very first thing Georgie did . . . and Colin went and *touched*

218

the flowers, as if he had never seen one growing before – close to, that is. . . ."

"And what did the little one do?" asked Gervase, intrigued in spite of himself.

"She hugged Archimedes and wouldn't let him go."

Gervase was touched. "Did he let her?"

"Oh yes! That cat knows when he is appreciated." She looked at Gervase with a touch of mischief. "Do you realize that this whole thing is all your fault – and his?"

Gervase laughed. "What a responsibility."

"Come and look at it," she coaxed, "while supper's cooking. You might even approve of it!"

"Very well," he said sedately. "But I shall reserve judgement."

So they went quite companionably down the stairs to the basement to have a look. Archimedes, who had retreated under a chair when the discussion began, clearly fearing the worst, now came out and joined them on their tour of inspection. He seemed to take a proprietorial interest in the whole affair.

"I do believe that cat thinks he is in charge," said Gervase, watching the clever black head with its golden eyes turn this way and that in inquisitive interest, and possible approval.

"I'm sure he does," agreed Isobel.

They looked at each other and laughed. "In that case," said Gervase, capitulating gracefully, "how can I object?"

It was soon after this that the letter came. When Isobel saw the stamp and the postmark from that small town in southern Ireland, her heart gave a mistaken leap of hope that it might be from the errant Katie Broadbent. But then she realized that Katie couldn't know of Isobel's existence, or her connections with the motherless family – let alone know her address. No. This letter went back much further into the past than that – to a time that Isobel had spent a lifetime trying not to remember. And it seemed ironic, after that curious conversation with Gervase about her early life, that this reminder of the past should come back to haunt her now.

She looked at the letter in her hand, and wanted passionately not to open it – not to know anything – not to go through all that anguish of choice again. But Isobel was no coward. After

219

a moment's silent thought which might almost have been a prayer, she opened the envelope and drew out the folded sheet of notepaper from inside.

'Dear Isobel' (it said),
'I hope I may still call you that, for although we have not communicated for many years (except over your occasional generous gifts to the convent), we do still remember you with affectionate regard. I did not have your present address, but your old school in Edinburgh gave it to me. I hope you do not mind.

"My reason for writing to you is that I have had a request, and I do not know how to answer it. To be direct, the Adoption Society in Dublin has been asked by your son whether there is any way that he can trace you or be put in touch with you. I believe it is not a question of simple curiosity, but a matter of some importance to him.

"I do not know how you are placed at the present time, or whether the sudden arrival of your son – he is still called Bruce, by the way – would cause problems? I believe your father died some years ago, and you now live in a very different area. But of course you may very well not wish to be involved in anything to do with the past.

"I can only ask you to think very carefully, if you will, and then let me know your decision, and I will pass it on to the Adoption Society, who will in turn make it known to your son. I know you made a very great sacrifice at a very unhappy time of your life, my dear Isobel, but perhaps now the time has come to heal more wounds than one.

"Whatever your decision, we will pray for you and your future peace of mind and happiness.

"Your affectionate old friend, Sister Ursula. (Reverend Mother now, since our dear Mother Agnes went to her rest some five years ago.)

"P.S. We still sing the hymn you wrote for us about the Forgiving Sky."

For a long time Isobel sat with the letter in her hand, while the memories of that distant time washed over her with painful clarity. But at last she got up slowly, put the letter away in her desk, and went out for a walk on the Downs.

She walked until she was tired, but she came to no conclusion. Her mind was in a turmoil of doubt, and every course of action seemed likely to be wrong or to cause hurt to someone. What about the adoptive parents? Wouldn't they be upset by the knowledge that their chosen son was seeking out his natural mother? And what about the boy himself? Wouldn't he be disappointed by this rather dull elderly (well – late middle-aged) woman who had given him away so long ago? Boy! she thought grimly. He'd be thirty-six now. Not a boy at all. Probably married. What good would it do to stir up things now? . . . Not that she had ever succeeded in burying the past in a place where it didn't hurt. . . . There hadn't been a single day in all those years when she hadn't thought of that unknown child, and wondered how he was growing up and whether he was happy and well loved. . . . But that was her own private grief. Was it fair to put anyone else through that kind of pain, those kind of choices? Wouldn't it all be best left alone?

She did not know. She could not see her way clear. It was all impossible, and she was afraid of her own temperament, her natural predilection for making swift decisions and sticking by them even if she was wrong. . . . She longed to have someone she could ask about it – someone whose judgement she could trust. And then, of course, she thought of Alan.

Could she tell him? He would probably not be shocked or critical – would almost certainly take it in his stride, like most things. . . . Whereas Gervase – Gervase would look at her in horror – or embarrassment – and disappear out of her life rather fast, rather than get involved. . . .

Yes, Alan might be willing to listen. But was it fair to ask him? She had lived with this secret of hers long enough, sternly repressing any desire to tell anyone – to cause hurt to anyone. That had been the whole idea. Why change it now?

By the time she got to this point in her thoughts, she had walked round in circles, and she suddenly remembered that she was due at the Broadbents' to discuss the arrangements for the move, and Alan was due there, too to offer transport and

221

help from the Likely Lads. Sighing, she left the open spaces of the Downs and went down towards Hotwells and the crowded streets round Cliff Broadbent's flat.

When she arrived, Alan was already there, and they were clearly waiting for her, with tea and buns at the ready. She immediately felt guilty for being late, and for being so obsessed with her own problems that she forgot the time.

"Sorry I'm late," she said, summoning cheerfulness out of nowhere. "But I have some good news – and a couple of things to ask you." She looked at Trevor now, since he was clearly the one who would be doing most of the organizing.

The boy still seemed a bit grey and tired, she thought. It would be a good thing when all this was sorted out and accomplished. (And how could she begin to think about her own dilemma till the move was over, and the family were safely settled in their new home?)

"First of all," she said, keeping her mind firmly on present issues, "the housing officer came back and approved all the new work."

"That's splendid," said Alan, smiling.

"And he says you can move when you like – since this flat is their property, they can let it when they like, and you don't have to give more than a month's notice, which you have already done."

Trevor looked pleased but worried. "How soon does that mean?"

"Next weekend, I should think," said Alan firmly, knowing it was what Isobel wanted, and that it would be better for everyone concerned to get it over. "Then the Likely Lads can help, and I can bring the car for your father." He remembered then to look to Cliff for support. "Would that be all right?"

Cliff nodded, already a bit bewildered by the speed with which things were happening.

"I'll bring some tea-chests round tomorrow," Alan added, "and you can pack up all the small things yourselves."

"What about the furniture?" Trevor still seemed a little alarmed by the whole process of removal.

"I've hired someone," said Isobel. "They'll collect it and deliver it. You've only got to be here to see it go, and then dash round on your bike to see it in the other end. They'll put it anywhere you tell them." She smiled at his anxious face. "But I wanted to ask Cliff about his day-bed." She turned to Cliff easily. "Would it be better in the new living-room, like here, or would you like it in one of the bedrooms? . . . And is it the right height for you to get in and out of, or would you like a new one? Because the Social Services say you are entitled to a special orthopaedic bed, if you want one?"

Cliff looked even more confused by this, but Trevor said sensibly, "Let's put the old one in the living-room for now – where he's used to it. And they can put a new one in the bedroom for him if they want to. Then he can decide which he likes best." He looked at his father, signalling reassurance. "OK, Dad?"

"OK," said Cliff, clinging to sanity. At least his old bed would be more-or-less where it ought to be.

Georgie, who had been listening to all this, went up to Cliff and wound her arms round his neck consolingly. "It'll soon feel just like home," she said.

"Just like home!" agreed Goldie, dancing about as usual.

And Colin added, honestly, "Better, really!"

"What about the carpets?" asked Georgie suddenly, eying the shabby living-room one with some misgiving.

"I've had carpeting put down all through," said Isobel. "To keep it warm. Those old stone floors are rather cold, you know. . . ." She grinned at Georgie. "But you can put down any of the old rugs or carpets over the top if you want to."

Georgie nodded, her practical little housewife's mind satisfied. "We'll just bring the rugs, then. They're brighter."

"And then," said Isobel, also sounding practical and cheerful, "you can try out the other new ramp as well and all come to tea with me on moving day. That'll save you having to search for the kettle!"

There was a grateful laugh of relief, but Trevor was looking at Isobel harder now, and he said suddenly, "Could you come and look at the bunk beds, and tell me what to do with them?"

Surprised, Isobel agreed, and followed him into the children's bedroom, leaving the others behind.

But once there, Trevor turned to her and said shyly, "You look – sort of worried. Are you sure it's all right for us to come?"

223

"Yes," said Isobel. "I've never been surer about anything in my life."

He was still regarding her with a faintly puzzled stare. "Well then," he asked simply, "What is it?"

How observant the boy is, Isobel thought – and how sensitive to other people's moods. He is behaving like an adult, and a rather special one at that . . . I do believe I could tell him about my unknown son, Bruce, and he'd know what I ought to do. . . . He has had to take so many grown-up decisions of his own already. . . .

But she didn't tell him anything, of course. She merely said, "It's all right, Trevor. Just something else on my mind. Nothing to do with you or the move."

He said doubtfully, "I don't like to see you worried."

She smiled at him. "I don't like to see you worried, either! Let's call it quits, and get this move safely over, shall we?"

He submitted to that fairly gracefully, though he was not entirely satisfied. "Quits then," he said, and grinned back. "If you say so!" And they solemnly clasped hands and laughed.

They went back to the others then, and discussed one or two more details, and then Alan said, "Come on, Isobel. I'll drive you home. We've given this lot enough to think about for the time being!"

Isobel agreed, rather tiredly, admitting to herself that her head was aching with too much thought. But before she could leave, she had to say something reassuring to Cliff, who was still looking bewildered and a little at bay. It would never do if he suddenly refused to come at all.

She went across to him and said quietly, "It won't be so bad, Cliff. We'll take it gently. There won't be any hassle, I promise."

He struggled to smile, though he was obviously a little apprehensive. "Better – when we're – in," he got out, trying to be co-operative.

"Yes," she agreed, smiling. "*Much* better. For everyone!" Her eye fell on the old record player and the pile of LPs in the corner. "You'd better choose a special record to play!"

"And we could play the Tunes," added Georgie, "just to say – to say—"

"To say we're pleased," said Colin, stoutly supporting her.

"Pleased," echoed Goldie, twirling. *"Just to say we're pleased!"* And she made it into a song and danced to it as she sang, and the others joined in, like a pop group backing chorus, finding it easier to say it this way than any other.

And during the general rejoicing, Alan and Isobel slipped quietly away.

"Where are we going?" asked Isobel, seeing that Alan's car wasn't taking the direct way to her house.

"We're going to buy two take-aways and a bottle of wine," said Alan. "And then we're going home to your place, and you can sit down in peace and tell me what's on your mind."

Isobel looked at him. "Alan, I—"

"It's all right," he said peaceably. "you're tired and confused about something – and you need a rest. I can wait." He grinned at her sideways, and before she could answer, he was out of the car and into the Chinese take-away on the corner.

Isobel sat back and closed her eyes to hide the fact that Alan's sudden kindness made her want to weep. It was almost too much to be understood so completely. She wondered, vaguely, how understanding he would be if she told him all her story.

And presently, when they were sitting together over two empty plates and two more glasses of wine, she did. She hadn't meant to – she didn't quite know how it happened – but Alan was oddly persistent, and she was so tired of taking decisions all alone.

"Come on, Isobel," he said, his deep musical voice very gentle and persuasive. "Something is troubling you very much – and I want to know what it is."

For answer, she got to her feet and went to fetch Sister Ursula's letter from her desk, and handed it to Alan without a word.

He read it in silence, and then gave it back to her quietly. "I see," he said, with a half-smile of affectionate reassurance. "So it's decision time."

Isobel stared. "You don't seem very surprised."

He ignored the faint question in her voice. "Isobel, I have always known there was something enormously sad deep

225

down inside you. . . . You cover it up very well, but it's still there. Isn't it time you told me all about it?"

She sighed. "It all happened so long ago, Alan . . . But it seems the past is never really over . . ." She took a deep breath, and wondered where to start.

"Begin at the beginning," said Alan softly. "It's easier."

But where did it begin? she wondered. I suppose, with my father. My upright, honourable, fanatical tyrant of a father, and his fierce religious convictions. "I hate religion," she said suddenly. "It makes people so—"

"Full of pride and prejudice? Yes." He understood her very well.

She smiled at his quick response – but a little shyly. "I told you my father was a Scottish Presbyterian minister," she said. "Out in the mission field in Africa for most of his working life. He was – very strict and rigid in his beliefs. We lived in – in the shadow of his displeasure, my mother and I. . . . We did what we were told, and asked no questions. It was easier that way. My first experience of teaching was out there, in a small, open-sided mission hut, before I was even trained." She shut her eyes for a moment, remembering the hot sun, and all those brown, eager faces . . . "I loved it, really, as long as I was busy and useful . . . but I – I suppose I led a very restricted life – very sheltered. I knew very little about the real world outside my father's unbending rule. . . ." She glanced at Alan briefly, almost as if pleading with him to make allowances for all of them. "And then he was sent home to Scotland – invalided out, really. He had malaria quite badly, And my mother . . ." She paused then, her voice wavering for a moment, "my mother had something much worse, though she didn't tell me then. . . ."

Once more she took a deep breath, summoning strength to face the host of memories that sprang into vivid life as she dared to recall them.

"Take it easy," said Alan. "There's no hurry."

She glanced at him gratefully, and went gamely on. "So they came home to a small, fiercely respectable parish where my father was looked up to as the perfect minister, the incorruptible man of God. . . ." Her voice had grown curiously bitter by now. "And I was sent to college." She looked at

226

Alan again, this time with open appeal. "I wonder if you can imagine what university life meant to me – the freedom – the laughter – the shedding of years of restriction and constant criticism . . . I loved every minute of it. I suppose you could say I blossomed . . . And of course I fell in love."

Alan nodded, and when she did not continue, he asked gently; "How old were you then?"

"I was eighteen. Well, nineteen when – when the crunch came." She gave a pale, self-mocking grin. "He was – much older than me. The classic syndrome of starry-eyed student and handsome senior lecturer. . . . And he was married, with children . . . I never really understood why he even noticed me. . . ." She blinked, and added in a breathless, rather humble voice, "I wasn't – wasn't very beautiful, or anything . . . but I loved him, and I think he really did care for me – in his way."

Alan made an indistinguishable growling noise at this, but he did not offer any other comment.

"I've seen it so often in my teaching life," she said suddenly, in a detatched sort of voice. "The mentor and the student . . . I think it is the attraction of a young, fresh mind and body ripe for instruction. . . ." But there was only a fleck of judgement in her tone, it was mostly just sad as she went on. "So I – the inevitable happened, of course, and I got pregnant. I didn't tell him. There didn't seem much point. I knew he wouldn't leave his wife and children for me. And a scandal would hurt him just as much as me . . . I wasn't sure what to do or where to go. I only knew I wanted to have the baby, and keep it if I could." She sighed again, driven back into a time of torment and turmoil she could hardly bear to remember. "And then my mother came to see me."

She stopped then, and she was silent so long that Alan had to prompt her again. "Yes? What did she say?"

Isobel was very pale by now, and her voice was even more shaken by memory. "She told me she was dying of cancer, and she wanted me to come home and look after my father. But when I told her about the baby, she gave me an ultimatum. She would help me to go away and have it in secret, and arrange to have it adopted, so that I could come home to be with her and my father. But if I insisted on keeping the child, I must never come home again, never let my father know about it, or it would break his heart – and ruin him in the eyes of his upright, respectable flock."

Alan snorted with undisguised contempt. "Some man of God!"

Isobel shook her head. "He couldn't help being what he was. His religion was his life. The wages of sin was death. You know the type."

It was Alan's turn to sigh. He did indeed know the type.

"And you must remember this was over thirty years ago. Being an unmarried mum was still considered pretty scandalous, especially in my father's upright community."

"I suppose it was," Alan conceded.

"It was an impossible decision for me to make," she said sadly. "And, of course, the idea of an abortion was quite outside my kind of moral upbringing, and my mother's, too. . . ." She smiled at Alan, a little wistfully. "But somehow I couldn't desert my mother. She had so little time left, and she needed my support so much . . . what else could I do?" She was not really asking Alan now, she was asking herself. "So I – I let her arrange things for me – as far away as possible. I went to the convent in Ireland for the last three months, and when the child was born I called him Bruce, because – well, because he was a Scot in a strange land, like me. . . . And then they just – took him away." Her voice was so bleak and flat by now that it made Alan ache, but he did not dare to interrupt. "So I went back to Scotland, changed universities so that I could live at home, nursed my mother till she died, and then took on my father."

She was staring beyond Alan now, but the most painful part of her story was really over. The rest was just grey endurance, and a lifetime of regret. She didn't have to tell Alan that. He would know it anyway. . . . "What a programme you set yourself," he murmured, and it sounded more like praise than blame.

"But I did enjoy my teaching life," she protested honestly. "That was one consolation. And at least my father couldn't disapprove of that!"

There was silence between them for a few moments, and then Alan said, "What did you tell the – the man in question?"

Isobel smiled a little grimly. "Nothing. I simply said I was going home to look after my mother. That it was over. I think he was rather relieved, really. We had both got in much deeper than we knew. . . ."

Alan looked into her face, and then got up without a word and poured her out some more wine from the half-empty bottle on the table. "That's enough of the past, Isobel. It's now you have to think about."

She nodded, and took a gulp of her drink. "I don't know what to do," she said, sounding like a small child in the midst of nightmare.

He watched the colour slowly return to her face, as the wine steadied her. "I think you should see him," he said. "What have you got to lose now?"

She looked suddenly vulnerable and shy. "Yes, but – maybe *he'd* have something to lose?"

Alan stared at her, and then began to laugh. "My dear, silly girl," he said, allowing all sorts of things to creep into his loving voice, "Don't you know you'd be an asset as a mother to any right-minded young man!"

Isobel made a strange sound between a laugh and a gulp. "Do you think so . . .? And what about his real parents – I mean, his adoptive parents? How will they feel?"

"He will have thought of that," said Alan. "You need not agonize over them as well."

"Needn't I?" She still sounded rather like a lost child, and Alan leant forward impulsively and took her hand in a firm, comforting grip.

"No. I think your Sister Ursula is right. It is the time for healing. You know you want to see him. Tell him so, and let things resolve themselves."

To Isobel's surprise, she found herself resting her tired head against Alan's shoulder and closing her eyes in a kind of weary surrender. "Do you think I dare?" she asked.

"I think you must," he said.

But there was the Broadbents' move to consider next, and Isobel knew she must concentrate with all her might on seeing Cliff and his family successfully transferred and installed. With this in mind, therefore, she found some courage from somewhere and wrote to Sister Ursula saying she would be willing to see Bruce, but not for another week. Give me time, she begged silently. . . . Give my unknown son time. Give Cliff and Trevor and the kids time. . . . They will need at least a week to get settled in, and I *must* be free to see that things work smoothly for them. That must come first.

And so, of course, it did come first. Isobel went over the night before to help Trevor pack up their remaining belongings, and to reassure Cliff in case he was feeling even more apprehensive.

"He seems all right," said Trevor, busily stacking the children's few books and toys in the last tea-chest. "At least he hasn't started yelling in the night." His voice was still a bit weary and flat. "But I think. . . ." he hesitated.

"Yes?" Isobel was also putting books into the tea-chest.

"I think he will need to have all his own things round him – as much like here as possible."

Isobel nodded. "We'll manage that, won't we? It can be the first thing we do tomorrow when you get there. . . ." She was picking up the last of the books when one of them – a handsomely bound copy of Shakespeare – fell open at the title page, and her eye fell on the written inscription on the flyleaf: *'Katie O'Sullivan – English Prize – Form IVA – Convent of St Clodah – Senior School.'*

She looked at it with a faint stirring of hope within her. It was the first clue she had found to Katie's Irish background. If she had been at school at this St Clodah's Convent, was there a chance that she might have gone back there? Or might her family live nearby . . .? Anyway, where *was* St Clodah's? In Kerry, probably – since Katie always talked of Kerry. But where exactly? There was no address under the name of the Convent.

"St Clodah's?" she murmured aloud.

Trevor glanced from the gilt-edged leather to Isobel's enquiring face.

"Oh yes, that was Mum's. She was very proud of it . . . she used to read us bits sometimes."

Isobel laid it carefully in the packing case among their other treasures. "It's a lovely book. Did she often talk about St Clodah's?"

Trevor sighed. He knew very well what Isobel was really asking. "Now and then. . . . She loved it there. She could never understand why we didn't love school that much."

Isobel laughed. "I daresay an Irish Convent was rather different from a big English comprehensive in a tough district of a big city."

Trevor nodded and gave her a brief, illuminating grin. But he didn't enlarge on the subject.

"Tell you what," said Isobel, having an idea, "If we got all your father's personal gear together, we could take it round there now, and arrange it all ready for him tomorrow. I've got my car here. What do you think?"

The boy looked visibly relieved. "It – it might make it easier for him to sort of settle in tomorrow."

So they took the things round to the clean, empty rooms, and arranged them as best they could on Cliff's usual small table where he would be able to reach them from his chair. And after this, they stood together looking round at the newly-painted walls and the soft silver-grey carpeting on the floors, and then looked at each other with mutual satisfaction.

"It looks nice, doesn't it?" said Isobel.

"Colin would say smashing!" grinned Trevor.

But Isobel was suddenly grave. "You will be happy here, won't you? All of you?"

"How can you even ask?" countered Trevor, sounding almost fierce. His glance moved to the new ramp outside the window, and the darkening garden beyond, and then returned to her face. "Brave new world!" he said, for he had read his mother's Shakespeare, too.

They smiled at one another then, both of them giving pledges to the future which they knew they must keep.

It was not surprising then, really, when they finally got the whole family and their possessions safely moved over, that Cliff pulled out his favourite record – the New World Symphony – again, and asked Isobel to put it on his old record player. He pointed to the title on the label, and looked up at Isobel, smiling, offering her the only thanks he knew how to give. "*New* . . ." he said.

Isobel had intended to keep Cliff upstairs in her own quiet

rooms until the rest of them had put things into place and got the new place habitable. But on second thoughts, she decided that he would want to know what was going on and have some say in the matter, even if it took him a while to make up his mind what he wanted. It was his flat, after all – his home and his castle – and he would like it all the better if he could help to arrange it. So she left him where he was, in his chair near the window of the big, sunny kitchen-living-room, with his record player beside him, and hoped the ensuing chaos would not upset him.

But Cliff seemed determinedly calm and cheerful, as if he knew this initial moment of arrival was important to all of them and must not be spoiled by a tantrum or a fit of nerves. So he just smiled lopsidedly at Isobel as the first notes of his favourite Dvorak began, and said, "All – right – here. P-perfectly happy . . ." and gave himself up to the music.

Isobel smiled back, repressing a sigh of relief, and went to help the others. She had already made new curtains for all the rooms and hung them in advance (after consulting the others, particularly Georgie, about colours). The carpets were laid. It was only the furniture now. They put up the bunk beds for the children, inspected Cliff's new bed which had been delivered that morning, and made sure his old one was in place and ready for him in the corner of the new living-room. They unpacked the china and the small amount of food they had brought with them, and plugged in the washing machine and the fridge and the brand-new cooker.

Georgie rushed about with blankets and duvets, while the Likely Lads and Alan shoved bits of furniture into place under Trevor's instructions, and Colin made sure that the electric iron and the kettle had the right leads and plugs. Goldie did very little except dance about to Cliff's Dvorak when nobody was looking, until Archimedes came down to have a look at the proceedings, and then the two of them settled down side by side on Cliff's day-bed and dreamed the day away together until Cliff's record came to an end.

By this time, most of the furniture was in place, and the children looked pleadingly at Isobel and said, "Can we go in the garden?"

"Of course," Isobel told them, smiling. "It's all yours." And

232

she watched the three of them streak off to the green and gold world outside. Georgie, as before, went straight to the end of the garden to look at the trees. Colin, as before, stopped to look at every flower. And Goldie accompanied Archimedes on his stately promenade round the garden paths, talking confidingly to him all the way.

Isobel turned from her smiling observation of the children, to find Alan and the Likely Lads beside her, waiting for instructions. And Trevor was standing beside his father, saying hopefully, "What do you think?"

Cliff came slowly back from Dvorak's American Dream, and looked round him with approval. "Nice," he pronounced. "Just – like – home!"

"It *is* home!" said Trevor, grinning.

And Goldie, who had suddenly reappeared without Archimedes, just to make sure her Dad was all right, repeated it happily with her usual dancing twirls. "It *is* home – it *is* home!" she chanted.

Isobel, seeing the time had come for ceremonies, offered her own forthwith. "Tea for everyone upstairs in fifteen minutes!" she announced, including Alan and the Likely Lads in her invitation.

But as regards ceremonies, the children had forestalled her. Georgie arrived breathless from the garden, and went straight to where she had laid down her precious violin. Colin produced his penny whistle, and handed Trevor his father's mouth organ which had mysteriously appeared from Colin's anorak pocket.

"The Tunes," explained Georgie. "We must play the Tunes – to show we've arrived."

"*To show we've arrived,*" echoed Goldie, with yet another twirl, and went to find her tambourine which lay (very conveniently) on top of the box of toys. "*To show we've arrived!*" she repeated, twirling again.

"Well, just one Tune," amended Georgie, and looked at Isobel with her strange gold-flecked green eyes. "We've chosen it specially. It's called '*The Garden of Daisies*'."

Isobel did not answer. She was not sure she could at that moment And the others gathered round her and listened quietly as the little band began their chosen Tune.

Goldie did not sing this time, since it was a dance tune anyway, but just softly stroked her tambourine with rhythmic fingers as if it was an ancient tabor, and managed a few twinkling dance steps as well, and Georgie sawed away valiantly on her violin, fingers flying because it was a tricky, fast-moving tune, and Colin's fingers flew even faster on his penny whistle. Trevor was steady and circumspect, as usual, filling in as much warmth and basic harmony as he could muster on a not-very-special mouth organ. But the effect was lively enough, and made the heart want to dance too. Even Cliff was smiling and tapping out a small tattoo of his own on the arm of his chair.

When it was over, ending in breathless laughter because it was really too difficult, everyone went into the garden with Cliff in his chair, and pushed him cheerfully up the new ramp and in through the garden door to the laden tea-table in Isobel's big kitchen. She did not know it then, but it was the first step in what was to become an established ritual – that Saturday evening family meal – with everyone chattering happily, barriers down and dark tensions forgotten . . . or at least laid aside for the moment.

"Here's to the new flat," said Alan, waving his teacup.

"The new flat!" they chorused, and waved their cups as well.

"And Mizzibell," added Georgie, waving some more.

"And Mizzibell!" they chorused.

"And Alan and the Likely Lads!" Isobel countered, wondering whether Dave and Mitch minded their nickname. But it seemed they didn't, for they were laughing with the rest.

"And my Dad for letting us come!" Trevor put in, knowing it was necessary to make Cliff feel like the decision maker. But it was at Isobel that Trevor looked, and bright sparks of reassurance and thankful relief seemed to dance in both pairs of eyes.

"And Archie – Arky – mee – dees," said Goldie, who knew the story now, and was determined to get the name right. "Because he found it!"

"Archie!" they chorused, waving their cups again.

And right on cue, the sleek black velvet silhouette came into view, walking sedately on elegantly lifted velvet paws,

234

and sprang on to the windowsill where he sat surveying the assembled company with a benevolent eye.

"I think he approves," said Alan.

"'Course he does," agreed Goldie, and got down from the table and went to lean her marigold halo of red curls against the cat's furry flank. "Don't you, Archie?"

And Archimedes winked.

Chapter Fourteen

'The Fair-haired Boy'

Jig

During that first week, Isobel carefully made herself available for any crisis that might arise in the basement flat, but in fact there were few problems. She had arranged with Trevor to keep to her usual arrangement of coming in twice a week to keep an eye on Cliff while Trevor (rather unenthusiastically) went to school. On the first day, she kept the routine familiar and simple, except that she and Cliff managed between them to get his wheelchair up the ramp into the garden. Cliff's arms were very strong by now, and he could push the wheels forward with his hands while Isobel shoved from behind. It was still a bit of a struggle, but Isobel had plans about how to deal with that. So on the second day when she came down to keep Cliff company, she brought someone with her.

"This is Harry Stevens," she said, smiling. "And he thinks he might be able to get you a powered wheelchair."

Harry Stevens was a stocky, grizzled man, with the kind of lived-in face that radiated quiet competence. He held out his hand to Cliff. "It's a society I belong to," he explained, carefully not calling it a charity, which it was. "We fix things if we can to make life easier for wheelchair people to become more independent."

Cliff looked back at Harry's calm, neutral gaze, and decided there was no pity or condescension in it. "S-sounds good," he said.

"You're an engineer, Miss Frazier tells me," smiled Harry. "Should be able to manage it – even if it goes wrong!"

This was clever of him. Cliff was immediately intrigued. "Ex – plain it to me?" he suggested.

"Better still. I've brought one along for you to try," said Harry. "I'll fetch it."

Before Cliff really knew what was happening, he had been skilfully transferred into a chair with magical levers and buttons that sent him forwards or backwards at the touch of his hand.

"Let's try it up the ramp," said Harry. "It should manage all right."

They tried it, with Isobel following slowly behind. The new chair went gently up the slope without any difficulty. Cliff leaned forward a little, urging it on like a horse, but he needn't have bothered.

"Splendid," said Harry. "Now turn round and try going down. Don't forget the brake."

They descended the ramp again, slowly and steadily, and Cliff manoeuvred it in through his new kitchen door in triumph.

"Well done!" grinned Harry. "Now you can say you've executed an electric chair without it executing you."

Cliff's eyes met his delightedly, and the two of them laughed.

Isobel breathed a quiet sigh of relief. It was one more step towards freedom – and Cliff had accepted it without a qualm.

"I'll leave it with you, then," said Harry. "Seems to suit you all right." And he flashed a swift grin at Isobel and went away without another word.

The next problem that had to be solved was Gervase – and with that in mind, Isobel cooked him an extra-special Friday night supper so that he would not feel neglected, and then promptly asked him to tea the next evening as well to meet the whole Broadbent family.

Gervase was clearly doubtful. "Well, I don't know—" he began.

But Isobel interrupted brusquely. "Oh come on, Gervase. Don't be so stuffy. You've got to face it one day! They won't bite. They're really quite harmless. Come and see. You might even find you actually like them!"

Gervase looked at her determined face and capitulated, though not very graciously. "Oh, all right!" he said peevishly, and went home to his own quiet rooms full of misgiving.

But when he arrived the next evening at 'six o'clock sharp. Cliff likes his tea on the dot!' he found them all in the garden, with Cliff proudly demonstrating the manoeuvrability of his new wheelchair, and the assembled family applauding. That is, most of them. For Colin and Isobel were stooping together over one of the flower beds at the end of the garden.

"Who does the garden?" Colin was asking, still looking round him with fascination.

"Oh, I do," said Isobel, briskly pulling up a weed.

"*All* of it?"

She straightened her back and joined him in surveying the ordered green spaces. "Mostly. There is an old man called George who comes to cut the hedge and help with the digging – and sometimes he does the mowing if I'm too busy."

Colin's gaze was now fixed longingly on her face. "Could I . . .? Could I help?"

Isobel met that pleading glance with surprise. "I don't see why not. Do you like gardening?"

"I don't know," said Colin simply. "I've never done any."

"It's hard work," warned Isobel. "But growing things is rather fun."

"I've never actually *grown* anything," Colin admitted in a dreaming voice. "Except some cress at school . . . but I'd like to try."

Isobel smiled. "I'd better give you a small patch of your own then, and you can experiment," she said, and saw by the boy's expression that she had offered him riches.

But now Gervase was coming towards them over the lawn, looking wary but not actively hostile, and she turned back to make the necessary introductions. But she needn't have bothered, for she realized that it had all been done for her by Goldie, who now had Gervase firmly by the hand and was chattering to him happily between small skips of irrepressible *joie de vivre*.

"An' you found Archie, didn't you? So you found us the flat!" she was saying, looking up at him with innocent admiration. "Isn't it lovely?"

238

Gervase didn't know if it was lovely or not, but he was clearly hooked, and Goldie had yet another devoted admirer.

Isobel saw his softened glance with satisfaction, and understood that the battle was almost won before it began. And then Alan arrived (she had asked him to come as well, hoping his calm good humour would help to keep the peace – though it seemed unlikely that it would be needed after all) and the whole party went in to tea, following Cliff's triumphant progress up Isobel's new ramp.

Gervase, meanwhile, with Goldie still firmly in possession of his hand, had been talking to Colin about flowers as they walked past the borders, and now he stopped for a moment on Isobel's dismembered terrace.

"I've been thinking, Isobel," he said, almost shyly, "about those front steps of yours, and this terrace. . . ."

She looked at him in surprise. "Yes?"

"You could do with some pots of flowers, couldn't you?" He glanced from her to Colin and hurried on before she could interrupt. "This young fellow says he likes flowers. . . . Maybe we could become Keepers of the Pots, as it were?"

Then Isobel saw that Gervase was making a real peace offering, and smiled at him with grateful affection. "What a brilliant idea!"

"Brill!" echoed Colin, and smiled even wider.

It was a cheerful meal, and the undercurrents that Isobel had feared did not seem to develop at all. Trevor and Georgie seemed to be aware that Gervase's approval mattered to Isobel, and they were at their most charming and attentive – and Cliff was so pleased with his chair and the new freedom that it brought him, that he sat there in happy silence, dreaming of roads and paths and hills and beckoning distant places. Trevor knew that his father was happy, and he looked across the table at Isobel and said softly, "Dad's very pleased with his new chair."

"It's smashing," agreed Colin, who really did have rather a one-track mind.

"Colin!" protested Georgie. "You mean *magic*!"

"*Magic!*" confirmed Goldie, and was only prevented from doing a twirl by Trevor's heavy hand.

"Sky . . ." said Cliff suddenly.

They all looked at him in surprise.

"Sky's . . . the . . . limit!" he got out, and laughed.

And then the telephone rang in the hall. Isobel went to answer it, her mind still vaguely on Cliff's surprising remark, but as soon as she heard the voice on the line, she knew who it must be. There was something about the overtones of that unfamiliar voice that were nevertheless familiar. . . . They brought back a host of distant memories.

"Is that – er – Isobel Frazier?"

"Speaking."

"Oh." There was a fractional hesitation – an indrawn breath. "This is Bruce – Bruce Conolly." Again the faint pause. "I hope – I hope I'm not ringing too soon . . .?"

"No," said Isobel, also taking a deep breath. "No, of course not."

"The thing is, I'm going to be in Bristol on Monday. I was wondering whether . . ." The deep voice wavered a little, sounding distinctly shy, and then continued, "Would it be possible for me to come and see you?"

"I – on Monday?" Isobel was clutching wildly at straws. "Yes. That would be all right."

"I'm sorry to sound so – so insistent," said the hesitant voice. "But it is rather – er – important. To me, that is." He lapsed into deprecatory laughter. "I hope you don't mind?"

"Of course I don't mind," Isobel said, trying to sound less shy and awkward than he was. "What time will you come?"

"Would twelve o'clock be all right?"

"Perfectly." She drew another tremulous breath. "I shall look forward to it – Bruce."

"So shall I," he answered, all sorts of strange emotions pulsing in the resonant voice. "Till Monday, then," and he rang off before Isobel could say any more.

She went back to the kitchen looking rather white, but she did not say anything about her caller – not then.

It was not until the party had broken up, with Trevor rounding up his family and watching his father steer himself back across the garden, and Gervase had gone home, looking slightly stunned by all the children's chatter, that Alan turned to Isobel and said, "You look a trifle shaken. Was that who I think it was on the phone?"

240

"Yes," said Isobel, sinking into a chair. "It was. And – Oh God, Alan, I'm frightened!"

"What of?"

"I don't know. . . . Recriminations – regrets – criticism – too many memories . . ." She paused, and then laughed at herself a little. "D'you know, Gervase accused me of suffering from frustrated maternal instinct! . . . But I should think Bruce might accuse me of having no maternal feelings at all!"

Alan shook his head at her. "No, he won't. Not if you tell him all that you told me. And you will, won't you?"

She sighed. "Yes. I will – if he asks me."

He glared at her. "Whether he asks or not. You owe it to yourself – and to him."

"I suppose so. . . ." She looked at Alan with sudden, almost child-like appeal. "Will you . . .?"

"You've got to see him alone, Isobel."

"I know that. Of course. But afterwards . . .?" She pushed at her hair with distracted fingers. "I may need – some more of your sound advice!"

He grinned at that, but he knew she was serious and answered tranquilly: "Yes, if it helps. I'll come round later."

At his instant response, she felt ashamed and said fretfully, "I'm using you."

"I should hope so, too," said Alan, and got up to go. "You're tired Isobel. It's been quite a day, hasn't it? And you've been remarkably successful over Cliff and his new chair, and over Gervase, too. . . . And the kids are happy. What are you worrying about?" He creased up his eyes at her in the old, familiar gesture. "I think you're very skilful at skating on thin ice. Tomorrow will be a doddle!" And he went away, laughing, knowing quite well that Isobel was in two minds herself whether to laugh or cry.

When the doorbell rang, promptly at twelve, Isobel was almost afraid to answer it. She stopped in the hall for a moment to look in the mirror, wondering what he would make of her. An alert, questioning face looked back at her, framed by a springy curve of swept-back iron-grey hair (was it neat enough? She gave it a swift pat). And those eyes of hers, iron-grey like her hair, looked distinctly worried, but fairly honest for all that.

Yes, they would have to do. And Bruce – whatever he thought – would have to take her or leave her. She straightened her shoulders, suppressed a sigh, and went to the door.

The young man standing on the step was fair – fair and blue-eyed, with a square-cut rugged sort of face that seemed so familiar to Isobel that she nearly cried out another name than Bruce. For he was like his father – so like him that she almost felt she was back in the past, looking into a face that she knew and loved. . . . But it wasn't that face, of course, and when she came to look at it more closely, she saw a certain strength and determination in it that she had the honesty to admit to herself had not been in the one she had loved so much. . . .

"Come in," she said, suddenly not shy at all, because she saw that the young man was desperately nervous. "I can't treat you as a stranger, Bruce, can I? Come into the kitchen and have a cup of tea . . . or would you like coffee?"

He followed her, relieved that the ice was broken. "I'm Irish," he said, half laughing. "It has to be tea!"

She looked at him in surprise. "I didn't realize – do you live in Ireland?"

"In Eire, yes. I'm an accountant, based in Cork. And my – my parents live in Killarney. I was brought up there."

Isobel was astonished. She had gone all that way to have the child in secret, and when they took him from her, she had supposed he would go far, far away, out of her reach for ever. . . . And he had been sent to some people only a few miles away! "To think I called you Bruce because you were a Scot!" she said, laughing. And then grew serious again. "Tell me about your parents. Do they know of this visit?"

"Yes," he said, and rightly interpreting her anxious look, he added, "They don't mind. In fact they are quite glad. I'll explain why in a minute . . ." He looked at Isobel again, as if still faintly surprised by what he saw. "They are – a lot older than you – and quite frail, now."

Isobel nodded, a small, wicked gleam of satisfaction flicking inside her that she looked 'younger' and could stand up to the comparison. But she was shocked by the thought, and sternly admitted that she was being vain and foolish.

"I – perhaps I'd better explain why I sought you out – and

242

why it's so important to me," he began awkwardly. "Not that I haven't often wondered . . . but until now, I never *needed* to know, and I thought . . . maybe things were better left alone?"

"Yes," Isobel agreed, understanding him that far. "But now?"

"It – it's my wife, you see – my young wife, Caro." His voice softened as he spoke her name, but his eyes, looking honestly into Isobel's, were filled with a kind of painful appeal. "She's – we're expecting our first child soon – and something went wrong, so she's confined to bed – they were afraid she might miscarry. . . ."

"I'm sorry," murmured Isobel, beginning to understand the problem.

"The thing is," Bruce rubbed his hair up the wrong way distractedly, "she's got it into her head that – that there might be something in my genes – or yours – that might make a full-term pregnancy difficult. The doctors keep telling her there isn't, but she won't believe them. I suppose, lying there, she has too much time to think." He gave Isobel a shy half smile. "I mean, I've told her, I'm OK, aren't I? So you must have had me quite successfully!"

Isobel grinned back. "Yes. I did." She paused to think, and then added, "What about your wife's own mother?"

"She's dead, I'm afraid. That's part of the trouble. She was killed in a car crash some time ago, and her father is . . . well, a man is not much help in these matters!" His smile grew a little less shy. "And, of course, my parents – my adoptive parents, I mean – are no help at all from that point of view. They were unable to have children, that's why they adopted me."

Isobel sighed. "Yes. I can see why she thought I might be the only one who could help. . . . But there was no physical problem with me. It was all too simple."

He was waiting now for her to tell him the whole of it – and she felt a great reluctance to do so. But she knew she must. There were a lot of fears and doubts to be allayed, one way and another.

"It must have been hard for you," he said, assuming the most important fact of all without question – and Isobel blessed him for it. "Giving up your own child would be an awful choice."

243

"Yes, it was," said Isobel.

For a moment there was silence between them, while Isobel tried to summon up the courage to talk of that anguished time again, and Bruce wondered if he was right to ask it of her. But at last he said gently, "Can you tell me about it?"

"Yes," she said. "It's time I did." And she told him the whole of it – except, even now, the identity of his father. "I kept his name out of it then," she said, "and I've never mentioned it since. He's dead now, anyway. But – from your point of view, he was a good man (except for this one lapse, and we were very much in love, I suppose). He had two children of his own, and they were quite healthy. I met them once. And he was a fine teacher, much loved by his students. Nothing to be ashamed of there."

"Except seducing an eighteen-year-old and leaving her in the lurch," said Bruce, bristling with indignation.

"I didn't tell him," said Isobel swiftly.

"Don't you think he might have guessed?" retorted Bruce. "Why else would you drop out of your degree course and go away without any explanation?"

Isobel shook her head at him sadly. "I don't know . . . I gave the excuse of my mother's illness, anyway. . . . He may have guessed. But it was better that way, for him and his marriage. . . . It's all old history now, Bruce. It's too late to blame anyone . . ." She looked at him and smiled with sudden affection at his troubled face. "At least you've turned out all right, haven't you? A son to be proud of, I'd say."

He laughed, shyness receding. "You don't know anything about me – yet!"

"At least I know you care about your wife," she said. "And I wish there was some way I could help her."

He seemed to draw himself together then with sudden resolve. "But I think there is," he blurted out. "If – if I can persuade you . . ." And then he stalled, seeming almost afraid to continue.

"Yes?" prompted Isobel.

"I – I wondered if you would agree to come and see her." He began to talk rather fast now, the nervousness returning. "I know it's a lot to ask. But if she saw you, looking so – so young and active and healthy . . . and if you could have a word with

244

her doctors, just to reinforce the argument that there could be no inherited weakness or anything, I think she'd be satisfied then, and stop worrying. . . . She – she's like a child in the midst of a nightmare," he said, his voice uneven. "And we've got to get her out of it."

Isobel was silent. Go back to Ireland? Eire, that is. To what had been to her a place of shame and exile? Could she bear to? But she owed this boy something – of course she did. She owed him a lifetime of not being there when she was needed – as a mother should be. . . . How could she refuse now?

"I – er – it would be all expenses paid, of course," he said, seeing her hesitate.

"That wouldn't be necessary," said Isobel, and smiled at him.

"Then – you'll come?" He sounded almost incredulous.

She took a long, slow breath of decision. "Yes, I'll come . . . But you mustn't expect too much. It may not do any good."

He nodded. "I know. But at least we'll have tried." There was quiet thankfulness in his glance. "When – when could you come? It is – it is rather urgent."

"I can see that."

"I suppose – you couldn't come back with me, could you? I could – we could travel together?"

"How soon must you go?"

He looked at her, half disbelieving her instant agreement. "Well, I – I could wait another day or two . . . I don't like to leave Caro for long."

"Of course not," agreed Isobel. But she was thinking furiously. There were the Broadbents and all their problems. It was too soon, really, for her to dash off and leave them on their own. And there was Alan – and Gervase – and Archimedes to be considered . . . And there was another thought in her head which she had hardly had time to explore yet, and that would involve a serious talk with Trevor . . .

"Give me two days," she said at last. "There are things to be arranged. Then I'll come."

His strong young face lit up with a smile that was curiously like Isobel's own, though she did not know it. "That's wonderful!"

It was on the tip of her tongue to ask him to stay, but she

245

held back, thinking of the other people she had got to talk to first, and how difficult that might be if Bruce was present as an already established part of her life. No, there would be time enough to get to know him on the journey – and over there in that soft green country she was afraid to re-visit.

"I wouldn't be able to stay over there very long," she warned.

"No, of course not. It's marvellous of you to come at all!" he said, and got to his feet, shyly aware that she needed time alone.

"Come to supper tomorrow evening," she suggested. "I should be sorted out by then, and we can plan accordingly."

He agreed, smiling, and took her hand in his. "I can't tell you what this means to me." He didn't try to say any more, but the two pairs of eyes met in mutual relief and gladness. The awkward meeting was over, and they had discovered that they rather liked each other, could even be friends.

"I'm glad you came," she said softly.

"So am I," agreed Bruce.

The future, all at once, seemed full of promise.

Alan, when he came, listened quietly to all Isobel had to tell him and made no comment until she asked him.

"I felt I had to agree to go with him, Alan. I couldn't refuse, could I?"

"No," he said, after a pause. "Being you, you couldn't. But have you thought, it may not do any good?"

"Yes," Isobel nodded. "I told him that. But he said we'd got to try." She looked at him rather anxiously. "But there are all sorts of complications about leaving. What about Cliff Broadbent and the kids . . .? They'll need someone around to turn to, with everything being so new to them."

"I could manage that," said Alan tranquilly. "Trevor trusts me, I think."

Isobel smiled at him gratefully. "I suppose I knew you'd say that. Using you again!"

He laughed. "A devious woman, you are."

But there was something else on her mind, and she badly needed his advice about it. "Alan – there's another possibility in all this. Bruce lives in Cork, and his parents are in Killarney. Neither place is very far from Kerry."

He looked at her and gave a slow nod of comprehension.

"And one of Trevor's books had the name of Katie's convent in it . . . if I can find it."

Alan looked dubious. "Do you think she's likely to be there?"

"N-no." She was as doubtful as he was. "But they might know where she is – or where her parents live – or at least have heard from her. . . ." She gave a small bleak smile that was laced with memories. "The Catholic convents are very good at keeping in touch with their girls . . . and if Katie was in some kind of trouble, I'm sure they'd help her. . . . After all, it wasn't the upright Scottish Kirk that helped me, was it?"

Alan smiled at her. "I see what you mean!"

"But," Isobel went on, "if I am to try to contact them about Katie, I *must* know whatever it is that Trevor is hiding about it – and that means I must tell him why I want to know. . . ." She looked at Alan again, with anxious honesty. "But ought I to – to raise his hopes? It may come to nothing – and then I'll wish I'd never brought it up at all."

Alan sighed. "Yes, that is a problem." He thought about it slowly. "But Trevor's surprisingly tough and practical, isn't he? My guess is, he'd want you to try – whatever the outcome. But I think he'd say don't tell the kids or Cliff where you're going."

Isobel nodded again. "That's rather what I thought. . . . Then – you think I should ask him what really happened?"

"Yes." Alan sounded quite definite now. "Apart from anything else, I think it's time he stopped bottling up all his private worries . . . Here, in this new place, he ought to shed a few of them and become less haunted – don't you agree?"

She smiled at him, acknowledging his good sense. "Yes, I do. It would be nice to see him become a normal, mischievous boy!"

"Give him time," said Alan. "The thaw has already set in!"

But here Isobel sighed again, once more filled with doubts. "Oh Alan, I hope I'm doing the right thing. There are so many issues at stake."

"I think you're doing fine," said Alan. "But you can only work miracles one by one. Not all at once!"

She shook her head at him in half-laughing reproof. "Come to supper tomorrow and meet Bruce. I don't have to hide him from you!"

He looked at her with faint mischief. "And Gervase?"

She laughed, though a shade ruefully. "Not yet. I'd rather tell him when I come back. Then he can't lecture me about going off with an unknown stranger."

"Maybe I should do that, too?"

She saw that he was half serious, and answered him directly. "Alan, he's as straight as a die. I could see that. And desperately worried about his young wife. He even offered to pay my expenses!"

"Then he isn't after your money?"

"*Alan!*"

But he was only teasing. "No, it's all right, Isobel. I trust your judgement. I'm only saying what Gervase would say – and he is only concerned about your welfare, after all."

"I know," she said soberly. "And that's why I won't tell him till it's all over . . . That way, nobody will be upset!" Then a brief grin flashed out. "But you can come and meet Bruce – and form your own opinion."

He grinned back. "I can't wait," he said.

Isobel thought the best way to get Trevor to talk was to offer him a confidence of her own. So she told him about Bruce, and most of the back history of that long-ago affair, though in a slightly shortened version. And she told him about her proposed trip to Ireland and the reason for it – and then plunged in headfirst to the core of the matter.

"I thought I might call at that convent of your mother's, Trevor – if I can find it. . . . They might have news of her." She looked at the boy's clever, listening face for signs of alarm or reluctance, but so far there were none. Only a faint, tired eagerness. He *wanted* to find her – but he thought it improbable. "But if I do," she went on, now sounding as firm and determined as she could, "I'll need to know a bit more about what really happened that day, before she went away. And I think you know. Don't you?"

There was a long silence while Trevor tried to think what to say. But he knew Isobel by now. She wouldn't be fobbed off with half-truths – and somehow he couldn't bring himself to lie to her. She was too honest herself for that.

"You must see that it's important," Isobel persisted. "I'll need to know what to say to her – if she's there, or what message to send to her – if she can be reached. . . . Do you understand?"

"Yes," said Trevor. And could not utter another word.

"I've told you something in strictest confidence, because I know I can trust you," pointed out Isobel. "Can't you do the same?"

The boy's candid eyes seemed to cloud then with some inexplicable emotion which he could not put into words. But he saw that it *was* important – and his long-held silence must be broken, at whatever cost to his father . . . or to anyone else.

"I – don't want my Dad to get into any trouble. . . ."

"There's no reason why he should," said Isobel. "Is there?"

He shook his head doubtfully. "I don't know. . . . It's probably too late now, anyway. But you must promise not to – not to tell the – the Welfare people or – or anyone. . . ."

"Not even Mr Selwyn?" she asked, knowing that Alan would want to know how to help.

Trevor hesitated. "I don't mind him – he wouldn't say anything to harm Dad, would he? But – but no one else."

"All right," said Isobel, wondering whether she had been wrong in her estimation of Cliff Broadbent and his capability of real violence, after all. But she had given her promise now, and Trevor was prepared to talk. He almost seemed glad, at last, to be able to share this long-endured burden of knowledge with someone else.

"I came home from school early," he said. "I often did, when I could cut a class, so that Mum could go shopping. . . ."

Isobel nodded.

"And when I came in, I heard this funny sort of drumming noise – almost like hammers tapping – and Dad kind of *roaring* . . . He used to roar then, when he was angry, because he couldn't get the words out. . . ."

Again Isobel nodded comprehension. She did not dare to

249

interrupt. Trevor's eyes were fixed now on the distant past, and his voice was rough with remembered terror.

"I went into the living-room to see what was going on, and my Mum was – the drumming noise was my Mum's heels kicking against the wall. . . ." He stopped there for a moment, as if he could not bear to go on.

But Isobel knew it all ought to be said now, so she prompted him gently, "Yes . . .? *Against the wall?*"

He shot her one wild glance, and then went on, doggedly remembering. "She was – Dad had his hands round her throat. She couldn't breathe – and he wouldn't let go. . . . He was shaking her, like a – like a doll. . . ." He took a long, shaky breath. "I was just going across to them when she – my Mum – sort of arched her back and tried to pull herself away, but he held on, and the whole wheelchair tipped over so that he fell on top of her on the floor. . . ." He looked at Isobel, less wildly now, but with a kind of desperate appeal. "I – I don't think he knew what he was doing . . . He was – sort of over the top, somehow . . . and he just couldn't let go . . . his hands wouldn't let him. . . ."

Isobel did not let her own sense of horror show in her quiet voice. "What did you do?"

"I – tried to pull his hands off, but I couldn't. He's very strong, my Dad, when he likes. At least his arms are, and his hands . . . So I – I went and got a big bucket of water and poured it all over him. It – it usually worked when he was having one of his rages. . . ."

"Did it work this time?"

"Yes. He let go – and stopped roaring – and I picked Mum up, and got her into the bedroom on to one of the beds. She couldn't really stand, and she was making an awful gasping noise . . ." He shut his eyes for a moment, and then compelled himself to tell her the rest of the story. "I wanted to get the doctor, but when I said so, Mum got all upset and said no. Well, she couldn't really speak, her throat was all bruised and swollen, but she did get out 'No!' in a kind of whisper. So I – I said I'd get her a cup of tea, and she'd better rest a bit. . . . She seemed to agree to that all right, and lay down on the bed quite – quite willingly. . . ."

Willingly? thought Isobel. What does he mean? "And what

about your father?" She asked, picturing the scene with awful clarity.

"I went back and got him into his chair – and then I had to get him a clean T-shirt and another pullover, because the water had made his clothes all wet . . . and he was – sort of crying by now." His voice was bleak with weary understanding. "He often cried when the temper was over." He looked at Isobel with a kind of shamed entreaty, as if he was to blame for something. "I – I suppose I was rather a long time getting the tea . . . but when I took a cup in to my Mum, she'd gone."

Isobel stared. "Just like that?"

He nodded. "I suppose . . . she was too scared to stay. Or she knew it would do no good, he'd only get furious again about nothing . . . Anyway, she went."

"Did she take anything with her?"

"No. No clothes or anything. Only her handbag. And her scarf. I noticed that because she always hung it near her bed on the chair . . . she was very fond of it. We – the kids and me, I mean, – we bought it for her birthday. It was blue, with roses on it . . . Goldie chose it." He gave a sort of stifled gulp, and then went on, "She left most of the week's money on the table, and the note for me that I told you about . . . I don't know where she could have gone, with hardly any money – unless she hitched a ride somewhere. . . ." His pleading glance met Isobel's again. "I – I did try to look for her a bit, on my bike – and I asked her friends down the street, but no one had seen her . . . And I – I didn't like to tell the police, in case they – thought Dad was too violent to be left at home, and took him away. . . ." He took another shaky breath, and asked piteously, "I mean, if they saw the state Mum was in, would he have been up for – attempted murder, or something?"

Isobel shook her head. "I don't think so . . . they would know it was his illness that was responsible. Just as you knew – and your mother knew, too . . . But you are right, they might have tried to take him away."

Trevor sighed. "That's what I thought . . . and we'd have had to go into care . . . that's why I—"

"Why you kept silent all this time?"

"Yes. And Mum, you see – she understood, too. That's why she didn't want the doctor to see her. . . ."

251

All this time, thought Isobel. That terrible burden of knowledge. No wonder the boy looks so haunted sometimes. . . .

"But he is much better now," she said gently. "Isn't he?"

"Oh yes. Much better." He smiled painfully. "Especially since you came."

"I think it was happening anyway," she said, offering reassurance where she could. "He hasn't been – violent like that again, has he?"

"No." Trevor was honest. "Not as bad as that. Though he did . . . still roar and hit out quite a lot at first – but he always ended up crying and being sorry. . . ." There was the same note of curiously adult compassion in the young voice. "And lately – since he began to talk again, he hasn't done it at all. . . ."

Isobel laid a comforting hand on his arm. "You've done an awful lot for him, Trevor, to get him this far . . . And I think he'll go on getting better, now that he's got more freedom."

Trevor smiled again, this time with more certainty. "He's much happier. So are we all."

Isobel's answering smile was warm with encouragement. "That's good to hear." Then she grew serious again. "I'm sorry to put you through all that, Trevor. But you do see why I needed to know?"

"Yes," he said simply.

"And you do realize that I may have no luck at all? They may not know anything about her over there?"

He nodded. "But it's worth a try?"

"Yes," she agreed. "It's certainly worth a try."

"You – you won't tell Dad or the kids where you're going?" he begged, just as Alan had predicted.

"No. Of course not. I'm not sure I even ought to have told you," she admitted sadly. "It may only disappoint you."

He looked at her with sturdy self-knowledge. "I'm used to disappointment," he said. "It's – not being able to do *anything* I can't stand!"

Isobel understood him. It was exactly how she felt herself. "Well, don't expect too much," she warned. "But I'll do my best."

He smiled then, with sudden blazing certainty. "You always do," he said.

* * *

252

In the end, Isobel changed her mind and asked Gervase round to supper as well, telling herself that she didn't like deceiving him anyway, and he wouldn't be able to make a scene with both Alan and Bruce present.

Alan came early, and she was able to tell him most of Trevor's story of the horrific events of that night before his mother left home – getting it all said and shut away quietly between them before the others arrived.

"The poor kid," said Alan, his voice deep with pity, "Carrying all that inside him all this time."

Isobel agreed, and added fervently, "Oh God, Alan, I hope I can find out *something*. He said – and he sounded so absurdly grown-up about it – that he was used to disappointment, but it was not being able to do anything he couldn't stand!"

Alan looked at her with open affection. "And that goes for you, too, I suppose?"

She laughed, and pushed the hair out of her eyes in the old, distracted gesture. "Suddenly there seems to be an awful lot to arrange," she murmured, and then shot a swift appeal at Alan's compassionate gaze. "You will – you will keep an eye on Trevor – on them all – while I'm away?"

"Of course."

"They probably don't need help exactly – only reassurance."

"Don't we all?" agreed Alan, smiling. And then the others arrived, together, on the doorstep, and Isobel had to introduce them.

"Oh, there you are," she said, summoning a brisk and cheerful smile. "Come in, both of you." She led the way into the sitting-room where Alan was waiting, and turned to Gervase first. "Gervase, this is my son, Bruce, who is taking me to Ireland for a few days to meet his young wife, Caro." Then she turned back to Bruce and added, more easily, "And these are two old friends of mine, Alan and Gervase, who are going to look after things for me while I'm away."

Bruce took it very calmly, smiling and shaking hands without any embarrassment. And Gervase, after a moment of stunned silence and a slight gulp, murmured greetings and expressed no obvious surprise at all.

Alan, of course, was already primed, and anyway found

fraught situations easier to handle than Gervase did, so his smile was genuine and easy. But his bright, intelligent gaze summed up the young man before him very shrewdly, and liked what he saw. It made it easier, too, that the boy was so absurdly like Isobel – with the same illuminating smile and the same clear, strong features.

They drank a ceremonial sherry together. Gervase liked his sherry. Alan really preferred whisky, she knew, and she suspected that Bruce probably did, too, but they both of them accepted their glass without demur. Alan took charge of the conversation then, asking about southern Ireland and the countryside around Cork, and recounting earlier trips of his own to the green hills of Eire. He was a skilled talker, and did not let anyone have time to feel awkward.

Bruce seemed well aware of what Alan was doing, and played up with beautiful Irish manners, and though Gervase said very little, and looked at Isobel from time to time with covert amazement, he did not seem unduly put out. In fact, if anything, Isobel reflected, passing round the potatoes at the dinner table, he seemed to be registering approval rather than dismay.

At last, they were all four sitting over coffee round the fire (for the spring evenings were still chilly), when Isobel said, "Well, Bruce, I think I can safely leave things in the capable hands of these two kind people." (Best to assume they are going to be kind, she thought grimly, and then they can't refuse!) She turned, smiling, to Gervase. "Alan has promised to look in on our little family below stairs, in case they need anything. Could I ask you to do the same? Especially now that Goldie and Colin have taken such a shine to you."

"Have they?" Gervase looked pleased. "Well, I – yes, of course I'll come and see them." He looked from her to Alan, trying to sound as warm and willing as he knew Alan would. It was hard for Gervase. He didn't find it easy to be generous-hearted. But he tried. "Alan and I had better take it in turns!"

Isobel grinned at them both, well pleased with their alliance. "Goldie will look after Archimedes," she mused. "She'll love that . . . and Colin can look after the garden – so long as he doesn't pull up anything till I get back!"

They laughed at that, and Gervase privately decided to keep a sharp eye on the fate of Isobel's plants.

"Georgie can look after the household, and Trevor will have enough to do looking after his father," she went on, half to herself, and then looked up at her two old friends with a sudden flash of brilliant intensity. "So it only remains for you two to try to instill a sense of confidence," she said. "Make them feel wanted and protected – till I return!"

The two men looked at her, both touched by her open trust in their goodwill.

"We'll do our best!" said Alan, smiling.

"Our *very* best," echoed Gervase, surprised by his own fervour.

Bruce had been watching all this in some amazement. But Isobel turned to him then with a quiet explanation. "It's just a young family who have taken over my basement," she said, smiling. "I'll tell you all about it presently."

He nodded, waiting for Isobel to return to their more pressing travel arrangements.

"I'll just have to tell them what's happening," she said. And then a thought struck her. "Why don't we all go down and see them now? They won't have gone to bed yet. It won't take long." And then she added as an urgent afterthought, "But don't mention Ireland. I'll explain why later."

There was no denying Isobel in this mood. They all followed her meekly, swept along in the tide of her swift decisions. And Archimedes, hiding as usual from too much company under a chair, came out and joined the procession.

Isobel had installed a Yale lock on the door to the basement stairs, and a bell that she could ring if she wanted to visit the Broadbent family. That way, she thought, they would feel more private and in charge of their own domain. So now she rang the bell and waited for someone to come running up the stairs.

It was Georgie who came, and she greeted Isobel with a beaming smile of welcome.

"Brought some friends to see you," said Isobel. "Just for a moment. I've got something to tell you."

So everyone trooped downstairs to the cheerful, sunny living-room. It really did look nice, Isobel thought, admiring

255

her own curtains and the silvery carpeting, and rejoicing secretly that the setting sun had chosen that moment to send a last, golden shaft of light through the windows.

She went first to Cliff, and the three men followed and shook his hand, rightly assuming that ceremonies of arrival and departure mattered to this wary man marooned in his wheel-chair. Isobel explained about going away for a few days, and watched the children's expressions grow a little apprehensive as she did so. Cliff's eyes were rather panic-stricken, too, and she hastened to reassure them all.

"I won't be away long. And Alan and Gervase have promised to come and see you and find out of you need anything."

Alan and Gervase nodded solemnly, and chorused, "Yes, we have."

Goldie, though, was not convinced. She took Isobel by the hand and gazed up at her with the searching clarity of a suspicious child. "You are coming back, aren't you?"

"Of course I am," said Isobel, suddenly aware once more that this was a child whose mother had gone away one day, and not come back at all. "It will only be for a few days . . . and you are going to look after Archimedes for me, aren't you? I'll give you all his tins of cat food for *just one week*. Is that all right?"

The child looked at her for a moment longer with that clear, probing gaze of truth, and then seemed at last to be satisfied. "All right," she agreed. "Archie will be safe with me." And she picked up Archimedes and hugged him close to make sure.

Then Colin and Gervase went into a huddle about the garden, Georgie produced cups of tea for everyone, and Bruce looked from Alan to Isobel and from them to the Broadbent family with smiling appreciation and said nothing at all.

"We'll be all right," said Trevor sturdily, signalling a strange mixture of reassurance and hope with his eyes to Isobel.

"I know you will," she answered. "I'll be home again soon."

"*Home again soon!*" chanted Goldie, and tried to dance with Archimedes.

Then Isobel took her party of half bewildered, half enchanted menfolk back up the stairs, trying not to look back at the row of upturned faces below. Archimedes, she noted, was among those faces, too. He had elected to stay in Goldie's arms.

Only Trevor followed her, ostensibly to open the door politely. But as he did so, he grasped Isobel for a brief moment with a convulsive hand, and murmured, "Good luck!" before he let her go.

Good luck? she thought. Oh God, I shall need it – in more ways than one. But aloud she only said to Bruce, with smiling decision, "Now the decks are clear. We can go."

Chapter Fifteen

'Happy to Meet and Sorry to Part'

Double Jig

The girl lying in the high hospital bed looked heartbreakingly young and frightened. Fair hair spread out on the pillow, blue eyes wide and beseeching, she gazed up at Isobel with a mixture of trepidation and hope.

"It was so good of you to come . . ." she said, her face lighting with a pale, shy smile.

"I wanted to come," stated Isobel simply as she sat down beside the bed. "But I'm not sure I can be any help."

"Oh but you can," said the girl. "Just seeing you . . . looking so—"

"Ordinary?" suggested Isobel, smiling.

"I was going to say – young," protested Caro, also smiling a little. "And – and so healthy and calm," she added. "Bruce was quite right."

Isobel had insisted that Bruce went in to see his young wife alone before bringing Isobel in to meet her. There must be things the two of them needed to say to each other, and it would also give him time to tell Caro as much as he cared to relate of Isobel's past history. It would save a lot of painfully repeated explanations. Now, she thought, the girl had already accepted her, Bruce had done a good job. She seemed willing to allow the past and all its pressures – including Isobel's reasons for giving up her son to another's keeping – to be laid aside while they considered the urgent problems of the present.

"Tell me what you want to know," Isobel said gently.

Caro looked at her with a kind of desperate candour. "Everything," she said. "About how you had Bruce – whether you were well – whether it was difficult. I know it must have been frightening for you, all alone among strangers – Bruce told me. . . ."

"The nuns were very kind," said Isobel, in a soft, reminiscent tone. "It wasn't so bad."

Then Isobel deliberately began to talk, describing everything that had happened, including the perilous, pain-fraught hours of labour and the final sad but triumphant moment of birth.

"So there he was," she concluded, smiling at Caro's anxious, listening face. "Perfectly formed and perfectly healthy – a lovely, lusty boy who yelled with rage at the wicked world as soon as he saw it!"

Caro laughed, but it was a shaken sound.

"And you must admit," went on Isobel, the smile still lingering, "that he has turned out to be what they call 'a fine figure of a man'!"

"Yes," admitted Caro, her laughter sounding a little less uncertain. "He has!" But she was still troubled. "I did wonder – I did ask the doctors – if there could be anything in his genetic make-up. . .? I mean, I believe sometimes a man's sperm can have—?"

"Abnormalities? Yes." Isobel had been reading up on it, so that she could sound positive and well informed. "But Bruce has been tested for that, hasn't he?"

"Yes," Caro sighed. "They told me he was quite normal. . . . Nothing there that could cause a miscarriage."

"Have you had a scan?" asked Isobel suddenly.

The girl turned her head away, moving it restlessly from side to side. "Yes. When this – when things started to go wrong, they did one . . . but I was too frightened to look."

Isobel smiled at her. "Next time, you must have the courage. It's a bit of a miracle, you know, being able to see your own baby. . . . They couldn't have done it in my day!"

The girl sighed again. "I know. I'm an awful coward."

"I think you've just got run down and overtired," said Isobel cheerfully. "Did you have a bad bout of flu or anything?"

"Yes," Caro said, surprised at the connection. "Why?"

"Flu makes cowards of us all," smiled Isobel. "And it can cause all sorts of odd complications. Didn't they tell you that?"

259

She looked uncertain. "They did say something about a viral infection – could cause it. . . ."

"There you are, then." Isobel's voice was deliberately brisk. "I bet you that's been the trouble." She laid a kind, steadying hand on Caro's nervous fingers which were still plucking restlessly at the bedclothes. "I'll tell you what I'll do, though, Caro – if it will relieve your mind. I'll go and talk to your doctors – and if they want to do any blood tests or anything that they think would help, I'll tell them to get on with it!" She grinned at Caro's doubtful face. "But if, after all that, they can find nothing to worry about, you *must* believe them. Understand?"

"Yes," agreed Caro, somehow caught up in Isobel's insistence.

"By the way," asked Isobel, her voice entirely innocent, "Does Bruce like music?"

"I – yes, he does," said Caro, sounding somewhat bewildered. "Why?"

"They say, you know, that babies in the womb are affected by what they can hear – or what they can feel of their mother's emotions. . . . The nuns used to play a lot of music – and plainsong chant is very soothing. . . ."

Caro was silent for a moment. But she was not a fool. She knew very well what Isobel was saying. "You are quite right," she said at last. "I have been very selfish."

"Not selfish," murmured Isobel. "Short-sighted, perhaps. . . . A tranquil baby is much easier to live with, I'm told!" She grinned at Caro in a conspiratorial way. "You'd better get Bruce to sing you some plainsong!"

And when Bruce came back to see how they were getting on, he found the two of them laughing together, and his young wife already looking a different girl – the shadows already receding.

True to her word, Isobel went with Bruce to talk to Caro's doctors. The gynaecologist and Caro's GP, who also ran a clinic at the hospital, saw them together, pooling resources, and both assured Bruce that there was nothing organically wrong – things had already settled down, and there was no danger to the baby now, if Caro took reasonable care and had plenty of rest.

Even so, Isobel explained Caro's fears in clear, straight-forward terms, and both doctors listened to her. Whether they were impressed by her air of authority, or just careful and compassionate doctors, she did not know, but they seemed to take the matter seriously.

"I think she's been reading too many medical books," said Isobel, with a faint smile, "or listening to too many old wives' tales!"

The two men smiled back. "That's something I often have to contend with," remarked the GP ruefully.

"What I'm trying to say," persisted Isobel, "is that you'd better do whatever tests you can think of that might be relevant – if you and the Lab can spare the time, that is – and then you can safely tell her that all her fears are groundless!" She looked at the doubtful faces and added firmly, "I think it may be important for her recovery. She's got two or three months to go yet. She can't spend all that time lying down in a blue funk!"

They laughed then at Isobel's forthright words, and Bruce laughed, too – but they agreed. And Isobel cheerfully submit-ted to whatever was required of her. Then it was just a case of waiting for results – and in the meantime, Isobel had other tasks on her mind.

She was staying in Bruce's house, at his insistence, and now they went back together to the pleasantly leafy suburb of Cork where he lived, and settled down in his kitchen over a cup of tea.

"I hope it will work," said Isobel, looking into Bruce's face with anxious affection.

"She's much better already," he answered, smiling. "You've worked wonders!"

"She's only frightened," Isobel told him gently. "Birth is a big thing to undertake. . . . She's got a bit too much imagination, that's all."

Bruce nodded. Then he seemed to remember that he was the host here, and Isobel had already put herself out considerably by coming at all. It was time he offered to do something for her in exchange.

"You said you had a couple of other errands . . . Can I be of any help with those?"

Isobel looked doubtful. "I don't know. . . . Maybe I ought to hire a car."

"You don't need to do that. I'm here, aren't I?"

"What about your work?"

"Oh, I took a week's leave to come and find you. We haven't used it all up yet. The firm can get on very well without me for another day or two."

Isobel was still regarding him doubtfully. "And Caro?"

He smiled. "I usually go in every evening. She has other visitors during the day. Her friends are very good." He saw that Isobel was still hesitating, and decided to be direct. "Where do you want to go?"

She took a firm breath of resolve. "To my old convent first – where you were born."

"Where is it?"

"Near the Ring of Kerry – just off Kenmare Bay . . . I could take you there."

"Then take me there you shall. Tomorrow morning?"

"Fine," she agreed, smiling. And then added half laughing, "Come to think of it, Sister Ursula would probably love to meet you – since she brought you into the world."

"What a responsibility," said Bruce solemnly. "But I'd like to meet her, too. Being alive is no small thing!"

Isobel laughed. Then grew serious again. "Talking of thanks, Bruce – there's something else I'd like to do – but I don't know whether it would be a good idea, or if you'd approve?"

"Try me," he said, fairly convinced by now that anything Isobel suggested would probably make sense.

"I'd like to meet your parents – and thank them for all they've done . . ." She saw his surprise and tried to explain her reasons. "Bruce, I've seen this situation before, many times – at school, and in my welfare work. . . . Foster parents, adoptive parents, grandparents and emergency aunts! They do everything for the children in their care – feed them, clothe them, teach them how to cope with the world, and, most of all, love them . . . and then what happens? Either the so-called 'natural parent' turns up and demands to take the child back, whether anyone likes it or not, and usually entirely disregarding the child's own wishes . . . or the child

262

itself grows up and suddenly demands to know its 'natural' mother or father. Though there's often nothing 'natural' about the supposed bond between them at all – not compared with the wonderful bond of love and trust that has been built up between them and the parents they know. But off they go, with never a backward glance, to find a perfect stranger – and never stop to think how much hurt they may be causing."

Bruce looked at her, astonished at her sudden eloquence. "I didn't realize you felt like that!"

She smiled at him. "Oh, I don't. Not about you. I know why you had to come and find me. And for my own sake – as well as for Caro's – I'm truly glad you did. . . . But – what of your own adoptive parents? You said they didn't mind. But are you sure?"

"Yes, I think so. They were only concerned with trying to help Caro – and feeling a bit frustrated and useless because they couldn't." He saw that she was still uncertain, and hastened to reassure her. "But I'm sure they know how I feel about them."

"Have you ever told them?"

He stopped short at this, considering it. "I – perhaps not . . . It's not something a man of thirty-six finds easy to say!"

Isobel did not smile. She was deadly serious. "You must tell them, Bruce. It's important."

"Yes," he admitted, sighing. And then, more certainly, "Yes. You're right."

"You say they're getting frail," pursued Isobel remorselessly. "People spend half their lives regretting the things they didn't say before it was too late. . . ."

He nodded, well aware of the implications. "All right," he agreed, in smiling acquiescence, "we'll call and see them, too. Killarney's not much farther. Satisfied?"

"Quite," said Isobel demurely. "You're very obliging!"

They drove in glancing sunlight and dazzling white cloud through a landscape of green hills, looming mountains and silver water, turning off the road from Cork at Pounds Bridge towards the long sky-reflecting tongue of water that was the Kenmare River estuary. It was a long time since Isobel had been that way, but she remembered it – remembered, too, how timelessly tranquil and beautiful this gentle land was.

Eventually, they found the small unmarked side road that led to the convent, and finally pulled up outside the soft grey stone of the gatehouse. There was an unobtrusive wooden door set in the wall, with an old-fashioned bell-pull hanging beside it. Isobel rang the bell and waited. A young, rosy face came to the grille and looked at her enquiringly. Isobel thought, with a faint flick of regret, they will all be old now – the faces I knew. A whole new generation – perhaps two – of green young novices and desperate sanctuary seekers like me. But I suppose their needs will be the same, and the peace that this place has to offer will be the same.

She smiled at the young face, and stated her business. "Tell Sister Ursula – I mean, Reverend Mother – that Isobel Frazier is here with her son, Bruce, and would like to see her."

The face retreated, and feet scurried away. Presently, they returned, and the rosy face smiled even more cheerfully at Isobel. "Reverend Mother would like to see you."

"Both of us?"

"Yes."

So they went in through the wooden door, and followed the tripping young novice across the open courtyard and into the familiar stone corridors that Isobel remembered so well. The central corridor was wide, with doors on either side, and ended in an open archway leading to a paved cloister with a glimpse of green gardens beyond. Isobel remembered those gardens. Herbs, flowers, vegetables, venerable fruit trees – she had tended them all and loved every stick and stone of that scented, sun-drenched space. . . .

Reverend Mother's office was the last door on the left, Isobel recalled, and she could not help a small frisson of remembered apprehension as she stood on the threshold of that small, spare room with its plain silver crucifix on the wall. She had been afraid of Mother Agnes then – afraid of her disapproval and censure, of the condemnation in her eyes and the rejection of her strict, shocked mind. But she had received nothing but kindness and acceptance. No word of blame was ever said – no judgement given to make her feel ashamed. . . . And now, this time, it was her old friend Sister

Ursula behind that door – the gentle, laughing nun who had helped her through the darkest days of her exile and brought her safely through the frightening ordeal that childbirth had seemed to an inexperienced girl.

"Isobel, my child!" said the soft voice she knew. "At least, I suppose I can't call you my child now! But maybe I can say it to Bruce with impugnity?" And the tall, black-clad figure came unhesitatingly up to Isobel and embraced her fondly, and then turned and did the same to Bruce. "Come in," she said, "and tell me all about it," and shooed the little novice away with a smiling nod.

So they did, and the stately form of Reverend Mother who had been merry-hearted Sister Ursula, leant forward in close attention and listened to all they had to say.

"And your wife, Caro, is feeling better already?" She looked smilingly from Bruce to Isobel. "That is good news. So your journey was not wasted."

"No, indeed," said Bruce fervently, and glanced at Isobel with undisguised affection. "She – my mother – has worked miracles."

My mother, thought Isobel. How strange that sounds. But it won't do. "I think you should call me Isobel," she said, her eyes meeting Reverend Mother Ursula's almost shyly, as if seeking approval. "It's easier . . . especially if we are going to see your parents."

Ursula nodded, not giving Bruce time to reply. "That sounds very sensible. I always liked the name Isobel."

The three of them found themselves smiling companionably, as if all kinds of past tensions had been resolved.

Then Isobel made her next request. "I wonder if you can help me to find another convent in Kerry – at least I think it is in Kerry. I have no address, only the name 'St Clodagh's Convent School'." She saw Ursula looking at her in some surprise and went on to explain a little of Trevor's history, and the urgent need to trace the missing Katie.

Bruce had already heard as much of the Broadbents' story as Isobel was able to tell him, and was prepared for her sudden request but even he had not expected her to follow it up so soon. . . . My mother – I mean, Isobel – is a fast worker, he told himself, smiling a little. She doesn't let the grass grow under her feet!

"And you think this young mother, Katie, might have returned to St Clodah's?" If Ursula guessed Isobel was leaving out certain crucial facts, she did no say so.

"I don't know," Isobel confessed. "It's a very long shot, I'm afraid. But it's the only real clue I've got . . . I thought they might have news of her – if they've kept in touch . . . And also, from my own experience," she smiled at Ursula with sudden warmth, "a convent is the most likely place to offer help and comfort, if she was in need of it."

Ursula smiled back. "I hope you are right." She thought for a moment, and then said, "Wait here a moment. Our librarian might have a list of all the various foundations . . . It is not a name I know – but we shall see," and she went quietly and purposefully away, leaving Isobel and Bruce looking at each other with a mixture of hope and perplexity.

"She's a very nice person," said Bruce appreciatively. "I'm glad you had her to help you."

"And to help you!" countered Isobel, smiling. "We both owe her a lot."

"Don't we, though?" agreed Bruce, and fell silent, overwhelmed by the complexities of the past.

There was another view of the garden from the small window in the outside wall of Reverend Mother's room, and Isobel felt a curious wave of nostalgia assail her when she looked out at those orderly rows and neat box hedges. She had spent many happy hours out there, working among the others, away from the pressures and anxieties of the world outside.

"I used to help in the gardens," she said in a dreaming voice, "until it got too difficult to bend!"

She glanced at Bruce, meeting a smile that was almost tender. "Caro's a gardener," he murmured. "Or she was."

Isobel nodded. "It would be nice to see her out of doors again in the sun . . . it would do her so much good."

"We probably will soon," agreed Bruce, "the way things are going now – anything could happen!"

But before they could say any more, Ursula had returned, carrying a slip of paper in her hand. "This is the only St

Clodah's we could find," she said. "Near a small village on the edge of Tralee Bay."

Isobel looked at the address in some doubt. "If it was a school, wouldn't it have to be near a town?"

"Not necessarily. It could be a boarding school, with a few local day girls. That is often the pattern."

Isobel nodded. "Well, it's certainly worth a try. I'm very grateful to you." She paused, and then added, smiling, "In fact, while we're on the subject, Bruce and I were just saying we both owe you an awful lot!"

Reverend Mother Ursula laughed. "I don't think it is *awful*," she said. "As far as I can see, things have turned out remarkably well in the long run!" And she gave them both another sedate, smiling embrace before sending them on their way.

They drove on, past the wooded foothills of the MacGillycuddy Reeks, and the slopes of the Purple Mountain, past waterfalls and flower-filled hollows to the magical silver lakes of Killarney – black sentinel trees and snow-bright cloud shapes reflected in their tranquil, unbroken surfaces.

"Beautiful," breathed Isobel. "I'd forgotten how lovely it was."

Bruce glanced at her sideways. "Lots to see. It's a pity you can't call this a real holiday and take your time."

Isobel smiled. "Another day, perhaps. . . . Things are too pressing now."

And they were, of course. Not only Caro and her recovery from panic, but the Broadbents, too. In fact, Isobel was surprised to find that she minded being away from them, and kept fretting about their welfare. So much so that she made up her mind to ring Alan this evening and find out how they had been getting on . . . that little, beleaguered family had somehow wound itself round her heart.

"Won't be long now," said Bruce, as they came into Killarney. "Just down the road."

The Conollys lived in a modest house in a quiet tree-lined road on the edge of the town where there was plenty of space to breathe, but not too much distance between them and the local shops. They were both in their seventies now, and did not venture very far afield unless Bruce came and fetched them.

267

Maeve Conolly had cataract and could not see very well, and John, her husband, was stiffened with arthritis, and found driving a bit hazardous. But they were cheerfully unharassed by their various disabilities and still game for any new venture if it could be undertaken without too much physical exertion. And they always welcomed Bruce with open arms.

They did so now, and then turned to Isobel with more reserve, but with the same hospitable warmth.

"This is Isobel," said Bruce unnecessarily. "And she has already worked wonders with Caro . . . I think things are going to be all right."

"That's good news," Maeve said, smiling at Isobel.

"Glad to hear it," growled John. "Time someone drummed some sense into her!"

"*John!*" Maeve protested – but her eyes met Isobel's in the age-old conspiracy of women who said to each other: Men! They don't understand a thing!

Isobel recognized that look and smiled back. But she also recognized the unmistakable undercurrent of fear that these two generous-hearted people were trying hard to disguise – and she could not bear it. She took a step forward and impulsively took Maeve's hand in hers.

"There's something I want to say to you both – that I've wanted to say for many years, only I had no means of reaching you. . . ." She took a deep breath, and looked into Maeve's anxious, milky eyes with a kind of honest bravado. "Thank you for being the ones who wanted Bruce – and for everything you've done for him – and for me. And I want you to know that although it is wonderful for me to meet him, and to meet you, this is where he belongs, with you, and I would never try to change things."

She hoped she had made everything clear, and that they would not be too embarrassed by her straightforward approach. Bull at a gate, that's me, she thought. Well, I'd rather be like that than sly and evasive. . . . They'll have to take it or leave it.

But Maeve knew just what to do. She reached up her arms and hugged Isobel, saying in a shaken voice between laughter and tears, "Oh, what a relief! Now we know where we are!"

"How about coming out to lunch with us?" suggested Bruce,

aware that everyone needed a bit of ordinary good cheer. "The Blue Boar does a lovely steak and kidney pie!"

John Conolly laughed. "Now you're talking!"

So they had a friendly, comfortable lunch, remarkably free from undercurrents, accompanied by a lively folk group playing traditional Irish tunes. Swaying infectiously to the irresistible rhythms of jig and reel, performing prodigies of dexterity on violin, tin whistle and bodran drum, they worked their way through the old favourites. Announcing each one in their soft Irish voices, they gave the listeners in the bar '*Hurry the Jug*,' '*Saddle the Pony*' and '*The Cuckoo's Nest*,' and several others that Isobel did not know. But they reminded her so much of the Broadbent children, fingers flying on fiddle and penny whistle, Goldie dancing, and Trevor seriously trying to hold things together on his father's mouth organ, that she found herself telling Maeve about them, and their unshakeable belief that playing the Tunes would bring their mother home.

"That's sad," said Maeve, touched by the story, "and very Irish! Do you really think it will work?"

Isobel was about to give a noncommittal answer, when John Conolly suddenly joined in. "You never know. Stranger things have happened in Ireland!"

They laughed, and Isobel turned back to hear one last jig from the group, who had just finished the '*Dandy-O*,' and were now embarking on '*Youghal Bay*'.

"They're pretty good," said Bruce, smiling at Isobel's rapt attention. "But we'd better move, if we want to go on to Tralee."

Isobel looked at him doubtfully. "Have we got time?"

He nodded tranquilly. "It's only twenty miles. We can easily make it."

"And get home in time for Caro?"

"Certainly. I don't imagine you'll want to spend all that long at St Clodagh's?"

"No," said Isobel slowly. "But I'll have to see them on my own this time – that is, if they are the *right* St Clodagh's. Will you mind waiting?"

"Of course not." He did not ask what was so private about this second visit, and Isobel did not try to explain.

Maeve and John Conolly had got to their feet by this time

– a little dazed by the insistent beat of the music – and Bruce steered them out of the noisy bar into the car, with Isobel close behind them, and drove them all home.

When they got to the Conollys' front gate, Bruce left Isobel in the car for a moment while he saw his parents safely to the door. Once there, he said something to them that made them both stare at him with rather incredulous smiles, and look quite rosy with pleasure. Isobel did not hear what was said, but she could guess. Bruce had not forgotten her fierce lecture about ingratitude. . . . Then he hugged them both and came back to the car, leaving the smiling Conollys waving from the door.

"You were quite right," he said.

"Was I? What about?"

"Oh – a good few things," he grinned, and let in the clutch and drove off into the sun.

It was sun and shadow all the way to Tralee, and then it rained suddenly and there was a brilliant rainbow over the sea. They followed its miraculous, iridescent colours down the long, silvery curve of the coastal road that skirted Tralee Bay, and only left it behind them when they turned off onto the small side road, and then on to the narrow farm track that was supposedly leading them to St Clodah's.

They were driving through green fields now, and a sharp turn brought the rainbow back above another glimpse of silver sea ahead of them. The colours were fading now, slowly dissolving into gossamer-thin mirages – a hint of rose here – a shimmer of purple there – a green that was brighter and clearer than any leaf – touching sea and land with a brief wash of unearthly brilliance before it vanished in the rainwashed sky. Isobel hoped it was a good omen, but she was not sure.

"That must be it," said Bruce, as a squarish, handsome stone house came into view, standing in pleasant grounds at the edge of the village. This time there was no question of difficulty about admission – St Clodah's was no enclosed order, but a school, and Bruce drove up the drive through an avenue of chestnut trees just coming into leaf, and parked on the sweep of gravel by the front door.

There was a stretch of green playing field across the drive, and groups of girls were strolling about there, while others were emerging from the house in twos and threes to join their friends on the sunlit grass.

"It looks like a nice place," commented Bruce, and left Isobel to find her own way in.

A pleasant nun met her in the entrance hall, and listened attentively while Isobel stated her errand. At length she said, smiling kindly; "Well, you may be lucky. School has just ended for the day, so Reverend Mother may be able to see you. I'll go and ask."

"Wait," said Isobel. "Take this with you," and she handed over the precious copy of Shakespeare with Katie's name in it, which she had brought with her all the way from home.

The nun accepted it gravely and carried it away. And presently she returned, without the book, and said simply, "Reverend Mother will see you. Come this way."

It was clear that Reverend Mother was also the headmistress of the school, and the study to which the young nun brought Isobel was suitably large and impressive – very unlike the small bare cell where Reverend Mother Ursula presided. But the woman confronting Isobel was neither formidable nor pretentious. She was dressed in the usual austere nun's robe, and her face was thoughtful and questioning rather than severe.

Isobel explained again, carefully, that she was seeking news of Katie Broadbent, who had been Katie O'Sullivan, and whose present whereabouts nobody seemed to know. She pointed to the volume of Shakespeare which lay open on the desk, and added sadly, "This is the only clue I have."

The woman opposite her had clear, very observant grey eyes, and they were now fixed on Isobel's face in shrewd appraisal. "Who wants to know?" she asked, admitting nothing so far.

"Her children," said Isobel promptly. "All four of them. And her husband, in his wheelchair."

There was a long silence, and then the other woman sighed and said, "I was not the headmistress when Katie was a girl here. I was just the English mistress then, but I knew her very well." Her gaze raked Isobel's with searching enquiry. "I think you'd better tell me all about it."

So Isobel did. She began at the beginning – with the stolen

271

milk bottle, and went on to the end, and did not leave out Trevor's account of that awful final day when Katie fled. She was breaking her promise to Trevor, but she knew that he would realize that this was the one place where the whole story had to be told.

The silence this time was even longer, and then Reverend Mother looked at Isobel with much compassion and said, "What a story! I thought it must be something like that – but she told me nothing."

Isobel spoke eagerly. "Then she is here?"

"No." The troubled headmistress sighed again. "She *was* here – for a long time. She was very ill – but now she has gone."

"Gone where?" asked Isobel, her heart giving a lurch of dismay.

"We do not know," said the headmistress slowly, and then seemed to make up her mind – like Isobel – to breach a confidence. "Since you have been so frank, I think I had better be the same." She folded her two hands together in front of her on the desk, looked away from Isobel out of the window, and began to talk. "She came here in a pitiful state – I don't know how long she had been wandering, or how she got here, but she was wet through, and scarcely able to stand. She had a scarf round her neck – a blue one – which she refused to take off at first, but when we did finally get it off, we found that her throat was so bruised and swollen that she could scarcely swallow, let alone speak. I understand why, now." Her straight, candid gaze returned to Isobel's face. "We got the doctor, of course. She had collapsed completely by this time, and he diagnosed pneumonia and some kind of shock. She couldn't stop shaking – even her teeth were chattering. But when he suggested that she would be better off in hospital, she made a dreadful scene and refused to go." Once again her eyes met Isobel's. "She was . . . very distraught."

Isobel nodded. "Trevor – the eldest boy – said the same. She wouldn't even let him call the doctor. . . . He thought she was afraid of what the authorities might do to Cliff – her husband – if they found out about his violence."

Reverend Mother agreed. "That must have been the trouble all along. . . . She would not talk – even if she could. She

272

wouldn't see a priest – or go to confession. She just lay there in silence – and shook all over."

Isobel could picture it, and sighed with pity. "The poor girl. . . ."

The nun's long, ascetic face reflected the same pity, but her voice was still crisp, still reflected faint criticism. "Yes, well – she got better very slowly, but she still would not talk, and we felt it was best to leave her alone and not try to put more pressure on her. . . . Of course, we did not know about the children—"

Isobel interposed then, "She left this curious note. Trevor was sure she meant the Social Services to take over and put them all into care, where they would be safe and looked after. . . . It was her way of trying to protect them – or so the boy believes."

The headmistress nodded. "I think I can believe that, too . . . It might be how a frightened woman would think – especially if she was at the end of her tether. And it might be a way of forcing a decision on the authorities about how to deal with her husband, too – a decision she could not make herself. . . ."

"It makes a kind of desperate sense," acknowledged Isobel. Then she prompted the troubled nun to go on. "So what happened to her next?"

The truth-loving grey eyes looked even more troubled. "She tried to run away again, twice, before she was well enough to cope. . . . Each time, one of our staff found her and brought her back . . . and each time she got ill again, as a result. But the third time . . ." She shook her head sadly. "She could talk by then – though only in a kind of hoarse whisper – and she kept saying she must earn some money – *a lot of money*, she kept whispering. But when I offered her some, if she would tell us where she wanted to go, she would not say."

The two women looked at each other in mute dismay, and then the crisp voice went on, a little more gently now. "We tried every way we could think of to gain her confidence – but she was still afraid to speak. When I suggested the confessional again, she shuddered, and said '*It's too late for that . . . I can't go back. . . .*'"

Isobel sighed again, and again murmured: "The poor child – she was so wrong."

273

"It was soon after that," went on Reverend Mother, somewhat grimly, "that we discovered she had gone again – and this time we did not find her."

"How long ago was that?" asked Isobel, clutching at vain hopes.

"About a month . . . no, less – three weeks."

Oh God, thought Isobel, why didn't I come sooner? I might have found her then. "Can you think of anywhere else she might go? Are her parents nearby?"

The nun's face became a little stern. "They are not all that far away, but I doubt if she would go to them."

"Why not?"

There was faint reluctance in the crisp voice now as she replied, "I gather there was no love lost between them. Katie married against their will – and a non-Catholic, at that. She ran away with – Cliff, do you call him? And they told her never to come back."

Isobel shook her head in disbelief. "How can people be so unforgiving?" She looked into the saddened, slightly sardonic gaze of the woman before her, recognizing its weary acceptance of all the hopeless tangles of human frailty, and added wonderingly, "How did Katie meet him? Do you know?"

"I do, as a matter of fact," said the headmistrees. "Katie was still a pupil here. He was working over in Cork, on the boats – a casual labourer, and that annoyed her parents even more. She met him at a dance – some local hop or other, in the holidays. . . . It developed from there, and of course parental opposition only served to make it stronger. . . . They ran away to England together . . ." She allowed herself another sigh. "And it ends like this!"

"I don't think it is ended," said Isobel. "She loved those children – and from what Trevor has told me, she loved her husband, too."

"In spite of . . .?"

"In spite of everything. . . . Why else would she keep silent . . .? In her way, she has made an enormous sacrifice . . . But we have to convince her, somehow, that it was not necessary – that she *can* go back."

Reverend Mother agreed. "Well, at least if she returns here, we'll know now what to say to her. In the meantime, I can give you her parents' address, though I'm afraid it won't be much help."

"You never know," said Isobel, summoning a whole new surge of courage and determination. "At least I can try." She got to her feet then, knowing they had said all that could be said at present. "Thank you for all your help," she said, "and for all you have done for Katie."

Reverend Mother smiled then. "I think you have done more," she said. "I do hope you succeed. Will you let me know?"

"Of course," promised Isobel, and held out her hand. But she left the Convent of St Clodagh filled with a disappointment bordering on despair.

"Tomorrow," said Bruce, seeing her despondent face, and having heard her brief account of her interview with the headmistress. "We'll try that address tomorrow. You've had quite enough for one day. What you need now is a drink, and a hot bath and a rest."

He drove her home to the empty house in Cork, and made valiant attempts to be hospitable and kind. But Isobel hustled him off to see Caro, and stayed behind, not to rest but to ring up Alan.

He answered readily enough – almost as if he had been waiting for the telephone to ring – and Isobel was shocked to find how much the mere sound of his voice brought comfort and reassurance.

"Oh Alan, I only missed her by a month! If only I'd found that book sooner!"

But Alan was, as usual, positive and optimistic. "You probably wouldn't have been able to reason with her then. It sounds to me as if she is already thinking of how to get home." He had heard the disappointment in Isobel's voice, and realized that for the first time since he had known her, she was feeling defeated. "You've got that other address to follow up. Try her parents in the morning. They may come up with something. . . . You can't give up yet, Isobel."

"No," she said, ashamed of feeling so dispirited. "Of course not. I expect I'm just tired tonight."

275

"So would I be, if I'd dealt with two Reverend Mothers in one day!" said Alan, and was relieved to hear her laugh.

"What about the Broadbents, Alan? Are they all right?"

"They're doing fine," he told her. "I went round last night – and Gervase is looking in today to talk to Colin about the garden. Everything is under control."

"Alan, I don't know what to tell Trevor."

"You needn't tell him anything yet – not till you come home. There may be more positive news by then."

"Yes," she sighed. "I hope so. At least we know she's alive and survived the attack. I think Trevor was afraid she might not have. . . ."

"I'm sure he was," agreed Alan, grimly. "Well, at least we can scotch that terror."

"Maybe," said Isobel doubtfully, "we ought to tell him that much . . .? It would save him some worry . . .?"

Alan thought about it. "Not yet," he said at last. "We won't raise hopes – or dash them. Leave things as they are a bit longer. . . . He's lived with them long enough, a few more days won't hurt."

Isobel was still not certain – but she trusted Alan's judgement. "All right. We'll wait."

"Ring me again tomorrow," commanded Alan, sounding deliberately autocratic, "Whether there's any news or not."

She was just about to promise meekly to do just that, when Alan added, "By the way, what about Bruce's wife – Caro, is it? . . . You haven't said a word."

"Oh!" She was instantly contrite – and ashamed to admit that she had been so obsessed with Katie's problems that she had almost forgotten Caro altogether. "She's much better, Alan. We had quite a long talk – and the doctors agreed to do some tests—"

"On you?"

She laughed at his anxious voice. "Only blood tests, Alan. Harmless, and probably totally unnecessary, but if it relieves her mind. . . ."

"Yes, I see."

"Bruce is with her now . . . I'll probably go and see her again tomorrow. And I've met Bruce's parents today. That was a success, as well, much to my relief."

276

"Good grief!" said Alan, "And you were feeling all down-hearted because you hadn't done enough!"

Isobel sighed. "Nothing is enough, Alan, is it? That's the trouble."

There was close warmth and laughter in his voice as he replied, "I think that should be written on your tombstone! But what is enough right now, is the expense of this phone call! Go and have a stiff drink and an early night and you'll be your usual fighting self again in the morning, I promise."

Isobel realized as he spoke that she really was rather tired, and something about the extra warmth in his voice brought her close to tears. But she also felt, illogically, that if Alan promised she would be all right in the morning, she probably would.

"I – bless you, Alan. I don't know what I'd do without you," she murmured.

"Well, you don't have to, do you?" he said, laughing, and rang off before she could reply.

The address given to Isobel was in a village outside the small inland town of Mallow, and she and Bruce drove over there the next morning through a green and rainy landscape aglow with spring flowers. It was the warm Gulf Stream, Bruce told her, that made everything grow with such lush abandon all through the soft valleys of Kerry, and even here, near Cork, everything seemed to bloom and burgeon in profusion.

"Why here?" wondered Isobel, considering the whereabouts of Katie's parents. "When they sent Katie to a school in Tralee?"

"They may not have lived here then," Bruce pointed out. "How old did you say Trevor was? Thirteen? That makes it all of fourteen or fifteen years ago."

Isobel nodded.

"And in Ireland families do this, you know – send their daughters to convent schools miles from home . . . especially if they don't much like the co-ed comprehensives nearer home."

"Would you?" Isobel asked. "If this coming one is a girl?"

Bruce laughed. "Give us time! It depends what Caro wants – and the child herself, too – if she is a girl!"

"Glad to hear it," grunted Isobel. "It's a – a rather loaded sort of life – all that conscience-searching and going to confession! Gives one a permanent sense of guilt!"

He glanced at her sideways, understanding her very well. "It must have been hard for you," he said, smiling a little. "Strict Calvinistic code on the one hand, and Catholic nuns on the other. I don't know how you survived!"

"I sometimes wonder myself," admitted Isobel.

But by now they had arrived at the neat white cottage where the O'Sullivans lived. Isobel took a deep breath, grasping at courage. She knew this interview was going to be difficult – perhaps even stormy.

"I won't be far away," said Bruce, seeing her faintly apprehensive look. "If they get violent, yell for help!"

She laughed and patted his arm. "You are a great comfort, Bruce. I hope it won't come to that." Then she got out of the car and marched purposefully up the white-washed front steps and rang the bell.

The woman who came to the door was about Isobel's age, but looked older and more worn. . . . Her hair had probably been red once, but was now mostly grey and wispy with reddish glints, and the face beneath it still had a hint of earlier prettiness, overlaid by a tired acceptance of the many and various blows that family life could give. And her eyes, looking sharply out at Isobel, were greenish-gold, and so like Georgie's that Isobel almost started back in surprise.

"Yes?"

"Mrs O'Sullivan? Reverend Mother at St Clodagh's gave me your address," began Isobel. "She thought you might know the whereabouts of your daughter, Katie."

A look almost of fear crossed the woman's face, and she glanced nervously over her shoulder at the passage behind her. "I'll – come outside," she said, and pulled the front door almost shut behind her. "Katie is not here," she told Isobel bluntly. "Her father would not – that is, she could not—" and she failed to finish either sentence.

Isobel looked at her with all the entreaty she could muster. "It's very important that she should be found."

"Why?" It was a flat, almost angry question, but those strange green-gold eyes were not hostile – only anxious.

"She is needed at home," Isobel said. "Her children—"

"Who is needed at home?" barked a new voice from behind, and Isobel saw the nervous figure of Mary O'Sullivan cringe even further as her husband came down the steps and stood glaring beside her.

"I – this lady was asking – asking after. . . ."

"Katie, was it? I've told you before, woman, I won't have that name said here! And I won't have you hob-nobbing with strange women about her, either." He transferred his glare to Isobel, and made it even more ferocious. Ned O'Sullivan was a ferocious-looking man if he liked, red-faced and bristly, shirtsleeves rolled up over powerful arms, and grey eyes under their fierce grey eyebrows positively sparking with resentment. "You'd better be off, Madam," he said, in a voice between a snarl and a growl. "We have *no* daughter called Katie now. We know nothing about her – and if she was foolish enough to come here, she would *not* be welcome. She would be sent packing – as she was before!" And he turned on his heel then and went back into the house, pulling his wife sharply round by the arm and taking her with him. "Come in, Mary. You have no call to stand gossiping outside!" He dragged her inside and slammed the door, leaving Isobel speechless on the step.

Sighing, she retreated to the road, and was just about to get into the car beside Bruce, when the house door opened a crack, and a hand came out, waving a bit of paper, and behind it, Mary O'Sullivan's frightened face peered out, finger to her lips, enjoining silence.

Isobel crept back up the steps, feeling like a conspirator in a Victorian melodrama.

"Her brother . . ." whispered Mary. "Try her brother, Dermot. She'd go to him. . . ." and she thrust the slip of paper at Isobel very swiftly and closed the door.

"Phew!" grinned Bruce, when Isobel finally got back into the car. "I thought you were a goner there!"

She laughed. "He was a bit ogrish! I feel sorry for his wife."

"So do I," agreed Bruce, looking down curiously at the new bit of paper in her hand. "Where to now?"

Isobel looked at the address in surprise. "It's in Cork, look! I can go there this evening, while you're seeing Caro."

279

"Don't forget, she wants to see you again, too."

"I could go this afternoon, couldn't I? And the results of those tests ought to be through by now. Maybe we can do a bit more reassuring then?"

Bruce grinned at her companionably. "Honestly, Isobel – it's all go with you, isn't it?" He examined the scribbled new address, and looked up at her questioningly. "Are you sure you can handle this on your own? Might there be more fireworks?"

"I shouldn't think so," said Isobel, smiling at his concern. "It's only her brother. He won't want to shoot me, will he?"

They drove back towards Cork, but on the way Bruce insisted on stopping at the prettiest and most welcoming village pub he could find – and he seemed to know most of them in the area – where he treated Isobel to a large Guinness and a bar snack lunch, followed by an Irish coffee with plenty of whiskey in it.

"After all, you must have a little bit of fun amidst all this turmoil," he said, "and I'd like you to think Ireland had some places worth visiting besides convents and unfriendly village houses inhabited by ogres!"

Isobel laughed again. She was feeling quite merry now, what with the Guinness and the Irish coffee, and although the scene at the O'Sullivans' had been another setback, there was this new address to follow up, and she was surprisingly optimistic about it, somehow.

" . . . And a few beauty spots," added Bruce, with his eyes on the green and silver landscape of water meadows and small rivers that gleamed with sunshine and spring rain all around them.

"But it is full of beauty," said Isobel softly. "Everywhere. And that rainbow over the sea yesterday was – out of this world!"

He smiled at her then, pleased that she had noticed it in the midst of all her preoccupations. "A lot of Ireland is out of this world . . ." he murmured dreamily, and then pulled himself together and drove Isobel back to the busy city of Cork.

Caro, when Isobel arrived that afternoon, was looking a lot better, propped up higher in the bed and presenting a much less haunted picture. She greeted Isobel with genuine warmth and held out a hand to grasp her by the arm. "I'm so glad to see you. They say I am much better, and if I go on like this, I can go home at the end of next week . . . I just have to spend a few days here when I first get up . . . to make sure I'm not going to start anything up again. But they are sure I'm not!"

"That's very good news!" smiled Isobel. "What about those tests of mine? Have they said anything?"

Caro grinned, looking rather like a small girl who has been naughty but is now determined to appear angelically good. "They said they ought to tell you first – but I had absolutely nothing to worry about there!"

"Told you so!" said Isobel, grinning back. "I'll go and ask about them, shall I? Then we'll know where we stand."

"Where you stand," said a voice behind them, "is blissfully and blamelessly in the clear. I've never seen such a healthy, ordinary, unremarkable, perfectly normal set of results!"

And they both looked round into the cheerful, laughing face of Caro's gynaecologist as he stopped beside them on his afternoon rounds.

"Splendid!" beamed Isobel. "Now Caro won't have a leg to stand on!"

"Yes, she will," contradicted the specialist. "Two, I hope. For we are going to let her get out of bed tomorrow." He gave Caro a reassuring pat, and Isobel a swift wink, before going on his way.

Isobel turned back to Caro, not missing the faint flick of fear in the blue, candid eyes. "That'll be a blessing, won't it? Back on your own two feet, and in charge of your own life again."

"Two lives," said Caro, admitting where the fear really lay.

Isobel's expression softened. "When we were looking out at the convent garden," she said in a dreaming voice, "I remembered how I used to help out there while I was waiting for Bruce to arrive . . . and I thought of you. I wanted to see you out in the sun – not lying here."

"Sunshine and flowers?" Caro murmured, in a half-mocking, half-accepting tone. "Just as important as music?"

"Of course," agreed Isobel, smiling.

Caro leant back against her pillows and sighed. "You are nice, Isobel. You make everything sound so simple."

"So it is," said Isobel, "if you think about it."

But before they could indulge in any more cheerful platitudes, Bruce came in, armed with more flowers, and said, "Isobel, I've changed my mind. I've come to take you home for a bit of a rest before you go off on your next jaunt. And then I'm coming with you."

Isobel looked surprised. "I don't think it's necessary."

"Well, I do," said Bruce, mouth set in an expression very like Isobel's own fighting look. "It's a roughish area down by the docks – and you don't know the city very well." He saw her doubtful look and added, "It won't take long, will it? Plenty of time to come back and see Caro afterwards."

Isobel hesitated, looking from one to the other of them, but before she could make any further protest, Caro interrupted. "Bruce is right, you know . . . I don't think you should go alone."

"Oh, very well," said Isobel, capitulating. Then she thought she had been a little ungracious, and added, smiling, "I must say, it's rather nice to be so well protected!"

They stayed a little while longer, while Bruce was told about the results of Isobel's tests and the doctor's promise to get Caro out of bed the next day.

"That's wonderful!" he said, signalling secret gratitude to Isobel. Already, the future for his young wife, and for himself, looked more hopeful.

But Caro decided that she still wanted Isobel's support and a bit more of the mysterious confidence she seemed to instill. "You won't be going back to England *tomorrow*, will you?"

Isobel hesitated. "I – I'm not sure. It depends on what happens this evening . . ." She glanced at Bruce, almost apologetically. "But I ought to go soon."

Caro was still looking at her with open entreaty. "You'll come back and see me again first, though?"

"Yes," said Isobel. If there is time. But she did not say it. How could she to those childlike, beseeching eyes? "Yes," she repeated firmly. "Of course I will."

And she went away then, with Bruce beside her, not daring to meet his eye.

It was not yet dark when they went down into the city, and the old streets of the port area, many of them built over ancient boat channels, seemed to glow with the rosy light of the sunset sky, and the early bloom of streetlights along the waterfront shimmered over the harbour. But Bruce did not let Isobel linger to admire the reflections in the water, he drove on past the warehouses and boats till he reached the small streets on the edge of town where Dermot O'Sullivan was supposed to be.

Once again, Isobel went up some steps, slip of paper in hand, and reached out to ring the bell. But before she could do so, the door flew open and a group of children spilled out into the street and ran off, laughing. Behind them, a young man with unruly red hair stood on the top step, looking after the scattering children with an indulgent smile. There was a muffled scolding from a woman's voice within, and the young man only laughed and said over his shoulder, "Ah, let them go . . . It's a beautiful evening."

Then his glance fell on Isobel hesitating just below him, and his smile did not so much diminish as become questioning. "Are you looking for someone?"

"Yes," said Isobel, holding out the scrap of paper. "Are you Dermot O'Sullivan?"

"I am that." He looked down at her with a light of unmistakable dancing mischief in his eyes. (They were green, Isobel noted – the same strange green-gold mixture as his mother's, and Georgie's, too.) "What can I do for you?" he asked, still smiling and untroubled.

"I – your mother gave me your address," said Isobel. "She thought you might have news of your sister, Katie."

The smile died then, and the eyes became more wary and looked at Isobel more sharply. "And who is it that is asking?"

She took a deep breath. "I am Isobel Frazier. Katie doesn't know me but I know her – through her children and her husband, Cliff – who are all waiting for her to come home."

There was a silence while Dermot took this in and continued to look at Isobel. Then he gestured quite politely at the open door, and said, "You'd better come in, then."

Well, at least I haven't had the door slammed in my face this time, she thought as she followed him into the house.

"Who is it?" called out a woman's voice from the kitchen.

283

"A visitor," said Dermot. "Bring us a cup of tea, Molly, will you?" And he took Isobel into the front sitting-room which was small and shabby and full of children's toys, but somehow not unwelcoming, especially when the distant 'Molly' came in and planked down two steaming mugs of tea on the table and went out again without speaking. Isobel looked after her retreating figure and thought: she's quite pretty in that dark, wispy sort of way, though she looks tired. Those children, I daresay. . . .

"Now," Dermot said, the smile back but still a little cautious, "what is all this about? Can you tell me?"

"I can," said Isobel grimly – and did.

Since Dermot was Katie's brother, there was no need to gloss over anything, she reflected, so she omitted nothing. And at the end, she said, "So you can see why she is needed desperately at home – and there is no reason why she should stay away any longer."

Dermot's face had grown almost as grim as Isobel's as he listened to the story, and it was filled now with a kind of incredulous pity. "She didn't tell me the half of it," he muttered, and then seemed to realize that Isobel was waiting in hope and fear for him to tell her what he knew. He sighed, and the green-gold eyes seemed to cloud a little. "You are right," he said slowly, "she did come here – but she has long since gone."

"How long since?" asked Isobel, once again feeling fear and disappointment wash over her.

He seemed to count up in his mind before answering. "About ten days ago, I'd say . . ." He looked at Isobel now almost as if he were apologizing for something. "She wanted to borrow some money . . . I gave her what I could – and the name of a mate of mine who works on the ferry."

"Which one is that?"

"Cork to Swansea . . . She wanted to get over somehow on the cheap . . . I thought he might let her help in the cafeteria or something. . . ."

Isobel looked a little more hopeful at this. "You think she was planning to go home?"

He shrugged helplessly. "How do I know? She didn't say much – only that she had to get back to England. . . . Well, Wales it would be." He paused, as if thinking back to that

284

meeting with his sister, and added suddenly, "She kept saying: 'I need to earn some money first – but I *must know* . . .'."

"It sounds to me," said Isobel, working it out, "as if she was planning to set up a new home for her children and get them out of care. . . ."

He looked puzzled. "But they aren't in care, you say. They're with you?"

"Yes, but she thinks they are."

Dermot whistled. "It's a tangle, and no mistake."

"Never mind," said Isobel, daring to sound almost hopeful. "If she's on her way home, it may be all right in the end."

Dermot shook his head uncertainly. "I don't know for sure that she is . . . only that she *might* be – and I *may* have put her in the way of making it possible."

"Well, that's something to be going on with," said Isobel, smiling at him. "You've done what you could."

He sighed again, looking young and troubled, the latent mischief quenched for the moment. "I didn't know things were that bad . . ." he said.

Isobel got to her feet, feeling that she had found out all she could, and there was nothing more she could do here. But there was one more thing she could say: "If – I don't suppose she will come back here, or you can get word to her – but if she can be reached, someone should tell her it is all right now to come home. I think she was afraid, for Cliff's sake, more than for anyone's."

He nodded. "Yes. She was always like that about Cliff – and he was about her, too."

Isobel looked surprised. "You knew Cliff?"

He laughed, a shade bitterly. "As a matter of fact, I introduced them. He was working here on the boats, and I took him to this disco, and Katie came over. . . ." He had followed Isobel to the door by this time, and now stood there, looking at her sadly. "You never know what you're starting, do you?"

"No," agreed Isobel, "but you never know the ending, either. There's still a chance it may be a happy one."

The green-gold eyes regarded her soberly. "Do you think so?"

"I hope so," said Isobel fervently. "I hope so – with all my heart!"

285

Then, as a last minute afterthought, she handed Dermot her card with the Clifton address on it, and went back down the steps to Bruce, waiting patiently for her in the car, and allowed him to drive her home.

Isobel rang Alan again that night, as promised, though she felt, sadly, that she had little enough to tell him.

But Alan was as determinedly optimistic as ever, and refused to be cast down. "It sounds hopeful," he said. "If she's trying to raise some money and get back to England, she must at least be *thinking* of coming home."

Isobel, remembering Dermot's doubtful face, said wearily, "I hope you're right."

"You sound exhausted, Isobel. All these difficult interviews are bound to take it out of you."

She sighed. "It isn't that, Alan. I just feel – I haven't really found out anything, or done any good at all."

"Oh, but you have," Alan protested, swift to defend her. "You've found out that Katie is at least alive, and well again . . . And who knows how far your reassuring news about Cliff and the kids may reach . . .? Especially if her brother is as sympathetic as you say. . . ."

"Yes," Isobel admitted slowly, "I did get a – a faint impression that he might know more than he said about how to reach her. . . ."

"Well, then, we've got to leave it to him, and be patient," said Alan. "Come on home, Isobel – you've done everything you could."

She found herself smiling into the phone. "I'm coming. I've just got to tie up a few loose ends with Bruce and Caro first."

"Well, don't leave it too long. The kids are getting anxious."

"Are they?" She was suddenly worried. "Why?"

It was Alan's turn to sigh. "Oh, Isobel! Don't be so humble. They miss you – especially Trevor. He's come to rely on your support. And Goldie is still very suspicious of anyone going away."

"I know," said Isobel, remembering how Goldie's small hand had clung to hers. *'You are coming back, aren't you?'* "Tomorrow!" she said, making up her mind. "I'll fly back tomorrow. Tell them I'm coming."

286

"You bet I will!" laughed Alan, sounding jubilant. "The kids aren't the only ones who've missed you!" And once again he rang off to prevent her replying.

So it was just a question of saying goodbye to Bruce and Caro in the morning. She found Caro sitting up in a chair, wearing a dressing-blue gown that just matched her eyes and made her look younger and more vulnerable than ever. But she smiled quite cheerfully at Isobel, and said, "Everything is under control. They're pleased with me . . . and I've made up my mind to stop being a wimp. I don't want a wimpish child!"

Isobel laughed and put an arm round her in a comforting hug. "I shouldn't think that's very likely. You've put up a pretty good fight for this baby so far, you and Bruce."

"So have you," countered Caro, also smiling. "A born fighter, if ever there was one!" She grew serious for a moment and then added shyly, "What was Bruce's father like? I mean, Bruce told me he was strong and healthy and had healthy children. But what was he really *like*?"

Isobel smiled at her without embarrassment. "He was a very nice person, really. Clever and visionary – a very fine teacher . . . He just – let his heart rule his head for once, that was all. And so did I," she added fairly.

Caro nodded and did not pursue it. Isobel had already told her what she wanted to know.

Then Bruce appeared, carrying yet more flowers, some for Caro, and some for Isobel. "We'd better go," he said, "if you are to catch that plane." He ruffled Caro's hair affectionately. "You look lovely sitting there – I'll be back this afternoon."

Isobel turned to Caro and gave her another even more enveloping hug. "Keep it up," she murmured. "Music – and sunshine and flowers! And you can't lose!" She turned away with Bruce, hoping she had somehow instilled enough confidence into Caro to see her through.

"You've done wonders for her," murmured Bruce, steering her out of the hospital and into his car. "Stop worrying! She'll be all right now."

They drove to the airport and said their farewells in the little departure lounge. Isobel was a bit saddened by this parting, for she knew very well that she ought not to expect to keep up the

287

tenuous relationship with Bruce. He belonged in Ireland, with Caro and his adoptive parents and the steady, useful life he had built up for himself and his young wife and the new child to come. It would be wrong of her, she told herself sternly, to want to see more of him. She had done what he asked of her – as well as she could – and now she must let him go. As she had told those two kind, apprehensive people, Maeve and John Conolly, Bruce belonged with them, and she didn't want to change anything.

"Well, goodbye Bruce," she said briskly. "I hope everything goes well from now on. Let me know when the baby comes. I'm dying to be a secret grandmother!"

Bruce laughed, and put a warm arm round her shoulders. "I can't begin to thank you. And we're not going to lose touch now, whatever you say."

Isobel looked faintly reproving. "Aren't we?"

"Certainly not. And you needn't look like that. I haven't forgotten what you said to my parents."

"Oh, that's all right then," said Isobel and smiled at him somewhat roguishly, and marched off through the boarding gate to her waiting flight.

Soon the little plane took off, pointed its nose to the east, and climbed up over the sea to a dazzle of cloud. But the memory of that magical green and silver land that had so beguiled her, followed her all the way home.

288

Chapter Sixteen

'The Woman of the House'

Reel

The home-coming was better than she had dared to hope. To begin with, Alan was at the airport to meet her, and the sight of him waiting there caused such a surge of relief and pleasure inside her that she was almost scared.

"How did you know when I was coming?"

He grinned, and tucked her arm through his, taking her small case in his other hand. "Did a deal with Bruce. Made him promise to ring me when he had actually seen you take off!"

Isobel laughed. "How is everyone?"

"Fine," he told her cheerfully. "Fine – but dying to see you."

They drove peacefully back into the city and up the hill to Clifton, not feeling the need to talk very much.

"The kids have asked you to tea. I know you must be tired, but I don't think you'd better refuse!"

"Of course not." She grinned, and then contradicted him roundly. "And I'm not a bit tired. Only a trifle disappointed because I haven't come back with better news."

"You've done quite a lot, one way and another," said Alan. "Don't reproach yourself."

"What have you told Trevor?"

"Nothing. I waited for you. Better that way."

"Is it?" Isobel's voice was rather bleak. "How does one tell a boy that his mother is wandering about Ireland, and might or might not decide to come back?"

Alan patted her hand, recognizing the slight bitterness in her voice as a kind of grieving pity. "You'll find a way. And

Trevor has a very adult awareness of human frailty. . . . He'll understand."

Isobel sighed, and flashed him a small, grateful smile. "You are a comfort, Alan . . . but I'm not sure I ought to let you beguile me with soft words when I've done nothing to deserve them!"

"That's only your Scottish Presbyterian conscience talking. Relax. We're going to make the very best we can of the situation we've got – and that in itself is a hundred per cent better than it was, thanks to you. What are you worrying about?"

"Trevor," said Isobel bluntly. "He doesn't say very much – but it goes very deep."

Alan nodded, accepting that. But he turned his head and smiled at her in a curiously tender fashion. "He's got you back. That's enough to be going on with." And before she could think of an answer, he had pulled up by her front door, and the next surprise was confronting her.

The whole front of the house where the old grey stone steps led down to the dingy dark well of the basement had been transformed. The walls and steps had been painted a brilliant light-reflecting white, and every available space on the ground and on each stone step was filled with pots of flowers. There were even extra containers hanging from the walls in a riot of spring colours. Polyanthus, primroses, pansies, forget-me-nots and pink and white daisies frothed and cascaded from every side. There were even clumps of narcissi and early tulips, which Isobel's experienced eye told her had been newly transplanted from expensive spring collections into their brand-new sunshine yellow pots. It was like a whole garden of flowers crammed into one small space, and the dazzling array of brilliant colour almost made her blink with its intensity.

"Oh!" she breathed, pausing to admire each glowing potful in turn. "How absolutely lovely! Where did it all come from?"

Alan laughed. "Gervase and Colin, of course. I expect they'll be lurking somewhere about. . . . They wanted it to be a surprise."

And then Gervase and Colin appeared from the garden gate, and behind them were Georgie and Goldie, both hopping up and down with excitement, and behind them still was Cliff in

290

his wheelchair, with Trevor close beside him – and everyone was smiling. "Welcome home!" they cried in a cheerful chorus, and Colin asked breathlessly, "Do you like it?"

But before Isobel could reply, Gervase answered for her, "She'd better – or we'll crown her with one of her new yellow pots!"

Amid the laughter (which was perilously close to tears in Isobel's case) Georgie came close and whispered in her ear, "It's like the Garden of Daisies. But we've got another Tune for you after tea," and purposefully led Isobel into the garden and down the ramp to the splendid banquet waiting below.

On the bottom of the ramp sat Archimedes, surveying the approaching procession with a slightly smug expression, but when he saw Isobel he actually got to his feet and made welcoming signals with his tail. Then he rubbed himself sinuously against her legs and began to purr.

"I believe he's glad to see me," said Isobel, pleased.

"So are we!" agreed Goldie, and danced before her down the smooth ramp, singing, "So are we . . . So are we . . ." to a tune of her own devising.

"So – are – we . . ." echoed Cliff, stopping his chair at the bottom of the ramp and smiling up at her.

Only Trevor had said nothing, but his eyes were fixed on Isobel in joyous welcome. His main support and ally had returned.

I must get that boy away upstairs for a few moments, thought Isobel. I can't keep him waiting for news all through tea – and a Tune as well, if Georgie has her way.

The feast spread out on the table was impressive. There were sugar buns and currant buns, iced cakes and biscuits, crisps and peanuts, and plates of bread and butter. And knives and forks, Isobel noted with relief, so there must be something cooking. It might just give her time.

"How long will you be?" she asked, looking at Georgie, who seemed to be in charge. "Have I time to go upstairs and unpack one small bag? I've brought back a few small things. . . ."

"Five minutes," said Georgie blithely, "while I make the tea. The rest is in the oven."

"Good." Isobel turned easily to Trevor. "Come up and give me a hand, will you, Trevor? We won't be long," she added

291

over her shoulder, and went rather swiftly up the stairs, with Trevor behind her.

When they arrived in Isobel's own kitchen, she said quietly, "Sit down, Trevor, and I'll tell you all I can. But don't expect too much."

"I never do," he said, with equal quietness, and waited for her to begin.

She told him everything that had been said or done about Katie, including the furious rejection by Katie's father.

"You told me they disapproved of your father," Isobel said, "but I didn't realize relations were that bad."

Trevor sighed. "She never said much about it – but I suppose the row was too bad to be mended. . . . My Dad once said – before he was ill – that Mum's father was an obstinate old dinosaur!" He grinned at Isobel rather bleakly.

"I think that's a fairly accurate description," said Isobel, grinning back. Then she grew serious again. "But Dermot – your uncle – was much more helpful, and much kinder."

Trevor nodded. "She did talk about him a bit. He knew my Dad, too. . . . They were mates on the same job on the boats in Cork, I think."

"Yes," confirmed Isobel. "They were. . . ." And Dermot had introduced Cliff to Katie, and perhaps regretted it ever since. But somehow she did not think Cliff had ever regretted it, nor Katie either, deep down, in spite of all that had happened. "He said," she told Trevor softly, "your Uncle Dermot – that Katie and your father were. . . ."

"Mad about each other? Right from the start?" There was a curious, grim, adult knowledge in his voice. "Yes. Mum told me. . . ." He looked at Isobel, the same thought in his eyes as in hers. "I suppose they still are – in a funny kind of way?"

"Yes," Isobel agreed. "I think they are . . . and that's why she's stayed away so long . . . to make sure she could bring him no harm."

Trevor nodded. He had already worked that out in his own mind long ago, and come to terms with it in his own way. "I'm glad she's all right," he said finally. "I did wonder. . . ."

He did not say any more, but Isobel was rather amazed that he understood so much – and spoke of it so calmly and rationally.

"She only needs telling it is all right to come home," she went on, trying to be positive, "and then I think she will. . . ."

Trevor straightened his shoulders in a familiar, stoical gesture. "Then we'll just have to wait," he said.

It was a splendid tea. Gervase admitted, somewhat sheepishly, to helping Georgie with the casserole.

"It won't be as good as yours," he said, smiling, "but we're learning."

Isobel was rather amazed at Gervase. She had expected him to be difficult and scratchy about the Broadbent family invading her house – and he was not. She had expected him to express a certain shock and disapproval about the sudden appearance of Bruce in her life – and he had not. In fact, he had not said a word of criticism about either event, and on top of this forbearance, he had obviously spent a lot of time and money over the transformation of her front steps and her churned-up terrace. For she had noticed from her windows as she passed that this, too, was mysteriously refurbished and full of new pots of flowers.

"Gervase," she said, as they carried a couple of dishes out to the kitchen, "you ought to let me pay you for the pots of flowers. You must have spent a fortune!"

"Nonsense." He sounded quite testy, but when he turned to look at her he was smiling, almost shyly. "My contribution to all this . . ." He waved a vague hand at the sunny, re-painted flat. "You're the one who's spent a fortune!"

She grinned. "Yes, but I wanted to."

"Well, I wanted to." He became half serious for a moment. "I know I've been a bit – um – unenthusiastic about the whole thing, but I – you were quite right – when I actually met them all, I changed my mind." His smile became almost roguish. "In fact, I've changed my mind about a lot of things."

"Oh?" Isobel sounded entirely innocent. "Such as what?"

"Ah," he said. "You're a bit of a dark horse, aren't you? And I find, to my own surprise, I rather like dark horses." He sounded absurdly sedate about it, but Isobel knew he was teasing her, and at the same time indicating that he was not going to ask any awkward questions.

293

"Bless you, Gervase," she said, laughing, "you *have* relieved my mind!"

They were still laughing together as they returned to the living-room, where Georgie was impatiently waiting for Isobel to cut the cake. It was a very grand cake, large and pink, with a small bunch of garden daisies in a tiny vase on the top. Georgie confessed, grinning proudly, that Alan had bought the cake, but she had iced it. She had also set round it a ring of ordinary kitchen candles stuck on saucers, in lieu of birthday cake candles, and a box of matches conveniently to hand for Isobel to light them.

"We didn't know anyone's birthday," explained Georgie tactfully, "but it was the new flat's birthday, anyway, so we put one candle for everyone who helped."

And here Isobel suddenly noticed that the Likely Lads, Dave and Mitch, had mysteriously appeared from the garden, and were sitting with the assembled company round the table. "Sorry we're late," they said, smiling round. "But at least we're in time for the cake." And Alan, catching Isobel's glance, gave her a solemn wink.

So there were ten candles round the cake, and Isobel had to light them all, one by one, with Colin and Goldie chanting each name in turn, until Goldie suddenly added at the last minute, "And Archie! We can't leave out Archie. He began it all." So they had to find another candle to add to the rest. When the ring of candles was alight, it suddenly made Isobel think of the Ring of Kerry and the rainbow over the sea, and for a moment she was not quite sure which world she was in – the green and silver world of Ireland, with Bruce and Caro and their urgent problems of new life, and the tenuous, disturbing snatches of news about Katie – or here, with this warm-hearted young family surrounded by their friends, trying so gallantly to rejoice while they waited patiently, and in diminishing hope, for their mother to return.

"Mizzibel . . ." said Georgie, interrupting her thoughts, "will you cut the cake?"

"But we ought to blow out the candles first!" protested Goldie, who liked her ceremonies to be exactly right.

"No," said Georgie sharply – for it was her ceremony after all. "Leave them . . . they look lovely like that."

294

So the golden ring of light was allowed to go on burning, and when everyone had been served and was quietly munching cake, Cliff suddenly spoke, as if he had been saving up precious words for this moment.

"*Wings* . . ."

They all looked at him in surprise. "All – of us," he added, looking at Trevor, and then at Isobel.

"All God's chillun got wings?" murmured Alan, who was very quick off the mark.

Cliff nodded, delighted. "Gotta record . . ." He glanced at Isobel, waiting for her to put it on for him, and then added, almost quickly for him, "b-before Georgie's Tune . . .?"

Isobel went over to the old record player in the corner, and Cliff came up behind her in his chair and handed her the chosen LP. But it was not Alan's negro spiritual. It was Vaughan Williams' 'The Lark Ascending', and Isobel understood him at once.

They were all silent when the violin began its first hesitant flight, trying to rise, failing, beginning again, rising a little higher . . . and higher . . . the sound of its beating wings, its brave, pulsing heart, clear in the music, strong behind the supporting strings. . . . They all, in their separate ways, felt the poignant anguish of that struggle towards the light, the sudden quickening ecstasy of the soaring bird as it broke free from the slow pull of the earth into the limitless freedom of the sky. . . . They all held their breath as the singing, joyous creature rose higher and higher into the pure, clear air until it was out of sight, too far for the human eye to see, and the sound of its tireless singing grew fainter and fainter until it faded into pulsing silence. . . .

When it was over, they were almost afraid to break the spell – even Goldie looked up at her father with round, wonder-filled eyes and said nothing at all. But Cliff had not finished with his own magic-making yet. He turned to Trevor, and said very quietly, "Is – it – dry?"

Trevor nodded, and smiled at him encouragingly as he held out something to him in his hand.

"No," said Cliff. "*You*. You – give – it." And he pushed quite gently at Trevor's hand, urging him on.

So Trevor turned to Isobel and held the small object

295

out to her. "Dad made it," he said. "He's getting quite good at it."

Isobel looked down and saw that what he was holding so carefully in his hand was a small clay bird with wings outstretched in urgent upward flight. It was beautifully modelled, even to the crisp outlines of the flight feathers, and it had been carefully dried and then painted a gentle, unassuming brown, with a lighter wash of pale buff colour on its breast.

"It is very like a lark," she said, and looked up at Cliff with rather over-bright eyes. "I can almost feel it flying!"

"Not – not only me," said Cliff again, making it clear. "All – of – us."

And if most of them had seen a picture in their mind's eye of Cliff whizzing across Clifton Downs in his new wheelchair, chasing his laughing children in the sun, they did not tell him so.

"Can we play our Tune now?" asked Georgie, releasing everyone from a silence they did not know how to break.

"Yes," agreed Cliff, having made his own small gesture. He smiled lopsidedly at Georgie's eager face, and added, "Make it – l-lively!"

"It's called '*The Wanderer's Return*'," announced Georgie, smiling innocently at Isobel. "We've only just learnt it!"

And it was certainly lively. Fingers flew and feet tapped, and even Archimedes' tail began to wave. But when Georgie asked if they should play the *Kerry Dancing* again as well, Trevor said quickly, "No. Save it for later," and did not explain. But the brief flash of awareness in his eyes as he met Isobel's glance made her long to resolve this final, most important problem for him. Freedom to fly was not the only thing his family needed – and Trevor knew it.

And though she carried the little Bird of Freedom so carefully in her hand, and smiled her thanks at everyone, Isobel knew it, too.

During the next few days, Isobel deliberately returned to the routine she had set up for the family in the new flat. It seemed to her that continuity mattered, and would give them a sense of stability. So on two days in the week she went down to keep Cliff company while Trevor attempted to put his mind on school work – something which Isobel could see he found increasingly difficult and irrelevant, though he did not protest. Cliff, however, did protest a little that he was 'or-right' and could manage, but he was clearly glad to see her there, so she took no notice. Instead, she asked them all up to tea again on Saturday, and reminded Trevor that she would be expecting him for his usual morning cup of tea after the paper-round. That way, she reflected, she should be able to find out how things were going, and whether there were any problems.

As regards the two men in her life, Isobel had been surprised by both their reactions to her return. They had both shown more pleasure about it than she had expected, but both had been a bit fierce about her determination to keep up her routine of acceptable care and kindness with the Broadbents.

Alan, that first evening after the tea party downstairs, had simply laid a startlingly tender and demonstrative hand against her cheek for a moment and said, "You have used all of yourself up, Isobel. . . . Go and get some rest."

"A good night's sleep!" ordered Gervase, backing him up.

But Alan needed no support. "Sweet dreams," he said, smiling. "And I'll come and take you out for a spin next Sunday, shall I?" And before Isobel could answer, he had gone off, as usual, taking Gervase with him, and not looking back.

Gervase, apparently taking his cue from Alan, was still a bit protective when he came to his appointed supper engagement on the Friday, and said, rather shyly, "Isobel, would it be a good idea if I came to supper – I mean, tea! – with the children and Cliff on Saturdays instead?"

Isobel looked at him in surprise. "Wouldn't you find it too noisy?"

He shook his head. "I'll tell you something, Isobel. I know I'm a dyed-in-the-wool old fuddy-duddy who likes his life orderly and not too exciting – or I was! But I find that I – I rather like being a proxy uncle – just as I rather like Dark Horses!"

It was only the merest hint of a question, but Isobel responded. She knew she ought to tell him about Bruce anyway – Gervase deserved her confidence – so she smiled and said, "Sit down, Gervase, and I'll tell you all about it You've been very patient."

297

When she had finished (and she did not dwell too much on the harrowing details), Gervase smiled at her rather more warmly than she had expected, and said, "I'm sorry you went through such a lot . . . but I'm glad you were naughty once!"

She laughed. "Did I seem so righteous?"

He considered the matter, head on one side like an inquisitive sparrow. "Well, your air of impregnable virtue is rather formidable!"

"Help!" protested Isobel. "And now that you know the worst, does that make it any easier?"

"I'm not sure," Gervase mused, half teasing. "But it makes me understand a lot more about you than I did."

"What is that supposed to mean?"

"That it's high time you had a little fun of your own, instead of providing meals for self-indulgent old men like me!"

"But I like your company," she protested.

"I like yours too – and I would hate to be deprived of it altogether!" He grinned at her. "In fact, that was one of the reasons why I changed my mind about the Broadbents in the first place."

Isobel looked confused. "What?"

"I thought if I went on being disapproving, I might lose you altogether."

"Gervase, you are a fool!"

"I know," he agreed, laughing. "But anyway you were right. I have come to like them very much – and I have a great admiration for Trevor . . . though as a matter of fact, it's Colin I've taken a shine to, because of the flowers."

"That is good news," said Isobel, really pleased.

"And I also think, compared with that lot, I've lived a very sheltered life – and it's high time I made myself useful!"

"Oh good," grinned Isobel. "I'll hold you to that."

He looked at her seriously for a moment. "I can't change the way I am, Isobel . . . or the way I live. It's too late for that – and I'm a creature of habit. But you warned me once that life was rather barren without affection – so I'm going to make the most of what I've got."

Isobel was touched. For she realised that Gervase was telling her something a great deal subtler and more important than he made out.

298

"Well, at least keep *some* Fridays free, as well as Saturdays," she suggested.

He smiled. "I might do just that . . . but I suspect you may have better things to do with your time in the future, one way and another."

Isobel was about to demand what he meant by that, when something in his glance silenced her, and she looked at him wide-eyed and almost beginning to blush. "The trouble with you, Gervase, is you know too much."

"Yes," he agreed cheerfully. "Isn't it a bore?"

When Trevor came in for his cup of tea on Saturday morning, he looked at Isobel doubtfully, and began to apologize for not being enthusiastic about fitting in time at school. He tried to explain to her that he was finding it increasingly hard to concentrate, or even to believe in his school work or its purpose. He seemed to be light years away from his peers with their favourite pop groups and football idols. Their preoccupations seemed to him totally meaningless, and he knew it was partly his own fault. "I don't seem able to be – er – silly enough," he confessed, with an apologetic grin. "I mean – there's so much to think of at home, what with Dad and the kids and everything – the rest seems . . .?"

"Trivial?"

"Yes, a bit." He looked at her a bit sheepishly. "Am I – do you think I am getting too solemn?" He wanted to say 'priggish' really, but it sounded out of date somehow.

She smiled at him. "No. Not really. The things they worry about *are* trivial, probably, compared to your problems." Her smile grew more impish. "But you do need to *play* a bit, Trevor . . . we all do!"

He grinned back. "Even Dad's learning to play volleyball. That new chair of his is brilliant!"

She laughed, and then grew serious again and asked her most important question so far. "Is Cliff settling in all right, do you think? No more shouting nightmares or anything?"

"No," said Trevor slowly. "At least – only one."

"When was that?" Isobel looked at him sharply.

"It was while you were away. He suddenly woke up crying. . . . He hasn't done that for a long time . . . I didn't

299

know what to do. He kept saying '*Changed* . . . changed . . . It's *different* now . . .' And when he woke up properly he asked me if he was *really* better, and I said 'Yes,' but he kept on asking, on and on. . . ." He looked at Isobel helplessly. "I tried to make him believe it, but I'm not sure if he did. . . ." His eyes were troubled, but also full of a curious, suppressed eagerness, as if he had seen something in his father's behaviour that offered a strange kind of hope for the future. "Do you think—?" he began, and then broke off, afraid to put his thoughts into words.

"Yes?" asked Isobel.

"Do you think he actually *wanted* Mum to go away then – when he was so ill – because he couldn't handle it – and now that he's better, he thinks she might want to come back?"

It had occurred to Isobel too, but she did not say so. "I think it is more than likely," she agreed, and smiled at those anxious eyes. "And I also think it will be much easier for both of them – when she does come back."

Trevor nodded, accepting that word 'when', though Isobel was still interchanging it with 'if' in her own mind. "Dad *has* changed," he said.

"So have you all," Isobel told him. "You are all much more responsible now – even Goldie. It won't be nearly so hard for Katie, will it, with all of you to help her? Life will seem quite good again then."

"It does already," said Trevor, with an extraordinarily vivid and loving smile.

So then it was Sunday, and Alan was coming to fetch her. And Isobel found herself in a strange mood that was a mixture of unexplained happiness and a certain grim determination to keep her feet on the ground.

Strangely enough, Alan voiced her thoughts, laughingly but with equal determination. "No climbing trees today, Isobel. Feet firmly on the ground! We've got things to talk about."

"Yes, but—" began Isobel.

"No buts!" He grinned at her sideways, and let in the clutch and drove off eastwards. Then he softened a little and added, "I thought we'd go to Avebury Ring. . . . Plenty of ancient

300

magic there, though I don't think you need it – you seem to bring your own magic with you."

Isobel glanced at him in surprise. "Do I . . .? That was a rather amazing moment with The Lark Ascending, wasn't it? I'd no idea Cliff was such a romantic."

"Hadn't you?" Alan was smiling at her.

She looked at him rather suspiciously. "Who got him on to clay modelling? Was it you?"

Alan made disclaiming noises. "Not really – it was Goldie. She 'does' clay at school . . . I just got hold of some for Cliff. It seemed a good idea. Trevor says he is still very good with his hands, in spite of everything."

Isobel nodded. "It *was* a good idea. He needs something to do."

"I don't see why he shouldn't take up something like electronics or computer assembly when he's better. . . . There are part-time jobs available for the disabled."

She agreed, but with reservations. "Don't let him hear you call him that."

"Disabled?" He shook his head impatiently. "He's got to face up to it one day."

Isobel sighed. "Yes, I know – but don't be too tough on him – yet."

Alan's smile returned like the sun. "When was I ever too tough on anyone? That's my besetting sin."

"Being too soft?"

"Soft in the head, more like," he grinned. And added, with intent, "Unlike you."

"What's that supposed to mean?"

This time when he looked round, his glance was sober and oddly tender. "I mean – you are always too hard on yourself."

"Am I?" She was a little startled.

"Yes. Even now, you are worrying about the errant Katie, aren't you? And wondering whether you could do anything more about it."

Isobel stared. "How did you know?"

"I usually do know when something's bothering you," said Alan blithely. "But this time I can't do anything about it."

"None of us can," admitted Isobel sadly. "Though I did

301

wonder if I ought to have gone to Swansea to look for her."

"You'd never have found her."

"No, I suppose not." She sighed again, almost angrily. "But I feel so – useless!"

He laughed, but there was still a fleck of tenderness in his eyes. "You are absurd, Isobel. What more could you have done?"

"I don't know," she said, sounding a bit like an obstinate child. "But there must be *something!*"

"Waiting is the hardest game of all," he said, smiling, "especially for someone like you! But you don't know what you may have set in motion over there. The Irish are fey enough as it is, without your brand of magic as well."

He put one hand out and patted Isobel's arm. "Stop fretting! This is a holiday. And now that I've got you safely back from Ireland, we're going to celebrate."

"*Safely?*" said Isobel, surprised again. "You weren't really worried?"

"That you might have decided to stay with young Bruce and never come back at all?" He grinned at her shocked face. "Well, it did cross my mind! But I know you, Isobel. You've got too much sense of responsibility for that! And too much conscience," he added soberly.

"It wasn't only conscience," said Isobel, admitting the truth to herself as well as to Alan.

"I'm glad to hear it," he retorted crisply, and drew the car to a halt in the car-park below the tall green slopes of Avebury Hill.

They walked for a long time on the soft, springy turf, not talking much, peacefully companionable – all anxieties and tensions set aside.

"We might hear a lark up here," he said, gazing up into a sky that was clear and blue and flecked with white cloud. "It's the kind of place for miracles. I can feel my toes tingling."

"Yes," agreed Isobel quietly, and did not say any more.

He looked at her with sudden pleading. "What is it, Isobel? Something's still troubling you."

She took a long, slow breath of resolve – for this was the

302

moment she had been dreading most, and she did not know how to say what she knew she must say. "It's – you, Alan."

"What about me?"

"I – you mustn't – I mean, you shouldn't spend all your time – all your spare time, that is – being kind to me. . . ."

"*Kind?*" said Alan, in a kind of muted roar.

She looked at him with piteous honesty. "You ought to – to be going around with someone younger."

He laughed then, understanding the trouble. "Isobel, you are *miles* younger than me! Who climbed a tree and yelled 'Jerusalem' at the sky? Who ran after a kite with the kids, and danced along the promenade with Goldie, following the band . . .? Who took off her shoes and socks and ran into the sea?" His eyes were crinkled up again now with their old tenderness. "And who swanned off to Ireland with an unknown young man without turning a hair? I tell you, Isobel, I can't keep up with you!"

She was half laughing by this time, but still determined to make things clear. "Alan, I'm fifty-seven."

He grinned. "And I'm fifty-five. I know men mature later than women, but I'm not exactly an adolescent!"

Isobel grinned back despairingly. "Will you listen? You should find someone more – more . . .?"

"Respectable? After all, you are a woman with a past."

She began to giggle. "I meant—"

"Dizzier? More dashing . . .? No one could beat you on those, Isobel. Braver? More compassionate? More loving?" His voice was deep and serious now, and Isobel did not dare to laugh any more. But she could still fight back.

"*Dishier?*"

He stared at her, and then gave a shout of happy laughter. "As far as I am concerned, with *that* profile you could beat Nefertiti and Cleopatra into a cocked hat!"

She shook her head at him, somewhat tremulously. "Alan – be serious."

"I am serious," he said.

Even so, she made one last, desperate attempt at reason. "I – commitments are so – so restricting, Alan. I just – I just want you to – to keep your options open."

His smile this time was entirely loving, his voice deeper

303

than ever with certainty. "Don't you know," he said, "that it's much too late for that?"

Then Isobel capitulated. The walls and towers of her pride and independence fell down all round her, and she was left vulnerable and helpless before the truth in his eyes.

"Oh Alan," she said, her voice shaken between laughter and tears, "what am I to do with you?"

"Love me," he said simply. "Just love me a little. That's all I ask." And he laid his arms round her gently and drew her close.

"That won't be hard," she murmured, into his hair.

And just beyond them in the soft spring grass, a lark rose suddenly at their feet with a flurry of wings, and flew singing into the air.

She stood outside on the pavement, looking up at the windows of the flat – a tall, slender girl – almost too slender for comfort – and fragile-looking as if even the soft spring wind might rock her off her feet. The windows of the rooms up on that narrow second floor were closed, in spite of the warm day, and there were different curtains framing them – secretive white net ones across the central glass, shutting out the light. There was no one up there any longer that she knew. . . . No one waiting for her, or looking out for her return. . . . As she watched, a strange face peered out, tweaking the net curtains aside – an old, suspicious face that gave the watcher one sharp glance and then let the swathe of white muslin fall back into place, rejecting the world outside. It was not a face she knew. They were all strangers up there now. They wouldn't know where the others had gone.

Drawing a sharp breath of resolve, she walked up the steps and pushed at the front door. It always used to be open, just to the hallway and the other closed doors of the flats. But now it was shut, and locked. Local vandalism, and the exploits of the Blatchford Gang and their friends, had made everyone doubly cautious. Everything was bolted and barred nowadays. There was no way she could get in, except by ringing one of the bells and asking for someone by name. But she didn't know any of their names, and they would not know hers.

Sighing, she went back down the steps, paused irresolutely for a moment in the street, and then walked away.

The garbled message, when it reached her via Mick, the steward on the ferry, simply said it was all right to go home. . . . What did that mean, exactly? He had said something about a card which had blown out of his hand overboard, he was sorry, he hoped it wasn't important. Was it? she wondered. And what exactly did it mean *'all right to go home?'*

Maybe, she thought, I could risk the Social Services office? . . . They would be bound to know where they had gone, wouldn't they . . .? But would they then begin to ask awkward questions about why and how and what had been happening to her, and who was to blame? *Who was to blame?* She shuddered at that thought, and actually stopped in the street. She couldn't risk those questions being asked, could she . . .? Or was it too late now to matter . . .? She did not know.

Uncertainly she made her way down to the Social Security offices, still not sure she was doing the right thing, but unable to resist the need to find out where they all were.

Where are they? she thought desperately. Are they safe? And happy? Is someone kind looking after them . . .? And is *he* safe? And looked after . . .? And not in any trouble of her making? She didn't know the answer to any of these burning questions, and somehow she had to find out. Yes, she had to take the risk. She simply had to know. . . .

The Social Security office was closed. A notice on the door said: *'Owing to new restrictions, this office will be open on Mondays, Wednesdays and Fridays only, from 10 am – 4 pm.'* And it was Saturday today.

Nothing to do here till Monday, she thought despairingly. And I can't wait that long. I *can't* . . . but then she gave herself a small, angry shake so that the flying red-gold hair glinted in the sun, and told herself grimly: I have waited long enough, God knows. A few more hours – a couple of days – won't matter. . . . If I have endured this long, I can go on a bit longer.

Sighing, she pushed the unruly hair back out of her eyes, which were already watering with disappointment, and walked on, not sure where she was going now. But her feet took her automatically back uphill towards the bright open spaces of Clifton Downs where she used to take them long ago.

It was late afternoon by now, and there were children running on the grass, kicking balls about, flying kites, queuing up for ice-creams at the van on the corner. . . . And parents – cheerful, untroubled couples, walking about in the sun, watching the antics of their children with an indulgent eye, and talking comfortably among themselves without a care in the world. . . .

Or so it seemed to her. . . . All those people playing Happy Families, while she . . .? While she walked around in a grey wilderness of loss, looking for those she could not find . . . *dared* not find?

And then she saw them. It was the laugh that alerted her – the clear, bubbling laughter of a happy small girl who was running in the sun, gold-red curls flying, with two other children after her, and a fourth one – taller and graver than she remembered – standing beside a man in a wheelchair who was manoeuvring himself around with cheerful skill in pursuit of the younger ones and their ball.

She drew back swiftly into the shade of a clump of haw-thorns and brambles at the edge of a dip in the grass. Her first instinct was to run to them – oh, to *run* to them and clasp them to her, and hold them and never let them go – not ever again . . . but she did not. She remembered the discipline that the nuns had taught her – the painfully acquired determination to think of those others first. . . . If they had gone somewhere that was good for them – if they were happy (as they seemed to be) ought she to interfere? Probably it was all arranged legally by now – fostering was a serious business, after all . . . and did she have the right to come back and upset it all? Upset *them* all, too?

But then, what about *him*? She hadn't expected to see this smiling, cheerful man, apparently well enough – and reliable enough? – to be out with his children in the sun? Where did he come in? Who was caring for him? He seemed to be safe enough out there on his own, zooming about in his chair – but she saw that the eldest of the four children – the tall one – was very watchful and protective. And something about that look of careful kindness and attention disturbed her terribly. It

306

didn't fit in with what she had thought was happening. It didn't belong with happy-go-lucky children who were cherished and cared-for as they should be. It was the look of someone who was doing the caring – and taking all the responsibility that she had thought they would have been spared.

Torn with doubts – and the anguish of long separation building up within her, she stood paralysed in the shadows, not knowing what to do.

But before she could make any move, the whole little party seemed to come together, encircling the wheelchair, and they all went off together towards the road and the tall houses on the other side – *towards home?*

Not quite knowing what she was doing, or what she was *going* to do, she began to follow them, keeping cautiously behind them, not daring to come too close. . . . She hadn't made up her mind yet about what was right. . . . Would they really be glad to see her? Or would they look at her as if she was a stranger who had come to disrupt their lives? Or as a traitor who had betrayed them and left them without a backward glance?

The cheerful little group crossed the road, the smallest one almost dancing, the older red-haired one restraining her – and they all turned along the side road leading to another row of tall and elegant houses.

Carefully, she followed, trying not to get too close, though her feet kept wanting to hurry, to run, to catch up with them before it was too late.

Then the whole party disappeared inside a small gate in a garden fence, and unaccountably went suddenly downhill out of sight. She heard the little one laugh again, a door opening and closing, and then there was silence.

Slowly, she went up to the garden fence and looked over it. Beyond was a wide expanse of green lawn, and then a sloping concrete ramp, and a terrace with a riot of flowers on it. Below the ramp there was a closed door. Beyond the terrace was another ramp, leading to a closed french window. No one was in sight.

But there was a front door to this tall house as well. For a while she just stood and looked at it, wondering painfully what to do. She was so afraid of doing the wrong thing that she almost turned away and fled. But she couldn't do that. Not when they were so near. . . . And then she made up her mind. At least *I* can *ask*, she thought. I can *ask* how they are. She won't refuse to tell me that, whoever she is. Yes, I can go and ask.

So she went up the steps and rang the bell.

Isobel had been getting the tea ready for the weekly invasion of the children. Gervase had opted out this time, as he had a book sale to go to, so he had come to supper the night before instead – with Isobel rather guiltily making a fuss of him because she was so unfairly happy herself. And Alan – blessedly undemanding, as usual – had decided to wait till Sunday before 'sweeping her off her feet' again.

She was smiling as she thought this, and laid down a few more knives and forks on the table before she went to the door, still smiling, to answer the bell.

The young woman who stood there was unmistakable – that glorious, untamable red-gold hair, and those strange, green-gold eyes which were fixed on her in such piteous entreaty could not go unrecognized.

"Come in, Katie," she said gently. "I've been expecting you."

The great eyes filled with tears at the unexpected gentleness of Isobel's voice. "I only – I only wanted to know—" she began, "I – I won't disturb them – if – if they are happy with you – I wouldn't want to—" her voice broke then. "But I *had* to know!" she whispered, and began to weep.

Isobel put an arm round her and led her inside. She took her into the sitting-room and sat her down in a chair, and brought her the first thing that came to hand, which was a brandy.

"Now, listen to me, Katie, while I make a few things clear. The children are not 'with me'. They have not been taken away from you, or fostered, or anything. They are simply living in my flat, with their father – *while they are waiting for you to come home.*"

The huge eyes fixed themselves on her face with incredulous hope. "W-*waiting* for me?"

"Yes," said Isobel firmly. "And playing The Tunes for you.

They play them nearly every day, hoping they will bring you home."

The tears began to spill over faster then, but Katie seemed almost too disbelieving to speak. "How—?" she began. "How did they find *you*?"

So Isobel told her. She told the whole, long story of their struggle to stay together, and Trevor's rocklike determination to care for them all and keep up his mother's traditions until she came home. She told her about the gradual change in Cliff's health, his slow recovery, and she did not leave out his repeated demands for news about Ireland, and his strange belief that Katie would come when he was better. . . . But most of all, she told Katie in detail about how good a carer her eldest son had become, and how much of his own life he had given up to do so.

"I didn't know . . ." whispered Katie, appalled. "I thought – I thought they'd all be in care, you see, where they could be properly looked after, with a bit more money spent on them than I could get. . . ." She looked at Isobel, not making excuses for herself so much as blaming herself for not realising what would have happened. "And I thought Cliff – he needed help so much, and they wouldn't give him any, not while I was around to look after him . . ." She hesitated then, not knowing how to go on.

Isobel said, "Katie, I know what happened – and I know why you went away – and why you never told anyone about it – and why Trevor didn't, either. . . . But that's all over now. All done with and forgotten. No one can ever blame anyone for what happened – now. Cliff is much, *much* better. He is talking more every day, and he can manage his new wheelchair splendidly."

"I know," said Katie, in a small, tearful voice of shame. "I saw him. I saw them all . . . on the Downs."

Isobel smiled. "Then you will know it's all right to come back. You have nothing to be afraid of any more."

The wide, gold-flecked glance was still anxious and beseeching. "Are you sure . . . they'll want me back?"

"Of course I'm sure," said Isobel. "Haven't I just been telling you? Come down with me now, and meet them. Then you can see for yourself."

Katie still hesitated, but at last something about Isobel's calm assurance seemed to get through to her, and the soft, sad mouth began to curve upwards into a tremulous smile. "All right," she began, and then drew back again. "But I don't want to do anything to spoil things for them. They – they all looked so happy, out there on the Downs."

"They will be happier with their mother back," said Isobel. "And as for the rest – the flat is still theirs, and yours – and I am still here. . . . Nothing need change, except for the better."

"I – I earned some money – in Swansea," Katie began, still afraid to accept all this kindness, "I meant to put it down for a deposit on a flat. . . ."

"That won't be necessary here," said Isobel firmly. "The council are paying the rent, and they didn't see the necessity for a deposit, and nor did I!" She grinned at Katie. "I should use it for a celebration, if I were you!"

Then Katie at last began to believe that she was on the edge of coming home. So they went out together into the garden, and down the concrete ramp to the door in the new flat, and Isobel opened it without knocking and went inside, with Katie beside her.

"Trevor," she said, speaking to the one who was still head of the family and still shouldered all its problems, "look who's here!"

There was a moment of astonished silence, and then everyone began to rush towards Katie, laughing and crying out with excitement and welcome.

"*Mum!*" cried Goldie, and flung herself into Katie's arms.

"*Mum!*" echoed Georgie, finding another bit to hold on to.

"*Mum!*" shouted Colin. "Smashing! *Where've you been?*" But he didn't wait for an answer. He just joined in the general hug.

Trevor said nothing at all. But his eyes shone with the tears he was too old to shed, and he came and laid yet another arm round her shoulders.

And then Katie looked at Cliff. And Cliff looked at Katie, and quite silently and simply held out his arms.

Katie disengaged herself gently from the children, and went slowly across to him, and knelt down beside him and laid her red-gold head down on his knees.

"S-sorry . . ." said Cliff, laying a hand on that well loved, well remembered head. "So – sorry. . . ."

"Sorry . . ." agreed Katie, softly.

Then Isobel perceived that it was time to take all the children away for a brief spell, while those two tormented creatures made their peace.

"Come and help me get the tea," she said, smiling at them, but signalling urgent things to Trevor. "And then you can come back down and fetch them when it's ready."

The children came, without making any demur, and once again Isobel reflected how disciplined they were, and how well aware of the perilous nature of family emotions. But Goldie could not help a few extra special skips of delight all across the garden.

When they got up to the big kitchen, Isobel set them all to work on one task or another, and went to telephone Alan. But Trevor followed her, looking a little anxious.

"Will they – be all right?" he asked, remembering all too clearly how it had been the last time they were together.

"Yes, they will," said Isobel firmly. "They have *both* changed, Trevor. Everything is going to be all right now."

He sighed, and voiced yet another anxiety his quick mind had already foreseen. "We – we won't have to leave here, will we?"

"Of course not. The flat is yours. The garden is yours." She had nearly added, "And I am yours," but she thought she had better not.

"And you?" he persisted, saying it for her.

"I am still here," she said, smiling. "Tea on Saturdays, as usual!"

He grinned then, full of relief. "And Saturday mornings?"

"That's your special time, Trevor. As long as you have problems to discuss!"

"There'll always be those!" he said, and began to laugh.

Then Isobel looked at her watch and said, "I think it's time you went down to fetch them." (They've probably had long enough, she thought. And coming up here to tea may make the transition easier all round.)

"Did *you* persuade her?" Trevor asked, before turning away to collect the others.

311

"No, Trevor. She didn't need any persuading. She came of her own accord."

"Oh good," he said, meaning much more than those two inadequate words. "Thanks," he added quietly.

"What for?"

He looked at her, suddenly blazing with certainty. "*Everything!*" he said. Then he took the children downstairs, and Isobel telephoned Alan.

"Are you free? Can you come? *Now*? I have something to show you."

And Alan, hearing the suppressed excitement in her voice, did not wait to ask questions. "I'll be round in five minutes," he said.

Isobel smiled at his instant response, and went back to the kitchen to set out the last of the tea. And while she was doing it, Alan arrived, and she took him into the sitting-room and gave him a drink, not explaining anything, and stood beside him by the open french windows waiting for the little party to come up the ramp on to the grass.

But as they stood there, a sound caught their ears – a familiar sound of fiddle and pipe and small beating drum, and a clear childish voice raised in a special song.

"Why, I do believe they are playing her home!" said Isobel softly, and took Alan's hand in hers because she was almost too moved to speak.

"So the miracle worked!" murmured Alan. "Katie has come home?"

Isobel nodded, afraid the tears might actually spill over and disgrace her. Alan touched one with a gentle finger. "And now we can allow ourselves to be happy?"

She nodded again – for truly there was nothing left to be said.

And now the little procession came into view – Georgie leading, fiddle jigging madly, red hair aflame in the evening sun, and Colin close beside her, fingers flying as the famous Tune of the *Kerry Dancing* began, and between them, Goldie, lifting up her face to the light as she sang, her flower-petal halo of red-gold curls glinting even more than her sister's as she danced along, chanting, "*O the days of the Kerry Dancing . . .*" in her sweet, pure voice. And Trevor and

312

Katie, both protectively on either side of Cliff as he swung his wheelchair over the green grass towards them. Trevor and Cliff were smiling, but Katie was actually singing with her small daughter, and the two voices rose together, alight with a strange, compelling magic that seemed to encompass the whole rejoicing company and the listeners beyond.

> *"O to think of it, O to dream of it,*
> *Fills my heart with tears . . ."* they sang.

But the lilt of the music drowned the tears and filled the soft evening air with a joy that could not be denied.

The names of The Tunes are taken from
the collection of Irish Folk Dances
by Captain Francis O'Neill (1910).